Named One of the Best Fiction Titles o. ___ **W9-AZX-690**
by THE WASHINGTON POST

"I love Susan Isaacs! Her books come straight from the heart, and her characters are smart, funny, and feisty enough to be your best girlfriend—not only for three hundred pages but for life. *Past Perfect* introduces Katie Schottland—a terrific gal pal who packs her kid off to summer camp and sleuths as a CIA analyst with equal style. Put simply, *Past Perfect* is perfect!" **—Lisa Scottoline, author of DIRTY BLONDE**

"There has to be a name for the literary form Susan Isaacs has invented: the funny scary book. The woman who made us laugh as well as shiver in fear over a murder investigation in *Compromising Positions* has done the same thing for the CIA and international espionage. *Past Perfect* made me laugh, but it also [had] me jumping out of bed every time a floorboard creaked in my old house."

—Sara Paretsky, author of FIRE SALE

"Susan Isaacs has an incredibly good ear for dialogue and a very sharp eye for the silly and stupid things people really do. Picture yourself laughing out loud while sitting on the edge of your seat and furiously flipping pages. The clever plot, the quick pace, and the pitch-perfect writing are good clues that *Past Perfect* was written by a master storyteller."

—Nelson DeMille, author of WILD FIRE

alone. Often I longed for the other mommies. Yet writing a novel did have its compensations. Instead of lunches with them and getting regaled with tales of toddlers choking to death on their daddy's carelessly dropped Turnbull & Asser cuff link, I could spend time in a universe in which a soigné deposed prince and an ex–New York cop with a badass past protected the free world by chasing down scummy Eastern Europeans peddling old Soviet nuclear warheads.

Right after my book came out, we'd gone to my parents' for brunch. Being the daughter of a shrink, I of course comprehended what it meant when I searched my handbag and found I'd left the *Cosmopolitan* review at home. Look, there were certain periodicals you didn't wave in front of a family that embraced serious poetry, serious psychiatric literature, and serious money. Adam, whose usual behavior chez Schottland was to smile, nod, and avoid lox, was staring across the table at Maddy's sour expression and flared nostrils. My sister didn't like all the bright chatter about my just-published *Spy Guys.* No one had yet said a word about her two-year-old collection, *Soft Fruit and Other Poems.* Her upper lip lifted into an expression between a sneer and outright repugnance as my father was telling me, "The manager of our Galleria store in Dallas said he loved the part where Jamie pretends to be an oversexed flight attendant." My mother looked like she was holding herself back from telling my sister, *The manager loved your book too, Maddy.* Maddy's nose twitched as if she were sniffing the stink of American literature decomposing after my having ax-murdered it.

Suddenly, Adam had a voice. He quoted the *Cosmo* review verbatim to my mother. He informed my father of the one-hundred-thousand-dollar advance my publisher had offered for a sequel. As my mother raced around the table to kiss me ("Katie, sweetie, what a lovely quote!") and my father reached across Nicky to squeeze my hand ("If you don't watch out, Katherine Jane, I'm going to hit you up for a loan!"), I saw the look on my husband's face. Pleased. He had gotten me my due. Then he tuned out my family by carefully applying cream cheese and plum preserves on a bagel in a clockwise swirl.

My mind was like a cyclone, spiraling darkly, lurching crazily, trying to come up with a way to locate Lisa that would not only prove to myself that I actually had a higher cognitive function or two, but would also get me from where I was—no place—to someplace. Also, I was feeling the pressure of "what if?" What if, as she'd said, the matter was huge, vital? What if she was in danger? The sooner I could act, the better. Naturally, I came up with nothing. It took me two and a half days after my dinner with Dix to find a way of moving forward, and that happened only because the show's CIA expert technical adviser made his annual, unannounced drop-in to the set.

Years earlier, a couple of weeks before we shot the first episode of *Spy Guys*, our producer, Oliver, contacted some association of former Agency ops and came up with Harry "Huff" Van Damme as an expert adviser. Hiring an ex-spy had been my suggestion. Since I'd never stepped outside headquarters in Langley on any business, I felt we needed somebody who had been Out There. Huff had been all over the world—according to him—risking his neck and his soul for his country. He actually had a scar on his cheek, though it ran unromantically in a horizontal line from under his nose to his ear, so it appeared he'd wiped something thick and pink across his face with the back of his hand. He claimed to have gotten knifed while taking over a boat on the Rio Grande de Buba in Guinea-Bissau, though for all anyone knew he could have walked through a glass patio door in Kansas City.

I'd always gotten on dandily with Huff because, right from the start, I'd chosen to accept whatever he said. This wasn't because he seemed like a born truth-teller, but simply because I wanted somebody to be able to give me an authoritative "His Highness could be wearing an ankle holster," so I wouldn't have to spend hours fighting with Oliver and a costume designer over a line in the script like

HH pulls snub-nosed revolver from ankle holster. Within a week of our first meeting, I recognized Oliver would be the type who'd be bellowing, "Only dykes wear ankle holsters!" and I would find myself screaming back, "It's make-believe, for God's sake! What does it matter?"

While the cameras rolled, Huff spent about half an hour on the set, sitting on a dirty wing chair abandoned by some other production company. Resting his head against soiled yellow damask, he stretched out his long legs and half closed his eyes to show how unthrilled he was. Once the director called, "Cut," Huff moved excessively close to Dani and told her breasts (as the rest of the cast and crew gathered close to listen to him) about machete fights with rebel commandos in the Philippines and outwitting the KGB in Romania. Having listened to Huff's guts/gore/glory oeuvre many times, I told him I'd meet him in my office.

"Hey, K," Huff said to me an hour later. *"Que está acontecendo?"*

"What?"

"It means 'What's happening?' in Portuguese."

"Nada," I answered tentatively.

"Your other half still cutting up elephants at the Bronx Zoo?"

"Whenever he can."

"He must have a strong stomach!"

I decided not to take that personally. "Besides what we talked about on the phone, Huff, about how someone Dani's size could take out a man built like a defensive lineman, say around six-feet-five, three hundred pounds: I need something else."

"What?"

"I'd like you to track down an Agency alum for me."

"From your era or my era?" Chutzpah, though technically not a dig. Huff was at least ten years older than I was. But he had retired from the CIA only five years ago. I hadn't been there since 1990. My time there now seemed so over that my colleagues could have been flying reptiles.

"She's definitely from my era," I told him. "For all I know, she could still be there. Her name is Lisa Golding. She was involved with training foreign nationals whom the ICD unit brought over here to live." His forehead looked about to crease at the acronym, so I added: "International Cooperation Detail." He still looked puzzled. "The unit that placed people who did us huge favors. The people we promised to bring here if things got hairy for them." Little doubt we'd promised many, many more, but the ICD was responsible only for those promises higher-ups determined were worth keeping.

"Oh, I know what you're talking about. It's called the JLC now. I'll have to check what it stands for."

"You don't have to—"

Huff didn't let me finish. "This is for the show?" Was he annoyed at having to do a little extra work for his flat fee? I wondered. He was eyeing my toile wallpaper with a pissed-off expression.

Okay, I shouldn't have been surprised by the sudden withdrawal of pleasantness, but I was. And I had no idea how to respond—a perfect example of why I was so much more comfortable with fiction than with life. In books and on TV, it's always easy: that next line of dialogue comes right away. What if it takes three weeks to think up? No one knows how long it took to create the next sentence, the next page. You never wake three nights later at 4 A.M. with the perfect rejoinder. So I blurted out, "Of course it's for the show."

From the start, Huff made me nervous. I was never sure what he knew about me, other than at one time I had been a writer at the Agency. Had "writer" sounded so boring that he never checked me out? Or did Huff know everything, especially all that I didn't? Every time I spoke to him I was dying to ask, *What happened to me? Do you know? Can you find out?* Except I always remembered my mother telling me in fourth or fifth grade, "If you think somebody's a little creepy, don't tell yourself he's not. Stay away from him. Trust your judgment." So I had never asked what he knew because I sensed there was something strange about him.

Huff ran his tongue back and forth over his top teeth. The mannerism was especially disconcerting because operatives were trained to suppress any personal characteristics that might hint of discomfort. I'd assumed he was made of sterner stuff. "Fine," he said. "What do you want me to get on her?"

"Anything you can. I'd like to get in touch with her."

"Why?"

"Why?" I repeated. Why was he asking "Why?" Curiosity? Hostility? I flashed a girly smile. "I want to contact Lisa because she's material," I started to explain, talking too fast, smiling too broadly. "She dealt with brave people who risked everything they had for the Agency. And she probably dealt with others who were the scum of the earth, but who we owed big-time. I want to get in touch with her because she's capable of noticing even the smallest detail of a person's style. And most of all, because she would make a terrific minor character for the show."

Huff shrugged. "I'll make a few calls." But I could see from the way his mouth pulled to the side that he knew something was odd with this assignment. He just had no clue as to what it was.

The remote possibility of being deprived of his annual fee as well as his personal panorama of the Dani Barber boobs must have posed a sufficient threat because Huff called that evening, minutes after I got home.

"Your Lisa Golding is out of the Agency," he said.

"As of when?" I had started to set the table, so I stood in the middle of the kitchen with a phone in one hand and a bouquet of knives, forks, and spoons in the other. I was about to set down the implements on the counter, but I didn't want Huff to hear the housewifey clink of silverware.

"She left in December, a year and a half ago."

"Retired or fired?"

"Retired. Not working anywhere else as per the latest info." His words were so clipped he sounded like an early version of computer-generated speech.

"Do you have an address for her?" He gave me an address in the Adams-Morgan section of Washington, an area that had gone from decaying town houses/has potential when I'd lived there to unequiv-ocally hip. When I'd known her, she'd lived elsewhere, in a great house in an up-and-coming neighborhood just outside Georgetown. Obviously she still had a sense of style and real estate smarts, plus money far beyond a CIA salary to indulge these gifts. "Do you know if she rents or owns?"

"Owns."

"What about a phone number?" He gave me her home and cell numbers. "Did you happen to pick up any news or gossip about her?"

"Just that she doesn't seem to be in her house. And nobody has a clue as to where she is."

Chapter Seven

Ⓘ F A PERSON FROM YOUR PAST SUDDENLY RE-appears and offers to change your life, or at least your understanding of it, you'd expect that person would be someone who'd been important to you. Like that witty, silky-haired boyfriend from senior year who dropped you for a lute player from the High School of Performing Arts. Or to jump ahead ten years, like Benton Mattingly.

What you don't expect in the coming-back-into-your-life department is someone who didn't mean much in the first place. Like Lisa Golding. She was one of those people who had been stuck between acquaintance and friend. Someone with a discerning eye to shop with. Someone eager to go to the theater—and it didn't have to be a Kennedy Center revival. Someone whose tales of being propositioned by powerful men were either amusing lies or tiny naked truths bedecked in outré clothes. Someone you would never open your heart to.

Lisa had come back into my life pleading urgently for my help.

Then she'd said, "It can wait till tomorrow." I'd been straining to recall something more I could use to track her down: who her parents were, where she'd grown up, names of friends. All I could come up with was that once she'd told me she'd been an army brat and had lived all over the world. However, another evening, at a bar with a bunch of people from the office, I'd heard her talk of her father, who had been a highly paid international troubleshooter for American-something-Airlines, Express—and that her family had moved some ridiculous number of times—thirty or forty—by the time she'd been sent off to boarding school in Switzerland at age fourteen.

Again I Googled, this time like a woman possessed, which I guess I was. All I was able to come up with was more of the same, an impossibly long list of Goldings—military Goldings, American Express Goldings, American Airlines Goldings, American Standard Goldings, Bank of America Goldings. There were Goldings all over the world who might or might not be related to Lisa.

A couple of days after my meeting with Huff, the name Tara floated into my consciousness. Somewhere in Lisa's genial babble, there was Tara the gourmet cook, brilliant golfer, daredevil skier, and the sweetest, most loyal friend a person could have. But I'd never met Tara and had no idea what her job or her last name was. I sat at my computer for about ten minutes staring at "Tara" in the Google box, trying to bring up another association, sensing that "amazing swing" wouldn't get me far. I squeezed my eyes shut to concentrate. When I opened them, it hit me that Lisa could have created Tara, the way kids invent imaginary friends. Then I tried the phone numbers Huff had given me. All I got were generic recorded messages to leave a message.

So I finished making dinner for Adam and me. I was still as far from finding Lisa as ever. Farther, because now I knew from Huff that she'd dropped out of sight. Had she phoned me with someone holding a gun to her head? Or as part of some crackpot scheme she cooked up? Should I be as frightened for her as I was beginning to be? Should I be frightened for myself?

Well, at least I could agonize and not give any thought to dinner. The advantage of being married to a guy whose mother served green Jell-O mayonnaise squares with radish and carrot circle "surprises" as the salad course was that Adam appreciated simple cooking. My salad was baby spinach from a bag and sliced mushrooms from a box with a thirty-second lemon juice and olive oil dressing. I defrosted a container of my father's Bolognese sauce, dumped it over a bowl of fettuccine. Voilà, dinner was served.

Sitting across from Adam, I knew that if I continued to flake out about what Huff had told me about Lisa, my husband would pick up my remoteness. Either he'd be annoyed or start wondering if I'd gone from obsessed to unglued. He was eying me as I tossed the salad with excessive gaiety. My vivacious act wasn't playing.

So I went into my genial bit—smiling with an excessive number of teeth. I also crinkled my eyes adorably. "You know what I need from you?" I asked him.

"What?" Cautious, looking at my smiley face almost the way he would at an orangutang trying to cadge another banana.

"I need advice about something for the show."

"Oh." A slight upturn of the right side of his mouth told me he was pleased, or maybe just relieved, that what I wanted had nothing to do with Lisa or my years at the CIA. "What kind of an animal could someone use who's trying to terrify His Highness—not that he's terrifiable."

"I don't know. Depends. A lion, a—"

"No. Something small. They have to sneak it into his bedroom. Like the scorpion in James Bond's bed in . . . I think it was *Diamonds Are Forever*. Except obviously it can't be a scorpion."

Adam pierced a few leaves of baby spinach with his fork but was too busy thinking to actually eat them. "How about a vampire bat?"

I nodded. It was a good idea, but now, being in possession of actual information, I'd have to write it into a script.

"The common vampire bat can walk, which looks pretty strange," he said. I nodded. "But there was something recently published, from Cornell, I think. They can run too. Like this." He demonstrated by elongating his arms. "See, my arms are the forelegs. They're strong. Vampire bats run more like a gorilla using its arms. Not like a dog that uses its back legs. It would be nice and creepy."

"Great! It's just what I needed." What was great was that suddenly it also came to me that there might be one more lead to Lisa.

I kept nodding and smiling and half listening while he told me how vampire bats have a bum rap, that they're kind of shy. Nice to each other too: after a new baby is born, other bats help by feeding the mother.

When he finished I thanked him profusely and served up the pasta. "I think that old box of Len Deighton novels is down in the crypt," I muttered a few minutes later. "I'll need to run downstairs for a couple of minutes."

"Okay."

Everyone in our co-op called the storage center in the basement "the crypt." Each apartment came with a caged-off space about the size of a prison cell where they could keep anything from a camp trunk to an old dining room set they'd loved until the new decorator informed them that sets of anything were middle class. Adam lingered over his usual dessert, two Mallomars. Each night, he'd patiently lift off a segment of the thin chocolate coating from the marshmallow cushion with his front teeth. As I left, he made a few grunts I interpreted as, *I'll load the dishwasher.*

Forget the Len Deighton novels. I was after something else. I took the elevator to the basement and walked through the long corridor past the laundry room. The lights in there were out now. The washers along the right wall and dryers on the left stood like opposing armies waiting for dawn to attack. The comforting baby-powder scent of fabric softener lingered in the damp air, but as always, the basement was spooky. As I turned the corner and walked down the long corridor toward the crypt, I started singing "Born in the U.S.A.," which had always been my have-courage anthem, even after someone informed me it was meant to be ironic. The song drowned out the creaks and squeaks that came from behind the old brown-painted walls as well as the gurglings in the pipes that ran the length of the ceiling; those squeals and glub-glubbing always sounded to me like someone whose head was being forced underwater.

When I opened the heavy fire door to the crypt, the baby-powder scent was overpowered by the storage room's perpetual stink: dead mouse, or rotting wood from some tenant's flea market side chair. The super had hung air fresheners—plastic pineapples—on several of the chain-link walls of the storage area, but they merely made matters worse. The freshener/stink combo became what's usually described in horror and mystery novels as "the sweet stench of rotting flesh." I prayed I wouldn't inadvertently tread on a dying mouse.

I began to breathe through my mouth, which effectively ended my "Born in the U.S.A." bravado. What was really scaring me was what I'd come to the crypt to find—my notes on the reports I'd written for the CIA. Stupid to have done something like that? Illegal also? Sure. Yet I'd come home to my (later Adam's and my) apartment in D.C. from Langley and two or three nights a week jot down short summaries of what I'd worked on during the day. The question did occur to me at the time: *Are you totally insane?* Yes, though not totally. But at least 90 percent. Before I'd settled on home scribbling, I'd even pondered tearing a rough draft of my reports into sections of ten pages, Scotch-taping them to the small of my back, and saying, "See you tomorrow!" or "Have a great weekend!" to the security guards who checked through our handbags and attaché cases as we left. But I worried that the computer paper had been treated with a chemical that would sound alarms throughout the building, or that there was a secret meter that measured how many printer pages a person had used and then either passed along or shredded. Besides, a random crinkle of paper during no-coat season could give me away.

Was that what had gotten me fired? Did someone sneak into my apartment in Washington and find my summaries? Almost definitely not. To the best of my knowledge, no one ever looked, much less discovered what I was doing. If they had, I wouldn't have just gotten fired. I'd have been interrogated and prosecuted and they would have confiscated the pages.

I was never completely clear on why I was doing it. Years later, after I'd written *Spy Guys* and the TV version was in development, I decided it had been my artistic ego that compelled me to make those notes. Deep down, I wasn't a spook, I wasn't a geopolitical analyst: I was a writer. Okay, a writer, not an author. My work at the Agency wasn't going to make F. Scott Fitzgerald turn over in his grave from jealousy. I was merely a CIA word wiz, clarifying and occasionally enlivening other people's communiqués and ideas.

However, the key word was *I*. Or to use the possessive pronoun, *mine*. *Mine*, the way a three-year-old clutches a toy to her chest and shrieks the word when another kid gets that acquisitive gleam in her eye. Yet, my report, "In Transit: The Likelihood of the Hungarian Government Opening the Border to East German Refugees," was not mine. I knew that. Yet it *was* mine, although my name never appeared. The chairman of the Senate Intelligence Committee and the members of the President's Foreign Intelligence Advisory Board would never put down the report and sigh, *Geez, that Katherine Schottland sure made that paragraph on the inferior quality of East German diesel fuel come alive!* Even though I understood the reports really weren't mine, I couldn't let them simply disappear into the great government information maw.

I knew then that if I asked my mother her opinion about what all this *mine* business was about, she'd turn around and pose a few questions in her offhand, I'm-just-a-curious-mom way. (It was a point of pride with her not to be intrusive, i.e., crazy, like other psychiatrist-parents with their Let Me Tell You What You're Thinking games. Of course, she loved to tell us what everyone else was thinking: just not the family.) Anyway, I'd wind up giving her a few off-the-cuff answers and suddenly I'd know something about myself I didn't want to know. So I never asked her opinion.

I opened the padlock on the storage area. Agency-trained enough not to make the combination something obvious, like the year we got married or the last four digits of an old phone number, I'd chosen 1-8-2-1. That was the year James Fenimore Cooper wrote what was supposed to have been the first spy novel—which he called, with an appealing directness, *The Spy*. I figured that if Adam and I simultaneously became senile and couldn't remember the number, we could always look it up by the title.

Except the lock wouldn't open. I must have been treading along the edge of hysteria without knowing it because I started yanking on it, pulling so hard that my hands became sweaty. I envisioned losing my grip on the lock and falling backward, my head crashing onto the cement floor. Adam would come looking for me sooner (if he wanted sex) or later (if he was in his recliner studying the centerfold of *Neuropathology of Primates*), but by then I'd be in an irreversible coma. I took a relaxation breath, let it out *slooowly,* then leaned down to try the combination again. Oh, the little red line was directly above the 2. I moved the dial to the 1 and the shackle popped out. I opened the high, chain-link door and walked into our little storage space.

To look at it, you'd think most of the Grainger-Schottland net worth had been invested in wicker baskets and rattan boxes. They were arranged, unintentionally, into stacks of differing heights, some as tall as I. All they'd have needed to have gone into the window of a funky store in a college town would be a few strands of beads, silver earrings of doves, and those ugly brown leather sandals male graduate students with repulsive big toes insist on wearing.

I saw the baskets with the usual boxes of checks dating back seven years, with Nicky's first everything—shoes, baby spoon, blond curl from first haircut, *Pat the Bunny,* Winnie the Pooh potty seat—as if I were planning to make a bizarre collage to replace him in his room when he left home to get his own apartment. I inched my way behind some medium-size boxes and lifted a sheet off an old treadmill I'd given up on. Books and books. Both Adam's and my sets of *Lord of the Rings* from high school, our college texts, his graduate school tomes, the novels, classics as well as espionage, I would never read again but couldn't part with, his books on wilderness adventures, all of which seemed to have titles with colons, like *Ice: Recollections of My Year in Ultima Thule with a Rabid Wolf.*

The only books I cared about at that moment were my economics textbooks. Following page 107, a number I chose for its arbitrariness, were the notes I had made when I came home each night after working on the final draft of a report for the Office of Eastern Europe Analysis. I'd stuck one page of notes between every few pages of the books. I picked up *A History of Economic Thought from Aristotle through Friedman* and said to myself, *Holy shit, I once actually knew this stuff.* Now all I could do was notice that its covers, like those of the other texts, were no longer slightly bulgy by the addition of my notes; over the years the weight of the books on top had pressed them until they'd regained their original shape.

I clutched the book against my chest and, since for two seconds I hadn't felt anxiety over anything, I started worrying that either my notes or the book's pages were not on acid-free paper and that I'd leaf to page 107 and find dust. That not being sufficient, I worried that the Agency had traced Lisa's call to my cell phone and had planted some sort of device in the heels of all my shoes when Adam and I were at work and right now its operatives were looking at a diagram of my building. Seeing me as a blinking red light in the basement storage area, they'd already dispatched someone to kidnap me to a safe house and question me—*What do you know about Lisa and when did you know it?*—while doing the pull-the-fingernails-out-with-pliers business. Or maybe they'd just kill me in situ.

Since my mother had never berated me for having an overactive imagination, I'd learned to give myself the business. Like now: it was

one thing to envision imminent doom, another to picture it in such detail that I could almost see the dirt-blackened elbows of an Agency operative shaking the chain-link gate of our storage area in the crypt to get at me. From there it took only an instant to conjure up the op's hand pulling metal shears from his pocket, then cutting. Each time a link split, it made a sharp clanking sound.

Stop this craziness! I yelled at myself silently. I wondered whether it was mainly screenwriters who saw their worst, crusted-elbow fantasies in high def, and then felt obliged to add sound effects. Or did everyone with rampant anxiety live their nightmares in such sickening detail?

But then I thought, All kidding aside, it didn't have to be my hyper imagination. Maybe I was just picturing a very real threat: i Lisa had troubling information, she might have led people to m simply by making a phone call. And those people didn't necessaril have to be from the Agency, or from the FBI acting on the Agency behalf. It could be some rogue op from any part of the U.S. intell gence community. Or an agent acting on behalf of a foreign gover ment. Right then my esophagus decided to do a couple of spasm causing acid reflux à la my father's pasta sauce.

Talk about parents. It was so embarrassing: me, the daughter o shrink, having such banal anxieties. At least *anxieties* had a nice, n mal, urban ring to it, unlike *paranoia*, which always seemed to me affliction suffered by people in red states who wouldn't go to mo with subtitles.

Maybe I was being overly sanguine about the man of my ni mares. He didn't have to be a representative of any country, like F sia's KGB or Italy's CESIS or Turkey's MIT. He could be Mafia a random maniac with enough technical expertise to trace a call f Lisa to me. *Crazy,* I told myself.

Crazy. That very instant, I heard a strange basement sound my God! Footsteps. Clutching an economics textbook agains chest, I held my breath. And heard it again. A *shhh* sound, like s

ers shuffling over a rug. Except there weren't any rugs in the base-ment. Someone breathing through a gas mask then?

I had to laugh at myself. Except I couldn't. And I couldn't tell myself that *shhh* was a mouse noise, unless there were a great, Busby Berkeley chorus line of mice. I would not think, Rats. Cut it out! The sweat from my palms suffused with invisible dust and suddenly the cover of the book felt so slimy I had to set it down.

Was that the sound again? It could be someone with gum-sole shoes on the damp floor of the laundry room, pacing, waiting for me to emerge. Or thinking up a plan of attack. A weapon: that's what I had to have. I peered around, but we hadn't stored any tables I could rip the leg off of to use as a bludgeon. I pictured a set of old ski poles, in case I had to stab someone, then remembered we'd decided it was cheaper to rent equipment than buy. What idiocy! Like the stuff I wrote into *Spy Guys*. Real danger required a real defense, and I didn't have any. *Shhh* again, definitely. A real sound, not a product of a fevered imagination. My hands, drenched now, trembling, managed to grab the lock off the gate of the storage area. But there was no gizmo for it to go into, so I couldn't lock the gate from the inside so he couldn't get to me.

Frantically, I began shoving my notes back into the textbooks, ripping a few pages as I searched out page 107. Hurry. Put everything back where it was: that made sense. Then I could cover the treadmill, grab a basket of 1999 check stubs, padlock our storage area, and stroll out. Say *Oh hi,* casually, as I passed whoever was outside the door. Except what if instead of a hi in return, he grabbed my neck with one huge, filthy hand and squeezed. I wasn't the type to write anything like, "She sniffed the scent of fear rising from her own body." Except it was rising and smelled like an unsuccessful attempt at roasting garlic.

Enough! I had to face this. Leaving the treadmill uncovered and the gate to our storage area ajar, I headed out. Then I stopped.

The closer I got to the door, the clearer I heard *shhh*. I was so

scared my mind retreated into the safety of blankness. I couldn't even pray. Maybe I managed a silent *Dear God*. I yanked open the door, prepared to knee someone in the nuts, or go for thumbs in eyeballs. The corridor outside the crypt was empty. Someone had been in the basement, though. In the laundry room. With each rotation, the drum of the dryer went *shhh*.

Chapter Eight

Back inside the crypt, pretending not to be humiliated, I returned to my old textbooks. I would have taken them up to the apartment to read through my old notes, but I didn't want to watch Adam's clear eyes turn opaque as I strolled by him with ten mildewed econ texts. Adam, true, had never known about my note-taking, but with one look at my face he'd know whatever I was after had nothing to do with the ten-pound *Macroeconomics and Growth Theory* in the crook of my arm. Plus, I'd told him I'd gone for my Len Deighton novels. So I opted for the crypt. Surprisingly, there was cell phone reception in the thick-walled basement, so I called and told him, "I can't find the damn books. But I got a second wind and I want to straighten up a little—throw out some of the junk I've been saving since practically kindergarten."

I folded the sheet that had been over the treadmill so it became a cushion and sat atop a large wicker box to examine my books. The first two were from the end of 1988 and, blessedly, my notes had not disintegrated, although the paper I'd used seemed to have degraded; its texture was somewhere between *The New York Times* and regular Charmin. In '88, I'd spent a lot of time on a project predicting what the effects of the Soviets' withdrawal from Afghanistan would be on the countries of Eastern Europe. If that was a clue to what Lisa had wanted from me, I couldn't figure out what it meant.

I found 1989 in one of the books from my seminar "Labor, Industry, and the International Economy," one of the few bright spots of my final semester at Connecticut College, which included getting rejected from every MBA program I'd applied to. (When I came home for spring break, my mother hugged me excessively, kissed me a lot on the forehead, and called me "my sweetie." My father told me Harvard and Columbia wouldn't know a good thing if they fell over it. Maddy shrugged and told me, "If you'd really wanted an MBA, you would have applied to at least one school where you had a shot.")

As I remembered, I'd been writing up a storm in 1989 at the Agency. Besides all the brouhaha in Eastern Europe, I'd also been doing some editing work for the Office of Transitional Issues between April and June, their writers being overwhelmed by explaining the massacre at Tiananmen Square. I skimmed my notes on that, sadly unable to recall who Hu Yaobang and most of the other names were. Then I tried to decipher what I'd jotted down about my work on the rapidly disintegrating Soviet bloc. Naturally I couldn't make sense of most of it. In 1989 I must have known what "ert G 2 fin" meant, but all I could do was guess that it had something to do with Germany and Finland, or Germany (East? West?) to finance something or other.

I shivered and rubbed my arms. They felt cold and loose-skinned like an apple left too long in the fruit bin. Our building was older than most in the neighborhood of prewar apartments; ours was pre–World War I. Because of its age, the walls and foundation were so solid that no summer heat could penetrate the basement. I regretted my tank top and open sandals. My bones were chilled as if I'd caught some old-fashioned-sounding illness, the grippe or pleurisy.

I couldn't concentrate. Besides being cold, I had a Mallomar sitting pristinely on a napkin, waiting for me in the kitchen. So at that moment I decided not to try to figure out every mysterious jotting I had made fifteen years ago. Lisa Golding was my problem. Ergo, I should look for her in my notes.

From what I could gather from them, I'd worked with Lisa twice in '89. The first instance, in February, was when I'd interviewed her about the daughter of General Corbajram, the highest-ranking general in the Albanian army. I was never let in on what aid or information Drita Corbajram had given that made us decide she deserved to be settled discreetly in the United States. All I was supposed to do was to write a report on why she had wound up running a plumbing supply store in Wilmington, Delaware, instead of being placed, as she'd requested and had been promised, in a fashion-related business in L.A. . . . and also what we could do, short of a well-placed bullet, to stop her from squawking and going to the media. "You wouldn't *believe* that this woman wanted to go into fashion," I recalled Lisa saying. "I mean, she was so incredibly, incredibly nearsighted that when she put on makeup she had to hold the mirror against the tip of her nose, and she wound up putting on hideous flamingo-colored lipstick like a total spastic. Check with *anyone* who dealt with her. We had a small L.A. sportswear company and a fabric design place ready to cooperate, but one look at her and they said, 'Not even for my country. Not even for a fortune in money.' It took us another six weeks to find another situation, and then we had to practically sell our souls to get the plumbing supply guy in Delaware to even sit in the same room with her."

I sat on the folded-up sheet on top of the wicker box and tried to think up a way the daughter of a psychotic Albanian general could spring to life fifteen years after being stashed in Delaware to become, even in Lisa's mind, a matter of "national importance." I, whose speciality, professionally speaking, was absurd plots, could come up with nothing.

I was so cold that I decided to pass on the Mallomar and instead make a cup of hot chocolate when I got upstairs, which would cause billions of teeny flavanols to launch an immediate power surge in my immune system and stave off any incipient sniffle.

I read on. The second time I worked with Lisa that year was in December, a month after the opening of the Berlin Wall. I was putting together a report on what had become of our "resources" in East Germany, the people in that government who had been working for us. Lisa had been charged with settling three of them.

You would think that by the age of thirty-nine and a half, I'd have figured out how to think, or at least to get myself mentally from A to Z. Or even A to B. Instead, teeth chattering, I kept repeating *three East Germans, three East Germans* silently, over and over. Was I waiting for my thoughts (like a TV script) to SLOW DISSOLVE and suddenly, there the three of them would be, in focus, doing whatever they did for the camera of my mind? Naturally, nothing came to me except that one of the Germans wound up in Cincinnati. As for what any of the three had done for us, I thought one might have been a double agent, an East German spy who was actually working for the United States.

Three East Germans, I persisted. Nothing: a blank screen. Finally, I put back the textbooks, fluffed out the sheet as if I were doing a laundry commercial, re-covering the books on the treadmill. Then I went upstairs, put on a sweatshirt, and enjoyed hot chocolate and a Mallomar.

Adam was in the room we'd called, after much discussion (on my part) and two shrugs (on his), the den. Sitting back in a recliner, his neck supported by a revolting blue velour-covered pillow he'd picked up in an airport, he was engrossed in a book on how we'd come to be in such a mess in Iraq. His eyes were on the page, and the reading light made his thick lashes cast a shadowy fringe on his cheeks. "When did you get that book?" I asked.

"Don't know." I guess my face suggested I needed something more so he added, "Last week." He'd changed into shorts when he came home from work. Even at forty, Adam's long legs and big bare feet gave him the air of a teenage boy in his final growth spurt.

"It's funny," I said. "You just go out and buy a book. I mean, if I'm going to read something serious like that, you know I'll make an announcement three weeks before, like, 'I want to read that book about Iraq.'" He nodded once, as much as he could with a pillow behind his neck. He wasn't sure whether I was making an observation or had begun a discussion—though from his longing glance down to his book, it was clear what his preference was. "Then the next week I'll say something like, 'Oh, I saw that Iraq book on Oliver's desk and he said it was good.' And the week after that, I'll tell you, 'Adam, I'm going online to buy that book on Iraq. Do you want me to get you anything?'"

"Uh-huh." He was not one for casual conversation. Okay, that wasn't fair. Adam didn't make conversation just to fill a silence. In his family, it was considered not the least hostile to sit through an entire dinner saying only, "Please pass the potatoes," and "Thank you."

"You know, we can call Nicky tomorrow night," I went on. "Remember, they said after ten days we could call? Or I can do it from the office late afternoon and conference you, because at about four-thirty, the lines won't be as busy. Do you have any preference?"

"Four-thirty," he said, and added, knowing my fondness for complete sentences, "is good." I could see how much he wanted to get back to his book. After all, we'd had a genuine conversation during dinner. For him, more talk would not only be distracting, but draining.

My parents went through their entire marriage talking, and that's what I'd always thought being married would be like. When my mother wandered into the kitchen, where my father was peeling apples, one of them would invariably blurt out, "Oh, you know what I forgot to tell you . . . ?" as if the last time they had spoken had been weeks before, not moments. On the other hand, soon after Adam and I started living together, I discovered the comfort of being in a room with another person who didn't mind if I kept my thoughts to myself.

"I'm just going to flake out in here," I said, grabbing a white afghan with white roses crocheted into it that I'd bought for fourteen dollars at a yard sale not far from my parents' house in East Hampton. It was one of my treasures. "Feel free to read." I stretched out on the couch to do some more *three East Germans* thinking, but fell into one of those states where your body remains but your mind checks out and goes someplace where you can't follow it.

When my mind returned, it reported that the guy who was being sent to Cincinnati was named Manfred Gottesman. A major guy: he'd been third in command of the Stasi, the East German secret police, and had been passing us a few names of people spying against us or against West Germany. He'd also reported on the agendas of meetings between the head of Stasi and the then leader of the East German government, Erich Honecker.

I remembered Lisa showing me his "before" picture. Stylewise, Manfred looked like a casting director's vision of a communist apparatchik: hair darkened and flattened by some oily commie pomade, shirt collar so ill-fitting it looked like it was compressing his trachea.

"You should see what I did with him," Lisa had said. "I mean, seriously check him out. Can you see he has cuteness potential?" After a few seconds, I did. A box of a face, with roughly chiseled nose, cheeks, and chin. Gottesman looked like a movie actor who might never be a star, but who would still get lots of interesting roles. A manly man, intelligent-looking too. "And guess what?" she'd continued. "He's Jewish, so now you can feel free to fall in love with him. Oh, I forgot you didn't marry one. Anyway, his parents came from . . . wherever, someplace in Germany. They were communists. They must've been *big* communists because somebody helped them escape from Nazi Germany and into Russia. He grew up in Moscow and he's fluent, almost no accent, in Russian, German, *and* English. You have no idea what a pleasure it is, because he can fit in anywhere and has a really, really good body. He looks great in a suit *or* jeans. Not your usual East German refugee who looks like Porky Pig no matter what you put him in. I *loved* doing him."

That was all I could remember, but at least it was something. I couldn't come up with any scintillating memory of the other two, though I was 75 percent sure one of them had been a woman.

Nearly a week went by. Even though I went down to the crypt twice more and reread my notes, nothing new occurred to me. On the phone, Nicky told us he'd lost three pounds, hated swimming because the lake was so cold one of the kids had seen actual ice near the raft, and totally loved basketball but needed sneakers. At work, Dani and Javiero got into their bimonthly fight in front of the entire crew. This happened after he said the line "I wouldn't do that," and she expelled an angry mouthful of air, then snapped, "I hate to say this, but for God's sakes, it's not 'I wooden.' You're supposed to have gone to Eton and Oxford. You should be capable of pronouncing the letter T." To which Javiero replied, "If I wasn't a gentleman, I'd punch your fucking teeth down your t'roat." To which Dani responded, "'Throat,'" and they had to be pulled apart by the boom operator and a production assistant. We lost the day's shooting when both their managers came to the studio to scream at Oliver and threaten litigation.

One evening I drove up to the zoo to see a four-day-old zebra foal. Adam had his arm around me, and I felt a surge of love for him not only for being tall and having really masculine hands, but because for all his science, he had tears in his eyes over this beautiful striped, leggy baby. The glow remained for a couple of hours over dinner, though it ended when he saw me in a sheer black nightgown and, after an appreciative "Hey," felt somehow obliged to add, "Just give me a minute to floss."

It would have been a perfectly normal late June/early July except for my being unable to get Lisa out of my head. My desire to know . . . no, my *need* to know whatever she could tell me about why I'd been fired, did not lessen in intensity with each passing day. If anything, it became stronger. Where was she? Why had she disappeared?

I guess I was desperate, because I put so much effort into trying to remember anything more she had said about Manfred Gottesman and the two other East Germans. To add to the problem, Manfred's name would no longer be Manfred Gottesman. The three of them would have wound up in different cities with different identities, that was standard procedure. But nothing—no name, no place—came to me until I remembered an old trick I'd overheard my mother telling one of her friends years before: "Just imagine putting whatever it is you can't remember into a car and watching it drive away. Then put it out of your mind. It often comes back when you least expect it."

I stuck Manfred and the other two Germans into an imaginary BMW and pictured them driving off. The following day, while reading an e-mail about what great fun the Deering School's twenty-first class reunion had been ("a reprise of our unforgettable twentieth, though sadly with fewer attendees . . ."), I had a genuine flash: Lisa complaining about Manfred's insistence on calling his company Queen City Sweets: "Queen City is a nickname for Cincinnati and, okay, sweets are candies, but nobody calls them sweets except someone in England in 1922 and Queen City sounds *so* gay. It's like calling it Cincinnati Boy Whores, Incorporated. I told him that straight to his face, and he told me, very, very snottily, like a real stick-up-the-ass German, that *his* business was none of my business. I mean, we were setting him up in candy distribution to the tune of . . . I can't even begin to tell you what it's costing us."

After all those endless days of waiting for my cell phone to ring, this was a twinkle of hope. I Googled Queen City Sweets. Yes! It still existed! One thirty-four Corporate Drive. The home page of its Web site was framed by bouquets of lollipops, chains of candy canes, and beribboned boxes of chocolates. Could it be the Web site of an über-

Stasi goon turned American entrepreneur? When I read the "About Us" page, I figured it was safe, though certainly not a given, to assume that QC Sweets was owned by my man Manfred. "About Us" was actually a long welcome letter that wound up with, "We think you'll find sugar and spice and everything nice here at Queen City Sweets, the home of sweet deals!!" It was signed Richard ("Dick") Schroeder, President, a name which definitely had a Teutonic ring. Because you couldn't take a guy who had even a little German accent and call him Ciaran O'Connor. Of course not. You'd call him Richard Schroeder.

If life were like art—or at least like *Spy Guys*—we'd cut to a sign saying WELCOME TO CINCINNATI in an airport. There would be a rear shot of Javiero as His Highness carrying an elegantly well worn Vuitton garment bag over a hooked index finger and Jamie schlepping a too large suitcase close to bursting. In the next scene Jamie would be sitting in Dick Schroeder's office wowing him not just with her hot body, but with her near-encyclopedic knowledge of candy-making and distribution that she'd mastered in twelve hours of reading. As Jamie was getting Dick to fall in love with her and reveal state secrets (ours and the East Germans'), HH would be collecting the gossip on him from the youngest daughter of the Duchess of Blenningshire, who had married a Cincinnati potato chip tycoon.

But life wasn't like art. Sure (as my mother-in-law once observed in a birthday card accompanying a pen and pencil set), I was the creative type. Yet for all my supposed imagination, I couldn't come up with a way I could meet Dick Schroeder—assuming he was the person who had once been Manfred Gottesman. Could I drop into his office on Corporate Drive and ask if he knew anything of the whereabouts of his former American Manners and Mores teacher, Lisa Golding?

Bottom line, Dick Schroeder didn't look like much. But when you have nothing, not much starts looking good.

Chapter Nine

THE OFFICE SUITE IN WHICH MY MOTHER WORKED was too blue to be gray and too gray to be blue. Whatever its color, it was calming. If your psyche was unsettled, there were few other venues in all Manhattan so kind to frayed nerves as her gray-blue waiting room with its up-close and arty photographs of seaweed growing out of a sandy ocean floor.

Inside, her diplomas and certifications hung behind the slab of pale blue slate that was her desk. The other three walls of her office featured more undersea pictures, but taken by a different photographer from those outside. Starfish this time, and not just the usual five-armed guys: such diversity! Shells with spikes, shells like brown velvet. My favorite had always been a pinkish one with twenty arms. The creature seemed to me to be ridiculously lovely, as much flower as animal. But these starfish photos were murkier than the seaweed ones in the waiting room; you could see the undulations of water, tiny explosions of sand rising from the seabed. Three, however, had shafts of sun shining through the deep water gloom. That set them apart from the others. Despite the murk, if you looked in the right direction, you could find some light.

My mother stood out in the watery gray-blue. In all her life I'd never known her to wear anything that could blend into that color. Decoration was background. She was foreground. We were sitting on her analyst's couch, which was upholstered in nubby gray silk. She sent it out to be re-covered every August so those patients who wanted to lie down during their sessions wouldn't be distracted by smells and smears of other patients' hair products as she herself had been during her own psychoanalysis. She could have gotten a couch covered in leather or a dirt-hiding tweed, but while she approved of the moral fiber of people who bought long-wearing furniture and energy-efficient automobiles, her taste prevented her from becoming one of them.

As always, my mother was the total land creature—that morning, in black linen. Her dress was cut so elegantly that even if you knew next to nothing about fashion, you'd recognize this as the work of a preeminent designer. From their luster, you might even guess that those big white beads she was wearing around her neck truly were pearls. You'd be right. My father's present for her fiftieth birthday. He'd confided in me—and in everyone he knew except my mother—that buying them had doubled Tahiti's gross domestic product for the year.

"I *love* your shoes," I told her.

"Thanks." She stretched out a leg and swiveled her foot right and left. What looked like two slender grosgrain ribbons formed an X over her instep. They were all that kept the rest of the shoes—soles and four-inch heels—from falling off as she walked her usual half mile from home to office and back again. "I decided they were very practical, being black." She smiled. "They had them in taupe too."

"You were tempted to buy both," I said.

"Of course." Maddy and I had not inherited her chic gene. We dressed reasonably well only because we'd been raised by a woman with innate good taste and a long list of fashion dos and don'ts. In fact, I had no idea what we inherited from our mother other than mitochondrial DNA and some ambition. Physically, we both took after our father, which meant that if our school had had a girls' wrestling team, we would have been recruited. Granted, I had one up on my sister because I had a discernible waist. But even though my sister and I were somewhere between okay-looking and pretty, with our high color and almond-shaped eyes, we appeared to come from people precisely like what our father's family must have been before they left Hungary for America: small-town Jews who could carry fifty-pound sacks of chicken feed on their backs—and that was just the women. My mother, on the other hand, had the height and grace to look as if her antecedents had been Tolkien elves.

"Look at it this way, Mom. You can congratulate yourself on your restraint, not buying the second pair."

"Believe me, I've been patting my own back for a week. And it allows me to deceive myself that somewhere up there"—she pointed heavenward—"it's written that I'm owed another pair of Manolos." She thought a moment, shrugged, and said: "It's a blessing I'm not Catholic, because I'd probably believe there was a tenth circle in hell for people who spend on shoes as I do."

Looking at my mother, I couldn't believe she had just turned seventy. That was a number that had nothing to do with her. She was still as willowy as she was in her wedding pictures, in which she'd worn an unadorned ivory satin gown that fit her body so perfectly it seemed to have first been poured onto her skin in liquid form before turning to fabric. Her eyes were a lively green. When I read *Gone with the Wind* for the first time, I was thrilled that Scarlett O'Hara had my mother's eyes.

My mother's hair was dark brown, expertly dyed now, and she wore it as she had all her adult life: she pulled it back as if to make a long ponytail, but instead she looped her hair into a knot at the base of her neck. It was kept in place by four tortoiseshell hair combs. When I was little, I'd stand beside her, watching as she sat at her vanity in the morning putting on makeup. I'd play with her four combs, pretending they were Mommy, Daddy, Maddy, and me. No doubt, given her training, she knew more about me than it was necessary for any mother to know.

She wasn't vain in that Upper East Side of Manhattan laser/dermabrasion/face-lift way of women whose skin is pulled so far back that they wind up looking like trout. She had minor wrinkles and a softening around the jawline, but somehow she'd reached seventy with only deep smile lines around her mouth and undeniable worry furrows between her brows. Her face said what she probably believed: life is neither all good nor all bad, but it always takes a toll. Looking at her, though, it was evident her life had been mostly good.

"I'm so glad my ten o'clock canceled," my mother said. "And then you called! I love spending time together, just the two of us. How are you? Missing Nicky?"

"Very much," I said. "Although part of me is starting to think of myself as a free woman instead of a mother. Don't worry, I feel appropriately guilty."

Naturally, my mother said, almost word for word, what I expected: "Ambivalence is human, sweetie. I've always said summer camp is for parents as well as children."

Simultaneously, we each sipped from our cans of Diet Coke, then set them on the floor where her rug stopped and the wood began. "Listen," I said, "I need your professional advice."

Her subtly mascaraed lashes flickered twice, the only sign she feared I was about to give her bad news. Otherwise she remained bright-eyed. I'd seen her I-am-a-mental-health-professional expression enough times in my life to know it well. It declared: *I'm interested but I don't want to smile in case you're about to inform me of some sickening secret that's lacerating your soul.* "Sure," she said pleasantly. "For you, my rates are cheap."

"There's a woman I used to work with at the CIA, Lisa Golding. I don't think I ever mentioned her because I wasn't all that friendly with her. She was a shopping friend, not a confidence-exchanging friend."

"Jewish?"

"No. Anyway, the Agency would occasionally bring foreigners over here to live—because we owed them something, and it might be dangerous for them in their old country. Lisa's job was showing them how to blend in to American life in whatever part of the U.S. they were settled."

"Did she teach someone who was going to be settled in Mississippi how to talk like a Southerner?"

"No. Because if she'd taken someone from Romania who barely spoke English to Mississippi, no matter how much she trained him, he wasn't going to sound as if he'd been born in Biloxi. What she did was give them some tools so they could behave as if they were ordinary immigrants. They couldn't appear to be special cases who came out of nowhere and were suddenly plopped down in a community. They had to act as unremarkably as possible. Lisa taught them how to dress American, given where they lived and what their social class was supposed to be. I'm not sure if she worked on their cover stories, but it was up to her to make the person and the story match. She lived with them for a few weeks, took them driving and grocery shopping, to movies, fast-food restaurants—or concerts and four-star restaurants if that was the case—and tutored them on how to behave, what to expect. A person from the Balkans might view a line of highway tollbooths as a border crossing and suddenly feel threatened."

"Well, that's interesting! One job description I never heard before," my mother said. Even as kids, Maddy and I noticed that her voice took on an upbeat tone, what my sister called "the wows," when she talked to us. Maddy said that was because she was trying to compensate for the fact that though she loved us, she found us slightly boring. I told Maddy she was crazy, that our mother just got happy being with us. But after Maddy's revelation, or maybe before, I always did feel slightly boring in my mother's presence. While I made a cute and/or insightful observation on occasion, nothing I ever said was worth such an ardent *wow*.

"Lisa had a theater background, set design. She also had a terrific eye for style. Not necessarily good style, like how to pick shoes like those." I pointed to her feet and she nodded a thank-you, pleased with the compliment. "She could take a walk through any neighborhood in the country and when she was done, she'd have absorbed amazing knowledge of how the people there lived—clothes, furniture, what they watched on TV, what they ate for breakfast."

"Uh-huh," my mother said encouragingly.

"The first time I met Lisa was to interview her for a report on how some big shot from the Polish labor movement was handling life in the Midwest—Chicago, I think. I thought she was cool. Lively and fun-loving, in a non-CIA sense. No har-har at witty observations about the Bundestag. On the other hand, no throwing parties built around tasting flavored vodkas."

"That's a party?" my mother demanded.

"It happens outside New York. Anyhow, I never thought Lisa was terribly bright, but she was good company."

"How come you never got past being shopping friends?"

"Lots of reasons. I'd just met Adam, so I wasn't all that anxious to go anywhere without him. We both were working hard and had so little free time that we wanted to spend it together." I looked down at my shoes. Black, but they were to my mother's shoes as a minivan is to a Ferrari. "But mostly, my relationship with Lisa never got past shopping and going to whatever play I couldn't drag Adam to because . . ." My mother was good at waiting. Finally I said, "I never could be real friends with her, well, because she was a liar."

"Oh." She gave a wise nod. Of course, I never really knew whether my mother's nods were wise, but they always looked it. "What kind of lies did she tell?"

Chapter Two

As the voice-over intro to *Spy Guys* observes every three or four episodes when some new hell breaks loose: It all started so simply. And only four weeks ago. It was around two in the afternoon. I was home on the Upper West Side of Manhattan packing a few of my things into a small duffel, preparing to take Nicky, my ten-year-old, to a weight-loss camp in Maine. His trunk was already up there, filled with large-bellied shorts and new athletic gear. Camp Lionheart required a parent to remain nearby for the first twenty-four hours of a camper's stay, probably to soothe any kid unhinged by half a day of sugar deprivation.

That kid would not be Nicky. Mere empty carbs were not his downfall. Food was. Naturally there was Ben & Jerry's. But there was also grapefruit. Calf's liver with sautéed onions. Giant Caesar salads with bony anchovies no one else under twenty-one would eat. He loved each block of the food pyramid equally. Nicky was a kid of huge enthusiasms. Yankees, Knicks, Giants, Rangers. Megalosaurus, tricer-

as some Blondie concert I went to when I was fifteen. All right, what the hell was I originally thinking I had to do here behind the toolshed? Oh, try to remember what I wrote in the journal I began a day or two after that first disturbing phone call. Maybe something I'd unthinkingly jotted down could help me now, or could at least allow me to delude myself that this episode will be yet another of my . . . *and they lived happily ever after.*

It's so dark. No moon, no stars: the earth could be the only celestial object in a black universe. And it's hot. Even at this late hour, there is no relief from the heat. My shirt is sweat-drenched and so sucked against my skin it's a yellow-and-white-striped epidermis.

I cannot let myself dwell on the fact that my danger is doubled because I'm so out of my element. Me, Total Manhattan Sushi Woman, cowering behind a toolshed in fried pork rinds country with unspeakable creatures from the insect and worm worlds who think my sandaled feet are some new interstate.

Adam, my husband, would probably be able to identify the nocturnal bird in a nearby tree that refuses to shut up, the one whose hoarse squawks sound like "Shit! Shit! Shit!" Adam is a vet. A veterinary pathologist at the Bronx Zoo, to be precise. Were something that feels like a rat's tail to brush his toes in the dark, he wouldn't want to shriek in horror and vomit simultaneously, like I do. He'd just say, *Hmm, a Norway rat.* Adam is close to fearless.

I, of course, am not. If I concentrate on what's happening here in the blackness, the slide of something furry against my anklebone, the sponginess of the ground beneath the thin, soaked soles of my sandals, a sudden *Bump!* against my cheek, then something, whatever it is (bat? blood-swollen insect?) ricocheting off, I will literally go mad, and trust me, I know the difference between literally and figuratively. I'll howl like a lunatic until brought back to sanity by the terrible realization that I've given away my precise location to that nut job who is out there, maybe only a hundred feet away, stalking me.

Feh! Something just landed on the inner part of my thigh. As I brush it off, its gross little feet try to grip me.

Don't scream! Calm down. Taoist breathing method: Listen to your breathing. Easy. Don't force it. Just concentrate. Listen. All right: three reasonably calm breaths. What am I going to do? How am I going to survive? Will I ever see Adam again? And our son, Nicky?

What used to be my real life back in New York seems as far away

Chapter One

O H GOD, I WISH I HAD A WEAPON! NATURALLY, I don't. Of course, if life in any way resembled *Spy Guys,* the espionage TV show I write, I'd pull off the top of my pen and with one stab inflict a fatal wound, and save my life. Except no pen: just two pieces of chewed Dentyne Ice spearmint wrapped in a receipt for sunscreen and panty liners.

When I began making notes on what I naively thought of as Katie's Big Adventure, I hadn't a clue that my life would be on the line. How could I? This would be my story, and every ending I'd ever written had been upbeat. But in the past few weeks I've learned that "happily ever after" is simply proof of my lifelong preference for fantasy over reality.

Unfortunately, fantasy will not get me out of this mess. So what am I supposed to do now? First, calm down. Hard to do when I'm crouched behind a toolshed, up to my waist in insanely lush flora that's no doubt crawling with fauna.

Past Perfect

SCRIBNER

A Division of Simon & Schuster, Inc.

1230 Avenue of the Americas

New York, NY 10020

First Scribner trade paperback edition June 2008

SCRIBNER and design are trademarks of
The Gale Group, Inc., used under license
by Simon & Schuster, Inc., the publisher of this work.

For information about special discounts for bulk purchases,
please contact Simon & Schuster Special Sales at
1-800-456-6798 or business@simonandschuster.com.

Designed by Kyoko Watanabe
Text set in Stempel Garamond

Manufactured in the United States of America

1   3   5   7   9   10   8   6   4   2

Library of Congress Control Number: 2006051203

ISBN-13: 978-0-7432-4216-5
ISBN-10:   0-7432-4216-5
ISBN-13: 978-1-4165-7208-4 (pbk)
ISBN-10:   1-4165-7208-2 (pbk)

SUSAN ISAACS

Past Perfect

Scribner
NEW YORK LONDON TORONTO SYDNEY

ALSO BY SUSAN ISAACS

"Her fans will delight in the exploits of another of her smart, somewhat neurotic amateur sleuths."

—*Hartford Courant*

"Susan Isaacs has made a career out of conjuring up gumptious gals. . . . The action is heart-thumpingly fast."

—*The Miami Herald*

"A riveting read."

—*Toronto Sun*

"This is a novel with buckets of attitude."

—*The Boston Globe*

"*Past Perfect* is perfect! I love Susan Isaacs! Her books come straight from the heart, and her characters are smart, funny, and feisty enough to be your best girlfriend."

—Lisa Scottoline, author of *Dirty Blonde*

"Picture yourself laughing out loud while sitting on the edge of your seat . . . *Past Perfect* was written by a master storyteller."

—Nelson DeMille, bestselling author of *Wild Fire*

"There has to be a name for the literary form Susan Isaacs has invented: the funny scary book. . . . *Past Perfect* made me laugh, but it also [had] me jumping out of bed every time a floorboard creaked in my old house."

—Sara Paretsky, author of *Fire Sale*

Praise for Susan Isaacs

"The jauntiness and frothy exuberance of Susan Isaacs's style carries you along as if on a wonderful joy ride. She is superb at quick character sketches, the deadly battles between fathers and sons, family frictions, and generational antagonisms. Her effervescence convinces you that everything will turn out all right in the end. Which it does. But just barely."

—*The Providence Sunday Journal*

Praise for *Past Perfect*

"Katie is vintage Isaacs: a sexy, successful woman with all her insecurities up front and no illusions about her own failings."

—*Newsday*

"Isaacs is so good at what she does that her deservedly loyal fans are bound to be charmed."

—*The Washington Post*

"The story moves buoyantly thanks to sharp dialogue, brisk plotting, and an eminently likable protagonist."

—*Los Angeles Times*

"The best part of this novel is Isaacs's Katie—glib, funny, discursive, semiparanoid, smart, and blessed (or cursed) with an eye for detail."

—*St. Louis Post-Dispatch*

"Isaacs's thrillers are always witty, informed in the ways of both women and the world, and *Past Perfect* is no exception."

—New York *Daily News*

"The engaging result is a light, fast read."

—*The Denver Post*

"Ms. Isaacs . . . is feisty, funny, and smart."

—*The New York Times*

"Readers always look to novelist Susan Isaacs for smart, sassy, funny, first-person heroines."

—*The Seattle Times*

"Isaacs knows how to write women you love to love . . . [she] has defined herself as a champion of smart, lucky, heroines."

—*Publishers Weekly*

atops, pteranodons. Yet, even as the Megalosauruses gave way to Game Boys and Game Boys were eclipsed by *His Dark Materials,* there was always that one overarching passion, food. Walking him to school when he was little, I had to allow an extra twenty minutes for him to stop and read (aloud and lovingly) every menu posted in the windows of the local restaurants, lifting him so he could read the appetizers. *"Gambas al Ajillo,"* he'd sound out. "What's that, Mommy?"

Sitting on the edge of the bed beside my duffel bag, I glanced inside. I'd folded the sleeves of my pink and aqua tattersall shirt across the front. They looked like hands pressing against a heart. The shirt was crying out to me: *What kind of mother are you? How could you do this to your child?* Not that Nicky would be one of the weepers, no *Mommy, Mommy, don't leave me here!!* Not one of the whiners either. While his father was a Wyoming strong, silent type, Nicky was a blabby New York kid. Still, he had inherited Adam's tough-it-out gene.

So there I was, beating up on myself, trying to figure what deranged thought process had led me to convince myself and then argue with Adam that a fat-boy camp was a stellar idea. I was packing off my only kid, giving him an entire summer to reflect on the fact that his mother couldn't accept him as he was. And his father too, since Adam and I were Present a United Front parents, a concept we'd both gotten from our own families, the eastern Schottlands and the western Graingers. Not that we'd ever consciously decided on such a strategy. Like so much in marriage, we did as our parents did, not necessarily because they were right, but because what they did was what we knew. Since we two were speaking as one, Adam could not blare out the truth: *I can't believe your mother is so shallow and easily gulled by those hysterical "Danger: Childhood Obesity!" reports in the* Times *and on CNN.* My eyes filled, though I can't remember whether it was at the unfairness of Adam's unspoken criticism or because it was so close to the mark.

I actually started crying genuine stream-down-the-cheeks tears when I remembered that Adam wouldn't be driving up to camp with us. It felt like desertion. It wasn't. He had to deal with an outbreak of duck plague. Five Muscovy ducks had dropped dead, admittedly not a big deal, unless you're one of those "there's a special providence in the fall of a sparrow" types, which obviously they were in the zoo's pathology department. Truthfully, my tears weren't flowing because I couldn't bear to be without my husband's company. After fifteen years of marriage, most people can tolerate forty-eight spouse-free hours. But I wanted Adam along to witness for himself, once again, my devotion to Nicky, to observe what a splendid mother I was, and how leaving our son in a weight-loss camp was not the act of a neurotic New Yorker who had a block of ice for a heart.

At that instant, my phone rang. I picked it up and uttered a tremulous "Hello."

"Hey, Katie Schottland," said a squeaky, cartoon voice, as if the speaker had come from some primary-colored, two-dimensional universe whose inhabitants did not have genitalia. "Do you know who this is?"

I sniffled back about a quart of as-yet unshed tears, then wiped my eyes with the three-quarter sleeve of my new, cantaloupe-colored stretch T-shirt that gave my skin the golden glow of liver disease. Shaken as much by my weepiness as by the intrusion of the call, I stood, marched to the dresser, and, holding the portable phone between ear and shoulder, yanked open a drawer. I wished I were one of those tough dames who could bellow, *I don't have time for this shit!* What I actually said was: "If you don't tell me who this is, I'm hanging up."

It's not in my nature to be that snippy, but I'd gotten home late from the studio in Queens where we taped *Spy Guys* for QTV, a network that called itself "The People's Choice for Quality Cable." (Its detractors called it Quantity Cable.) Besides being rushed and sick with guilt about what I was doing to Nicky, I was again trying to dig up the old dark blue bandanna I'd been searching for obsessively, as though it were a talisman that would protect both me and my son from my folly. Why couldn't I find it? I pictured myself wearing it knotted casually around my neck, the implication being that I'd be using it as a sweatband, or, in a pinch, as a tourniquet as I gave first aid to a fellow hiker who'd suffered a hundred-foot fall from a precipice. Not that I was actually considering the Parent-Child Hike option scheduled for Camp Lionheart's opening day, but for my son's sake, I needed to look like a gung-ho mother who delights in vigorous exercise.

Meanwhile, the person on the phone shrilled, "Come on, Katie. Lighten up." Now I could hear: definitely a woman's voice. Not unfamiliar. Her identity was right on the tip of some neuron, although she was not sister, close friend, mother, or anyone connected with the show. Still, I couldn't access the name.

"Fine," I said, "I'm lightened up. Now please tell me."

"Actually, this is serious. Terribly, terribly serious."

"Lisa!" I exclaimed.

For all the time I'd known Lisa Golding, since our sunny days more than fifteen years ago in the CIA, she'd had a habit of repeating adjectives: "The German translator has a gigantic, gigantic pimple on his chin." "Ben Mattingly's wife is so filthy, filthy rich that he actually doesn't find her embarrassing."

Anyway, back on that afternoon four weeks ago, Lisa Golding declared, "Katie, I've *got* to talk with you. This is a matter of national importance!"

National importance? Years earlier, when we were both in our twenties, Lisa's job at the CIA had been an extension of her brief career as an assistant set designer at a regional theater in exurban Atlanta. She set up houses and wardrobes, and coached foreign nationals in American lifestyles. She worked for the International Cooperation Detail, the CIA's equivalent of a witness protection program. The ICD brought people whom our government owed big-time to the United States to live.

"Do you know why I'm calling you?" she demanded.

"You just said something about a matter of national importance," I muttered, at last finding the blue bandanna. I crumpled and twisted it until it looked wrinkled enough to pass for hiking gear. I know I should have been paying more attention. Yet even though I hadn't heard from Lisa in years, I couldn't imagine her saying anything compelling enough to make me slow down my packing. I just assumed her call had to do with my writing *Spy Guys*: She was coming to New York and could she visit the set; or a friend had written a screenplay and did I know an agent.

Perhaps at this point I ought to put my conversation with Lisa Golding on hold and explain the spying business. First and foremost, I was never a spy.

My career path actually began years before I even heard of the CIA, when my big sister, Madeline, copped both the Deering School's fifth grade's Vance Poetry Prize and the Kaplan-Klein Essay Award. Uh-oh. At that moment I thought, Okay, I'll be a theoretical physicist—probably because "mathematician" sounded too pedestrian. That vocabulary does sound a bit much for an eight-year-old, but consider the extenuating circumstances.

Maddy and I were privileged mini-Manhattanites who lived in a co-op on the Upper East Side with gifted, solvent, and articulate parents. Our father was the founder and CEO of Total Kitchen, a small but quite profitable chain of kitchenware stores for people eager to spend nine hundred dollars on an espresso machine. His hobbies were listening to jazz, mostly that stuff that repeats the same phrase fourteen times—until you can't bear it anymore—and collecting colonial American cooking equipment. Our kitchen was decorated with shelves and shelves of ugly black iron shit with wood handles.

Our mother was a psychiatrist whose patients—chichi bulimics and natty manic-depressives—worked mostly in the garment business. She herself had such a brilliant sense of style that more than a few patients confessed they couldn't bear to quit treatment because they would miss seeing how she got herself up each week. My parents' friends were an urbane crew, journalists, theatrical producers, an academic here, a lawyer there, as well as their fellow minor moguls and shrinks. Thus, Maddy and I were not at all fazed by words like *soigné* and *Turk's head mold* and *astrophysicist*. While we were allowed only one hour a day of TV time, our reading was never censored or limited. My vocabulary grew. I read every book that caught my attention, from *Harriet the Spy* to *Wild, Reckless Love* to *The Big Bang: A Report from the Cosmos.*

Leap forward a decade. Ten years after I enchanted the guests at one of my parents' dinner parties by appearing in a pink flannel nightgown with itsy-bitsy unicorns prancing on the collar and cuffs and declaring how cool Einstein's relativity theory was, I recognized an obstacle in my way of becoming a physicist. One ought to like physics. Or at least have a talent for it.

Ergo, I majored in economics. What with the obligatory differential calculus and statistics, it was a subject comfortably distant from my sister's world of exquisite literature. Still, during my four years at Connecticut College, my true major was doomed relationships. I also educated my left hand to give my right a flawless manicure, and continued my life of intrigue going to spy movies and reading espionage novels. I read and reread the oeuvres of John Le Carré, Ian Fleming, Robert Littell, and, when in a rare philosophical humor, Graham Greene.

Upon graduation I was unable to find work reading spy fiction. I came back to New York to spend eighteen hideous months at Winters & McVickers, Investment Bankers. I worked eighteen-hour days among people who found discussions of the availability of government-enhanced equity for investment in venture capital more stimulating than either sex or going to Miami. I figured that was the price I had to pay for being an adult. (My sister, Maddy, by this time, had already had several poems published in *Pleiades,* one in *The New Yorker,* and had just gotten married to Dixon Cramer, man about town, gourmet, and a film critic for *Variety*.) All the above is the simplest explanation for how, shortly before my twenty-third birthday, I turned my back on family and the financiers of New York and ran into the open arms of the spooks of Langley, Virginia.

Even though the CIA had given me a fair idea of what sort of work I'd be doing, I was a little disappointed that when I arrived at Langley there was no *Surprise! You're going to be a secret agent!* welcome. I was placed in the unemotional, spreadsheeted world of financial analysis. But at least I was investigating money laundering. And I was at the CIA! The stuff that dreams were made of, or at least my dreams. They gave me a security clearance and an identity card to prove it. I'd never been happier. Every morning as I passed through the security checkpoints, I felt the thrill of being precisely where I was born to be.

Born to be slightly bored, I decided after a few weeks. But only slightly. There was zero James Bond glamour in my work. Most of it entailed reading communiqués from our own people, reports from other agencies, and analyzing illegally obtained financial data on the assets of certain world leaders and their associates. I was figuring out stuff like how much of, say, our thirty-five million in military aid to a certain country in Central America wound up in *el presidente*'s offshore account in a bank on the isle of Jersey. (Ans: $7,608,300.) Then I'd write up my findings in snappy, don't-fall-asleep language for reports to be read by congressional and executive branch staffers.

So snappy was I that my writing soon got me out of the Economic Study Group. Six months at the CIA and I got transferred to a completely different area. My new gig was working for the deputy chief of the Office of Eastern Europe Analysis, a congenial unit save for the über-chief, a nasty Kentuckian who had let his hair grow out with the Beatles and still, all those years later, sported giant gray sideburns and low-hanging bangs the color of aluminum foil. Nothing boring in this department. Every day I came to work feeling alive: something exciting will happen today. And usually something did. I walked through the halls with that confident, chin-up stride of an astronaut.

The nearly two years I worked for the Agency might have been a mere blip on the radar screen of anyone else's life. But this was my bliss. Twenty-three months of knowing not just that I loved what I was doing, but that my work mattered. To me. To my country. Nothing else I'd done or would ever do would feel so right. Then suddenly it was over. And I had no place to go. I couldn't find another job.

A prospective employer would call the Agency's personnel department and all he would get was a terse confirmation that, yes, Katherine Schottland had once been an employee. Had I left of my own accord or been fired? Was I competent? Stable? A patriot? A traitor? No comment. This went on for nearly five years, until Nicky was born; his birth gave me a sweet though colicky excuse to stop looking for work.

Throughout that time, Adam was so decent about my not finding a job that it only added to my shame. "Stop worrying about it," he told me. "Millions of women stay home and are perfectly happy. Go to museums, read, get a master's in something. I can handle it as long as you don't want a mink coat or rubies." But I needed to know I could do something worthwhile, or at least earn money, so until my eighth month of pregnancy, I did cooking demonstrations in my father's stores: deep-fried potato nests in Boston, food processor pastry in Palm Beach. I drove up and down I-95, staying in chain motels that seemed to mandate their chambermaids not to clean under the beds.

When Nicky was three, Adam took a job as a pathologist with the Bronx Zoo, and we moved to New York, to City Island, a salt-sprayed, yellow-rain-slickered boating community, one bridge and a few miles from the zoo in the Bronx. When my parents visited our small and perhaps too cutely decorated (by me) apartment for the first time, my father had an ear-to-ear grin that was so phony it could have been painted on. He managed to say, "Very sweet," as if that poor kid from Brooklyn he always talked about having been wasn't him after all. My mother opened a window, took a deep breath, and said with a too-toothy cheering smile, "The air here is so wonderfully bracing!"

Not that I felt any pressure about living the wrong life in the wrong neighborhood, but we moved to Manhattan the summer before Nicky went off to kindergarten. I tried again to get a real job and, once again, potential employers who seemed so interested at my interview became cold after checking my credentials. Why didn't I lie and say I'd worked for my father the whole time? He'd have me draft a brilliant recommendation he'd be glad to sign. How come I didn't merely drop the Agency from my CV as if I'd never been there? I don't really know. Maybe it meant too much to pretend it hadn't happened. Maybe if I couldn't have the CIA, I didn't really want to work at all.

My only credential besides demonstrating overpriced cookware was that, from both fiction and life, I had some knowledge of spying. Desperate for something to do, I decided to write a spy novel. Had I always secretly burned to write fiction? God, no. But as I read more and more espionage novels, I began thinking, *I could do this*. And I did. *Spy Guys*, the novel, took me two years. Writing it was so lonely and tedious that, in comparison, my days in due diligence meetings in the Winters & McVickers, Investment Bankers, fourteenth-floor, windowless conference room seemed like Fun Fest USA.

Surprise, the book was published, and with some success. While I was trying to write the sequel (a task my publisher seemed only slightly more interested in than I), QTV came along and inquired: Was I interested in developing *Spy Guys* as a weekly, hour-long television show?

"Listen, Kathy," the development executive I had asked five minutes earlier to call me Katie said, "let me be straight with you. Okay? Okay. You've got to be willing to make certain changes with one of the leads." He told me I could keep Jamie the tough but beautiful and lovable streetwise New York cop turned CIA agent. But I'd need to change the other main character from *Mitteleuropa* deposed prince with a goatee into a clean-shaven, minor Spanish royal.

Not just any minor Spanish royal. Development Guy went on to explain that through some labyrinthine link to Queen Victoria, His Highness would be fifteenth in line for the British throne. That way, his dialogue could include witty Prince William and Prince Harry references. Oh, and best of all, he'd be played by Javiero Rojas, a gorgeous but not-very-good singer from Chile turned egregiously bad actor, though still gorgeous. Then Development Guy said, "The truth, Kathy. Doesn't it sound like fun?" The truth was, creating a TV show sounded better than sitting alone in a room for a couple of years getting wired on Diet Coke and trying to write a book.

Back to the afternoon four weeks ago, when that voice from the past, Lisa Golding, called me. "Katie, you're the only one I know who has big-time TV connections."

If I hadn't been so pressed for time, I would have laughed. As it was, all I did was hoist my lower lip over my upper so that the impatient sigh I exhaled traveled north of the phone's mike. "Lisa, I'm really sorry but I'm in a huge rush to get out. Can I speak to you late tomorrow or—"

"Trust me," she squeaked, at which I did have to smile: within a few days after first meeting her, I'd realized the words *Lisa* and *truth* did not belong on the same page. "Your friends at CNN or wherever will owe you forever when you give them this."

"I don't know anybody at CNN. I don't know anybody at any other news outlet either. *Spy Guys* is aired by what's probably the most obscure cable network in the country. And my show isn't just not-news. It's unreality TV." Trust *me*, I was tempted to tell her: *Spy Guys* was a fluffy forty-seven minutes for viewers who enjoyed being willfully ignorant about the actual doings of the Central Intelligence Agency.

"What about your husband?" she asked.

"My husband has nothing to do with the media."

"Katie, I know Adam. I thought he might have a friend or something. It is still Adam, isn't it?"

"Yes, it's still Adam."

"Well then, remember when we were all in Washington? We were friends. How could I not know Adam?" The extent of her friendship with Adam, as I vaguely recalled, was when we once ran into her at a coffee place. She'd sat with us for the length of time it takes to sip a cappuccino.

"Anyway," I went on, "he's a pathologist at the Bronx Zoo. That isn't a job that puts someone in the media loop. I haven't had anything to do with anyone doing work of national importance for . . . whatever." Not for the fifteen years since the CIA fired me without an explanation.

"Oh, Katie, *please*."

"All right," I told Lisa Golding, "I'll be glad to listen to whatever you say, but honestly, if it truly is of national importance, I'm not your girl."

"Look, I know you think I tend to be frivolous—"

"Not at all," I assured her. Shallow, yes. Amusing on occasion. Not trustworthy.

"—and that, to be perfectly honest, you think I have a tendency to embellish the truth. And I do, or at least I did, to make for a more fun story. Believe me, I was dreading calling you because of the boy who cried wolf syndrome. But I've grown, Katie. And I swear to you, this is urgent. I need you to listen and I need you to help." Unfortunately, even if I'd thought of her as an honorable and contemplative person, Lisa had one of those top-of-the-treble-clef voices that, had she been discussing *Being and Nothingness,* would have sounded like she was talking about hair gel.

I think that was the moment Nicky strolled into my bedroom with a handful of dried apricots. He extracted the piece he was chewing on from his mouth with such delicacy I had a two-second flash about what a good surgeon he'd make. "Mom, what if . . . Oh." His voice fell to a whisper. "I didn't see you're talking."

I held up my hand in a wait-a-minute gesture. "Lisa . . ." I said into the phone. What was making me feel even worse was that Nicky wasn't fat. I studied him. A warm, smile-filled face. Okay, he was overly solid, and big for his ten years, five feet tall already, so his size seemed magnified alongside of his smaller classmates. But he wasn't flabby. And he didn't have the starchy pallor of a kid who was a couch potato. His ample cheeks were like peaches, warm gold tinged with red. Admittedly, his waist spread rather than tapered, but—

"Lisa, can I get back to you? I have to drive my son up to camp and I'm already an hour behind schedule."

"Katie, didn't you hear what I said? I swear, this is so huge . . ." Her high voice thinned, as if someone had taken the up and down line of an EKG and stretched it out until it was flat. *"Please."*

Okay, Lisa Golding did sound stressed. And my natural tendency has always been to offer an outstretched hand or comforting pat on the head to someone in need. However, my years in TV, an industry made up entirely of overwrought people, had taught me it was not necessarily my obligation to be the primary easer of angst, especially for those like Lisa who were given to overdramatizing and under-veracity, who popped up after a decade and a half of silence. So I met her halfway: "I'm taking my cell phone," I told her. "I could talk to you tomorrow afternoon, after the camp's opening day activities."

"Listen," Lisa said, "besides the urgency . . . Things have happened. . . ." I was shaking my head in a *she's-hopeless* gesture and Nicky responded with a grin of understanding, when she added, "Things are completely different now. I feel I don't owe anybody anything anymore." She took a deep and dramatic breath. "I feel absolutely free to tell you why the CIA fired you."

My body began to tremble from the inside out. I recalled the expression: shaken to the core. Well, my core was definitely shaking. Here was Lisa, offering an answer to the question I'd come to accept as unanswerable, except I couldn't really have accepted it—could I?—because at that instant all there was in the world was the woman on the phone who had the information I so desperately needed. My son had vanished from my consciousness as though he'd never walked into the room.

Truthfully, as though he'd never been born. My years as a mother dissolved and I was back in Personnel, thinking I'd been called in because I was going to get a promotion, given the title of communications coordinator. *Ms. Schottland,* the yellow-toothed placement officer would smile at me, *your higher level of clearance went through, so now you can go to meetings off-site, at Congress and the EOB. . . .* I almost floated into the office. Talk about job satisfaction! God, I was so happy. I greeted her with a smile.

She said, "Your clearance has been pulled." It was like a dead person speaking. Zombie tonelessness, eyes open, on me but not seeing me. "You'll have to leave the premises immediately. We'll have guards accompany you upstairs so you can take any personal belongings."

My mouth had dropped open. Somehow I made it say, "Listen, there's been some—"

"There is no mistake. You are Katherine Jane Schottland, Social Security number is 124—"

"Why? What happened?"

"You know we cannot discuss matters of Agency security."

"But I'm entitled to an explanation."

"No." When you're shot through the heart, you go into such shock that all analytical powers take flight. Yet I did have one thought: Just *no*? Not even a brusque *sorry*? She went on: "By regulation you are not entitled to anything."

I stood there, staring at the wall behind her because I couldn't meet her eyes. Two nail holes from a picture that had once hung there stared back at me. She picked up her phone, punched three or four buttons, then hung up: probably the Agency code for *Accompany security risk to desk to pick up coffee mug, cosmetic bag, and framed honeymoon photo of subject and husband on a Belize baboon pre-serve, then throw her off premises.*

"*Please,*" I said, but she ignored me.

Desperate, I tried to come up with some explanation. But what in God's name could it be? Before Adam, I had gone out a couple of times with a guy from the Israeli embassy, a trade attaché who knew his economics, if not much else. Could he have been Mossad? But why would they wait almost two years and then not even question me about him? What else could there be? All I could come up with was that my sister, Maddy, had joined a radical poets' cabal that some genius in the FBI had determined was dedicated to the violent over-throw of the U.S. government. Nothing. I'd done nothing wrong. Right? Yet I flushed, hot with shame.

And now, all these years later, Lisa Golding was on the phone offering me an answer. I was shaking so much that I had to sit on the bedroom's only chair, a silly armless thing with a flouncy skirt. Like the rest of the room, it was a red and white toile. But I missed the seat and took a hard flop onto the floor. Nicky hurried over to me, but I waved him away. "I'm okay, I'm okay," I whispered, not look-ing at him.

Half sitting, half lying on the rough sisal rug, I said in my casual voice, "Fine, let's talk now, Lisa."

"No, not when you're rushed," she said quickly, as if she was already having second thoughts about calling me. "It can hold till tomorrow. I'll speak to you then."

"Really, Lisa, if this is important to you . . ."

"It is, and I appreciate your trying to accommodate me."

Had I sounded too eager? "Well," I said, trying to come across as casual, "I'd like to help." I gave her my cell number.

"Tomorrow will be okay. I'll call you around four o'clock. Take care, Katie. And thanks so very, very much."

■ ■ ■

As it turned out, Nicky took to camp immediately. His counselor was a nineteen-year-old kid from Nîmes. When Nicky said something to him in French, he said something back like *Lonnnk, lonnnk* many times over, which, frankly, is what French spoken at a normal speed usually sounded like to me. Then they performed the latest, elaborately choreographed version of the *High Five Internationale,* which demonstrated to each other their mutual coolness.

The other boys in the cabin ranged from chunky to morbidly obese, the latter a blond kid from Louisville whose complexion was the creamy yellow of a Twinkie; his eyes darted, as if trying to determine which of the other kids would be first to be cruel. He didn't spend much time on Nicky, which told me his instincts were good. My son would not be unkind, and would no doubt wind up defending the kid by murmuring something like *Don't be assholes* to the others.

Nicky had always been one of those pudgy/hefty/husky boys with a buoyant personality that other kids recognized came from an innate cheeriness (his Wyoming antidepressant gene), not from any desperation to be liked. Nicky's self-confidence earned him a respect that might have been denied a child whose gregariousness was forced. Back in fourth grade, Billy Kelly, the school bully who tormented the lives and dreams of all the other boys, left my kid alone. He saw what other people saw: my son's gleaming smile, all white teeth and silvery braces. With Nicky's irresistible grin, bright blue eyes, and the perfect number of freckles on his nose and cheeks, he could be cast as the pudgy, friendly, true-blue neighborhood kid in any American movie.

So not having to agonize about my child beyond the usual mother worries about waterfront safety and bad mayonnaise, I sat beside him on a wooden bench during the parent-child Making Meals Count meeting in the arts and crafts barn and, gazing down at the planked floor, wondered what Lisa Golding would tell me about why my life had turned out the way it had.

Chapter Three

AFTER A DESSERT OF FRUIT KEBABS, AND AFTER kissing my son good-bye, I spent the requisite twenty-four hours close by camp, in and around the Woodsworth Motel ("All our rooms face beauty-full Manasabinticook Lake"), trying to think suitable maternal thoughts like, Oh my God! I won't see Nicky for four weeks! while admiring the scenery—water behind a lot of pine trees. I tried to reread the spy classic *Tears of Autumn*.

But pretty much all I did was obsessively check my cell phone for reception bars and battery stripes, of which there were always a bounteous number, and wait for Lisa Golding's call. It didn't come. Not at four. Not at five.

Maybe Lisa had called our home phone. Could Adam have listened for messages and, without thinking, deleted it? Dubious. Besides, I was the designated voice-mail listener. Still, I called him at work to tell him someone I knew from my Agency days had phoned about a matter of national importance.

"National importance? Is she serious or nuts?" Adam asked.

"Probably nuts." Then I tried a light laugh that came out as a choking sound. "But she did say she would tell me why I was fired."

My husband said, "I'm really busy now."

I drove the 350 miles back to New York with a hands-free device stuck in my ear, but heard nothing but the audiobook *The Bourne Supremacy*. I was playing it low, so I wouldn't miss the call, and I couldn't follow the plot. At home, wiped out from the long drive and ready for bed, I left the phone on and recharging on my nightstand. Adam, obviously exhausted from the duck plague crisis, was deeply asleep on his side. His shiny reddish-brown hair, unstylishly long in this era of neofascist buzz cuts, fanned out on the white pillow.

The next morning, he went out for his usual run with our two dogs, Flippy and Lucy, so there was no one to stand guard over my cell phone in case it rang. Not that I was a wreck or anything, fearing I would miss Lisa's call, but when I took a morning shower, I began agonizing that my Bluetooth earpiece would not pick up my phone's ring through the glass door. I moved the soap from its overpriced Gracious Home nickel-plated dish and rested my phone there, far from the spray. Naturally, it got wet. The second I emerged I frantically dried it. Despite being able to see the lighted display with Nicky's smiley face as wallpaper, I panicked that some audio microchip had kinked from the steam, rendering the phone mute.

Dripping all over the rug, I rushed to the bedroom phone on my nightstand and called myself. The cell jingled the opening theme of *Spy Guys*, an insipid tune the discount composer we'd hired claimed he had all but sold decades earlier to the Carpenters, except Karen died. As I stood there, the air conditioner blew iced air in the general direction of my knees, so within seconds my legs were covered with pink goose bumps and I was shivering. Pressing the "end" button only gave me the opportunity to brood that my call to myself had probably blocked one from Lisa, who, too fearful to leave a voice-mail message, had not only hung up, but had now given up on me in despair.

■ ■ ■

Funny about Adam. When I saw him for the first time, that day at the National Zoo, my initial thought was along the lines of, *Wow, he's hot.* Yet I thought I saw a world-weary sadness in his eyes à la Richard Burton in *The Spy Who Came In from the Cold.* But his smiling and saying hi in a friendly, open manner quashed any full-blown spy fantasy. I decided that the sadness in his eyes was because he was out of work, so instead of offering an encouraging hi, I nodded.

Except as I turned back to look at a lemur, my mind's eye was still seeing his strong, squared-off features and the way he knew how to fill out a pair of jeans. It made me reconsider—*Well, maybe he's just between jobs, not down and out*—so I amended my nod with a smile. It took only about three minutes of my native New York nosiness to learn that A) Adam Grainger of Thermopolis, Wyoming, had his Ph.D. and was a diplomate of the American College of Veterinary Pathology and B) the Burtonesque resemblance wasn't due to existential sadness, but to blue eyes (light blue with sparkles of darkest sapphire) that pulled down slightly at the outer corners. He took me for lunch in the employees' cafeteria and I could all but hear my mother and my friends singing *Don't let this one get away,* though my mother would be unable to exert enough self-mastery to resist a contrapuntal *Not Jewish.* She wouldn't sing it for long. Adam was smart, good-hearted, polite, and not so much of a workaholic and sports nut that he didn't read actual books.

Objectively, my husband was blessed with almost-handsome genes. Adam never looked dorky, though no one would ever think him a trendy guy. His hair was dark red-brown, straight, and a little mussed, and somehow you just knew he was two styles behind, not one ahead. He was sufficiently tall and lean that not even the most mean-spirited human being in Manhattan (i.e., my sister, Maddy, poet and sufferer of weltschmerz, a word that she actually used in everyday speech) ever held his lack of being cool against him.

Adam was a looker and had serious academic credentials but still he was a guy who had chosen to cut up dead animals for a living. Early on, the first few times we'd slept together, I'd done a lot of sniffing: attractive (or handsome, if your vision was 20/40), to say nothing of being Mr. Sizzling Sexuality Beneath Cool WASP Facade, but I had to make sure there was no subliminal smell of formaldehyde or, God forbid, something like a five-days-dead pit viper. Anyhow, then and through the years, Adam always smelled reassuringly of Adam, hay with a splash of sandalwood. Maybe it wasn't hay, but since he came from Wyoming and knew how to ride a horse, that's how I thought of it.

"I'm so glad you're not one of those science guys who wears T-shirts from a 1985 Dire Straits concert," I was telling him over breakfast, trying to sound lighthearted. I think I even attempted to toss my hair girlishly, forgetting I'd gone from shoulder length to chin length a year before.

"What would you do if I was one of those science guys?" he asked, clearly understanding I was in playful mode but not looking at me. He was concentrating on slicing his toast twice so it formed four nearly equilateral triangles, something I'd watched him do since the first morning we'd had breakfast together. "Leave town?"

"Probably leave the country. Do you want to know another thing I'm glad about?"

He glanced up from his plate and smiled. "Do you actually want a yes or no?"

"Of course not. I'm glad that you don't wear those stiff, baggy science-guy jeans that look like they were put in a charity bin and sent to some third world country where they said, 'Ugh!' and sent them right back."

As our dialogue indicated, Adam was closer to being a word minimalist and I was pretty much a maximalist. Still, when it came to thinking, I didn't know whether long and complex thoughts whizzed through his brain or if he was particularly gifted in the hunch department. But he did sense I was still upset about Lisa because he asked, "Did that woman you knew from the CIA get back to you?"

"No."

"She sounds like a pain in the butt."

"She was."

"Sounds like she still is. Well, she probably realized you couldn't do anything about . . . what was it? A matter of national importance." This remark was so you-doing-something-nationally-important-ha-ha! it brought to mind that breakfast table scene from *The Public Enemy* in which James Cagney smushes a grapefruit into his mistress's face. Not that I could imagine doing something like that to Adam, plus the only citrus fruit I had on hand was a lemon, which was in the refrigerator and I would have to cut it in half. Besides, even during our worst moments, my attacks on him tended more toward the oblique: *Your mother is a closet anti-Semite and don't deny it because every time we visit, her first dinner is always that greasy roast pork with bacon and chard,* though during one fight I threw his shaving mug across the bathroom. Actual belligerence was rare.

Most of the time, actually, we were more like the two demoiselle cranes that lived in the pond right next to the Bronx Zoo's hospital, where Adam worked. They were gray birds, a little smaller than regular cranes, with black on the front of their necks that extended down over their chests like chic, oblong black scarves. Not only did they mate for life, but they always seemed to do things together.

Each time I visited Adam at work, he'd point them out. "When one crane drinks," he'd tell me, "the other one always seems to be drinking too!" His hands would be on my shoulders so he could position me for a perfect crane panorama. Then, for the fifth or twenty-fifth time, he'd go on about their monogamous nature (human marriage, alas, being an institution in which you listen to the same observations limitless times, which would reduce mere cranes to insane philandering). "Amazing!"

Actually, Adam did not speak with exclamation points, being

your standard low-key Western guy, but I was pretty good at discovering the occasional maraschino cherry of emotion in his vanilla delivery. In any case, my husband was a one-woman man, and since the day he'd picked me up inside the Small Mammal House at the National Zoo in Washington, where he claimed I was smiling at a red-ruffed lemur, I'd been his woman.

And I stood by my man, albeit not while he was doing a necropsy — that's what an autopsy for animals is called — on, say, a deer he suspected might have succumbed to meningitis. Still, I was a traditional wife, delighted to sit beside him on the couch watching *24*, or to go along for an hour-long evening trot with our dogs, even listen to the old country music records he'd inherited from his grandfather — scratchy, mournful songs sung by a hoarse cowpoke who sounded as if he should get a chest X-ray.

"Why should you care if she doesn't call back?" Adam said. He eyeballed his sunny-side-up egg and expertly cut it so that not only did the yolk not run, but the piece fit perfectly atop his toast triangle. In vet school, his professors said he'd make a brilliant surgeon.

"I don't know," I muttered, trying to think of some topic that would make him believe I wasn't trying to avoid talking about Lisa. I sliced a humongous strawberry into my yogurt and quickly dismissed such potential conversation gems as Nicky's adjustment to camp, the war in Iraq, and the health of the duck population at the zoo.

"You told me you let go of this CIA stuff years ago," Adam said. "I hope you're not going to ruin your summer worrying about it again." He was cutting another egg triangle to match his toast, but even though he was concentrating, I could tell he was irritated. A couple of months into 1990, after I'd been fired, he'd advised me, "It's over. Give it up, Katie," and I guess he thought that was that.

"How can I ever say it's over and done without understanding why?"

"You have to for your own good. You were writing for the CIA, not *Ladies' Home Journal*. The Agency's a crazy outfit. You know it,

I know it, the whole world knows it. I thought we agreed back then that you'd be wasting your time trying to make sense of what happened. You'll never find out. Can't you accept it?"

"Obviously not." But I offered a sad, ingratiating little smile. As soon as it passed my lips, I knew I'd spend all day wishing I could take it back. Okay, not all day, as most of my energies would be spent on agonizing over why I hadn't heard from Lisa Golding. Listen, I wanted to shout at my husband, I was canned from the CIA without explanation. Cut off. Half my life was ripped away from me. You were there! Don't you remember how traumatic it was?

Forget how all of a sudden I was kicked out on my butt and couldn't find a job anywhere. Forget that on some government computer network there were probably terrible things written about me and nothing I could do would ever get them erased. Imagine how so many colleagues I'd cared for and respected now thought of me as a bad apple. Two years of cordial relationships with some of the smartest people in government, then, abracadabra! Katie Schottland went from respected colleague to a security risk. Maybe they guessed it was just crummy judgment on my part, or dubious associations. Perhaps I crumpled a page stamped "CONFIDENTIAL NATIONAL SECURITY" and stuck it in my pocket instead of feeding it into the shredder. Or they might have wondered whether, overburdened in the office, I'd tried to sneak work home on a floppy.

Or maybe they'd concluded I was genuinely bad, though there was not evidence enough of my badness to prosecute.

"Don't tell me to get over it," I said to Adam.

"Whatever you want." He went to the cabinet, reached for his New York Giants car mug. But instead of sitting back down, he poured some coffee, grabbed his second piece of toast, uncut and unbuttered, and (with a pleasant nod to show he was not an unfeeling bastard), headed off to the zoo.

■ ■ ■

Driving to the studio across Manhattan and over the Triborough Bridge, I didn't listen to NPR out of fear of getting engrossed in an essay on loganberries and missing a call from Lisa. Print Rite Studios, where we shot most of the interiors for *Spy Guys,* was a sprawling building of pockmarked yellow brick on a dead-end street in northwest Queens. As evident in its clever name, the building had housed a printing plant that closed in the early sixties. Now, whenever it rained for more than two days straight, the nostril-burning stench of midcentury ink would rise through cracks in the foundation up into the soundstages.

That day, however, was cloudless and brilliant. The only smell permeating the first floor was the ham and cheese from someone's fast-food breakfast reheating in a microwave. I climbed the two flights of steep, ink-blackened stairs to my office because the elevator was—cell phone–wise—a dead zone.

Starting right then, while climbing the stairs, I should have focused on the reality I was about to face: I'd missed a day of work taking Nicky to camp. That had left the producer, Oliver Waters, a man probably more suited to running a torture corps in Guantánamo than a TV series, to tyrannize the newest director and overrule him on any script issues the first day of taping a new episode.

However, reality and I had never enjoyed spending much time together, so my mind reverted from Oliver to its usual occupation, fantasy. As the riser of each stair was steep enough to qualify as step-aerobic gear for an advanced class, I had plenty of time to imagine my cell ringing. I would answer a little breathlessly and Lisa would say, *Sorry it took me so long to get back to you. I had to locate a safe land-line. A pay phone. These days it's so hard to find one that's working and not totally, totally crudded up so you don't even want to touch it.*

For some reason, that thought kicked off a memory of going to a big shoe sale with Lisa not long after we met. I'd watched as, with the concentration of a chef examining produce for a three-star restaurant, she'd scrupulously checked over the size sevens. She was in the middle of outfitting an East German national the Agency had spirited out and was resettling in the United States in some state that (the émigré's personal request being honored) had no harsh winters. Anyway, somewhere between flats and heels, Lisa got into a conversation with a woman about our age who was also checking out the size seven racks. Innocuous chatter about the fad of displaying what they were then calling "toe cleavage." As Lisa spoke, the woman, who'd been the one to initiate the conversation, started backing away.

Why? Something about Lisa's delivery put people off. I'd watched, fascinated that after retreating from Lisa's mile-high voice, the woman picked up a short brown boot and clutched it to her chest, almost like a shield. She edged back so far that she banged into a six-and-a-half rack just as Lisa was droning, ". . . makes your feet look crippled because the front, where your toes are, looks so wide and . . ."

I could hear too the personality glitch that was disturbing that other shopper. The unnatural slowness of Lisa's delivery. This tic might have been an asset working with foreign nationals who couldn't speak much English, but her too-slow talking obviously made her fellow Americans uneasy. No matter what she was saying, it began to come across as inappropriate after a minute or two. Flirtatious? Could "the front, where your toes are, looks so wide" sound like a fetishistic sexual innuendo? Or maybe the slowness made her every word sound teasing or snide: *There's more to what I'm saying than what I'm saying.*

Well, maybe there was.

Chapter Four

Lisa wasn't around the day the CIA got rid of me, or at least I didn't see her. She was probably in New Mexico or North Dakota teaching some ex-Polish commie big shot how to eat Kentucky Fried Chicken. But everyone else, from my boss, Benton Mattingly, to the woman wheeling the mail cart, had observed me being more conveyed than escorted to my office by two guys from the Office of Personnel Security, both of whom could be mistaken for albino gorillas. They were not all that tall, but they were hulking. Also, both had those small eyes and cone-shaped heads that connote the lack of a subscription to *The New Republic*.

They stood offensively close to me, glaring as I gathered up my mug and my pictures. Adam and I were scheduled to go to Wyoming to visit his family and there was a shopping bag full of presents for them I'd bought the day before during an overly long lunch hour—that couldn't be the reason for my disgrace, could it?—and had forgotten to bring home. The two gorillas made me take off all the ribbons and wrapping paper and pawed over my mother-in-law's blue flannel robe with green piping and my niece's white-gowned Barbie while half the unit, no doubt, hearing that something big was afoot, came sauntering by.

Even though I couldn't think of anything I'd done wrong, I felt so ashamed. I spotted my friend Martha, an Albania specialist, in the back of the group watching me leave and I tried to give her the look and a smile that would demand, *Isn't this the craziest thing?* Except my mouth wouldn't smile and the instant after we looked at each other, her eyes didn't move while mine began darting around as if I had hundreds of crimes on my conscience.

By the time I got home from Langley late that afternoon, I realized no one I'd worked with would ever speak to me again. And if I picked up the phone and called them at their homes? They'd cut off any conversation, plus, two seconds later, report my contacting them.

Those work friendships that lead to after-hours socializing: gone. No more women friends for drinks and dinner and movies. No more guy buddies who needed a smart woman to talk to when they wanted to show how sensitive they were. The people I'd worked with at the CIA weren't in Clandestine Services—operatives living overseas where people have a different identity and sometimes have to avoid each other to maintain their cover. We in Intelligence got together. We knew each other's lives.

Yet all those losses—job, friends—seemed small when it dawned on me that I'd also be cut off from Benton Mattingly for the rest of my life.

Okay, here goes. *Benton Mattingly: The Explanation.* Look, there's not a heterosexual woman alive over age fifteen who doesn't have some guy permanently in residence in the back of her mind—or hard-wired directly to her heart. The one who could have been. Sometimes it's simply an old crush that still has an overwhelming feeling of right-ness about it: *If only he'd gotten to know me, he would have loved me*

precisely the way I imagined he could love me. The guy could be someone she said no to, only to change her mind too late. Other times, it's
the great love that never worked out; that moment when you could
finally say, *Whew, glad I finally got him out of my system,* never happened. Benton Mattingly was my boss at the CIA, second in command
in the Office of Eastern Europe Analysis. He was the man who gave
me my assignments, evaluated my work, and passed it on to higher-
ups in the Agency, members of congressional oversight committees,
big shots in the executive branch.

And for a few months, he was also my lover.

Yes, dumb to start up with my boss—a married man seventeen
years older than I was. I should have just worn a T-shirt announcing,
Not only immature, but self-destructive! It wasn't as if I were a large-
eyed waif—the tremulous, can't-wait-to-be-victimized type who'd
be played by Winona Ryder. Early on, I heard all about Deedee
Dudek Mattingly, Washington hostess, the big-boned, big-voiced,
nonpartisan party-giver and partygoer. She'd inherited millions from
her father's foot care business (Dudek's Tween the Toes Creme,
Dudek's Cutting Edge Nail Clippers). The word around the Agency
was Deedee was so rich that even Ben, who'd won the gold in
upward mobility, hadn't had the grandiosity to dream of the life he
wound up living.

I knew all this about his life not just from office gossip and the
"Chronicles" column in *The Washington Post,* but from the teary
confidences of a Czechoslovakia analyst and, five months later, from
witnessing a microrage by a macroeconomist. These encounters both
occurred in the tiny antechamber to the ladies' room, the lone bathroom area reputed not to be bugged by Personnel Security, a unit said
to be committed to the axiom that the nearer a conversation is to a
toilet, the more reason to eavesdrop.

Ergo, before my affair with Ben began, those two fuming and
weepy women he had dumped had smartened me up. From the out-
set of those flings, he'd told them he would never leave his wife. "He

said so over our first drink, *days* before we even slept together," the Czechoslovakia analyst had confided in me, sniffling delicately. Yet apparently Benton's every word and act in his paramours' company persuaded them not to believe his words. He *would* indeed leave his wife and her money to marry them. Their delusions lasted around six months, which according to office gossip was how long it took, typically, from the beginning of one of his affairs until he said good-bye — reportedly with utmost civility.

So how could I not know? Willfully, that's how. Two and a half months into our affair, Ben began complaining about not being able to sleep. Sometimes I believed him: Ah, his knowledge of unspeakable government secrets keeps him awake; he's terrified of his own nightmares. Other times I was convinced his lust for me was so powerful he could not bear to sleep beside Deedee — the woman he was on the verge of walking out on for me.

One night Ben said, "Kate, I can't take it anymore." He was lying on his back, his arm around me as I rested my head on his chest in postcoital languor. What a chest! He was big, a former college athlete, but not one gone to seed. Okay, not rock solid, but he hadn't turned into one of those massive mounds of middle-aged flab. He had a chest the size of the Ozark Plateau, Popeye arms, with muscles both above and below the elbow. Maybe his legs weren't like twin sequoias, but they were damn impressive.

But it was Ben's face that got to women. His coloring was pretty much what you'd expect to come across in Fayetteville, Arkansas, where he grew up — gray-green eyes that in bright sunlight turned a wan hazel, skin more sun-roughed than tan, hair a short-cropped mix of blond and gray. Yet the bone structure beneath the skin might be described as Asian, with broad, high cheekbones and a wide-bridged nose. But Asian was too commonplace an adjective. Ben was exotic and beautiful, like a Mongol king: not what Mongol kings probably looked like historically, with blackened teeth and features disfigured by smallpox, but those triumphant Mongol kings on the covers of paperback romances who are always carrying off some virgin with waist-length hair.

With his free arm, Ben reached down to the floor beside my bed and patted the rug, searching for his undershorts. As there was that big age difference between us, I assumed by his gesture he was saying he couldn't do it again. But then I glanced up: gray shadows hung beneath his gray eyes. In an explosion of joy, I understood why he'd said he couldn't take it anymore: He couldn't take living without me! Yes! For him, every night was Insomnia City. My own eyes, brown, and at that point, shadow-free, must have started glowing because he almost tripped over his own tongue adding, "As much as I love you, we have to stop seeing each other."

"What?"

Ben came over to my apartment once more, three nights later. All that happened was he stripped down to his shorts, sat on the edge of my bed, covered his high-cheekboned face with his hands, and murmured, "Katie, I can't." When he removed his hands, there were actual tears in his eyes. That was it for more than a year, until I was fired.

Was he really crying that night? Did I ask myself: Is he a good enough actor to be able to turn on the waterworks at will? I did. But I couldn't allow myself to decide if I'd witnessed a performance or the real McCoy. Was I crazed enough from losing him to wonder: Had someone in the Office of R & D come up with a top-secret gizmo that could be hidden in boxer shorts and, merely by the wearer rubbing his knees together, bring tears to his eyes? Of course not! But who knew?

At least as far as my being fired went, I was confident the decision had nothing to do with Ben. I myself had seen both his other ex-conquests remain at their jobs and work side by side with him—their sides no longer accidentally brushing against each other, of course. I'd heard rumors about there being one or two other women. Three or four. Maybe they'd convinced themselves (as I would have in time) that because he was stuck with the rich and raucous Deedee, his freedom was far more painful to him than their rejection was to them.

For a few seconds, I managed to stop staring at the screen of my cell phone. I glanced around my office. I'd always been nuts for toile, the fabric that uses only one color for a design against a solid background of another color. Adam's and my bedroom was a red pastoral scene on white—eighteenth-century milkmaids, guys with George Washington–style wigs, and hunting dogs gamboling under trees—and our dining room was blue on white, this time with pagodas and less frolicsome Chinese couples. And no dogs.

So when QTV signed *Spy Guys* for a fifth season, Oliver, the aforementioned sourpuss producer, told me he'd allow me $2,500 to redecorate my office. "If it's even one goddamn penny overbudget, you pay!" he'd said sweetly. So now my office was a ten-by-twelve room whose walls and chairs were covered with ridiculously buxom yellow women playing yellow lutes and flutes while smirking yellow French courtiers danced under trees—all of them yellow—in a cream-colored universe. I sat at my desk, an old farm table that periodically shot splinters into my flesh, and looked back down at the "recently received" readout of calls on my cell phone. Of course, there was no number for a call that I might have missed from Lisa Golding.

This was merely the four hundredth time I had looked at it since I'd left to take Nicky to camp. What did I expect, that Lisa's number would morph onto the screen? I couldn't figure it out: Why hadn't she called back? Since my computer was already on, I began a list, using stars instead of bullets as I usually did in order to avoid feeling like a corporate, inside-the-box dullard. Now and then I did use smiley faces, but this time, dealing with CIA matters, I didn't want any interference from outside-the-Beltway ultra-femme vibes. So, stars:

★ Before she could call back, Lisa was shot dead in front of a Melrose Avenue boutique in L.A. / shot by a CIA op with a teeny poison-dart gun as she waited for a martini royale at a club in Miami Beach / garroted in the ladies' room of the Guthrie Theater in Minneapolis / mowed down by a Hummer in Houston. (Yes, I was being glib here, trying to mock the notion that such melodramatic doings could happen in real life. But keeping an ironic distance was hard because if Lisa was indeed planning to rat out the Agency, she'd left real life far behind. Terrible things could happen.)

★ Lisa had been drunk or high and going through an old phone book, trying to upset people she used to know and had always secretly despised.

★ She wasn't calling back because she wanted to keep me hanging so I'd be desperate. But desperate enough to do what? What could I have or do that she might need? I hadn't a clue.

★ Her call had been some sort of a lame joke in which she'd lost interest.

★ She was dying to call back but was being chased by evil forces aligned against the national interest and couldn't get to a phone. In *Spy Guys*, cell phones never died and evil forces were always vanquished. But real life meant real trouble.

★ She'd lost my number.

The night before, I had dug around the back of the coat closet and found the small carton with my pre-Adam Washington memorabilia; among all the papers and photos was the Filofax I'd been using in those years, its leather cover now so cracked it looked like alligator. I must have been anticipating today's big-time anxiety, because I'd copied down Lisa's fifteen-year-old Washington phone number. And I dialed it.

Someone's voice mail engaged after five rings. A man speaking a language that I didn't think I'd ever heard before said in Thai or

Yoruba or whatever, "I'm not in. Please leave a message." Of course, it could have been "I'm standing over Lisa Golding's dead body and there's nothing you can do about it, heh-heh," but the former seemed more likely. My guess was that Lisa hadn't had that number for such a long time that it had been reassigned.

I couldn't think of what to do next, so, even though I knew what would happen, I called the CIA's general number. The voice on the "You have reached the Central Intelligence Agency" recording sounded perky yet sincere—what you'd expect from the female cohostess of a show on a Christian broadcasting station. Eventually, I got connected with a public affairs person who, just as I'd expected, told me he could not give out any information on current or past employees if indeed this Lisa Golding was or ever had been an employee of the CIA.

Not that it in any way would be productive, but I began wondering whether I should be worrying about Lisa. Panicking about her? I had no idea when she'd left the Agency: Ten days ago? Ten years ago? Had she quit or had she been fired? If she'd been fired, was it for cause? Or, like me, had she gotten the ax and had no clue why?

The last few years, I'd noticed that whenever I was mulling over something at work, my eyes were drawn to the computer screen, as if any question I was capable of coming up with—*How hot is it in Tuscany in October?* or *Does God ever get vindictive?*—could be Googled and answered. The only answer I got from the screen now was that I had thirty-six unopened e-mails.

So I did a search on Lisa's name. Other than the Goldings I Googled before, there was nothing of interest, unless I cared to join up with all the Goldings spreading out the fruits of their family tree. And there was no trace of any Lisa I might have known among them. I closed my eyes and recalled a conversation (probably after she spent a January in Buffalo teaching some ex-KGB agent that you don't settle an argument with the owner of a Laundromat by slamming the man's head against a dryer) in which she had said may

she'd made a mistake coming to the Agency. True, she'd wanted out of theater, but maybe she should have tried film.

With that recollection, I checked for her in every area code in and around Los Angeles. Nothing. I looked at the online membership list of the Art Directors Guild, the group that represented people who work in movies and TV, but she wasn't there.

If this had been an episode of *Spy Guys,* His Highness would say to Jamie, "Wait! I had a little liaison with Countess Delphine, the one who's married to the head of Jupiter Studios." A fast cut to a mogul's pool in Belair (our location scout would come up with some successful CPA's pool in Hewlett Harbor on Long Island and we'd throw four or five potted palms into the shot). Javiero Rojas, who played HH, would be in a Speedo that looked like it was covering a giant chorizo. He'd lounge muscularly on a chaise next to an actress in a barely there bikini and a diamond bracelet—the latter would, of course, show she was an aristocrat—while a short, fat actor would take a cigar the size of an ocean liner out of his mouth and say, "Hey, Highness, my secretary tracked down that Lisa Golding you asked me about. She used to be an art director, but now she's living at 4107 Pecan Drive in Columbus, Georgia."

This being life, I was summoned to our producer's office because Dani Barber, the beautiful but intellectually challenged actress who played Jamie, would neither get in front of the camera nor stop fanning herself with script pages and saying, "Boooring!"—her way of communicating to us, every few days, that there was something in the script that displeased her.

"I'm not quite getting my motivation in the scene at the Venezuelan embassy," Dani Barber was telling me a few minutes later.

"What do you mean?" I asked, trying to sound as if I actually wanted to hear her answer.

She stroked her blond hair as if it were a lover she was trying to

arouse. Dani was our Jamie, the ex–New York cop turned CIA agent. She played her with a Brooklyn accent so egregious that there wasn't a week that we didn't get letters from Brooklynites with phrases like "I am outraged," "incredibly condescending," and "no-talent skank." Next, she put her nails to her teeth and pretended to gnaw on them, which of course she couldn't because they were plastic, and instead of a hangnail, she'd wind up with a chipped crown. "Where do I begin?" She sighed.

I kept silent, knowing one, she was on the edge and, if she went over, it would mean an hour of her *What do you want from me? Shakespeare is worth dying for and this piece of crap isn't, but can't you see it's killing me?* soft-voiced diatribe interrupted only by her dry heaves, all of which would delay the taping for another hour, and two, we were sitting in Oliver Waters's office. Oliver was leaning back in his leather throne of a producer's chair, giving the ceiling a view of his face, which, as usual, was probably contorted by some emotion in his customary range of pissed off to enraged.

For some reason, every time a pudgy African-American man is described in print, he's a "black Buddha." Oliver did have a fleshy, round face. His eyes were elongated, not from smiling but from being squeezed up by his balloon cheeks. As his mouth curved down instead of up, no one glimpsing him would come up with Buddha-ish adjectives like *benevolent* or *enlightened*. In the unlikely event anyone thought about him in religious terms at all, Oliver might suggest the god of dyspepsia.

Both he and I understood that Dani had been due before the cameras fifteen minutes earlier and was therefore costing us big money. Oliver went into his caring act, which was a wordless performance consisting solely of uttering that sound written as *tsk*. So I was stuck with having to be receptive to Dani's latest insight while listening to his incessant chirping: "Tsk, tsk, tsk."

"Let me put it this way," she finally spit out. "If I'm going into the embassy pretending to be a guest at the dinner and have to wear this dress with my boobs showing . . ." She adjusted the spaghetti straps of her costume, an emerald green cocktail dress. Her alleged boobs were grapefruit-size implants (albeit the larger, Indian River variety), but her narrow chest with its convexity of ribs seemed designed to support breasts no larger than kiwis. ". . . would I just walk in like the March of the Wooden Soldiers? Wouldn't I flirt, or grab somebody's arm and rub up against him?"

"I see your point, Dani," Oliver said. He had one of those husky Rod Stewart voices. Were he to say anything pleasant, someone might think, *Ooh,* sexy, *the way he talks,* but in the five years we had worked together on the show, no pleasant word ever passed his lips.

Oliver's head swiveled my way, signaling it was my turn. I had to take it. True, the show was based on my book and I'd been sole writer for all the years of its existence, but when there was a difference of opinion between writer and star, it was a TV fact of life: star wins. Oliver, who had the sentimentality of a block of petrified wood, would not hesitate to cut me down if I could not get along with Dani. The network, of course, would back him up.

"Dani," I said, "I have to give you credit: you're absolutely right."

"Then how come there was nothing, no guidance *whatsoever,* in the script?"

Oliver's office was around the corner from mine, and his door was open. Each time someone's cell tinkled or tooted, my heart seized up, even while realizing it was not Lisa calling me.

"Is it *totally* up to me to define Jamie's growth?" Her words jolted me back to the present; I knew there was no escaping what passed for reality in my life, *Spy Guys* in the person of Dani Barber. "Because as I see it, Jamie's changing a lot this season. Becoming stronger, and yet more humble." Dani offered this insight with high importance, as if she were Max Planck first declaring his constant. "Right, Oliver?" A grunt of agreement broke from his throat. "So in effect my entrance should display Jamie's femininity for everybody in the embassy, yet it would have a deeper meaning to the audience that even while she's quintessential Woman, she never forgets that she's an intelligence operative." Just to be certain I wasn't stymied by the complexity of her vision, she added, "Get it, Katie?"

"I got it, all right." What I didn't get was the phone call from Lisa Golding.

Chapter Five

"I KNOW YOU DON'T WANT TO HEAR THIS," MY ex-brother-in-law told me that evening.

"Hear what?"

At that moment, I wasn't so much listening to him as checking out his beard, or rather, lack of one. The last time I'd seen Dixon Cramer, his face had been darkly shadowed, the actor/artist look of *I get better sex than you.* Now he was so clean-shaven his tanned skin gleamed like a child's. God only knows what this change signified, but it was obviously cutting-edge face fashion. I didn't have to glance around the restaurant to know that slightly less cool men at other tables were unconsciously rubbing their jaws, regretting their scruffiness. Whenever I was with Dix, I always felt people must be wondering, How come he's with her? Oh, maybe she's a friend from high school.

"For someone who was a CIA analyst, you're not being very analytical," Dix was saying.

It had been four days since Lisa's call, and I'd opted to have dinner with someone other than Adam. He'd made it clear he thought any conversations about Lisa Golding, the Central Intelligence Agency, and why I'd been fired were pointless. And becoming tedious. A couple of times I'd noticed husbandly eyes following me. They were not aglow with desire. More like, How did I come to marry someone so crazy? But thinking me crazy didn't make him sympathetic to me, the way people shake their heads sadly when met with some poor soul in the grip of an obsession.

Adam had been patient. He'd been kind. He'd stuck by me way back then. He'd not only said all the right things, he'd thought them as well. But now: enough was enough. I could see it in his lips, compressed to the point of invisibility. If he'd been one of my mother's patients, she'd have jotted a note about him clamping shut his mouth so as not to allow himself to vent his anger.

"What are you talking about, Dix? Me not being analytical?" I started to diddle nervously with the flattened oil lamp on the table that looked like a frosted-glass version of Miss Muffet's tuffet, but it burned the pads of my fingers. So I peered straight into my ex-brother-in-law's dreamy eyes. "All I've *done* is analyze. I told you I've tried at least a million ways to track Lisa down. Not one of them led to anything."

We were sitting in Dix's newest hangout, a restaurant in Tribeca so exclusive that its name wasn't posted outside. Formally it was Giorno e Notte, but those hip enough to get a reservation simply called it Reade, after its street, a fact that simultaneously nauseated me with its in-group chic and made me long to be one of those in-people maître d's rush to kiss. Dix ran his finger around the rim of a red wine goblet large enough to be a baptismal font. No high-pitched squeal, but I shivered for a second as if there had been one.

"Katie, you and I have never been gentle with each other. Therefore"—Dix actually used *therefore* and *nonetheless* in conversation—"I feel free to tell you that tracking down somebody's phone number is not a test of the higher cognitive functions. And don't even think about giving me your hurt look." He thrust out his lower lip about a quarter of an inch and cast down his eyes.

"I stick out my lip like that when I'm insulted?" I asked.

"The Keira Knightley pout, which doesn't even look good on Keira Knightley."

Lucky for me, my ex-bro reviewed movies, not television. He probably would have given *Spy Guys* a scathing review. Okay, not scathing. Neither bitchiness nor blatant cruelty had ever been Dix's style. But with his combination of SAT vocabulary words, mastery of film history, and stealth humor you suddenly comprehended three sentences after you'd heard it—the best conclusion he could have come to about my show was *It's-lively-but-irremediably-trivial.*

The good news was, Dix liked or loved me enough to watch every new episode of *Spy Guys.* In lieu of reviews, he would e-mail me sprightly congratulatory notes: *Good show! Liked how His Highness's indecision over whether to order the Iranian caviar at the restaurant reflected his doubts about renewing his contract with the Agency.* It delighted me to learn I'd intended something so subtle.

Dix and I no longer shared my sister, but after their divorce we'd held on to each other, mostly out of affection, but also because of our mutual awe at Dix's cleverness. Both of us had wound up earning our livings from TV, a circumstance we each would have laughed at (with a single, condescending New York *hah!*) had anyone suggested it way back then. After getting his master's in film at NYU, Dix became one of the faceless film critics for *Variety.* A year of that and he'd jumped at a stint as number-three reviewer at the *Times.* As he was working his way up to number two on the long trek to the top spot on the paper, he'd gotten his own PBS show, *Sitting in the Dark.*

"I need your advice," I told him. "So go ahead. Tell me how I can be more analytical."

Maybe I was acting a little too wide-eyed because he snapped, "Oh, for God's sake! What is that face? Leslie Caron innocent?

You're too big-boned for that." I laughed, though his casual *big-boned* made me feel like Horton the elephant in my seersucker pants suit, which I'd realized was a mistake two seconds after I walked into the restaurant and realized every other woman there was in white silk or black gauze.

"Dixon, what's wrong with asking for help? You just told me I wasn't winning any awards in the higher cognitive department."

"That's because you're not *allowing* yourself to think, Katherine." He twisted off the tip of an elliptically shaped roll and dunked it into a dish of olive oil, then popped it into his mouth. For an instant, I feared a droplet might fall onto the front of his pale brown silk sport shirt and get sucked up by capillary action into a disgusting amoeba-shaped splotch—the sort of thing that routinely happened to me. But of course it missed the shirt entirely and wound up on the napkin he'd adroitly draped on his lap. Dix continued, "You're getting swept off your feet by your own need for—I'm actually going to utter the word—closure. Oh, this Lisa person will give me the answer I've been praying for all these years! I'll know why they fired me and it will turn out to be an idiotic keyboarding error and not a grave mis-judgment on my part that led to thousands of deaths in some obscure Baltic republic. I'll bring it to the CIA's attention and they'll be *dev-astated* that such an injustice occurred. Naturally, the head of the Agency, the one with the strange lips, will call a major news confer-ence and apologize to me."

"Don't make a joke of it," I snapped. "You of all people know what it's been like for me all these years. Every damn time I say to myself, Hey, I'm over it, the next thought that instantly pops into my head is, But seriously, what the hell did I do that was so wrong it made them get rid of me like that? It hurts as much now as it did then. Kicking me out with no explanation. Even if I made some stupid error, that Comrade X in Czechoslovakia sold a few MIGs under the table to Qaddafi and then stashed thirty million in a bank account in Geneva—except it turned out to be twenty-nine million in a bank in

Bern—someone was always checking my work. A huge mistake wouldn't have gotten by."

Dix's eyes widened. As they were green flecked with twinkles of gold, this was a very pretty sight. "Did something like that really happen? With Qaddafi?" he asked.

"No. It was one of my second-season *Spy Guys* episodes."

"Oh. Thought it sounded familiar."

"I didn't do anything original in Eastern Europe Analysis either. I wrote up other people's research and conclusions. If I needed more information, I interviewed them—and the session was always taped. That's *all* I was doing in that department for the year and a half before they got rid of me."

"Then why can't you live with the knowledge that there's a ninety-nine percent chance you did nothing wrong?"

Because in my heart of hearts, I didn't think anyone else believed that. Not Dix, not my sister, not my parents. Maybe Adam, but he was a scientist from Wyoming. How worldly could he be?

The waitress came with our appetizers: baby octopus with linguine for Dixon, warm arugula salad for me. She was wearing a white butcher's apron with the strings wrapped several times around, less out of necessity, I suspected, than because her waist was so small. The rest of her was too. She was one of those thin foodies who was either blessed with a metabolism like a smelting furnace or had a long, skinny forefinger that knew its way down her throat. She clunked down my plate so hastily that it was only chance that kept the arugula from flying into my lap. Then she placed Dixon's revolting baby octopus before him with the devotion of a priestess offering a sacrifice to her god. Her shining eyes and glory of a smile declared not only that she knew who he was, knew of his greatness, but truly, truly, truly, it was her pleasure to serve him.

Dix had always had the ego for fame, and now, with his own PBS show, he had the urban celebrity to match. Sitting across the mosaic-tiled table, I observed him as he attended to the plate before him and pretended not to notice how the other diners were giving each other that subtle Manhattan signal: Famous Person Sighting, a quick lift of the head to point out with the chin, *Look who's over there!*

Dix was not only telegenic, but he actually looked the same in person, somewhere between handsome and stunning in a dark, thick-eyebrowed way. As usual, he was dressed so you never doubted that under whatever jacket he was wearing lay genuine muscle, not shoulder pads. He reminded me of Sean Connery in *Dr. No,* if Sean Connery had been metrosexual enough to make people wonder if he just might prefer Bond boys to Bond girls.

Bond boys, as my sister discovered to her dismay, naturally acting as if I had caused Dix's homosexuality. This was because I suggested during their early dating days that (maybe, possibly, perhaps) he might be *comme ci, comme ça.* In any case, she and Dix went through what my parents referred to as a "civilized" divorce, which meant that Maddy didn't shriek, *You lousy fairy fuck, how could you deceive me like that?* As for me and Dix, my sister said she didn't care if I stayed friends with him. (Actually, what she'd said, poetry abandoning her, was, "Why should I give a shit?")

"What were you working on in the weeks or months before you were fired?" Dix asked. "Unless it's still top secret."

"Almost everything there was top secret. The rest was just plain secret. Technically there were lower levels of security too—classified and noforn, no foreign nationals. You want some CIA humor? There was a board in the cafeteria where they wrote the daily specials: someone painted 'Top Secret' across the bottom in big red letters. Funny."

"Excruciating."

"Everything I was working on was seriously secret. I mean, this was the Eastern Europe section and—surprise!—the Cold War was ending. That last day, before I could leave the personnel office and go get my things, I had to sign an agreement not to disclose what work I'd done or what discussions I may have overheard during my term of employment. I'd already signed an oath exactly like that when I started but they made me do it again . . . just in case it had slipped my mind. Anyway, Eastern Europe's stuff was all top secret."

"But can't you talk about what's public now?" Dix persisted, casually aligning the points of his shirt collar. He loved inside information. Film, theater, politics, but he could probably savor gossip about the Chicago Mercantile Exchange if no other inside info was coming his way.

I nodded. "I can talk about anything that's not classified. Plus, for you, a little extra." That wasn't true, but I wanted him to feel I was worth an evening. "The two top people in our unit had been in shock from how fast the regime in East Germany broke down. And then came the opening of the Wall between East and West Berlin. We hadn't exactly predicted it, at least the people in charge hadn't. All they'd done was insert those cover-your-ass sentences in reports: 'While it is possible that the East German bureaucracy may crumble under its own weight . . .'"

Even after everyone in the unit saw the first footage of ecstatic Germans holding up pieces of concrete—film gray from deconstruction dust and pollution brightened by a blue sweater here, a chunk of red-and-yellow-graffitied wall there, Ben Mattingly was making it clear that the NVA, the East German army, might just reanimate itself and send in tanks to quell "the uprising." Here he was, one of the Agency's top thinkers on the Cold War, and he couldn't comprehend that it was over. In government as in putting on a TV series, people in charge become so enthralled by their own story that the truth—it stinks—cannot get through. They throw their arms around their story to defend it from the assaults of the truth-tellers.

"You know," I said, "all these years I've been telling myself how lucky I am with the life I have, to forget all the crap with the Agency. Like the whole time after I was fired, Adam behaved like an absolute prince. He stood by me. He never acted as if he thought I was a traitor or had bad character, not one single time. And jobwise: after years of never being able to find work, I got to be a mother. And then I wrote *Spy Guys*."

"Remember how you were stunned when you heard the book was going to be published?" Dix asked.

"Stunned and then crazed with joy. And double that when QTV bought the TV rights and asked me to adapt it." Yet nothing with my novel or the TV show was as sublime as my two years with the Agency. But I couldn't keep saying that. No one wanted to hear it anymore. Not even Dix, who had a great capacity to tolerate my kvetching. "So here I am making probably ten times what I would be making at the Agency and doing something that's fun—at least most of the time. I have a son and a husband I love. Okay, Adam may not be a thrill a minute, but after fifteen years of marriage, name me one husband who is." Dix didn't even try. "I'm living in New York, which isn't just the greatest city in the world, but the small town I grew up in. I walk up Madison or Broadway and run into half the people I went to high school with."

"I know. But what are you getting at?"

"Why can't I let it go? Getting fired, I mean. It's so remote from my life now that in some ways it feels like it happened to somebody else. Why does it still have such power over me?"

"Hmm," he said, which was Dixonese for *You'll have to draw it out of me.*

"Go ahead. Say whatever you're thinking."

"You know how I adore your mother," he began. "And respect her work." Then he glommed down a baby octopus.

That meant it was my turn. "What does adoring my mother mean? Oh, you're going to give me a psychological insight into my feelings about the CIA."

"Katie, listen. You're stuck in 1990, obsessing about why. I can tell you why."

"This should be a treat."

"Quiet. Listen to me. Ever since it happened, you've tried to laugh off your inability to leave it alone. Time after time, you say you know the firing must have been a mistake or that if you did anything wrong, it was inadvertent. Deep down you feel—"

"I love the 'deep down' business."

"You can't make me lose my train of thought." He pointed his fork at me. "It's not that you feel guilty. It's that you failed—in your own eyes. And nobody in your family fails. The Schottlands are successful. It's in the DNA. Your father did some light cooking while your mother was in medical school and what happened? He turned a couple of copper pots into one of the most successful cookware chains in the country. Your mother's only departure from being a completely balanced person is her insane lust for fashion. And what do you know, she's now the shrink for three-quarters of the designers and garmentos in New York. Your sister was short-listed for the Pulitzer in poetry . . ."

Simultaneously, we broke into grins at the memory of Maddy's not winning the Pulitzer. Dix and I did tend toward heartlessness when it came to Maddy. We were also the only two people in the world who didn't worry that my sister—"sooo fragile"—would one day put her head in the oven. Well, not that, because Sylvia Plath had beaten her to it. But neither of us feared she would do away with herself.

Dix's opinion was that Maddy was far stronger than she behaved. That's why he'd finally been able to leave her, because he knew that after all her swooning and staring out of windows for days on end and suffering poet's block, she would inevitably recover. Dixon believed that Maddy would live because her need to create art was far stronger than her will to die.

My response to that was always the same: *Bullshit*. What kept my sister alive was the fear she could not make it as a postmortem literary saint. The Virginia Woolf, Anne Sexton, and Other Great Artists Who Offed Themselves Pantheon wouldn't accept her. "The Personal and Poetic Pain of Madeline Schottland" might not make it as the subject of a doctoral candidate's dissertation.

Dix could never accept that despite Maddy's shaky voice (especially tremulous when she gave readings—her too-many-people-I'm-so-frightened number), my sister was physically and emotionally strong enough to kick the shit out of Wonder Woman. She'd made herself a Poet of Note more by will than by genius.

Was this uncharitable? Yes. Cruelly competitive? Yes. But my sister was twice as competitive and uncharitable about me as I was about her. Three or four times.

Dix was about to begin his analysis of me again, so I kept going. "I'm not saying you're completely wrong about my shrinking from failure. My parents and sister are relentless achievers. But I set reasonably high standards for myself too, and getting canned was a shock. A double shock, really, because I thought I was doing terrifically well. It's a lot more than wounded ego, though. You know what's always hurt so much more than my failing? The injustice of it. I can't believe the unfairness. I didn't deserve to fail!"

"Then stop walking around the same block you've been walking around since 1990. 'It hurt. It was unjust. I was so surprised.' Where has that gotten you? Either use the brains you have or—"

"Or stop being a bore?" I inquired.

"Not just to other people, Katie. To yourself." It was hard to manage an amused little smile when I felt flushed with shame. Maybe rage. But Dix was right. It was time to tackle my problem with intelligence or drop it—for good.

Chapter Six

IN THE CAB GOING HOME, I HAD A QUICK FAN-
tasy about sticking my key into the lock and Adam pulling open the
apartment door. Definitely hot: his shirt would be open a couple of
buttons, his hair mussed from running his hands through it as he
anguished over having been so tough on me in the morning. That
reverie evaporated within ten seconds of opening the door.

I was hit with the familiar aroma of microwaved popcorn. In the
hallway, the dogs, who'd formed themselves into their usual inverted
V, were snoring outside our bedroom door. Inside, Adam was asleep,
though blessedly silent. Not only did he not snore, he barely moved.
Despite his size, our summer comforter was undisturbed, still tightly
tucked into the mattress. As always, he lay on his back looking swaddled. Every once in a while he turned onto his side, but his night
moves were mostly smiles playing over his lips and the sleep-time
erections pushing against the tight covers.

I went into the bathroom for my nightly business: toilet, hand wash, contact lens removal, de-makeup/tone/moisturize, floss/brush. How odd, I decided as I did an anti-garlic tongue brush with my Sonicare and almost choked as it slipped and hit my uvula, that someone like me, the anxiety queen, a woman given to imagining her own death from a freak accident on even the jolliest occasion (like catching fire while leaning over to blow out the candles on a birthday cake), would marry a man who appeared to be without a nervous system.

All right, that wasn't fair. My husband was capable of emotion: he loved Nicky, me, the dogs, his family, my parents, probably in that order, although there were times I sensed I'd moved temporarily to number one and Nicky had dropped down to two. But Adam definitely wasn't given to huge hugs and shouts of *I love you!* His waking hours were an extension of his sleeping hours: small smiles and, for me alone, erections.

Well, I assumed they were for me alone. Of course, I'd heard the usual marriage horror stories: *They always had fabulous sex—not just once a week—and then, out of the clear blue sky, he announced he'd been having an affair with one of the assistants at the Gymboree on West Seventy-third and wanted to marry her!* But I believed in my husband. From high school on, Adam had had only one relationship at a time. Whatever wild oats he possessed, he didn't sow them around.

Adam-wise, it was bad timing that the Lisa Golding call came on the very day Nicky was leaving for camp. Up to that point, I'd been viewing the summer as a chance to rekindle my marriage flame. Not so much our sex life. That had actually been good all along, both of us needing more than the national average. Also, for a guy from Wyoming, a state I'd never viewed as a hotbed of erotic creativity, Adam was extremely inventive, to say nothing of uninhibited. Maybe it was his nature, or perhaps during his years in veterinary school he'd picked up everything there was to know about mammalian anatomy and physiology, and to that he'd added the tricks he learned watching humping wildebeests.

What needed rekindling was our life together. When Nicky was away on a school trip or at a friend's, our dinner talk was less conversation than alternating monologues. Adam would tell me about his day. Knowing him to be a man of few words, I'd pepper him with questions, just to keep him going. When there was nothing more to say about zoo matters, it would be my turn. I had a lot more to tell, since I was a storyteller by trade and blabby by nature. From Oliver's rages over letters from Bible Belters complaining of clinging clothes that outlined both cheeks of Dani Barber's butt to what was going on with the makeup lady's love life, Adam heard it all. Any leftover moments got filled with politics, family news, or great issues like, should we go see *Doubt* with the Cassidys, who always want to sit in the cheapest seats?

Maybe this is what happened to all couples after fifteen years together. Could we have been like this right from the start? Were we both so taken with the novelty of each other and the New York–Wyoming contrasts that we mistook novelty for sparkle? For depth?

Oh, about depth: it was a quality my sister was credited with. Never me, not even once. Admittedly, depth was not a word applicable to *Spy Guys*. The novel wasn't even a millimeter deep, although it had got a great review from *Cosmopolitan*: "High-style CIA hijinks, told with wit and a wink."

Writing the book had had more to do with a homage to spy fiction than with any personal obsession, my not being able to stop thinking about the CIA. I was pretty sure of that. Sort of sure. I needed to have fun, to do something I could call my own after years of involuntary unemployment followed by Manhattan mommydom, with its incessant conversations about getting little Tyler and baby Zoë into whatever was that year's Harvard of nursery schools.

When I began the book, I was lonely. In fact, I hated working

9. After Jacques and Huff reveal to Katie why she was fired, she has the answer she was seeking. Why, then, does she continue to look into the circumstances surrounding her dismissal? What more does she want?

10. What motivates Katie to travel to Florida and speak with Maria Schneider in person? What warning signs does she miss during her conversation with Maria in the park?

11. Discuss the CIA's offer of restitution to Katie. Ultimately, does Katie get the closure she was seeking? Why or why not?

12. What is your overall impression of *Past Perfect*? How does this book compare to other novels you've read by Susan Isaacs?

ENHANCE YOUR BOOK CLUB

In the spirit of Ian Fleming's suave spy, James Bond, mix up a round of martinis—shaken, not stirred, of course. Or, like Katie does in *Past Perfect*, indulge in hot chocolate and Mallomars.

Make it an espionage-themed gathering when you discuss *Past Perfect* and show a classic film, such as *The Spy Who Came in from the Cold, Three Days of the Condor,* or *Dr. No.*

Visit www.simonsays.com to watch a video clip of Susan Isaacs discussing her fiction and the writing process.

2. The people in Katie's life offer opinions as to why she's so intent on delving into the circumstances surrounding her dismissal from the CIA—Maddy theorizes that Katie is looking for an adventure, while Jacques suggests it's because her fortieth birthday is looming. What is your theory as to why Katie so zealously pursues answers about her past?

3. In chapter one Katie reveals that she has had a "lifelong preference for fantasy over reality." At any point in the story, did you question Katie's judgment about the events taking place or the decisions she made? Why or why not? In what ways does her fascination with espionage stories hinder or help during her investigation?

4. With Nicky off to camp for several weeks, Katie had envisioned using the time to rekindle her "marriage flame." Why, then, does she prioritize her investigation above her marriage?

5. What is your opinion of Adam? How supportive is he of Katie's search for answers? What do you suppose the future holds for their relationship?

6. When contemplating why she might have been fired, Katie asserts, "I was confident the decision had nothing to do with Ben." What makes her so certain that Ben was blameless in her termination? How is her visit to Ben's Washington, D.C., office a turning point in how she sees her former boss?

7. Discuss Katie's relationship with her parents and her sister, Maddy. How much of Katie's concern about being fired from the CIA had to do with their opinion of her? How is Katie now viewed by her parents and sister?

8. "You've involved yourself in a dangerous business. . . . You know it, but you don't appreciate it," Maddy remarks to Katie. Do you agree or disagree with Maddy's observation of Katie, and why? What basis does she have for assuming Katie doesn't fully comprehend that she might be placing herself in harm's way?

Katie Schottland appears to have it all: a great husband and son, an upscale Manhattan lifestyle, and a dream job writing for the television series *Spy Guys*. But an unexplained incident from her past has long troubled Katie: fifteen years earlier she was dismissed from her post as an analyst at the CIA with no warning and no explanation.

When Lisa Golding, a former Agency colleague, telephones Katie out of the blue and asks for her assistance with "a matter of national importance," she promises, in exchange, to reveal the truth about Katie's firing. Lisa disappears soon after, and Katie finds herself drawn from a fictional spy world into a dark, intriguing real-life case of espionage.

As the body count begins to rise, Katie realizes she might be an assassin's next target but is determined to complete her self-imposed mission. Driven by a need to know what really happened all those years ago, she risks her marriage, her television career, and even her life to finally make peace with the past.

DISCUSSION QUESTIONS

1. For fifteen years Katie has obsessed over her termination from the CIA. Why was working at the Agency so important to Katie? How much of her fascination with the job stemmed from her interest in espionage novels and films? And why, as Katie wonders, does being fired "still have such power" over her?

Do you know the whole story before you start writing? Do you make an outline?

For me, making an outline is a way to work out the plot, since with me, the characters come first. Also, it's easier to see the structure of the novel that way, and I have the security of knowing where it's going. Sometimes, the outline is a snap. I guess that's when my subconscious has already done the heavy lifting. However, on a couple of books, including *Lily White*, I took almost a year to work out what was going to happen. Naturally, I was petrified the whole time that I was losing my marbles and/or having the world's most unconquerable writer's block. However, I know many authors who don't bother with an outline, who feel it's too constraining. There is no one right way to write.

Are any of your characters based on people you know?

I never consciously pick someone I know and put him or her into a book. The fun of writing, as well as the agony, is in creating a new universe and populating it. Also, I don't want to get a lot of grief from Uncle Joe or my down-the-street neighbor that I didn't portray them in a flattering light.

To learn more about Susan Isaacs
please visit www.susanisaacs.com.

And suddenly I had a new novel. Katie Schottland had her dream job in the CIA—and then lost it in 1990, just months after the fall of the Berlin Wall. She never learned why she was fired, but the pain of that dismissal still plagued her years later. Sure, she had what most people would say was a great life, but . . . That's one of the joys of writing fiction. Disparate ideas meet and suddenly, whammo. It's rather like falling in love.

Did you always want to be a writer?

As a child, I wanted to be a cowgirl. Perhaps that seems odd for a kid growing up in Brooklyn, but even then I had the ability to be anyone I wanted to be—in my head, if not in reality. Writing was always something I did reasonably well, but it didn't occur to me that I could make a living by it. After college I worked at *Seventeen* magazine. I began by writing advice to the lovelorn, and after a few years I became a senior editor. I left *Seventeen* to raise my children, and I worked part-time as a political speechwriter. When my second child was two, it occurred to me that I wanted to write fiction.

Of all the books you've written, which is your favorite?

There's a writers' cliché about books being like children. Well, it's true. You love all your children, even the goofy ones.

Do you write longhand or use a computer?

A computer and, more recently, speech recognition. I sit there with my headset, and dictate. To me, it's a boon because I speak faster than I type. Also, for some reason, I focus better using this method. Naturally, there's a downside. The program I use doesn't seem too comfortable with a New York accent, even with the extra training I gave it. So when I had the protagonist of my new novel say "I opened the door," what I saw on my monitor was "I opened the Torah." Ultimately, I don't think it matters what method a writer uses. Longhand, typewriter, quill and ink: they're simply tools.

Other writers use the big What If. Something arouses their curiosity and they ask themselves: What if a savvy businesswoman turned stay-at-home mother starts to believe her house is haunted? What if a couple in the midst of a bitter divorce finds themselves snowed in for a week?

Some authors may get intrigued by a story or situation they hear about on the news or just in casual conversation. Henry James is said to have gotten the idea for *Washington Square* from a story he overheard at a dinner party. Just a phrase or a word might get the creative juices flowing. "Seduced and abandoned," "Poor little rich girl," "Won the lottery." There are writers who give a new spin to an old work: a fairy tale such as Cinderella, or the biblical story of Job.

Finally, a would-be writer or an old pro can wonder, What's the book I most want to read that hasn't yet been written?

Where did you get the idea for *Past Perfect*?

Before I wrote *Past Perfect*, some random ideas were floating around in my head. The first was what a tight grip the past has on the present. For so many of us, a long-ago relationship (a lost love, a callous parent) or an event that happened years earlier (getting fired, being the victim of an unjust accusation) still has so much power in our lives. Friends advise, "You're thirty/fifty/eighty. Get over it." Yet we can't.

Another idea: Like so many other Americans, I was thinking about Iraq. How did we get it so wrong? More specifically, How did the CIA, an agency filled with supposedly smart people, make such bad calls? In *Shining Through*, which was set in New York, Washington, and Berlin during World War II, I'd written about America's spy organization, the OSS [Office of Strategic Services]. The CIA grew out of that group, and I'd read a fair amount about its development—everything from spy novels to books on American foreign policy to memoirs by ex-spooks. So I got to thinking how the Agency had gotten it wrong before: the Bay of Pigs invasion, failing to predict the rapid implosion of East Germany.

A Discussion with Susan Isaacs

Where do you get your ideas?

I don't think there's been a time since I've been answering questions that I haven't been asked where I find my ideas for novels. I hope my answer is enlightening, although I don't know if it will be helpful. That's because each writer's inspiration is as unique as his or her fingerprints.

My "ideas" come to me as characters. Before I wrote my first novel, *Compromising Positions,* I was reading a dangerous number of mysteries a week: three or four. Suddenly, a character popped into my head. Like me, she was a housewife on Long Island with two young children and a husband who commuted into Manhattan. Unlike me, she wanted to find out who killed . . . well, I had no idea who had been murdered, but since she seemed to be hanging around in my head, I decided to figure out a mystery for her to solve.

The same holds true for my novels that aren't mysteries. For *Shining Through,* a legal secretary came into my head wanting me to tell her story—about being in love with one of the law firm's partners, even though social-class differences supposedly put him out of her league. I wanted to give her some way to prove her worth, to herself if not to him. But it wasn't until World War II popped into my head, a time when ordinary people often displayed extraordinary courage, that I had my story.

"Dumb lies. About what her father did for a living. She told me he was an army officer. But then she told someone else he was a troubleshooter for a multinational company—the idea both times being that she'd been raised all over the world. Sometimes she made it sound as though her family just got by financially, but were no great shakes. Other times she talked about how her mother's family had been bankers in California since gold rush times. One time she said she spent Memorial Day weekend in Paris, except someone mentioned something about seeing her that Saturday at Bloomingdale's in Tyson's Corner. I don't get it. Why would someone lie like that?"

"Lots of reasons." She lifted her Diet Coke and sat all the way back on the couch. "It may have given her a temporary sense of power, presenting herself in the way she wanted to be presented at any one time. Typical American middle-class kid one day. Child of wealth with an upper-class pedigree another."

"But why would she lie to people she worked with? I mean, we weren't employed by a used car dealership. We worked for the CIA. Remember how thoroughly they investigated me before I got hired?"

"She might have told the truth on her application because she wanted the job, and then passed whatever security clearance with flying colors. But the truth might not fit her emotional needs. Look, children tell a type of wish-fulfillment lie all the time. 'My parents really aren't my parents. They adopted me, but I'm the daughter of a Hawaiian princess who's going to come and reclaim me any day now.' It gives them a feeling of gratification for a little while, even if it's unsustainable. But when that kind of lying continues into adulthood, it's a sign of pathology."

"But the weird thing was, sometimes she'd tell you something you were positive was a lie, like she was putting her condo on the market to buy a row house—out of Georgetown proper but still in a great area. I thought, Yeah, right. Then I got an invitation to her housewarming. Okay, it wasn't a mansion, but it was an absolutely incredible house. It wasn't a house you buy on a government salary.

None of the people I worked with lived like that. So maybe her mother's family were bankers."

My mother nodded. She was waiting for me to go on, but as I had fifty thoughts roiling about my head, nothing came out. Should I tell her about Lisa's call? Sure. Except then I'd have to tell her how I couldn't let go of getting fired and for a nanosecond she'd get a look in her eye as in, *Oh God, if you'd only told me about this obsession a year or two ago I could have helped you. Now that you're going to be forty, it's too late.* Then her customary cool would reassert itself and she'd look at me compassionately as if to say, *I understand. Go on.*

"Lisa called me about two weeks ago," I said.

"You hadn't spoken to her in all these years?"

"No. When someone is fired from the Agency, they're tainted."

"That's asinine!" my mother said. "'Tainted.' What is there, the mark of Cain on your forehead? I can't believe—"

"Mom, please just believe me."

Reluctantly, she nodded, then reached for a silk pillow and stuck it behind the small of her back. "So why was this Lisa suddenly free to call you? Is there an expiration date for taintedness?"

"It was a really weird call. She knew I worked in television. She wanted me to get her to someone high up in TV journalism."

"Do you know anyone—?"

"No! I mean, the only journalists I know cover entertainment, and then the story is usually about Dani or Javiero. Anyway, Lisa said it was a matter of national importance and it was terribly urgent that I get her to someone."

"Did she sound as if she were under a great deal of stress?"

"Definitely. But I still didn't take it all that seriously. Sure, it was somone from the Agency, but not someone of substance. A lightweight. I hadn't thought about her in years. Even if I had, I'd have thought, yeah, a lot of fun, but the second after thinking fun, I'd have gone, Yeah, fun, but what a liar—and not a very good one. Also, when she called I'd just gotten home from the studio and was rush-

ing around, throwing a few things into a bag to stay overnight when I took Nicky to camp. Maybe I should have been amazed that someone from the Agency was calling me, but this was Lisa, Miss Trivial. So I blew her off."

My mother's head moved up and down as if to acknowledge, *Oh, I see.* Except she didn't. Her eyebrows moved a little closer together. She seemed confused, as if someone had forgotten to film the fourth act of a TV show and was trying to pass off three as the complete story. What was this all about?

"As it turned out, I didn't blow her off," I explained.

"Oh. What made you change your mind?"

"She said if I would help her, she would tell me the reason why I was fired. I mean, it was like this: she said she no longer had any reason for loyalty or to keep quiet, and essentially would trade her knowledge for my help."

My mother peered into the depths of the diamond ring my father had bought for her sixtieth and asked, "Would she have been in a position to have had such knowledge?"

"I don't know," I said. "I don't know if there was anything in her job description that went beyond what I saw. The three little words at the Agency were *need to know*. Unless it was necessary to have information to do your job, you didn't get that information. It's possible that I knew only part of what Lisa did. Or after I got canned in 1990, her job could have changed, or she could have been given broader access to what was going on. She could have found out months or years after I was gone."

I'd always noticed that when people aren't ready to look you right in the eye, and when staring past you would be a dead giveaway of that reluctance, they get busy checking out the manicure situation. My mother stopped examining her ring and began studying the streaks of light reflected from the silvery sconces over the couch that glinted in her clear polished nails. "Is it possible," she asked her nails, "that Lisa made up the whole business about a matter of national

importance?" Her tone was gentle, as if she didn't want to unsettle her manicure.

"It didn't sound like an act," I replied. "She sounded genuinely scared."

"When someone repeats an exaggeration or a lie often enough, it can change from personal myth into a kind of truth for them. It can be as powerful as a real memory. That's because, in essence, it becomes a memory."

"It's possible. I can only tell you that I heard conviction in her voice."

My mother sighed. To give her credit, it was not one of those passive-aggressive sighs other mothers give that demand, *Why can't I get through to you?* Hers was more like, *Gee, I'm at a loss. I don't know what to tell you.* "So you decided not to blow her off," my mother finally said. "What did Lisa say?"

"Nothing, because she knew I was in a rush." I had a feeling I sounded a little pathetic, that I was trying to hide the fact that I'd been gulled or humiliated. I talked faster. "It was like this: I said I was in a mad rush to get my son up to camp, but that I was really willing to talk to her and help her. And she seemed incredibly relieved and said something like, 'It can wait till tomorrow. I'll call you.'"

"How would she call you if you'd be up with Nicky and staying at a motel?"

"I gave her my cell phone number."

I waited. She'd never been the kind of mother who posted her agenda in letters the size of the big E on the eye chart. I wanted to see what she was getting to. To be fair, maybe she didn't have an agenda. Maybe she was just thinking. Her lips were pursed. When she did that, the tiny wrinkles deepened. They looked like a child's drawing of the rays around the sun. I felt trapped, sitting there on the couch, having nothing to do but look at the lines in her skin. Finally she spoke: "So did she call the next day?"

"No." Maybe I snapped.

"Did she ever?"

"No," I said, more evenly. "I haven't heard from her again. She seems to have dropped out of sight. Maybe she changed her mind about wanting to talk to me. But something could have happened to her. I'm kind of worried."

"You don't have a number where you can—"

"There's an ex-CIA operative who is *Spy Guys*'s technical adviser. He gave me her home and cell. I tried them. Nothing. And he said she hadn't been seen lately at her house."

"Did you leave a message? Tell her you're concerned?"

"No. I probably watch too many of my own shows. I called from pay phones." My mother gave me her sweet almost-smile and nodded: *I understand.* "I was nervous about . . . you know. Everything."

"Katie, is this more about helping someone who might be in trouble? Or is it finding out why you were fired?"

"Truthfully? It has nothing to do with altruism. I need to know why. I was doing good work and thought I was in line for a promotion. What happened to me was an injustice. I want to say 'gross injustice' but that's so overused. How about 'huge injustice'?"

"Have you asked yourself why it means so much to you? Gross injustice, huge injustice, it happened—what?—fifteen years ago?"

"Mom, can't you accept that I just need to know?"

"Of course I can accept it." She paused for so long that in a script I'd have had to write: [LONG BEAT]. "Is there anything I can do to help?"

"I'd like your opinion. Do you think Lisa was lying?"

"About what?"

"About anything, for God's sake." That was not me at my most pleasant. "Sorry."

She nodded at the apology. "There's a pretty good shot she wasn't telling the truth," my mother said. "If she's as inventive as you say she is, why couldn't she call up Anderson Cooper or someone like that and tell him directly what her matter of national importance is?"

"What do you think she wanted from me?"

"I have no idea. I have no real sense of this Lisa other than that she was fun to shop with and that she lied. Possibly her call was the opening move of some sort of practical joke. But I don't think so. That's different from the type of lying you experienced from her in the past. Putting something over on someone in the practical joke sense is an act of aggression. Look, I just don't know, Katie. It is possible she's delusional and in this so-called matter of national importance, she's determined that your having a TV connection means you're a very powerful person who has entrée to every mover and shaker in the world."

"Do you think if she believes that she could be dangerous to someone?"

"If she's delusional? Sure. As a psychiatrist, but more as a mother, I'd feel much better if you stayed away from this Lisa."

Chapter Ten

JUST BECAUSE MY LAST GLIMPSE OF BENTON MATtingly had been of him watching me clean out my office as two security guys stood guard didn't mean I was to be totally cut off from him, never to hear about him again. Ben was a man in the news, even if it was often in the social columns standing next to Deedee, she of the big decibels and huge inheritance.

Through the years, even after Adam and I moved back to New York, I bought *The Washington Post* on Sundays, hoping to see his picture. I was also a regular in the research section of the library. Once search engines became a fact of life, I made a macro of "Benton Mattingly" so I could check him out in less than a second. Now and then a day would go by when I'd forget to do it, and I'd feel proud of myself: See? I have so much to do there isn't time for me to waste being obsessed by a man who had shown zero desire to obsess over me. Later, when Google Alerts came along, Ben's name would pop into my e-mail whenever it appeared on the Internet.

It's not as if I thought about him all the time. No one had to tell me, "Get a life." I had one. TV writer, and not just "Written by Katherine Schottland," but with a separate credit, "Based on the novel by . . ." I was an insider in the world of New York–based TV production. I was a wife and, after a few difficulties in the fertility area, mother. I had friends, extended family, two well-behaved (thanks to Adam) dogs, a beagle and a Newfoundland. I belonged to two book groups and was a volunteer math tutor one night a week at a church in East Harlem. So I wasn't a loser stuck in the past. I wouldn't turn out to be one of those osteoporotic women at her fiftieth high school reunion still waiting for That Certain Someone to notice her, except Certain never showed because he'd dropped dead the year before.

So I knew that Ben had left the Agency a couple of years after I had. No great shock. No doubt he had finally accepted that the Cold War was kaput. Having been one of the experts who thought it would never end, he wasn't exactly in line for the Agency's directorship.

He started a business, Mattingly Associates, advising corporate clients how to operate in the former communist countries of Europe. I tried to believe the company's name was Deedee's idea, because a) it was banal and b) it sounded like it was made up of a bunch of people associating with Mattingly, without Mattingly necessarily being around. Maybe he was, maybe he wasn't, but his name was in the first sentence of every press release. If nothing else, Mattingly Associates was committed to PR.

In 2000, he left to become president of Euro-fone, with offices in Vienna, Prague, Warsaw, and London. I'd thought, Now, with his big corporate salary and stock options, he can be free from Deedee. On the other hand, maybe she'd bought the company for him. One of the articles about him remarked it was no wonder he was in the communications business. He was fluent in seven languages: French, German, Italian, Russian, Czech, Polish, and Romanian. I was amazed, though whether it was true or not was another story. Dur-

ing the eighties, he had gone back and forth to Germany every couple of months for the Agency. But the only time I heard him speak anything but English was when we once had dinner at a bistro. He ordered in French and the waiter understood him. Personally, I thought he sounded a little mushy-mouthed, as if he'd learned the language in a former French colony that had been granted independence in 1953, but the waiter acted as though he thought Ben incredibly cool. Maybe that's because he came in every six months with a different CIA cutie.

As far as I could tell, even though Euro-fone was based in Europe, Ben got back to Washington fairly often. There was rarely a benefit or gala that did not produce a photo of him and Deedee, or at least their names in boldface. The big Bush administration/social conservative events were not his style, so there was no "Seen on his knees at the prayer breakfast beside the Speaker of the House . . ." For a political man in a political city, Ben had survived by being smart, charming, marrying well, and remaining nonpartisan. So two months earlier, I'd been more than surprised when I read he was the lead candidate for secretary of commerce after what's-his-name went back to his money.

Talk about surprised: I was surprised that after having spent nearly an hour with my mother, I still was crazy enough to sit in the parking lot at the studio and call Euro-fone in Vienna and ask to speak with Mr. Mattingly. I asked in the rich three-hundred-word vocabulary I'd managed to retain from German Studies 101 and 104. The woman on the phone replied in English: "Mr. Mattingly is in Prague. I can put you through to his secretary there." Surprised? I was über-surprised, or however you say that in Czech, when his Prague secretary said, "Mr. Mattingly is late for a meeting." Then, without missing a beat, she went on: "But he said he'll call you back within the hour."

He did. "Katie." Naturally, he knew he didn't have to go into a "This Is Ben" song and dance.

While waiting the hour for his call, I'd taped a WRITING — DO NOT

DISTURB!! sign onto my office door and pulled out the jack of the phone on my desk in case anyone didn't get the message. I'd learned from watching actors work that the best spontaneity is often meticulously rehearsed. I went through my opening a few times so I wouldn't blurt out *Sorry to call you. I know how busy you must be and I hate to disturb you.* I wouldn't even allow myself a *I wouldn't have called you if it wasn't important.* I simply said, "Thanks for getting back to me so quickly. Ben, you knew Lisa Golding, didn't you?"

There was a slight pause. "Sure. She was in the Welcome Wagon." Agency employees, past and present, had euphemisms for every aspect of CIA life. For instance, at Langley itself, the Weapons Intelligence, Nonproliferation, and Arms Control unit was called WIN-PAC, but on the rare occasion it was referred to on the phone or at an outside gathering, it was Shangri-la. "She's the one with that chalk-on-a-blackboard voice, right?"

"Right." I was so nervous I'd forgotten to chuckle at his remark. Too late now. Too bad. I never knew whether or not he needed it, but people always felt obliged to give Ben positive feedback. Someone else's marginally amusing statement could remain unacknowledged, but Ben's would invariably bring out a laugh worthy of a Chris Rock routine.

"Do you know if she's still with her old employer?" I asked.

"You know I can't—"

"Sorry. I should have remembered. I'm out of practice."

"Don't tell me that," Ben said. "I've seen your show. Cute." Cute? A backhanded compliment, WASP understatement? Or a mild slap in the face, barely felt yet still stinging? It was one thing for me to trivialize what I did, another to hear it from Ben. Well, here I was again, in old form, not knowing where I stood with him, afraid to ask for fear of learning the truth. "There's something up with Lisa?" he inquired.

"Yes. Or at least I don't know. That's why I'm calling." My heart

was banging against my chest as if it wanted to get his attention. "I got a call from her a couple of weeks ago. I hadn't heard a word from her since"—my throat did that involuntary pullback that's written as GULP! in comic books—"since I left the office. She sounded seriously stressed."

"Isn't she rather theatrical?" Ben asked. "If memory serves, I think she had a theater background." Wow, I loved his voice. Deep, husky, what's described in espionage novels as a voice "cured by years of smoking Gauloises and drinking Laphroaig," except Ben had never smoked, and, in a city where breakfast meetings were prized or scorned as the only time of mandatory sobriety, he drank hardly at all. "But I suppose theater people get stressed like everybody else. Did she talk to you about . . . business?"

I didn't hear him panting to know the answer. The impression I got was of someone who, having taken a phone call from a person out of the past, was now stuck with being polite. "Well, she said it was about a matter of national importance. I was pretty short with her—I was in a hurry. But I think I let her know I was willing to help." I didn't say anything about Lisa being willing to tell me why I'd gotten the ax. "Anyhow," I continued, "she said she'd get back to me the next day."

"And you didn't hear from her?"

"Not a peep."

"Do you remember who her friends were, or anything about her background?"

I'm not a moron, I wanted to tell him, but instead I politely said, "I wasn't able to find anything that would lead to her. And as far as her friends went, I can't remember. She did talk about someone named Tara years ago, but obviously that isn't much of a help. I'm tainted by having been fired so I have no old colleagues I could call. I took a chance on you." I took a deep breath and added, "I'm a little surprised you got back to me, Ben. But I'm grateful."

"Katie, how could I not?"

To avoid going GULP! again and choking on sentiment, I quickly said, "Do you have any way of getting a reading on her or—"

"I can't use any contacts who are still at the organization to find out where she is. You know that. I do know a couple of civilians, so to speak, who know as much as can be known. I can ask them. But to be brutally honest, Katie, I don't think she was at a level in the corporate structure that attracted much notice. I'll do what I can. If I learn anything I'll call you."

"Thank you." Despite all my rehearsals, I hadn't thought about a way to say good-bye.

"How are you doing, other than being rich and famous?" Give me a break, I thought as I was savoring the remark. "Still married?"

"Still married," I said. "And I have a ten-year-old son."

"Great! Okay, Katie, I'll do due diligence and if I hear anything, I'll get back to you." As I was about to tell him I'd heard he was up for secretary of commerce and wasn't that great, he said, "Bye." In the old days, even after we broke up and I'd married Adam, he always ended whatever conversations we had with "See you around."

"Bye, Ben," I said, but he'd already hung up.

Chapter Eleven

AFTER SPEAKING TO BEN, I GOT MILDLY HYS-
terical: a rush of adrenaline—gotta fight, gotta flee—but what actually occurred was that I fused with my office chair, like an extra
cushion. At the same time, half the water content of my body mysteriously evaporated. Talk about no sweat: mouth so dry my tongue
could have disintegrated into sawdust. Hands like emery boards. I
might have sat motionless till I entered menopause, but a production
assistant finally knocked on my door twice. Without opening it, she
blared, "Katie! The CIA adviser Huff! He's on the line!"

"Okay." I tried to sound soothing, or at least soothed.

"What?"

"I said—"

"What? I can't hear you, Katie." I stood and opened the door to
Toni Wiener, the most conscientious production assistant who had
ever worked in film or TV. She had a perfect oval face, a serious
expression, long blond hair, and bore a striking resemblance to Bot-

crime or character flaw. In other words, the Agency had let me go and destroyed my chances of getting another job for a reason that had been good enough for them. But it wasn't good enough for me.

My sister once called espionage novels "romantic pap, including Le Carré," though to be fair, which I rarely was when it came to her, she'd made the remark before I wrote *Spy Guys*. Long before *scum* became a popular word for lowlifes, Maddy had used that word to refer to the people who worked for the CIA, and that was after I joined the Agency.

But I felt pretty smart espionagewise. Having been trained by fiction and honed by my CIA tenure, I hadn't been calling any of the phone numbers for Lisa from my cell or from the office. This time, when I drove back to Manhattan, I double-parked my car in front of a Korean market on Third Avenue and used a pay phone. When I dialed the new number Huff had given me, it went right to voice mail. Not Lisa's own unmistakable voice squeaking she wasn't there: the same canned message announcing that the person whose phone this was wasn't taking calls. I could leave a message including the date and time I'd called. This time I decided to speak: "Hi! You said you'd get back to me. This is your friend from the old days. I'd love to hear from you, just to know if everything's okay and if I can do anything to help." For a nanosecond, the words *I'm here for you* passed through my brain, but my lips refused to have any part of it. So like the two CIA veterans I'd spoken to that day, I just hung up.

My mind wandered back, but not too far: to just hours earlier, late morning. While rehearsing my call to Ben, I had given a half minute's thought to explaining to him that my strongest connection to Lisa at the Agency had been that report I'd written about the three East Germans we'd brought over—including the Manfred Gottesman who had settled in Cincinnati and presumably become Dick Schroeder.

The three were brought here shortly after the opening of the

Berlin Wall, when there was panic among the recently powerful in East Germany. At the Agency, we heard about the mass shredding of files. Not long after, when shredding clearly became too monumental a task, Stasi officials began building bonfires of documents. Meanwhile, most of Europe and the United States were jubilant about the downfall of the oppressive government. But some in my unit, Ben included, couldn't accept that it had actually come to pass. I recalled one analyst who had quoted Ben as declaring, "They'll be back." The people in the unit who had predicted the rapid crumbling of the East German regime alternated between private delight at their colleagues' discomfort and off-the-record *See? I told you so!*s to their pet journalists or staff members of the congressional oversight committees, the so-called watchdogs of the CIA.

Anyway, the report on the three East Germans I was working on became a high-priority document. We had to explain why we had whisked away three communist high-ups, saving them from the anger and likely retribution of their fellow countrymen. Who were these three, and why were they chosen to get a new life in the United States? I remember thinking it was a no-brainer. The three had risked everything—lives, status, the safety of their families—for us. We owed them. Lisa had been one of the fifteen or twenty people I'd interviewed in the course of writing the report. Her account became my epilogue to show how well these CIA-certified good guys were settling in in the land of the free.

The details—what I needed to know—were lost somewhere in time-space, along with so many other items: how to do the regression analysis required for econometrics; who was the third boy I slept with. I'd always had a B-minus memory, unlike Adam, who could come up with a tome of trivia on any ant who happened to cross our picnic table, or Maddy, who could quote the entire oeuvre of every neurasthenic female poet who lived in the Cotswolds before 1940, and they were legion. My notes jogged what memories I retained, but they didn't help me come up with the big picture.

Now, fifteen years later, I knew objectively that Lisa could have sought my help in communicating with the press on any of a million matters, not just that report. Maybe she wanted to tell all or tell some about Islamic terrorists in Boca Raton or, for all I knew, extraterrestrials taking over the government of Honduras. But during her years at the Agency, she no doubt dealt with other report writers besides me. She'd had access to everything from radical Islam to experts on the demographics of Central America.

Okay, she had claimed she needed me to get to CNN because I worked in television. But half the employees of the Agency knew which journalists could be trusted to make good use of news leaks. And if Lisa was part of the other half? Washington was filled with reporters aching for a good spook story. She could cold-call almost anyone. Therefore, I decided Lisa had come to me because I had some particular knowledge that could help her, not because of my media contacts.

And what I knew, Ben Mattingly would know because he'd been my supervisor. So while I was rehearsing the phone call I'd thought, Let me see if he thinks Lisa was calling me over something to do with those three Germans. I'll mention Manfred Gottesman–turned–Dick Schroeder. Maybe Ben will remember something about the case that would have made it resonate with Lisa all these years later. But then I hadn't asked him. I was afraid he'd think there was something fishy in my remembering so much. Why could I recall in such detail a mention of some German in a report I wrote fifteen years earlier? Ben could probably recall enough about me and my work to know that my memory was no better or worse than anybody else's. He'd have to conclude that I had a copy of the report, or at least that I had taken notes.

So I decided to keep the Germans to myself. I would go to Ohio and pay Dick Schroeder a visit.

Chapter Twelve

I TOLD ADAM THE TRUTH, THAT I WAS GOING TO Cincinnati for a day or two to talk with a former East German communist who'd been brought over at the end of the Cold War. He accepted the trip as part of my job writing *Spy Guys*. Had he told me a comparable lie, that he had to go to Cincinnati to consult on wild boar entrails, I would have accepted it as part of his job as chief pathologist at the Bronx Zoo.

The question was, how would I find Schroeder? In my scripts neither HH nor Jamie ever acted directly. Finding an address, for instance: looking something up in a phone book wasn't visual enough, plus I had twenty-two minutes to fill between the first and the final commercial breaks. Finding where someone lived meant tracking down mysterious Mr. X's former personal trainer, who had a grudge against him and was glad to give out Mr. X's unlisted phone number and address.

This was real life, however. While I was considering whether it

was worth spending the money at some shady Web site to maybe get the hush-hush whereabouts of Richard Schroeder in Cincinnati, I did a quick switchboard.com search. Bingo! It got me three Richard Schroeders. For free. The first of these, with that variety of Midwestern accent a New Yorker would mimic by holding her nose, told me that the Queen City Sweets Richard—"He's in the business section of the *Enquirer* practically every month"—lived in an area called Indian Hill. "That section is the cream of the cream of the cream," he said. "If you get my meaning."

I certainly got his meaning the following day, Saturday, when the prissy voice of the global positioning system in the Jaguar I'd rented at the Cincinnati airport (hoping to blend into the cream with a sufficiently creamy car) announced, "You have arrived," as I pulled up in front of the iron gate that closed off the driveway to the Schroeders' gold stone Tudor mansion.

Old Manfred-turned-Dick had definitely arrived. The high noon sun beamed down on the colored slate tiles of the roof, making them look like rectangular gemstones. The central part of the house was a gold cube with wings extending on either side. Each of these wings had spawned wings of its own that sprouted dormers, bay windows, stuccoed areas striped with split timbers. The roof had brought forth several gables, a noble stone chimney, and three high-reaching cylindrical clay chimneys perched close together. All in all, this was a proper American dream house that had grown to keep pace with its owner's wealth.

About twenty feet behind the gate, a tall white flagpole flew Old Glory, or at least held it up high. There was no wind. The humidity seemed to have seeped into the flag's fabric, so it hung like a wet washcloth. But there was that matter of the gate. Closed. However, one of those boxy speakers sat atop a metal post, the un-high-tech kind of speaker boxes you see in noir movies in which all the men wear hats. Okay, I'd come on a Saturday on the chance of catching Manfred-Dick at home, but I hadn't pictured such an intimidating

residence—I guess you'd have to call it an estate—complete with a locked gate. I'd seen myself ringing the doorbell of an upscale suburban colonial with a Mercedes in the driveway. It would be answered by Dick Schroeder, who, when I smiled at him, would think, Hmmm, lusty, bosomy Jewess, and because he'd had an Oedipus complex, it would work to my advantage. Or if it was Mrs. Dick, my mere smile would establish an immediate sense of sisterly simpatico and she'd let me in and whisper to her husband, *Mein darling, you absolutely must talk mit her*. Naturally, I'd also imagined every horror. Dick siccing meat-starved Dobermans on me. An appointed-for-life CIA security detail shooting me down in cold blood. But since I could have filled the Library of Congress with all the self-help books I had bought over the years, I was determined to substitute all anxiety images with visualizations of me being successful.

I opened the car window to reach out and press the button on the speaker. I don't know what I was waiting for—maybe a butler's voice intoning, *What is it you wish, madam?* Instead, the gates opened slowly enough to give me time to get afraid. I drove around the circular driveway to the front door praying that the wave of nausea that suddenly contracted my esophagus and was rising to my throat wouldn't get any worse. I didn't want to choose between heaving over the tan leather passenger seat of the rented Jag or onto the stone entranceway of Schroeder Manor.

I rang the bell, which chimed a low-pitched, understated *Bong! Bong!* rather than the first fourteen notes of some Bach ditty. I heard high heels hurrying across a hard floor. The door opened.

"Oh," a woman said, pulling back her head in surprise. She looked around my age. Girl Child Schroeder grown up, I figured, since she was wearing a pale turquoise silk skirt with a matching sleeveless blouse that didn't look like any maid's uniform. Considering it was already an expensive outfit, what probably was a Pucci sweater was tossed over her shoulders. The sleeves hung untied down the front and looked awkward, as if they were trying to cop a feel. She was

softly pretty, blond-haired and blue-eyed, like an older sister of Charlize Theron—but a sister who ought to start considering hormone replacement therapy as she was looking a little thin-skinned and a lot jittery. Anyway, Girl Child was gnawing one of her nails. The edges of a few of them were serrated where the polish had been chewed off.

"Ms. Schroeder," I began. Having just spoken, I spotted a wedding band on her left hand. One second later I was worrying what it would do to my standing if she had taken her husband's name; I would come across as Total Stranger Who Knows Nothing. Or what if she was one of those right-wing types who gloried in being called Mrs.?

"Sorry, this is the time United Parcel usually comes," she said by way of explanation. "That's who I thought . . ." It wasn't as if her voice trailed off. She appeared to have lost the thought midsentence. Her accent was purely American.

"I apologize for dropping in on you like this," I said, "but I couldn't call ahead. My cell phone died and I didn't have my charger."

She nodded, though I wasn't sure she'd absorbed what I'd just said. "I know this may sound very pushy, but I worked with . . ." The words *your father* were just about to emerge when it occurred to me—in one of those odd, sixth-sense moments—that she might not be his daughter after all. Wife? Well, he'd been spirited out of Germany with his parents to spend World War II in Moscow, so the youngest he could be would be late sixties. Granted, Ohio style wasn't my area of expertise, but I began thinking she could be married to him because her coiffed hair and diamond ear studs were more rich man's country club wife than daughter.

"I worked with Mr. Schroeder when he first came to this country," I continued, "and he was incredibly kind to me." Hopefully he wasn't a first-class prick. In order to project benevolence, I tried to conjure up a vision of a Manfred transformed from tough Stasi hunk into a cheery, beery Midwesterner patting me on the head in a paternal manner. I failed. "I'm only in Cincinnati for the day," I went on, "but it would mean a great deal to me if I could thank him personally."

Though I'm generally the sort of person babies smile at, dogs wag their tails at, and strangers confide in on the M7 bus, I wouldn't have been shocked if she slammed the door in my face or shrieked, *Diiiick!! Call 911!!!* At that instant it also occurred to me I had no fallback position, no second lie to tell if this one failed. But she neither slammed nor shrieked. Her blue eyes grew teary. She swallowed and in a choked voice said, "Please come in."

She led me into a room with a ceiling so high it could have accommodated the Rockefeller Center Christmas tree, and so wide in every direction that the Rockettes in their Santa outfits could have spread out for line kicks. Because there was a huge Persian rug on the floor and a lot of Louis the Something chairs and a couch, a giant mirror in a gilt frame, and an oil painting of either a fat old lady in a white gown or a medieval pope, I assumed it was the living room. Except we then took a right into the living room, and I realized we'd passed through . . . I guessed what would be termed the reception hall.

This was a new level of money for me. Ever since I could remember, my parents had been well-off. A few of their friends—as well as a couple of the families of some of my day-school classmates—were what is so delicately referred to in Manhattan as obscenely rich. Still, I had never seen anything like this living room. I was pretty sure it was Gothic style. Anyway, the ceiling was vaulted and there were lots of tall, arched windows on either side of a fireplace that had some nasty faces—though not quite gargoyles—and a coat of arms carved into its black wood mantel. Was this the home Manfred Gottesman had dreamed of growing up in as a good little commie boy in Moscow?

"Please," she said, motioning to one of the two giant couches that flanked the fireplace, "have a seat." She sat beside me, about a foot away. Her back was straight, not resting against the cushion; her knees and ankles were together and angled sideways, a ladylike posture more in keeping with characters in 1930s movies than in women of my generation. "Forgive my manners. I'm Dick's wife, Meredith."

"I'm Daisy Green," I said.

"And you knew Dick when he first came here?" She leaned toward me as if she wanted to catch my answer the minute it came out. I noticed the skin on the bottom of her nose was rough and red. I added that to her teary eyes and knew it wasn't hay fever. Troubled, I decided.

"Yes, I worked for the organization that brought him over. You know, I doubt if he'll remember me, but at the time, I was so unhappy. At the end of my rope over some guy." (Both the name Daisy Green and her backstory came from a character in the novel *Spy Guys* who had never made it into the show because the actress who was going to play it got a feature film offer and Oliver decided to cut the character and use the money for an assistant to the location scout.) "I lost some of your husband's papers and couldn't get my act together. He could have reported me, probably should have. But instead he was *so* decent and sympathetic—" I was going to mention something again about thanking him, but that very moment, Meredith Schroeder began to sob.

"Forgive . . ." she managed to say.

"Is there anything I can do?" She didn't answer. Her hands were over her face. I reached over and patted one and gave it a little squeeze. She lowered her hands and gave me a small smile. "Thank you." She took a deep breath. "My husband is always saying I'm too emotional."

"Mine does too," I said.

Actually, Adam never said that outright. At the beginning of our marriage, I even thought it was one of my charms: designated emoter. Anyway, my response must have struck some cord because she patted her eyes dry with her fingertips and smiled. With her deep dimples, light blue eyes, strawberry lips, expensive clothes, and a tan like golden velvet, Meredith looked like an ad for the American Woman. After a childhood as a war refugee in Moscow and then a life in East Germany, the man who became Dick Schroeder seemed to have embraced not just the spirit of capitalism, but its embodiment.

"Is something wrong with Dick?" I asked softly.

"He's in the hospital." She shivered and, hugging herself, rubbed her upper arms, seeming to have forgotten her Pucci sweater. Sometimes it pays to schlepp a ten-pound hobo bag when you're taking a trip. I reached into it and pulled out a shawl I'd brought along for the flight, though I could have given her an iPod with a lot of Phil Collins and Dire Straits I'd recently downloaded, or a science fiction paperback about some ensign who was an agent of Imperial Terra. Even half a Snickers. Meredith just sat there, so I stood and draped my shawl around her. "Oh thank you. Such a nice wrap." She drew it tighter. It really wasn't nice: pale pink and so thin it looked like some sort of used medical dressing. I'd gotten it from a street vendor for ten bucks, which included a laughable label that said 100 percent cashmere. "All of a sudden, I just got chills," she apologized.

"I've come at a bad time," I said. "I feel terrible, not being able to call, dropping in on you like this."

"No, please. I'm glad for the company. He's in intensive care and was having tests all morning. I can't go to see him until two o'clock, and they only let me stay for ten minutes at a time. Then I have to wait again until three. Would you like anything? A bite of lunch?"

"No, thanks."

"Really, it's no problem. I have someone in the kitchen who can do it." I shook my head. I knew it made sense psychologically to break bread with someone you want to ingratiate yourself with. But Meredith seemed overwrought, and she definitely looked like the type who, unlike me, would lose her appetite when stressed. I didn't want to sit there chomping on a turkey sandwich in the kitchen while she either wept or excused herself and went upstairs.

Also, I was trying to figure out what to do now that one of my only links to Lisa and our mutual past was tubed up in intensive care. Granted, trying to see Dick Schroeder had been a long shot, but now I'd have to wait until he got better. If he did. Also, Meredith's tears looked real to me. It would take a first-rate actress to shiver so con-

vincingly. Even though she was around my age, I was getting the urge to mother her. I wanted to hug her and pat her head the way I used to do for Nicky when he'd get hurt or upset: *It's okay. Come on, it's going to be all right.*

"Did he ever talk about the old days?" I asked.

"Not really. He once told me, 'You have no idea what hell it was living under a communist regime.' He said President Reagan was so right when he called it the evil empire."

I had to give Dick credit. No wonder he didn't want to talk about the past: living in a totalitarian state, working for that government, and spying for us. "Did he tell you what it was like when he first came here?"

"Not too much. Mostly how shocked he was at the abundance of everything and also at the freedom to read criticisms of the government." She adjusted her watch, trying not to let me see she was looking at the time. "I remember something else he said . . . that the refugee organization that brought him over really had wonderful people. They even gave him a couple of thousand dollars to help him get started in business."

"Well, all of us did our best." Manfred-Dick must have done something extremely wonderful to have gotten here in the first place, and I wondered how many tens or even hundreds of thousands of dollars he was given, and for what. It might have been in my report, but I couldn't remember. "Would you like me to drive you to the hospital?" I asked.

"No, that's all right. We have a driver." She glanced at her watch. I assumed the trip to the hospital wasn't that long, because she finally leaned back against the cushion of the couch, slipped off her high-heeled slides, and tucked her feet beneath her.

"Has Dick been in the hospital long?" I asked.

"Four days." Meredith flattened her lips and blew out a long, slow breath.

"I bet it feels like four weeks."

"It does."

I was trying to think of a way to ask what was wrong with him, when she said, "They call what he has FUO, fever of unknown origin. He was just tired at first. I begged him to stay home. But you know what men are like."

"Sure. He went straight to work."

"Yes. And then one night he came home looking gray. Positively gray. And I put my wrist on his head. He definitely had fever. And I didn't like his breathing. I told him, 'I'm taking your temperature right this minute.' Then I couldn't find the thermometer. He said, 'I'll take a couple of Advils and get a good night's sleep and I'll be better.' But . . . you know Dick, I mean, he's older than I am by a lot and I worry. He was a little boy in Germany during the war and had rheumatic fever and didn't get enough to eat." I wondered if Meredith knew the truth about how his family had been taken to Moscow and protected, and she was just giving me the official biography. But maybe she too had gotten the cover story. "How was he then?"

I had no way of knowing whether she knew of his past as an Agency asset. Did she look at me and think, Hmm, old CIA hand or a nice social worker from some do-good group? "Do you mean how he appeared healthwise?" She nodded. "Fine." I decided to take a chance and added: "A little on the thin side."

She laughed, and it had a tender sound. "Trust me, he's not like that anymore. But it's all meat and potatoes. He's the second biggest candy distributor east of the Mississippi, and he never even takes a Lifesaver. If he has dessert once a year it's an event. Except since he's had this, he's lost a lot of weight."

"They have no clue as to where this fever came from?"

Meredith shook her head. "No. They've taken a million tests, asked me where we've gone on every vacation for the last . . . I don't know, five years. They keep wanting to know 'Mexico?' 'China?' And I keep saying no, we've never been to Mexico or China. I have the chief of the infectious diseases department on the case and he con-

sulted with NIH. They're getting back to him. And the rheumatologist and the hematologist are at a loss so far."

"Is the thinking that it might be some kind of an infection thing, not some side symptom of another disease?" I didn't want to say "cancer" because it might frighten her. If I called my mother, she could probably list another ten or twenty horrible possibilities.

"The tests say it's an infection. They even tested him for HIV, which I told them was ridiculous, but they said they had to. Nothing. They finally narrowed it down. It's not viral or bacterial. Now they're saying it's a fungus."

"Is he conscious?" I asked. I was getting nervous that any second she would decide she'd been nice enough to me and make it clear it was time for me to leave. Not that I really thought there was anything to learn by staying, but going would be so final.

"Yes, but he's so weak. He can't even talk anymore. All he can manage is a whisper." I murmured how sorry I was. "It's funny, he doesn't seem to be at all fearful or worried that something's going to happen. The only thing that upsets him is me. I mean the strain on me. He says things like, 'I don't want you coming here every day,' or, 'You've been at the hospital too long. Go out and buy yourself something beautiful from me.'"

"That's one of the nicest things I've—" I didn't get to finish the sentence because a maid in an actual uniform—the black dress with a white apron—came into the room and said, "It's Dr. Morvillo on the phone, Mrs. Schroeder."

A person with good manners might have excused herself at this juncture. I didn't. After Meredith left, I paced the length of the living room and by the time I sat down again, I'd walked the equivalent of a half marathon. On the wall opposite the fireplace, beside a pair of French doors, there was a formal portrait of Dick and Meredith. Formal, not just in the sense of it being an oil of her seated in one of their Louis chairs with him standing behind her, but with them in evening clothes. He wore a tuxedo and shirt with a wing collar, she a strapless

pink gown and diamond necklace. With his white hair and her com-
parative youth, it would have looked like father-daughter night at
some symphony benefit, except his hands, fingers splayed, were
spread over her shoulders as if he couldn't get enough of the feel of
her skin.

From what she had said about meat and potatoes, I'd expected to
see a stout burgher type, like photos in travel brochures of those
schmucks in lederhosen. But unless the artist did him a favor, he was
simply solidly built. Good-looking too, an elegant, older version of
the man in the photo Lisa had shown me years earlier. His dark eyes
and black eyebrows contrasted with his thick hair, now a sugary
white. The serene expression on Meredith's face told me she was not
one of those young wives of older men who had to fake it.

When she returned, though, her expression was not serene. She
was clutching a fistful of tissues. "Dick is in a coma."

Chapter Thirteen

I'D BEEN GOOGLING DICK SCHROEDER SINCE my return from Cincinnati, keeping my fingers crossed he'd pull through. Three days later, I was staring at the computer monitor, astounded. Dead! It happened so fast. I'd been too optimistic, expecting several weeks of nothing new, of being steered by search engines to the same articles about Queen City Sweets and the Richard and Meredith Schroeder Music Building at the University of Cincinnati.

I learned more from Dick's obituary than I had from his wife. He had come to the United States from Leipzig in 1989, after managing the state-run confectionery industry. Not a bad story. The obit talked about how he'd found himself in constant opposition to the authorities there. He was quoted as saying, "There is nothing worse than cheap chocolate," which, had I been an ex–German Jew, was an opinion I might have withheld.

The man in the obituary sounded like the nicest sort of tycoon— philanthropic, appreciative of his good fortune. He was a sports

lover; besides being a great fan of the Cincinnati Reds and the Bengals he was a golfer, boater, fisherman, and hunter. The piece quoted a chamber of commerce speech he'd made about how grateful he was to the United States. "This country gave me a life I thought was possible only in Hollywood movies."

The obituary said he was survived by his wife Meredith Spalding Schroeder. No mention of children or previous marriages. "Mr. Schroeder died from complications of a rare fungus infection, blastomycosis. The fungus, on very few occasions, has been associated with recreational activities around the Ohio River and its streams. This phenomenon occurs at times when the water gets a high level of moist soil rich in organic debris or rotting wood."

Even though I'd never met him, I felt sad, though admittedly not *ferklempt*. I had to give him credit: surviving all those years of hardship as a child, then having the brains and guile to thrive in East Germany. Then coming to America, making it big as a candy tycoon and having what looked like a loving marriage. But that's life: out of the blue, some weird-ass fungus comes along when you're fishing for whatever people fish for in Cincinnati, and it's *Auf Wiedersehen* forever.

That night—it must have been around two or three—I woke up. Adam and I, as occasionally happened, were sharing the same pillow. Mine. When I complained about it one time, he'd done his Willie Nelson impression, singing "Don't Fence Me In." Then he told me Wyoming guys needed more territory than New Yorkers. Anyway, we were lying on our left sides, spoon position, and his arm was around me, his hand warmly tucked in my cleavage, his breath stirring my hair.

Before I was conscious of having the thought, I must have stiffened because Adam turned over and, in his sleep, felt for his own pillow. What if Dick Schroeder hadn't, say, stuck his hand into some stream to grab a fish? What if instead the blastomycosis had been induced? Cut it out, I ordered myself. Those kinds of ideas come

straight out of espionage novels and spy movies, of which I had read an unhealthy number. They were not about reality, not about the CIA as I knew it. All that stuff about "wet work," "sanctioning," "executive action" doesn't happen to a mini-mogul in Cincinnati, even if he happens to be an ex-Stasi guy.

Okay, it had been known to happen elsewhere to, say, heads of state and insurrectionists who had seriously pissed us off. The most infamous case, the Agency's attempt to kill Fidel Castro with an exploding cigar, was alternately hilarious, inventive, and frightening in its wicked childishness. There had also been talk of an assassination attempt on a Hezbollah leader. Of sponsoring Salvador death squads to hit rebel leaders. None of that had anything to do with my time at the Agency, God knows.

If I'd had to put money on Assassinations, Yes or No, I would have said yes. Of course. There had been and still were political assassinations and attempted assassinations—though the old KGB was reputed to be not just a more frequent employer of such methods, but a hell of a lot more efficient. But outside of novels and movies, there was almost no chance the Agency would be going after U.S. citizens inside the United States. Could there be a rogue agent? Yes. A cabal of them? Unlikely but possible. Would they be out to get a guy who last wielded power in East Germany in 1989?

I had to laugh at myself, which I might have done if Adam hadn't been sound asleep. Well, I probably wouldn't have, because while I might be amusing enough to get *Entertainment Weekly* to call *Spy Guys* "occasionally witty," and self-deprecating enough to amuse guests at the usual Manhattan gatherings of the semiclever, laughing at myself, when by myself, had never been my forte.

I pushed my pillows into a mound of the proper height, but sleep wasn't happening. I alternated between uneasy and unglued. I remembered how Dix had told me I had to be more analytical. Okay. Was Lisa truly about to reveal some matter of national importance, as she had claimed? Assuming she was, could the late Manfred-Dick have

been somehow involved? And if so, what would the CIA have to do with it? Would they go into a SCIF, a room within a room where top-secret information can be discussed, and say, *Let's think of a rare disease someone living in Cincinnati could convincingly contract, something that would be hard enough to diagnose that the guy we're killing would be dead before the final lab test results came back?*

Anyhow, what did this have to do with me? Dick Schroeder was dead and therefore could not lead me to Lisa. The real question was, how come her call had set me off the way it had? And why couldn't I leave this whole business alone? Had I gone from my normal anxiety-ridden state to being overtly whacko? When Americans went nuts, I mused, probably half the time they thought the CIA was after them—or after someone important to them. If not the CIA itself, they'd think Mossad or the KGB was listening to phone conversations, or putting hypnotic drugs into their Starbucks, or sneaking transmitters into silicone breast implants. Just before I fell asleep, I sensed I was getting too close to the deep end. Time to stop thinking about some operative sprinkling deadly fungus over Dick Schroeder's muesli.

The last time I recalled seeing Dr. Jo-Ellen McCracken Hazan was when I was about fifteen, a day or two after I had misread some package directions and dyed my hair orange instead of the Debbie Harry blond I was aiming for. Naturally, I then insisted that garish orange was the color I had wanted all along. When my mother and I ran into Dr. Hazan in the shoe department at Saks, the two of them had squealed and hugged each other and launched into an extended *Oh my God, it's been ages* routine. In their case it was true because after being medical school classmates, Dr. Hazan had gone on to do a residency in infectious diseases and settled in L.A. The reason I remembered her, and fondly, was because she didn't recoil or blink at the sight of me.

I called her at noon, nine California time, and, amazingly, got through two secretaries without having to give my curriculum vitae. After a moment of chatting, during which I told her I no longer had orange hair and she assured me that what she remembered was that Carol Schottland had a delightful daughter, I asked her if she knew about blastomycosis. I was the writer for an espionage-adventure show on TV and, while I conceded it sounded brutal, I wanted to kill off a character this way.

"Well, if blastomycosis—it's sometimes called Gilchrist's disease—is not diagnosed and treated, it can be fatal," Dr. Hazan said. "It's considered a rare disease, you know."

"I heard about a man in Cincinnati who got it. He did a lot of fishing in and around the Ohio River, I guess."

"Well, that would be the place for it. It's found in the Midwest and the Southeast too. Farmers get it, and so do hunters, campers. And fishermen also, it appears. How is he doing?"

"He died." She made a doctor noise that I translated as *Too bad*. "They called it a fever of unknown origin. It seemed as if he had the flu."

"It usually presents with flulike symptoms," she said. "Fever, chills, night sweats, cough, muscle aches, chest pains. The usual miseries. But blastomycosis can turn into a widespread infection that affects the skin and bones, the genitourinary tract. Sometimes even the meninges." She must have read my silence as *Duh* because she added, "That's one of the membranes that covers the brain and spinal cord."

"How do people get it?"

"By inhalation. Breathing in airborne spores that come from contaminated soil."

"Could someone get it by injection? I mean, if I had a character who was pierced with a sharp object loaded with blastomycosis fungi, could he get it?"

"I've heard of primary cutaneous blastomycosis that can follow a

traumatic inoculation of the fungus into the skin. I've never seen a case. But you're an entertainment show, right?"

"Right."

"I think you'd be on pretty safe ground if you want to kill off somebody that way. Well, be sure to let me know if it's going to be on TV. How exciting! Oh, and send my love to your mother."

Since my father's business was selling high-priced cookware, there was an elaborate test kitchen on the second floor of his headquarters. He loved to cook and could have been his own best customer, so while an architect had been designing Total Kitchen's new location in a loft building in a down-and-almost-out neighborhood now called Tribeca, my father had told him he had another thought: Since there had to be plumbing for his fancy CEO bathroom, they might as well stick in a few more pipes so he could have a modest galley kitchen on the other side of his office.

Modesty was relative: the test kitchen had one of those six-burner restaurant stoves and a separate mini-dishwasher especially for glasses. Though his galley wasn't large, my father was the kind of cook who demanded a mandolin to slice red onion for a sardine sandwich. Therefore, it was equipped beyond all reason, with three different types of citrus zesters and an espresso machine that could make a latte or a café cubano at the touch of one of its sleek oval buttons. From where I was sitting, I could look into the kitchen and admire the gleam of copper pots reflected in the glass and stainless steel doors of his refrigerator.

"See?" He gestured to a spinach salad with grilled chicken and mango and the Sauvignon Blanc he'd set out for lunch. "I got one advantage over your mother." He was the same age as my mother, seventy. The black hairs that had once been on the backs of his hands had disappeared. The previous summer, when we'd been on the beach together, I noticed his legs looked waxed. I wondered if he

would eventually turn into one of those old men who were baby-hairless, except for the odd strip of fur around the edges of their outer ears.

"What advantage?" I asked.

"I can have a table in front of my sofa. She can't. Though I always said to her, Carol, would it be so terrible to give a patient a cup of coffee? Not the ones who lie down, because they'd dribble on the cushions. But almost all of them sit up. I'm not saying cookies or anything because that could interfere with the therapeutic alliance."

"There's one problem," I said. "I don't think she ever made a decent cup of coffee in her life. When I was about eight or nine you were in Europe somewhere on a buying trip. She made a pot of coffee for herself. When she tasted it, she spewed it out. I still remember the force of the spray, like from one of those things people have on their lawn. God, were we laughing!"

"I guess it wouldn't be so terrific, her patients spritzing and worrying that her lousy coffee symbolized learned helplessness." In their forty-six-year marriage, my father had picked up a lot of the lingo of my mother's profession, talk she rarely used at home. But she delighted in the way he tossed her words around—*magical thinking, rationalization*—often with whim, occasionally with precision. The only time she corrected him was when he specifically asked, "Carol, babe, did I use that right?"

While he dished out the salad with a chichi stainless steel server that unfortunately reminded me of something on a tray of forceps in Adam's necropsy lab, I tore off a chunk of bread from a baguette. The bread nestled in a cloth napkin in a wicker basket so heavily lacquered it looked carved out of rock. "Did Mom tell you I dropped by her office?" I asked.

He put my plate of salad in front of me. He had a talent. Not only would the salad be delicious, but it didn't come out on my plate in one giant mishmash of ingredients, the way it would have if I'd served it. Somehow, despite tossing it in the bowl, my father had

managed to get the greens on bottom and the chicken on top—with a fan of mango slices around it. "Yeah, she told me." Then he gave me the encouraging smile which meant *You can confide in me the way you do in your mother.* My father was a sixties guy who had mortified me throughout my adolescence with his pleasure in telling my friends, "I was one of the first feminists!"

He didn't fit the stereotype: someone scrawny and henpecked. Short and built like a shipping crate, my father could have been cast as one of Tony Soprano's lesser henchmen. Though much better dressed. Also, since he'd started going bald in his early twenties, he always had what hair he possessed chopped short, marine-style. That would have looked odd on anyone else, especially during the late sixties when most men wore antimilitary monster sideburns and hair to rival Rapunzel's. Yet my mother claimed that for some reason, he'd always been able to carry it off, year in and year out.

While he wasn't elegant in the way she was, he had good taste and an ability to make anything look its best. He could put a bunch of wire whisks into an arrangement so pleasing you'd want to use it as a centerpiece. Likewise, he always looked just right for the occasion, from a black-tie wedding to a football game to the kiln room in a ceramics factory in Italy.

But a feminist was what he was. He and my mother met in their freshman year at Brooklyn College. Not being much of a student, he'd dropped out after his second year and got a dead-end job with a company that designed and installed window displays for mom-and-pop stores all over the city. He did canned peaches beneath a fake ficus plant pretending to be a tree; a beach pail full of antacids in the middle of a mound of sand; sneakers that danced up a step ladder.

My mother, on the other hand, stayed in school, majored in chemistry, and graduated magna cum laude. When they married that August, her parents were as aghast at the union as his were when a few years later he quit his job to stay home with Maddy and me. That was when my mother was twenty-seven and decided to go to med-

ical school. He made ends meet—barely—working every other night plus weekends at a car rental company. But back then, he was the parent at home. My earliest memory was sitting in my high chair, banging a wooden spoon—confident I was helping him—while he stirred something in a pot. In those years, my father discovered not just the joy of cooking, but the potential in keeping cooks in pots, pans, gizmos, and crockery. He became a man inspired: once he was able to go back to work, we went from poor to rich in three years.

I spread my napkin on my lap. "I was telling Mom how I never really got over getting fired from the CIA."

"What do you want me to say, Katie?" my father asked.

"You mean that you always thought my going down there was a lousy idea."

"Far be it from me to rub it in, but I told you then: if you go to work for the government, you're going to be dealing with people who'll do anything to preserve their little piece of turf. The big three: lie, cheat, steal." At least he didn't add four: kill.

"I don't want to rub it in either," I said to him, "but how about people who want to serve their country?"

He shrugged somewhat wearily, but then we'd had this discussion more than once, in the mideighties, when I'd decided investment banking was as thrilling as watching alfalfa grow—not that I ever actually saw alfalfa. My father had wanted me to stay in New York and work for Total Kitchen: he'd demanded, "Who do you think I built up this company for, Katie? For me?" Before I could come up with an answer that didn't sound snide, he added, "Your sister's too sensitive to have a head for business. You're not."

I took a forkful of salad less out of hunger than to change the subject: "Terrific dressing!"

"Not too oily. The older I get, the more I'm moving away from vinegar and back to lemon juice. So listen, honey, like I said, they fight for their tiny piece of turf—and that's just in departments like Health, Education and Welfare."

"It's called Health and Human Services now."

"Right. Fine. You're the genius. I don't know anything."

"I didn't say that, Dad. I just—"

I had to get the last word in. As did he. "Katie, I'm only telling you that the CIA does whatever all those other departments do, except they're smarter. Or they think they're smarter. Plus most of their work involves sneaking and lying. That's how they do their jobs. What are they going to do, go to the president of Russia and say, 'Excuse me'—what's Putin's name?"

"Vladimir."

"'Excuse me, Vlad, but I need the address of all the nukes you haven't told us about.' No, they can't do that. So they bribe, they blackmail, they lie to get what they need."

"That's the Operations Directorate. And they don't act out of venality. It's their job to convince foreign nationals that it's in their best interest to . . . well, to betray their country. That's how we get information we need but aren't supposed to have. But I was in—"

"You worked for the Intelligence Directorate. I know. The point I'm making is that the CIA does what everybody else in Washington does, except they do it meaner and tougher and so out of sight no one ever finds out. You knew that even before you went down there, from all those spy books you read."

Then he got all damp-eyed. His tears had always made me cringe until I was twelve or thirteen, when I realized he got that way only in front of the family, about the family. My guess was, no one in his company had a clue that he possessed tear ducts. "Katie, don't you think Mom and I know what a hit you took?" He sniffled and wiped his nose with his napkin.

"I know you know." Even now, they had no idea of the extent of it. "Look, it wouldn't have come up again for me with so much force if someone I used to work with hadn't called. It made the whole thing seem like my firing happened yesterday. Did Mom tell you about that call?" Of course she had. As far as I knew, the longest they'd ever

SUSAN ISAACS

kept a secret from each other was the time it took for me or Maddy to leave the room.

"She mentioned it."

I spent the next fifteen minutes going over background and telling my father how Huff had gotten me information on Lisa, albeit reluctantly. As for Ben, I went on, he might have been less than truthful assuring me he would ask some civilians—not in the Agency—if they could check around about Lisa's whereabouts. However, if Ben had considered me reprehensible, he would never have taken my call. I also told my father about Dick Schroeder, and that with his death, I had lost my chance of learning if there had been anything in my past work with Lisa that had motivated her to phone me.

"Now listen, kiddo," my father said, "don't take offense, but this tracking-down-Lisa thing sounds to me like it could be a story for your show. I mean, you're going off to Cincinnati. Not that there's anything wrong with it, but you seem to be building—"

I finished his sentence for him—twice: "A mountain out of a molehill? Something out of nothing?"

"Katie," my father said, "tell me. What's the big deal now? You haven't been out of work for years. You wrote the book, and now it's playing on television and nobody's even breathed a word like *cancel.* You've got a career every single one of your friends would die for." I was about to list a decorator, two teachers, and a jewelry maker who loved their work even more than I loved mine, when he added, "Let's just say you've got a career that pays you so much you don't even have to ask me for money." He smiled, delighted. It wasn't that he loved me more because I was earning a good living. It was that I now pleased him in a way he'd never anticipated: in the way a son would have. I was holding my own in the world. I was a success. Even the most feminist of fathers, especially those of his generation, lapsed occasionally. "Not that you'd ever have to ask, moneywise, because if you needed it, I can honestly say I think I would know it."

124

"I know, Dad."

"Of course you know. But let me do something for you." He held up his hand in reassurance. "I'm just going to call Andy. Now you may be asking, what can a corporate lawyer do for me about all this business with the CIA and talk about 'national importance' and stuff?"

"Dad—"

"He's at Greenberg Traurig. It's a national law firm. I know they got an office in Washington." He held up his hand again, traffic-cop style. "Hear me out. He'll call one of his people in Washington he knows and he'll say, 'Listen, my friend, I need an attorney—maybe not in the firm—who can do business with the CIA.' You know, the guys who get documents declassified for different groups or whatever. Probably someone who used to be a lawyer for them. What we need, Katie, is a guy—or I should say a person—who can put the screws on them a little to maybe find out something about what happened to you." He picked up a piece of mango and held it aloft on his fork. "Would that help make you feel better?"

"It might."

He got up from the couch and stuck his head out the office door. "Get me Andy on the phone," he boomed, though his secretary was no more than three feet away. "E-mail him too in case he's at lunch because he never goes out without his BlackBerry." Then he looked back at me. "We'll get somebody good. Andy knows with me money is no object. If you need somebody to do a job for you, hire the best and the brightest. It always pays off."

He glanced at his watch. It had been thirty seconds and Andy hadn't called back yet. "So listen, you want to hear about real classified information?"

"What?"

"Relax. My kind of classified. You can't breathe a word about this. Well, except to Adam. I got a team. An engineer, an industrial designer, and a chemist working on a top-secret project. The ulti-

mate grill pan! How many people would give their right arm to get a grill pan that even in a studio apartment could give something that grilled, kind of charcoaly taste without making the smoke detectors go off? Seriously, with minimum smoke. More like almost no smoke. It'll be my pan, my patent. Williams-Sonoma will want to shoot themselves."

Chapter Fourteen

NOT MUCH MORE THAN TWENTY-FOUR HOURS later, I got a call from Constance Cincotta, the lawyer from D.C. my father's lawyer recommended. She'd spent a couple of decades in the Office of the General Counsel in the CIA. She told me to forget about getting anything out of the Agency. "Forget the Freedom of Information Act." She had a rich, opera singer's voice, but I sensed she was going to give me bad news from the last act. "FOIA is if you want to look at a certain national intelligence estimate, or want to learn about the Agency's investigation of UFOs from the forties to the nineties." So far, if there was any drama in this aria, it wasn't evident.

"I know," I told her. "It's not an issue I'm interested in, it's my own employment record. Or in my case, the termination of my employment there."

"I understand. Now under the Privacy Act, you could request the Agency's information on you, whatever is indexed to your name. But

I made a couple of calls, spoke to the second-in-command in the information and privacy coordinator's office, and there is no—repeat—no access to personnel records, other than the fact that you were employed by the agency. That's all they'll give out."

"But they were giving that out back in 1990, the year I was fired. And just to see what would happen," I went on, "when I was first interviewed by a couple of reporters when I was publishing my novel, I mentioned I knew about the Agency because I had worked there. One of them checked and found out, yes, sure, I had been at the CIA."

"Well," she said brightly, "that should have given your book a kind of credibility that a lot of others don't have." She cleared her throat. "I tried to find out, as subtly as I could, if I could at least get a sense about whether your termination was a serious matter or simply a question of downsizing or your taking home a box of pencils—"

"I don't steal pencils," I said. "That's number one, and number two, it was shortly after the fall of the Wall and the implosion of the East German government, so they needed more report writers, not fewer." I sensed my voice veering out of control, so I added, "Sorry to cut you off."

"I understand. And I apologize for the box of pencils remark, which was me at my impolitic worst. After twenty years at the Agency, what one gains in discernment one often loses in delicacy." Maybe she wanted me to say, *Oh, you're not at all indelicate.* Maybe I hesitated too long because Constance Cincotta went back to business. "Unfortunately, there was nothing I could find out. The wall of silence. Or rather, the law of silence. I can only say, don't take it personally. It's the law for everyone, not just you."

"Well, thank you. I appreciate—"

She interrupted. Fair play, since I had just done the same to her. "I've never had the pleasure of seeing your TV show, but I've heard some fine things about it. And I understand you come from a good, solid background. It seems to me, if you'll forgive my pontificating,

that you shouldn't let your experience with the Agency cast a pall on your life. Whatever happened back then, whether it was some misunderstanding or a genuine miscarriage of justice, you wound up getting off easy. Much worse could have happened and didn't."

For an instant, I contemplated telling her about Lisa's call, and seeing if that would make any difference in her attitude. What she was giving me was not so much a brush-off as a realistic forget-about-it. Perhaps if she knew that some recent event had kicked off my search for answers, she could . . . What could she do? Let some former colleague in the CIA's general counsel's office know they had a rogue ex-employee named Lisa Golding who wanted to blab to the media? Maybe it was something they ought to know. Or it might be something that would set off a chain of events ending . . . how would His Highness say it? A chain of events that could end in a most distasteful manner.

More likely, I would be the one branded the lunatic, not Lisa. And for all I knew, maybe I was. Maybe they would decide that if anyone posed a threat to national security, it was crazy Katie Schottland and something had to be done about her. No, that was lunacy à la mode. What would happen was that after a functionary in internal security muttered *Quel nut job* about me, two seconds later I'd be forgotten.

"Well, thanks for your time," I said. Rather mean-spiritedly, I calculated that time was being billed to my father at about eight hundred dollars an hour and mused that her call to the CIA on my behalf probably had not lasted more than five minutes.

"No problem," Constance Cincotta said. "I wish you lots of luck. And from now on, I promise, I'm going to TiVo your show!"

For what Adam and I paid monthly for our parking spaces in a garage just west of Broadway, we probably could have rented a pleasant little farmhouse on a hill in Provence. But without a car my commute to the studio in Queens would have taken just under two hours on

public transportation. And with the hours Adam sometimes had to put in, he could find himself waiting more than half an hour on a subway platform in the Bronx at ten-thirty at night.

I was coming out of Exquisite Foods, an unremarkable deli a block from my apartment where I'd just bought my lunch, a Muenster cheese, guacamole, and tomato wrap. While most of the cast and crew made gagging sounds whenever I opened my brown bag, I preferred my choices to those at the craft services table at the studio: bologna the diameter of a Dodge Ram tire, salad scented with either preservatives or insecticide; also, it was my belief that while steak might be aged, sliced turkey should not be.

I was halfway across Broadway when I sensed someone tall beside me. Whatever body language was being spoken between us — a slight forward movement of his elbow, a foot in a brown loafer too close to mine — I violated my native Manhattanite's no-eye-contact rule and, as I put my foot up onto the curb, glanced up.

"Good morning, Katie." Huff Van Damme.

Obviously he'd expected me to gasp, because his smirk vanished when I said, "Good morning. How's it going?" Maybe it would have been a goodwill gesture to express shock and awe, but that didn't occur to me until afterward. In truth, I wasn't surprised that a retired CIA operative was able to get my address, tail me as I left my building, and keep out of sight while I walked east on West Eighty-fifth, stopped at the deli, then continued on toward my garage. On the other hand, I did think to say, "Good shadowing. I'll have to write that into some script."

"It's always nice to be a muse," Huff said. I was pretty sure he wasn't serious, but saying something even vaguely amusing seemed alien to everything I knew about him. So I smiled, but refrained from chuckling. "You asked me to see if I could get a name for you," he murmured, "someone who knows what was going on in eighty-nine, with the East Germans and all."

"Right."

"Jacques Harlow," he said. "Ever hear of him?"

"No. I'm not sure."

"He was with DIA." Defense Intelligence, the agency that pro-
vided military information and assessments for the Defense Department and the Joint Chiefs of Staff. "Started out as a military attaché
in Eastern Europe, midsixties, I think, but went civilian." Huff
rubbed the side of his face as if checking his shave. I read the gesture
as a passing instant of embarrassment about the scar on his cheek in
the bright morning sun. He stuck his hand into the pocket of his
slacks. It was strange that I didn't feel sorry for him. "Jacques wound
up being their point man on East Germany. He called it right."

"Called it that the East German government was going to
implode?"

"Yeah." He actually peered around to see if anyone had overheard
this vital information.

"Would he have known what was going on at our Agency?" I
asked more circumspectly.

"Some of it. He liaised with the intelligence community."

We had reached the garage and I wasn't too keen on having Huff
walk down the ramp with me. The guys who worked there might,
God forbid, think he was my boyfriend, and they were extremely
fond of my husband. Adam was amazingly patient in answering their
questions about their pets, sometimes bringing them information he
downloaded. One of them—a guy who owned a couple of fighting
cocks—always sang a song from *Dr. Doolittle* every morning when
Adam came into the garage: ". . . If we could walk with the animals,
talk with the animals, *dum, dum, dum* . . ."

I stood on the sidewalk beside the entrance to the garage as if I
planned on opening an office right there. "Would this Jacques guy
have known any of our players?" I inquired. Lisa, I was afraid, hadn't
been at a level to be dealing with someone like Jacques Harlow.

"The ones dealing with the . . ." His voice fell. "East Germans, I
suppose."

"Do you have contact information for him?"

Huff handed me a folded Post-it. The sticky part had picked up some gray pocket lint. "Jacques took early retirement." Oy, I thought. That means he'll have no current connection to the intelligence community. "He has a place in the Blue Ridge Mountains." I nodded as if I knew where the Blue Ridge Mountains were. Virginia or Tennessee, I guessed. My mind's eye could see a picture of a guy who left his teeth in a glass in the bathroom. "Call, see if he'll talk to you. He's funny about people."

"In what way?" I asked.

"Who he'll see, who he won't see."

"Okay."

"Don't even think of going there unannounced."

I had to smile. "What is he," I asked, "one of those guys who shoots first and asks questions later?"

"All I'm saying is you'd be better off not finding out firsthand."

Chapter Fifteen

USUALLY, I LOVED GOING TO THE STUDIO — and not just to do what I was good at or what earned me a living. I treasured the tiny routines that figured into the sum of the workday. Buying my lunch, hearing the guy behind the deli counter announce, "Here she is, Miss No Liverwurst," since each day I gazed longingly at the liverwurst, so fat it looked ready to burst out of its skin, then never ordered it. I liked deciding whether to drive through Central Park, across the Upper East Side, and over the Fifty-ninth Street Bridge or up through East Harlem and take the Triborough. My ritual of choosing between the news on NPR or "The Big 80s" on my new satellite radio was a comforting self-delusion that I could let in as much of the world as I wanted. It pleased me that when I drove into the studio parking lot in Astoria, I got the security guard's unsolicited report on Dani Barber's mood: "Hungover and mean," he'd say. Or, "She smiled. Must have found a new drug." Or, "Dangerously quiet."

I loved getting out and about, being part of the city I was born in. The deadest period of my life was when I was writing *Spy Guys*. I was stuck in the apartment. Nearly all I'd seen of my city was with Nicky when he came home from school. What I'd experienced then was Soccer Mom Manhattan, the diminished borough a parent sees when accompanied by a child who needs attention—playground, school, Museum of Natural History, Sneaker Street.

Alone at the computer all those hours, writing the novel, numbed me. Even if I took a break, there was no one to talk to. My only relief was the rare few hours when I was transported into the universe of the story, and was more in HH's world than in my own. In one chapter, he was working the room at a party at the Moroccan embassy in Moscow. I wrote those few pages while glancing over at pictures in a book on Moorish architecture. But the room I was creating inside my head was far more real than all the photos and drawings in the huge book on the table, more tangible than my actual desk, computer, and mug of tea. I saw the room as HH did, with the discriminating taste of a deposed royal, an outsider who had grown up studying the accoutrements of wealth and privilege. But I could also view the world through Jamie's ex-cop's eyes. Fused with her in that cosmos of the book, I was as frightened as she was in her first meetings with the more worldly and sinister informants a CIA op depends on. With her, I longed for the foul-smelling, two-bit snitches she/I had known as an NYPD detective.

But most of the time, I hated the lonely life. Each day when I sat down to write, I couldn't believe I'd been stupid enough to announce to everybody that I was going to try a novel. Sure, I'd known it would be tough: I'd read all about first-time writers getting blocked by fear of failure. Still, I had to have a job, pay my own way, and that didn't mean earning a living doing deep-fryer demos in my father's stores. Once I started working on what would become *Spy Guys*, my problem wasn't fear of failure. It was fear of success. What if this book actually got published? What if they wanted a sequel? Two

sequels? Twenty-five? Reading spy novels and thinking, I could do that, had initially felt like a challenge. Now I saw it could be a life sentence. What good was making money if you were doomed to do it locked in solitary? My TV gig was my ticket out.

The morning after I saw Huff I decided I had to tolerate one day of home confinement. Having determined that I wasn't going to get involved with a crazy person who lived in the mountains named Jacques, it was time to face the unpleasant fact that because I'd been playing the Find Lisa game, I hadn't done my job: produce a reasonably clean first outline of the season's last episode to show to Oliver. Now I had only one day in which to do it. Deciding what to write about was a no-brainer because, short of having the Spy Guys mutilate their genitals or mock God, I could let them do anything. But I couldn't afford a single distraction.

In the fifth year of writing the show, I found I was running out of new villains and whimsical plot twists that held my interest. No matter what crazy concepts I brought forth—like a demented entomologist in Azerbaijan raising toxic carpenter ants to attack campers at Acadia National Park—no one stopped me. True, no one said, "Great!" but no one ever had. Viewers weren't writing to the president of Quality TV complaining of the diminished quality of the scripts either. What was worse, I knew if I told Oliver that I wanted to leave, to develop another show, he'd either offer me a close-to-irresistible raise or the coproducer credit I'd been pining for since I signed for the job.

Sure, by this time I'd made enough money that I could take a walk for a while and smell the roses people were always talking about. Except where would I go after that? I couldn't think of anything I wanted to write except spy stories. But a dark espionage drama, one that alternated anomie and angst with the occasional set of teeth being punched out, the kind of show that HBO would go for, wasn't my style. And I wasn't good enough at plotting to come up with a spy thriller like *24* or *The Bourne Identity*. And forget ripping-out-

eyeball spy fiction: describing torture would be too disgusting for words. As for espionage erotica, I sensed I could write a graphic sex scene with words like *throbbing*, but Nicky would inevitably read it, or some mean critic would write that it lacked vérité or verisimilitude or one of those words in my sister's everyday vocabulary. I took my laptop into the den, sat in Adam's recliner, and began an outline about terrorists trying to form a cell in the United States by having their people masquerade as Hasidic tourists from Poland. No doubt it would bring in the usual letters, invariably in boring Times New Roman font, that would begin, "I am disgusted that you would be so insensitive . . ." I finished the outline in three hours or so, interrupted by some bathroom breaks, making two cups of green tea, neither of which I drank, and downloading the audio of a spy novel, *Prince of Fire*, onto my iPod. That's when I decided to call Jacques Harlow. I dialed.

I heard a click on the phone. A definite click. Then a close-to-subliminal hum, followed by a basso buzz. As I waited for his phone to ring I pictured the signal going through a series of silicone chips and cyber switches up to a Cingular satellite a thousand miles below the moon, then bouncing back to Earth only to be captured by the NSA, where cryptographers would . . . Would what? I chewed off most of my lip gloss. A long *cleeeek*. I took a deep breath. Cut it out, I ordered myself. Is this the first time in your long life on the phone that you've heard a click? Half the time I was talking to a friend, one of us would hear a noise on the line. We'd mutter: "Did you hear that? What was it?" But what could it be? Some minor digital disturbance? Or a unit of the National Geospatial-Intelligence Agency whose sole purpose was to eavesdrop on U.S. citizens who were nattering on about why they hated sharing a bathroom with their husbands?

I heard another click. For all I knew, Jacques Harlow could live in some backwater where they hadn't yet changed from rotary dial to touch-tone. Or maybe he had a thunderstorm over his house. As his phone began to ring, I realized I hadn't rehearsed what I was going

to say to him. But if I hung up now, he could have a record of my calling. Who cared? *Hang up now!* I clutched the phone with both hands. If my right hand fumbled, my left could come to its aid, slamming down the receiver before the two syllables of his hello emerged.

"Hello," a man's voice said.

"May I speak with Jacques Harlow, please?"

"This is Harlow."

I wasn't bad at reading voices, or maybe I was just good at reading things into voices. But I couldn't get much from his. Maybe calling himself Harlow was his protest against the informal generation for whom "Hi! I'm your server, Scott" was the measure of distance between strangers. It could have been some snappy holdover from his military days.

"Mr. Harlow, my name is Katherine Schottland. I'm the writer of a TV show about two spies who work for the CIA." I was hoping for an *uh-huh* or some acknowledgment that at least he was still on the line. I didn't get any, so of course I immediately pictured him rolling his eyes at the imminent idiocy of what I was about to ask of him. How could I describe *Spy Guys*? Not with a word like *lighthearted,* which he might interpret as frivolous. I decided on: "It's a good-natured show. Not a *Three Days of the Condor* take on the Agency." I had to assume someone who'd been in Defense Intelligence had at least heard of that movie, one of the first—and best—about an evil conspiracy within the CIA. "I was speaking with Harry Van Damme . . . Huff . . ." I took a deep breath and went on. "I mentioned I needed to speak with someone who has a sense of what was happening in the Agency in 1989, when the Wall—"

"I know something about that." He said it matter-of-factly. So far, he didn't sound mentally unhinged.

"I have some questions I'd like to ask you. I realize this may not be a good time. I'll be glad to call back at your convenience. Really, whenever—"

He didn't let me finish. "We'll talk about that when you get here."

"Oh." I brought the recliner up to sitting position. "I actually didn't factor in the time to come and see you, Mr. Harlow. I was hoping we could do it on the phone."

"Don't think so. Do you have a fax line?" I gave him the number. "I'll fax you directions for getting here. I'm about three-quarters of an hour from the airport in Asheville."

"That's in North Carolina?"

"Yes." It was a cautious yes, but at least he didn't ask me if I thought I could follow directions.

"I'll have to check my calendar and get back to you," I told him. "We have a pretty tight shooting schedule right now. I honestly don't know if I have time—"

"I'll fax directions. If you show up, I'll know you were able to make time."

Chapter Sixteen

MY SISTER AND I DIDN'T GET TOGETHER BECAUSE we relished each other's company. Both of us, I think (because naturally we never talked about it), wanted to be able to tell our parents, *Oh, I saw Maddy/Katie the other day,* to reassure them that despite the psychological axiom of sibling rivalry and our vastly different takes on life, they had done a terrific job bringing the two of us up. See? We voluntarily spent time with each other!

Why both of us felt that we needed to buck up these two adults who seemed more richly endowed in the ego department than we were was an interesting question. I probably figured that if I pondered that question too much, I'd decide my parents could live with reality and I'd wind up telling my sister to fuck off permanently. I assumed Maddy never answered the question either, not even with her higher IQ, not with the help of any of the eight thousand psychologists, psychiatrists, and social workers to whom she'd gone

since I'd been born. She called me to get together as often as I called her. We were due, I decided.

So, after I hung up with Jacques Harlow, I wrote a first draft of the script in a couple of hours. Then I wrote a long letter to Nicky. That calmed me: my son was the antidote to all that could be odd or dangerous. I ate a yogurt and a plum for lunch. Finally, I couldn't avoid my sister. "I'm working at home today and finished early. How about I come downtown to you?" I asked. "We could take a walk or something." She ruled out a walk—the angle of the late afternoon sun made her head pound—but yes, of course, come over. She wasn't writing. She was blocked, though she had promised to read some new work at Bread Loaf in August. But now she would have nothing.

Her last comment underscored one of the many differences between us. "I'll have nothing," she repeated when I got to her loft. Three words, poetic parsimony. I, on the other hand, would have emoted: *I have nothing. Nothing at all! Nada. Rien du tout. Gornischt*—and that would have been just the preamble to my description of writer's block. If I got it. Which I didn't. Poets got existential despair. TV writers got a dental plan.

As for her emotional life, since she and Dix had been divorced she'd had a series of men. Maddy hated the word *relationship* so she referred to whatever she had going with them as *liaisons*. Liaisons sounds French, sophisticated, hookups with married men in nipped-waist suits who carry sex toys in Vuitton attaché cases. But her guys were mostly heterosexual variations on Dix: intelligent, better-looking than average, tending toward tight-crotched pants and trendy eyeglasses. What all the ones I'd met lacked, that Dix had, was humor.

Not only did these guys not do a thing for me, I couldn't see how they did anything for Maddy. She and Dix had had great repartee, and while he couldn't zap her congenital inertia and hypochondria, he'd lifted her spirits more than any of the antidepressants she'd

taken. The good news about her post-Dix men was she never married any of them. The bad news, or sad news, was that at age forty-three, she lived alone. Not even a cat. If she derived some delight or contentment from having no entangling alliances, like glorying in the freedom to turn on all the lights in her apartment at three in the morning and blast recordings of Edna St. Vincent Millay's poetry with no one to yell, *What the fuck are you doing at this hour?* it would have been fine. But *pleasure* was the one word not in my sister's vast vocabulary.

"You've never gotten blocked?" Maddy asked.

"Well . . ." I began.

"You haven't, have you?"

"Could I please finish?"

"Go ahead." My sister sighed. If I'd been feeling as lousy as she probably was, I would have slumped into a huge, comforting chair. Instead, I was in the chair with the big rolled arms while she sat in a straight-backed chair that looked as though she'd grabbed it from some flamboyant person's dining room. Her own living room was beige or white, 1990s good taste with lots of linen fabric. Most of her furniture looked as if it needed ironing. But the chair she was in was lacquered dark red, Chinese style, I guess, with a yellow silk seat. She moved her back around, then shifted her weight from one cheek of her butt to the other.

"Maybe I've never been truly blocked," I said. "But there are days when I call in and say I'm working at home. Then I drive to some outlet and buy stuff I don't need: plaid umbrellas one time, four of them. Or I go to the bookstore when it opens and buy a load of books and come home to read. I can't write those days. I don't even try."

"But that's never happened to you for months at a time," Maddy replied. The sentence may have started as a sigh, but there was so much feeling behind it that it sounded like a whimper from a baby.

"No. But most of the time I've been writing, there's been a dead-

line hanging over my head. Back at the CIA, when I was doing reports: there was nothing creative there. I put a lot of people's work into an order and . . . did some clarifying. Many of them were academics and I had to make their language more accessible. And now, in TV, I'm always under the gun. The only time I didn't have a deadline was when I was writing the novel."

"Did you get blocked then?" Maddy asked.

"No. I was so desperate for employment—in the sense of being used for something. I was afraid that if I slacked off . . ." She was crossing her legs, right over left, left over right, then back again. "Why are you"—I imitated her leg switches—"like that? Do you want to change chairs with me?"

"No." She flipped her hand toward the rest of the living room. "I have lots of chairs."

"You look uncomfortable," I said.

I thought she was going to say something like *Life is uncomfortable*, but she said, "I'm not."

"Fine."

There was a moment of silence that grew more awkward because each of us was waiting for the other to break it. We were both nervous about talking at the same moment, then simultaneously saying, *Oh, excuse me*, then realizing neither of us had anything to say. I got out the first word only because I'd always had the faster reflexes. All Maddy managed was a sound like the *i* in *if*, and then she stopped because I had won.

"Do you think there might be a positive aspect to being blocked?" I asked. "Look, I always say that my subconscious is my best collaborator. When we map out a new season, I sit down beforehand and make an outline of what I want to present. After months of not working or even thinking about work, I'm amazed at what comes out. I mean, it all didn't crystallize in that split second. Some part of my mind had been sitting in front of its own little computer and plotting out what ought to happen in the upcoming episodes."

"Writing poetry is different." It sure was. Maddy's most well-known poem was "Soft Fruit," about starting to eat a peach and having her teeth bite into a small, rotten spot and before she can pull back, there's putrefied peach all over her tongue—though she wouldn't use such an obvious alliteration as *putrefied peach*. But most of her other poems had the same idea: finding something terrible in the middle of a pleasant experience.

"Why is poetry different? Because there's not necessarily a story involved?"

"It's not just a question of narrative," Maddy said. Trust my sister to say "narrative" after I've said "story."

"What's it a question of, then?"

"I don't know." My coloring was more red and Maddy's more yellow, yet if we stood side by side, there wouldn't be a great difference between us. Normally. But now I noticed she had gone from slightly sallow to waxy. That happened when she was really low. Though I didn't think she'd gained weight, she was looking more blockish. Like my father, except while his cubelike physique came from sturdy forebears and playing tennis, hers suggested a loss of muscle tone. What curves there were to her body had become squared off by flesh.

"Is your mind a total blank when you try to write?" I asked.

"It's blank and in turmoil at the same time. I can't explain it. I get up every morning thinking, This is it. Today I'll take my notebook and put a new ink cartridge into my pen and I'll begin with the first word that comes to mind. At the end of the day, it's just the end of the day. The sun sets. Nothing's happened."

"You're depressed?"

"Katie, when have I not been?"

Before I was born, when there was only you. Naturally I didn't say that. "I know. But maybe this time is a little worse."

"No. I'm actually in a good mood—for me. It would probably be your major depressive disorder. For me I'm all right." I must have

looked dubious because she added, "I *am*. And for God's sake don't go running to Mom and Dad."

"I'm not—"

"I'm okay. I've gone through the usual dry spells before and I'll go through them again."

"Maddy, are you feeling suicidal?"

"No! Can't I talk to you? Can't I say I feel down because I'm not writing without you thinking—"

"Swear you won't pull a Sylvia Plath?" I'd always been so sure she wouldn't. But what if I was wrong?

"I swear," she said in a louder voice than she'd used since I'd got there. "I swear! Don't give me your skeptical face. I told you I won't do anything and I won't. I've been a lot worse than this."

"How about calling me every morning just to let me know—"

"'Good morning, sis! No carbon monoxide for me today!'"

"Something like that," I said. Great, Laughing Girl seven days a week as my first call in the morning. "It couldn't kill you to make a thirty-second call every day."

"Stop it!" Maddy snapped. "If I do start feeling . . . not right, I swear to God I'll call you."

"You're an atheist."

"I swear I'll call you. Now shut up about me. What's new with you?"

Of course I wasn't going to tell her. Yet somewhere in every younger sister's head is the notion that it is the older sister's duty, if not natural inclination, to take care of her. So what came out was, "Well, actually, a lot is new."

For an instant, Maddy stopped wriggling. "Tell me."

"It's a lot of narrative," I said.

"I can take it."

So I told her what had been happening since Lisa's call, except I left out dinner with Dix, less out of protectiveness than selfishness, because I wanted her to concentrate on me. She only clapped her

hand over her mouth once, when I told her how I faked my way into Dick Schroeder's house. "Are you crazy? What if they'd had a guard dog?"

"I thought of that, but I was more worried about getting shot."

"By him?"

"It's too embarrassing. Okay, I'll say it. I kind of pictured an Agency security detail pulling out Berettas and drilling me."

"That makes no sense," Maddy said. "Why would the CIA give him a security detail from 1990 until now?"

"It makes as much sense as slavering Dobermans ripping off my flesh."

"Why are you doing this, Katie? What can you hope to get?"

"Justice."

"Justice?" The sound she made would be noted in scripts as "[HUMORLESS LAUGH]." Then she added, "From the Central Intelligence Agency?" I could have written that response before she gave it. Maddy was so damn predictable.

But I chose not to make a cutting remark in case she decided to do a Sylvia Plath and needed one final hurt. Anyway, at that moment, my lunch of yogurt and plum stopped working. I was hungry. My sister, however, made a point not to be, as she put it, fetishistic with regard to food the way my father was. He wasn't, though admittedly he did whip up plates of sandwiches for the random plumber or the Time Warner cable-repair guy who passed through the apartment. He had to feed people. To me that was a lot better than not offering your own sister even a cup of tea.

"Maddy, do you happen to remember anything from around the time I was fired?" I asked, determined not to beg for food.

"What do you mean?"

"I mean . . . I don't know. Is there anything that struck you then that still sticks in your mind? The theory being that if it stuck, maybe it's because you picked up on something important."

"What's important to me may not be important to you." I braced

myself for one of her discourses on subjective reality. But all she said was, "I remember you felt betrayed by your boss."

"What?"

"You asked me what I remembered. I remember you telling me he was in the hall watching as you packed your stuff." I nodded. "You said you asked him, 'Wasn't my work good?' and he didn't answer. He didn't even say he was sorry this was happening to you. Nothing."

"That's right," I said. My stomach grumbled. "He just stood there the whole time. It wasn't as if he had to be there to make sure I didn't steal the paper clips. There were two goons from Internal Security for that. Isn't it funny? I'd totally forgotten this until you mentioned it. Anyway, there was no expression on his face to show he was thinking, Ah, too bad for Katie, or, Life is unfair, and maybe he was trying to ESP it to me." The minute that was out of my mouth I regretted not saying "communicate it telepathically" so she wouldn't think my vocabulary had completely degenerated from working in TV.

"Would you have been able to read him that well?" Maddy asked.

There might have been a flicker of sisterly sixth sense in her question. I simply said, "I'd worked for him for a year and a half. I knew him better than I knew anybody there, though I wouldn't necessarily put CIA employees in any Most Soul-Baring Colleagues competition."

"Think back. Did you read anything into his silence at the time?"

"That's such a Mom question."

My sister actually smiled, albeit a small smile that did not display teeth. "Are you avoiding answering?"

"I'll tell you what struck me at the time," I said. "He wasn't looking at me with hate, as if he thought I'd committed treason. I was taking things out of my desk drawers and when I looked up I saw he was still there watching . . . not that he was the only one. What was weird was that he didn't look away, you know, the way people do when they're uncomfortable because you've caught them staring at you.

Okay, Ben's a worldly guy. He's not going to turn bright red and start kicking the ground with embarrassment. But he didn't even avert his eyes, not for a second."

"And that seemed . . . ?"

"Strange. As if he expected me to somehow challenge him, or try to defend myself."

Chapter Seventeen

"I HAVE TO VISIT A SICK FRIEND IN NORTH CAR-olina," I told Oliver the next morning.

"It might be better to call her." He squeezed the very top of his nose, the part that was between his eyes—his private acupuncture point for calming himself while dealing with annoying people. "Visiting can be a really big strain."

"She's very, very sick." For someone who hardly ever lied, I felt I was doing well. I especially liked the quaver in my voice on the second *very*. I hadn't mentioned any particular disease because Oliver was one of those who shuddered during discussions of illness and death, but I was picturing a woman afflicted with a lady-like ailment that required lace-trimmed handkerchiefs; that way, I wouldn't have to feel guilty about giving her cancer, even though she was imaginary.

"Sorry to hear that. I'll tell you what." He picked thoughtfully at the pink polo pony on the front of his XXL green Ralph Lauren

shirt. "Send her one of those Harry and David baskets. The big ones with fresh fruit plus you get candy and nuts." Nearly all producers have a congenital aversion to spending money, but understand sometimes it is necessary. So he added, "Charge it to my account."

"She's past being tempted by food. For all I know, she may not be eating at all."

"Terrible, terrible." The conversation wasn't going his way. "Is she around your age?" I nodded sadly. "Sometimes it's hard to understand God." We both sighed. "I don't know," he went on, as if talking to himself. "A visit might be counterproductive. You make a long trip down there, she's going to feel obligated to see you. I remember when my uncle Fred got really bad, we all flew to Louisville. My aunt Cora said, basically, 'Thank you for coming but go home. He's going to use his energy to get better, not to say good-bye to you all.'"

"Did he get better?" I asked.

"A short rally. Katie, all I'm saying is you should think it through." He went back to squeezing the bridge of his nose. "Is she dying?"

"I think so."

"I can understand you want to say good-bye, but—"

"You said you liked the first draft of the final episode."

"Dani and Javiero haven't looked at it yet. They'll have a lot to say, as you well know."

"I'll call. I'll get their notes. You know I can deal with them."

"How long do you think you'll stay?" Forget empathy: even sympathy was not in Oliver's nature, but he'd worked with actors all his professional life and had mastered eyebrows-drawn-together-in-concern along with *tsk-tsk*ing. He was feeling big-time pressure over the deadline for getting the season's final episode in the can.

"I'll just be gone for a day. Tops two. And I'll be just a phone call away and I'll take my laptop. That way, I can redo whatever needs redoing and e-mail it right back to you. My phone will be on constantly."

"Most hospitals don't allow cell phones," he said sadly.

"She's at home. There's nothing more the doctors can do for her."

Oliver gripped the edge of his desk and half pulled, half pushed up his bulk. "To tell you the truth, this isn't a great time for you to be away. Is she that bad? I mean, is she going to, you know, go within the next two weeks?"

Was this a veiled threat? I preferred Blustering Oliver to Semi-Polite Oliver, because at least the former was predictable. Most of the time I thought I was indispensable to the show, but in this business, who could be sure? They could hire another writer tomorrow at half my salary. Or less. By midseason, the ratings might be hurtling downhill, but by then it would be too late for me.

I told myself not to think about having to reinvent myself at Total Kitchen, about learning how to amortize baker's racks or market electric lobster steamers. That, of course, led to a high-def image of my father's face as he tried to mask his anguish when he realized that when he retired, I would rapidly run his wonderful business into the ground.

I leaned toward Oliver and said, "I'm going. This is something I have to do for my own peace of mind."

Lying to Oliver was like a day in fields of daisies compared with lying to Adam again. A day trip to Cincinnati was one thing. Schlepping to the middle of nowhere in the Blue Ridge Mountains—which to me was already the middle of nowhere—to see a Defense Intelligence guy named Jacques who made Huff Van Damme nervous was another.

"I'll go with you," Adam said. We were walking the dogs in Riverside Park, watching the pink sky turn amethyst as the sun set across the Hudson over New Jersey.

"I'm really only going to be gone for one night. Fly to Asheville, rent a car, and get to wherever this guy lives. Then I have to interview him . . ." I suddenly realized I couldn't say I wanted to find out about East Berlin 1989, since *Spy Guys* was set in the present, ". . . about spying in Hong Kong." I chuckled, then added, "That means they're

going to have to get a lot of stock footage of Hong Kong and find a couple of locations or two in Chinatown. Maybe Flushing."

One of the dogs, the beagle Lucy, stopped to pee beside a maple that looked sickly, probably from having its roots burned by gallons of uric acid every day. I looked up at Adam and realized he knew my lightheartedness was phony. Unless he or she is being willfully ignorant, one spouse can usually sense when the other is lying. I can't say Adam's forehead had deep lines of concern, as if he were thinking, She's going to the Blue Ridge Mountains for a tryst with her lover and that's why she doesn't want me to go. It was more a recognition that he knew I was trying to put something over on him and couldn't figure out what.

"You can go, do your business with this guy," he said. "Then we'll spend a couple of days. I used to drive down there from Washington, do some fishing, camping. Before you, I think. We never got down there together, did we?"

"No."

"So how about it?" He peered at me quizzically, as did Lucy and Flippy. *How could you say no to such a good idea?* their looks seemed to demand. "We don't have to camp out," Adam said. "We could stay at a hotel someplace."

Say yes, I told myself. Why not? His being along wouldn't stop me from going to see Jacques Harlow. He could spend the time browsing in stores that sold fishing lures, which was the kind of shopping he liked. Then we could go hiking for a couple of days. But I couldn't say yes. Here I was, pulling away from him. Was it out of petulance? Adam hadn't been particularly supportive of any of my recent journeys into the past. He had wanted no part of it.

"I don't want to wait for the weekend to go," I told him. "It's not as though I'll be lolling about down there. Oliver wants me back ASAP." He picked up his pace, and because his legs were so much longer than mine, I had to racewalk to keep up with him. "Listen, Adam—"

"I have plenty of time coming. I could take a couple of days mid-week." It was barely a suggestion anymore. It was more like he was already in the middle of an argument, telling me that he'd offered me X and Y and Z and, coldly, unreasonably, I'd said no to all of them.

"It's not that I don't want to take advantage of being just the two of us this summer," I told him. "But I have to go and get back fast, get through the last episode. I think the first draft is pretty clean, so it's just a question of—"

"What you seem to want this summer is to take advantage of being the one of you, not the two of us."

"That's not true!" I scurried up beside him and tried to hold his hand. He didn't take it. Instead, he presented me with Flippy's leash, then jogged off with Lucy fast enough that I couldn't possibly keep up.

Chapter Eighteen

ROAD LORE SAYS AS LONG AS YOU'RE THE DRIVER
of a car, not a passenger, you won't get carsick. Not true. I'd been
doing fine: tooling around winding North Carolina mountain roads
with forests looming on either side. I'd gotten lost only twice. Ten A.M.
and merely queasy from a few hairpin turns. But then I got out of the
car. Bad idea.

The beginning of the gravel drive that led up to Jacques Harlow's
house had one of those galvanized-steel mailboxes on a splintery
wood post—the silvery ones that look recycled out of milk pails.
Suddenly I wanted to heave what had been listed on the coffee shop
menu as a "breakfast sandwich." Sausage, egg, and cheese: what a person from a blue state would order in a red state to display openness
to another culture and also a willingness to let bygones (segregation,
Bush versus Gore) be bygones. I also figured that a sandwich with
sausage had to be better than the other choice: a sandwich with liver

mush, egg, and cheese. I hadn't even been able to bring myself to ask the waitress what liver mush was.

Oh boy, was I sick now! The overgrown grass around the mailbox looked promising for heaving. Despite all the mountain air, I could smell only greasy sausage slices. But I had to try to control myself because just then I saw a Jeep careen down the gravel drive. It pulled up at a ninety-degree angle and blocked any entry. Two people jumped out.

"Hi!" a woman called. Resonant voice, friendly too, except she was carrying a rifle. "You Katherine Scotland?" Close enough. I would have nodded, but part of me was writing a scene in my head in which I smile and say, *Yes, I'm Katherine . . . usually Katie, but, hey, with that rifle you can call me anything you want,* and, instead of looking amused, she says coldly, *This is a shotgun,* then aims and shoots. "I'm Merry Slone," she said instead. *"S-L-O-N-E."* Her copper-streaked hair was pulled back into a ponytail that she wore high on her head, like someone in an old movie where kids jitterbug at sock hops. She laid the weapon in the back of the Jeep—the model without a roof, only a rollbar. "We were out after coyote." She sounded as though she thought that an excellent pastime. She was wearing jeans and a tight T-shirt decorated with two orange kittens: on it was written PURR-FECT! As another wave of nausea hit, I decided she was between five and ten years younger than I was.

The man, who had been driving, walked down the few feet of gravel from his car. He must have noticed I seemed disturbed because he explained, "Always open season on coyote!" in a voice even more cheerful than hers. I guessed he'd pegged me as a New York liberal coyote lover. He was one of those sun-reddened, tall, skinny guys with an Adam's apple that popped out almost as far as his turned-up nose. Men like that were usually not menacing, but there was something in the way he held himself that gave me the sense of a Special Forces type who could live in a cave and eat cactus for months at a time. "You are Katherine, right?"

I realized I had not yet said a word. "Sorry, I got a little fluttery in the stomach driving on the roads up here. Just needed a few breaths of fresh air. Yes, I'm Katie Schottland."

He must have picked up my unspoken *Who the hell are you?* because he said, "I'm Harv. Harvey Aiges. *A-I-G-E-S*." I figured that if they were planning on gunning me down, they wouldn't have been so precise about their names. Unless they were truly perverse. "We work for Jock Harlow. Help manage the place. Do whatever needs doing. I can call you Katie?" I was pondering the meaning of "do whatever needs doing." Splitting logs? Torturing trespassers? So I just nodded. Harv looked no more than a couple of years from forty either way.

"You feeling like you got to spew?" Merry asked.

"Fifty-fifty," I murmured.

"I got ginger ale at the cabin. Ten times better than Coke. That'll fix you up. Then we'll take you to Jock."

"Do you live in the house with Jacques?" I asked. Half a second later I realized they might think I was correcting their pronunciation. Not that they would shoot me for it.

"Oh no," Harv answered. "We have our own place, really nice, not too far from the house."

"We're married," Merry said as she walked around to the passenger door of my rented car. "I was going to change my name to Aiges, but at the last minute I thought, Gee, both my sisters took their husbands' names. For my Daddy's sake *someone* should carry on the Slone. Harv was okay with it and I think it really meant something to my daddy." The next thing I knew, she opened the door of my car and got in. "I'll keep you going in the right direction in case you lose sight of Harv. He drives like he's doing the Baja 500."

"How long have you been working here?" I asked as we waited for her husband to get back in the Jeep.

"Few years," Merry said. I was about to ask another question — where had she and Harv met, what had she done before coming

here—but Harv vaulted over the door of the Jeep, put it into gear, and headed up the road with a spray of gravel.

Chez Slone-Aiges looked like a small weekend house you might see on a lake in Connecticut or upstate New York. Except there was no lake, just a little clearing in front of a rocking-chair porch that ran the length of the cabin. The clearing of grass tufts and dark brown dirt was a countrified version of a suburban circular drive, a place for the car to turn around quickly and get back on the road. I was so sick I didn't want to get out of the car.

I did though and Merry said, "Hey, you look green around the gills!"

The interior of the cabin was so close to adorable it looked ready for its close-up in *Elle Decor*. "Art of the Artless" or something. The first floor was what I guessed was called a great room, with a couple of red and white quilts on the wall, plain chairs, and a long table that looked as though it had once been part of a barn. Whoever had put it together either had an eye for the beauty of simple things or a sophisticated aesthetic sense and knew from rustic. I would have bet it wasn't the woman with PURR-FECT! on her T-shirt.

In a kitchen with a wrought-iron pot rack, Merry handed me a can of ginger ale. It helped, but I would have felt better if she hadn't been standing six inches from me as I drank it. I would also have felt better, once I finally burped—and none too delicately—if she hadn't announced, "I got a million things to do. You can leave your car here. It's too complicated for directions. Harv will run you up to the house. One of us will be here all day, so have Jock call when you're done and we'll pick you up." Not that I was really worried, but I tried not to picture Harv and Merry using a backhoe to dig a separate hole for my car after they'd buried my body.

There was some solace in being driven. At first the rutted road seemed constructed like a maze in a puzzle book. On my own, I might have wound up facing wall after wall of trees. After a while we began to ascend one of those mountain roads that induced me to

recite the Twenty-third Psalm to myself when I glanced down into the abyss right below the car door. I thought about Adam. He would have been stretching out his neck to admire the view.

What was wrong with me that I hadn't simply said to him, *Okay, come along and while I go to see this North Carolina guy, you can spend that day by yourself*? Just knowing Adam was close by, hanging out in Asheville, not scared of being high up in the mountains and looking down, would have braced me. Why, I didn't know, except being nearer Adam, a man who knew his coyotes, would have made me feel less of an urban weenie who was out of her element in any area with more than three trees. Yet I'd pushed him away, and not subtly either. Adam was angry. Probably confused too. So was I.

I put him out of my mind by tuning in on Harv. He talked all the way without saying anything significant, though by sharing his thoughts about maybe buying Goodyear Wrangler MT/R tires he was baring his soul. I was listening so intently, working on not thinking about Adam, that I didn't notice we had pulled up to the house until Harv shifted the car into park, or whatever it's called in standard-shift lingo.

"Knock good and hard," he told me. "It's a big house." Understatement.

Jacques Harlow's house was huge, a log cathedral with tall, Romanesque windows topped with arches, except they were clear instead of stained glass. I wasn't sure whether it was the angle of the morning sun or some kind of film over the windows, but I couldn't see inside.

I marveled at the size of the house. It was what a seven-foot basketball star would design with the thought of having all his teammates over for long weekends. I suppressed a *Holy shit!* and instead asked, "Does he have a big family?"

"Just Jock."

Realizing only then that Harv wasn't about to vault out of the Jeep to open my door, I got out and said hopefully, "See you later."

Without even a *yup* or waiting to see if anyone answered the door, he was off.

I shouldn't have worried about my knuckles getting raw or shrieking *Mr. Harlow, Mr. Harlow, are you there?* then having my words echo from mountain to mountain, mockingly, until I wept. Seconds after my first knock, the door opened and a man who looked a wretched-life fifty-five or a blessed-by-fortune seventy said, "Good morning."

"Good morning," I replied.

He held the big wood door open, and I walked into . . . well, into a big wood house. I couldn't shake that cathedral feeling. Not in any St. Patrick's sense: with its giant gnarled wooden posts and vaulted and beamed ceilings, the place seemed built for the worship of some powerful tree god.

Jacques Harlow himself wasn't exactly godlike. On the other hand, he wasn't an eyesore. He had the even-featured, craggy face of a forgotten movie star, but with an older man's sun-dried skin and loss of lips. His eyes must have started out blue or gray, but now they were faded to that no-color shade that could only be described as pale. Nothing was new about him: after nine thousand launderings, his jeans had shrunk in length but not in size; they were just short of baggy, which admittedly was better than having to eyeball an older guy's package. His blue shirt, with its button-down, frayed collar, appeared to have been worn on a once-a-week basis since he was eighteen.

"Let's go into the living room," he suggested.

As with Merry and Harv's cabin, the public part of the downstairs was a single great room—living room, kitchen, dining room, den, and a massive alcove with a flat-screen TV so big that if he watched *Spy Guys*, Dani and Javiero would be taller than they were in real life. The entire downstairs area had approximately the same square footage as Macy's.

My stomach, which I thought was on the mend, did a nervous flip. I smelled fresh coffee and prayed he wouldn't offer me any. Even though he wasn't terribly tall—probably an inch or two under six feet—Jacques Harlow didn't seem dwarfed by the scale of his house. It could have been the remnants of military bearing, but he had a stature that wasn't measured in feet or inches. When we got to the living room, he gestured toward a chair that had all but Papa Bear's name on it. "You can sit there," he ordered, though not impolitely. If the idea was to make me feel diminished and/or cowed in an oversize piece of furniture, it didn't work because the tactic seemed so obvious to me. I inched back so I would have something to lean against, but that meant my feet had to leave the floor. So be it. Maybe he was doing a mental eenie-meenie-minie-mo because it took him a little while before he settled into a rocking chair—one of those made out of knotty sticks lashed together with rawhide. It struck me as a little Wyoming for North Carolina. It was catercornered to mine, so he had to turn his head to talk face-to-face.

"So Huff Van Damme is an adviser to your show?" he asked.

"Right. He gave me your name because—"

"Why do you need an adviser?"

"The show's about two CIA agents," I said. "Occasionally I'll need a few words of intelligence jargon so the characters can toss them around, sound more authentic. Like *collection management officer* or *angel assets.* Or I'll need to know what an operative would do in a certain situation." I was seated facing a stone fireplace so high and wide it looked like an altar. Four logs rested on a grate, all ready for a cold spell that might not come for months.

"How is Huff at advising?" Something in his question amused him. Jacques Harlow seemed like a guy pleased by his own company.

I didn't want to establish or confirm my status as a blabby female who could be dealt with in the most superficial manner possible, then sent on her way. So I simply said, "As an adviser? Huff does the job."

He had gone forward in the rocker and for a few seconds, he

stayed there waiting for me to go on. When I didn't, he rocked back and crossed his legs. His shoe, a moccasin aspiring to loaferdom, slipped from the back and dangled from his toes. His heels needed moisturizer. "What do you want to know about East Germany?" he asked.

"I'd be interested to hear a little about your background first."

"You could have looked it up."

"Maybe I did. Maybe I'm just asking to get a sense of how you present yourself."

He rose a bit from the rocker and turned it so that it faced me. "Here, I'm presenting myself." I guessed this was humor, but he wasn't the type to signal with anything like a smile. "Born in Chevy Chase. That's Maryland."

"I know."

"Well, you had to ask where Asheville was."

"True." The anti-babble stance was hard to maintain because it was so against my nature. I came from a talking family, a blabby city. Still, I'd been taught to trust my gut, and my gut at that moment was telling me to hold back, that the only way to win this guy's respect was by not having him view me as a lightweight. "So what happened after you were born?"

"University of Maryland. Math major."

I waited for him to go on, but he didn't—though he did stop rocking. "Assuming you didn't graduate last June, what happened between college and now?"

"Army. Military attaché. Eastern Europe. Left in seventy-eight and went into Defense Intelligence. Retired two years ago."

In some ways talking to Jacques Harlow was like trying to use a machine that needed maintenance: difficult to get anything out of. In other ways, he was uncomfortably human. The question was, human in what respect? Someone who in another era might have taken a vow of silence? Working alone, living alone. The huge house was almost soundless: no creaks despite all that wood, no drone of an air condi-

tioner or refrigerator compressor. His reluctance to talk was not simply a tendency to be reticent, like Adam and his family. Maybe he was holding back as some sort of test. Or maybe he was next to nuts, with a mind so assailed with crazy thoughts that he couldn't concentrate on the give-and-take of regular communication.

"I'm interested in what was going on in eighty-nine, when East Germany fell apart."

"Do you want coffee?" he asked.

"No thanks."

"Still sick to your stomach?"

"A little. Nice of Merry to call to tell you I was indisposed."

"Tea?"

Knockout drops. Poison. Tea bags that had been around since his differential equations final. "No, but thank you for offering." He got up and went to the kitchen. His walking did almost nothing to break the silence. I got busy rearranging my purse; what I wanted to do was see if my cell phone was working. It wasn't. Not a single bar of reception. I was out of touch with the world.

Chapter Nineteen

WhㅔN HE GOT BACK, COFFEE MUG IN HAND, I said, "How surprised were you when the East German government collapsed so quickly?"

"There was no reason to be surprised. The Soviet Union wasn't going to intervene militarily, or in any meaningful way, for that matter. East German industry had gone to hell in a handbasket. The people hated the government and the Stasi. Repression, corruption, monumental inefficiency. The only way you could miss the handwriting on the wall was if you never learned to read."

"Then how come some of the best minds at the CIA were said to be surprised?"

Jacques Harlow's pale eyes locked on mine. "'Were said to be surprised?' You were there. Don't you have any idea of how surprised they were?"

Talking about surprised, I don't know why I was. Of course Huff would have told him I'd been with the Agency.

"I was pretty low on the food chain."

"I gather your job entailed writing reports that went to the oversight committees." I nodded. "Good. Then why don't you cut the crap. You're not here about your television show. What is it you want?"

If there had been some ambient noise, as least I could have averted my head to one side—*Listen! Is that a ruby-throated humming-bird?*—and had a couple of seconds to come up with something. But there was only silence.

There had been moments on the flight to Asheville when I'd asked myself why I was doing this. Why had I dissed my husband and pissed off my producer to go to North Carolina? Yes, it was the sort of thing characters do on TV shows (with stock footage of a Delta plane, then an interior scene, shot close in so as not to show how low the budget was). I'd gone for movement. Action. Something happened so that something else could happen. But what could Jacques Harlow possibly tell me?

What I needed was a link to Lisa Golding, who might at that very moment be very, very dead. I felt a chill of fear, then argued with myself that she could be sunning herself on the Costa de la Luz having totally forgotten me. I had deduced or maybe induced—having always gotten them mixed up—that when Lisa called, what she'd wanted from me had something to do with the report I'd written on the three Germans. Yet I had no notion whether this conclusion represented clear thinking on my part or the mushy mentality of someone who earned a living by making up improbable stories and who was desperately looking for answers.

But, assuming any supposition was correct, where had all that thinking gotten me? Scared. Here I was, in a humongous and extremely remote house in the company of an ex–Defense Intelligence guy who at worst had slit a few throats in his day and at best wouldn't talk about anything that might be classified. Maybe he'd insisted I come down here because he'd decided that after two years

of retirement, it was time to talk to someone, but he now regretted it and couldn't wait to get rid of me. But how would he get rid of me? By being obnoxious and condescending? Or by other means? I had a fast, cinematic vision of me running through the woods trying to get away from his maniacal pale eyes and suddenly not only was I being chased (rather breathlessly) by Jacques Harlow, but also by Merry of the questionable taste in T-shirts and husband, Harv, both of whom were in splendid shape and carried rifles.

"I got fired in 1990," I said.

"I know."

"I'm here because I want to know why."

He looked at me as if I had just started speaking a language he'd never heard before. "You don't know why?"

"No. I haven't a clue. I've tried to find out and struck out. So you're sort of a last straw. Huff says you know what was going on in Germany in eighty-nine and ninety. Maybe something you can tell me can lead me to the truth about what happened to me. I need to know."

"What's so important about knowing?"

"Because . . ." I reminded myself of Nicky when he'd been seven or eight and kept saying "because . . ." when he didn't want to tell the truth but, whether out of fear or honor, didn't want to lie. ". . . it's been eating away at me all these years. The injustice of it."

I didn't think he could sit any straighter, but he did. "How old are you?"

"Forty in December."

"So you're thirty-nine years old and you're upset that in 1990 the CIA treated you unjustly?" He got that smirky half smile Europeans in Hollywood movies get when confronted by the naivete of Americans.

"Yes." That was it for my being a woman of few words trying to gain his respect. "Listen," I snapped, and then picked up speed, "even though I've only been in this house for a little while, I could

probably come up with something about you that would make me go . . ." I imitated his smirk. "I have no idea why you insisted I come down here, but whatever your agenda is, I didn't come to be condescended to. Most people have one or two things in their lives that still anger or disturb them five, ten, forty years later. And someone else can say, *Isn't that ridiculous, your letting something like that bother you. Get over it!* But you and I are both old enough to know that what's ridiculous to someone else isn't the least bit foolish to us."

He answered with a long, deep breath that puffed out his chest, the way birds do before mating to appear more impressive and resplendent. This was not exactly a satisfactory response. But since I had nothing more to say, I waited. He exhaled and said, "At the risk of being ungentlemanly . . . maybe your distress has something to do with your being about to turn forty."

"Like what?" I asked.

"I don't know," he replied.

"I don't know either. Look, even if I have all the predictable miseries about going into my forties—that menopause is coming and I'm going to shrivel up and look like a Greek olive or that my husband will leave me for a Dallas Cowboys cheerleader—I don't see what that has to do with my wanting to know why I was shafted by the CIA."

Jacques Harlow rubbed his palms on his jeans as if they'd been sweating. Maybe he'd been a warfare planner, maybe an operative who'd had to perform some extremely dirty tricks, but he didn't seem to be a man who easily discussed emotional issues. He was obviously relieved that the turning-forty business was over, but he made one more stab at psychology. "Did you get into writing your TV show because you thought espionage was marketable? Or because you'd been at the Agency?"

"Maybe a little of each. But I first wrote the novel the show is based on. That was because I loved the spy genre. Once I got to sixth

grade, I was reading spy fiction. When I got a little older, I started going to spy movies. I remember once being the only person in the theater watching a Japanese antiwar spy film with subtitles that seemed to have been lifted from some other movie." He sucked in a cheek so his mouth shifted to the left. "Are you trying to think of some diplomatic way to tell me something undiplomatic?" I asked.

"Yes."

"Well, go ahead."

He nodded a thank-you. "You want to right a past wrong. Has it occurred to you that your going back to the past is a means of reconnecting with the Agency, of giving yourself an adventure? So your life can resemble one of your television shows?"

Not bad. I wished I had the rocking chair, because I could have gone back and forth on that one for a while. I wasn't my mother's daughter for nothing. I just sat quietly, though. Finally I said, "It's a thoughtful question. I wish I could give you a definitive 'Absolutely not!' But I don't know. I don't think I want actual adventure. If I did, I would have applied to the clandestine service when I applied to the CIA. But if I had, I'm sure I couldn't have passed the psychological tests, because I don't have what it takes. I don't get thrills from danger, I just get scared. Look, Mr. Harlow, I've never even been on a roller-coaster." I was about to say the only way I'd ever get on one would be at gunpoint, but I decided to skip it.

"Fair enough. And you can call me Jacques."

"So where did you get the name?"

"It was my father's." My buddy Jacques was not overly generous in the information department. "Are you called Katherine?"

"Katie. Kate if you're the monosyllabic type. I want to clear something up, though. It's not as if I spent the last fifteen years rubbing my hands together and plotting how to get justice from the Agency." I made a big deal about swallowing because I wasn't sure of the wisdom of telling all, or even telling some, to Jacques. On the other hand, there was no other hand. He was my last and therefore

best hope. "A few weeks ago," I began, "I got a call from someone I had known at the Agency. Lisa Golding."

I looked at him long enough until he said, "Never heard of her." He stood and walked around and leaned on the back of the chair, which seemed, somehow, to know not to rock. "I'm assuming that's not the end of the story. Somehow this led you to want to speak to someone familiar with the situation in East Germany in eighty-nine."

"Yes." I considered getting up too, but the back of my chair was low enough that if I rested my arms on it, I'd look like Quasimodo. So sitting there, I told him how Lisa had offered to tell me why I was fired in exchange for my help, and then gave him a three-word character sketch—amusing, talented, untruthful—and a description of her job. Since I wasn't about to tell him of my notes down in the basement, in the crypt, I said, "I spent days trying to remember what I'd worked on with her. The only thing I could come up with that might still have meaning was . . ." I stopped for a moment, then said, "I'd feel better if you swore to me you weren't recording this."

"Swear to you? It's a damn good thing you didn't apply to clandestine services. You take somebody at their word?"

"Didn't you ever decide to trust someone?" I asked him.

"Yes. Yes, I did. All right then, I swear to you I'm not recording this." He smiled. "I'll have to watch your show now, learn how spies behave." I didn't smile. "I assure you, no one is hidden in the attic and taking this conversation down in shorthand either." To me, asking him about recording wasn't such a way-out question, what with him living alone in a huge house in a forest on top of a mountain with two chipper but slightly threatening people working for him. He wasn't exactly Mr. Normal.

"I feel more comfortable," I said, "and what good would it do me to be uncomfortable?" The names of the three Germans weren't in my notes. Considering my B-minus memory, it was a miracle I'd come up with the name Manfred Gottesman. The other two were

blanks, and I needed someone—hopefully Jacques—to fill them in. "Now I can tell you about stuff that's probably still classified. Not even probably." Casually, I wondered what the penalty was these days for disclosing top-secret information. "In late November of eighty-nine, December also, I guess, we took in three East Germans who'd helped us, who'd worked for the government. I could only remember one of their names." I was frightened, as if my next sentence would bring some terrible retribution that would not, as in the show, be followed by a commercial break. "One of them was a Stasi official named Manfred Gottesman."

"Jesus!" Jacques said.

"You've heard of him?"

"The Agency brought Manfred Gottesman to the States?"

"Yes."

"I'd heard it, but I really didn't believe it," Jacques said. "As far as I knew, whatever he did for us didn't merit a new life here."

"From what I heard, it did."

Had life been a 1940s British spy novel, the character would have harrumphed and looked down his nose. Jacques just said, "What did you hear?"

"That he'd been number three in the Stasi and had been passing along names of who might be spying against us—or against West Germany. Also that he filled us in on meetings between the head of Stasi and Honecker. So he helped us big-time. Anyway, for a dyed-in-the-wool communist, he turned out to be quite a capitalist once he got here."

"Do you know if he's still living here?" Jacques asked.

"Not anymore. He died about a week ago." I waited for him to say *Oh* or maybe *Too bad* or *Good riddance to bad rubbish!* but since he didn't, I added, "He died of a rare infection. Do you think that's significant?"

"Significant of what? People get rare infections. If you mean do I think someone emptied a syringe full of some exotic virus—"

"Fungus."

" —fungus into his vitamin pills, I'd say, 'I don't know.'"

"But you wouldn't rule it out?"

"Rule out that Manfred Gottesman died an unnatural death? No, of course not. He's the type of man I could happily have killed myself."

Chapter Twenty

By THE TIME I GOT AROUND TO TELLING JACQUES Harlow about how I tracked down Manfred Gottesman–Dick Schroeder by recalling the name Queen City Sweets, I wanted to call it a day. My stomach still wasn't a hundred percent. The emotional pogo stick of Jacques–good guy, Jacques-psycho had wiped me out and I found myself doing the close mouth/flare nostrils routine to hide my yawn. What I needed was a nap.

I didn't get it. Also, I didn't know what to do about Jacques's next words: "Let's go upstairs." Okay, maybe I had picked up a scintilla or two of sexual interest on his part, but I'd put it down to what could be expected from a recluse in the presence of a still-fecund female wearing lipstick. He walked across the expanse of room, not bothering to look back to see if I was following him; his stride was more than an amble, less than a march. "The more I think about Gottesman dying from an obscure disease . . ." He shrugged and his sentence faded into the mountain air.

Now he was only a few feet from the wide wood staircase that led up to a gallery—a kind of long hallway—that overlooked the downstairs. Since his musing about Gottesman's death didn't sound like a come-on, I figured I was safe. I rose from the Papa Bear chair and hurried to catch up with him. If he suddenly started making humping motions with his hips, I'd think of something.

"Poison, maybe," I heard him saying, "and even that's highly unlikely. Not by the Agency. Not in the U.S. I never watched your show, but murder by microbe sounds like something you'd see on television. From everything I know, the times that ops sidle up to somebody these days and stick them with something sharp that's covered with botulism or some kind of hemorrhagic fever virus? Zero. Just to be on the safe side, close to zero."

"So you don't think Dick Schroeder—Gottesman—was murdered?"

"I didn't say that."

I was on the stairs now, three steps behind him. "Okay, so what are you saying?"

"Right now," Jacques replied, his voice forty degrees chillier than room temperature, "not much of anything."

At the top of the stairs, he turned left and passed the first door. I followed. Downstairs there had been no decoration on the walls: no paintings, Indian blankets, deer heads. But along the hallway, there were a series of wood-framed photographs of sunsets, taken in different places. It was hard to tell where, because even the city sunsets lacked any identifiable skyline, just an occasional, undistinguished building of brick or stone. The typical "Nature at Sundown" ones differed from each other only in the intensity of their coloration and bits of landscape—palms or pines, desert or snowcapped mountain. I wondered if these untraceable mementos were Jacques's record of his life in the service of his country. Pictures without people, scenes without scenery.

The next door down was closed, but he opened the third. God

knows what I was expecting. Okay, probably a heart-shaped bed covered in pink quilted satin. Inside was a long table with metal legs, the kind caterers cover with a cloth and serve hors d'oeuvres on. It was bare except for a few pieces of electronic equipment under the table. Two identical large, flat-screen computer monitors as well as a mouse and one of those curvy, ergonomic keyboards were on top. The only other furniture was a secretary-style chair with wheels.

"Come in," Jacques said as he took the chair.

"How come you have two monitors?"

"Sometimes I need them." He pressed a button, and two towers and a cubish thing powered up. Tiny blue and green lights flashed busily. That was quickly followed by a full-volume "Ta-da!" and a blast of music that sounded Wagnerian, enhanced—if it can be called that—by an aggressive subwoofer. After all that fuss, one screen lit up and displayed only the conventional Windows XP logo; the other remained dark. I hadn't advanced from the doorway, and he stood, swiveled the chair a little, and said, "Here. Sit." Just as I was about to make the big *Oh, it's all right, I'll stand* declaration, he left the room. He returned carrying a bentwood chair that he placed directly in front of the keyboard.

Seconds later, I was seeing a document in German on the monitor. I couldn't exactly read it, but I was able to make out enough to get part of a sentence: "*. . . für den Staat DDR gehandelt hätten und somit Immunität genössen. Nachdem im February 1990,*" which I thought meant something like if East Germany had acted, then immunity would have . . . something-or-other . . . and then, after, in February of '90 . . . By the time I translated the little I could, Jacques was two or three Web pages ahead of me.

I couldn't be sure, but if he had deviously planned to put the chair he'd offered me far enough from the monitor so I would have trouble reading (but not necessarily think he was trying to keep me from seeing what he was doing) then he succeeded. Except the chair had wheels, so I came in closer.

Reasonably clever of me, until he said, "Back up. I don't like people reading over my shoulder." So I wheeled back, squinted, saw almost nothing other than him double-clicking a lot. Periodically I glanced at my watch, not just to check the time, but in the vain hope that I would discover a second hand so I could follow it around and have something to do. After twenty minutes, Jacques got up and said, "We can go back downstairs now."

Once we were in the hallway, I asked, "How come you asked me to come up here with you if you didn't want me reading over your shoulder?"

"I thought you'd be more comfortable."

"More comfortable up here than downstairs?"

"I didn't want to disappear and have you think I was busy preparing a syringe full of smallpox virus."

"Thank you," I said as we started to descend.

"You're welcome." He was one of those people who didn't put his hand on the banister going down.

"Actually, I would have thought of something more prosaic, like you were up there loading a semiautomatic pistol."

From the back, I saw him shake his head at my faux pas. "You wouldn't fire a semiautomatic weapon indoors," he said.

"A regular gun would do it?"

"Correct."

When we reached the bottom of the stairs, I asked, "Was I emitting waves of fear? I didn't think I was."

"No. I sensed you felt out of your element."

"Well, more like out of my league. Playing with the big spy boys and only knowing some of the rules."

We got back into the living room area and resumed what seemed to be our assigned seats. "This is what I got off the Internet just now," Jacques said. "From sites accessible to the public . . . and one not. Gottesman was charged with a number of crimes, including ordering the bombing of a discotheque in West Berlin in which two U.S.

soldiers were killed. There were a few specific human rights abuses, including kidnapping and murder. Also multiple manslaughter charges because he signed a shoot-to-kill order for East German citizens trying to escape to the West."

"Do you think there was actual evidence?" I asked. "There was wholesale burning and shredding of Stasi documents in November of eighty-nine."

"That's true, but if Gottesman hadn't escaped, there would have been enough officers and noncommissioned Stasi personnel to testify against him. They could make at least some of the charges stick without a lot of documentary evidence." He closed his eyes and started rocking back and forth.

I waited. For all I knew he was taking a quick nap so I announced, "I don't get it."

Without opening his eyes, Jacques asked, "Don't get what?"

"Why we would take someone who had committed crimes or abuses on that scale and give him our protection? Allow him to enjoy our freedom?" His pale, spooky eyes opened and he looked straight at me. "Are you going to say, 'Don't be so naive'?" I asked.

"No," he said, "I'm not. Maybe he had something to offer that was so valuable he was able to strike that bargain with us. From my point of view, Defense, there wasn't any priceless information someone like Gottesman, in the secret police, would have—unless he fell upon something. Or he could have been in a blackmail situation with someone in his own or the Soviet military. Except that didn't happen."

"So what you're saying is that he didn't have anything for you that would make you or the Secretary of Defense or whoever promise him the moon."

"Cincinnati," he said.

"Right. I stand corrected. Sit corrected. Anyway, your implication seems to be that he might have had other information that was priceless to some other intelligence agency."

"Yes."

"If that's the case, if we had all this fabulous information, then why did we mess up so badly in our intelligence estimates?"

He stopped midrock. "What do you mean?"

"We brought this man and the two other Germans over at the same time. They were treated as a package deal, although I don't think they worked together. As much as I can remember, which isn't much at all, Gottesman was the only one who had been with the Stasi. I don't even know if any of the three knew each other. But it was the perfect moment for people to get out. The only moment, really. The East German government had imploded and it was before whatever evidence that hadn't been destroyed could be examined. So we brought out these three movers and shakers. Former movers and shakers. What I'm saying is, if we'd have been found out, we would have seriously pissed off West Germany."

A shadow of displeasure crossed his face and I assumed it was because he wasn't a fan of women saying *pissed off*. Naturally, that made me want to shout all George Carlin's dirty seven. Instead I gave him a torrent of clean language: "We risked inflaming world opinion, for God's sake. The Wall coming down was a glorious moment. All around the world, people were thinking, How great! And now all those officials responsible for the repression are going to get what's coming to them. Except, because of us, these three didn't. Also, bringing them here cost us a fortune. This isn't like the FBI's witness protection program, where you're plopping down some low-level gang member in Albuquerque—and even that's not a discount deal. Look, we obviously set Gottesman-Schroeder up in business. What did that alone cost? A hundred thousand dollars? Half a mil? All that risk, all that money. For what? So the oversight committees could report we did a lousy job foreseeing what would happen?"

Jacques crossed his arms over his chest. "We've made bad bargains before," he said slowly. "Stupid deals. From funding the 2506 Brigade to invading Cuba to acting on the theory that WMD in Iraq was a slam dunk."

"I know," I conceded. "Sometimes we show a real gift for stupid deals. But that doesn't answer my question."

"What do you mean?" Jacques asked.

"The Cuban invasion, Iraq . . . they were ongoing operations. No one could predict with absolute certainty what would happen. The three East Germans were different. Their country was toast. We weren't in the middle of any operation that required their input. At best they could report to us that so-and-so wasn't just a cog in the wheel, that he was the wheel itself—and we could pass that information on to Bonn. But we put so much effort into bringing those three here. I remember my boss going to Berlin two or three times in November and December. Hush-hush visits. The only reason I heard about them was because I was working on time-sensitive reports he wanted to review personally. I guess he told his secretary it was okay to let me know when he'd gone and when he'd be back."

"Why was he going?"

"He'd been one of the guys who had guessed wrong, so maybe he had a little mopping up to do there to make himself look better. God, I wish I could remember more. But normally he only went to Eastern Europe once every couple of months. So at least part of what he was doing at the end of eighty-nine was grabbing these three and pulling them out before the authorities—or some of their fellow citizens—could grab them."

"So you think it was your boss's doing?" Jacques asked.

"I'm starting to realize that's the only logical conclusion. But putting him aside. What was Lisa Golding's role in all this . . . Could she have been perceived as a threat because of what she knew about the three? If she'd outed Dick Schroeder—or the other two—what would have happened to them?"

"If she'd exposed them now? Well, if she made an announcement that Mr. Schroeder was really Manfred Gottesman, who had been number two or three in the Stasi, there might have been a few raised eyebrows in Cincinnati, and even some legitimate moral outrage. The

statute of limitations on serious crimes committed by DDR officials expired in 2002. There's no time bar on murder, but unless they had a strong case, they couldn't have extradited an American citizen. And it's a basic principle of German criminal law that a defendant's presence is required at trial."

"So if the Agency wanted to stop Lisa from talking, it would only have been the social and business consequences they were worried about?"

"Seems that way." He rubbed his chin. He hadn't shaved that day because his beard made a scratchy sound. His hair was almost totally gray with just a touch of brown, but his beard must have been close to the ruddy color of his skin; I could see no trace of it. "Diplomatic consequences too. And keep in mind that if your Lisa had made such a public disclosure, she, herself, would have been liable for prosecution here. Everyone at the Agency signs an oath. You know that."

I felt myself flushing because I was certainly violating my oath. The proof that I'd disclosed classified information was that Jacques had long discounted rumors of Gottesman being brought to the United States and had been surprised when I'd told him about it. I could be prosecuted under some felonious verbalization statute.

On the other hand, why was he talking to me? Okay, he hadn't given away any secrets. But it was weird that such a solitary man would say yes to an interview and actually insist I do it in person. Jacques Harlow was not your celebrity-struck average Joe. Working in TV, I found I could call up almost anybody with a question, say I was a writer for the TV show *Spy Guys,* and he'd be glad to speak to me. Celebrity culture. Not that I was a celebrity. Dani and Javiero were, however. If people couldn't get the real thing, they'd settle for writer-in-glam-industry-who-deals-personally-with-celebrity. (If I were a poet, most of these same people would probably have told me to drop dead.) But Jacques struck me as Mr. C-SPAN. He also seemed as immune to celebrity worship as a person could get, probably because his interests lay elsewhere. He was

a reader of *Air & Space Power Journal,* not *Entertainment Weekly.*
So unless Huff Van Damme had said something wonderful about
me, which I doubted, how come Jacques had said yes?

As the sun rose higher over the mountain, the light streaming in
through the windows began to heat the house. If wood walls could
perspire, they were doing it; the place smelled like a lumberyard. I
was wearing what I'd thought were sensible black cotton slacks and
a yellow cotton shirt, sleeves rolled back, but they were both starting
to stick to my skin like Post-it notes. I felt a trickle of sweat mean-
dering down my Achilles tendon.

"Getting too warm in here?" Jacques asked at that moment.

While I didn't like being so easy to read, I was grateful either to
his intuition or his realization his own deodorant was on the verge of
meltdown. "Yes."

It was only when he said, "It's cooler outside" that I realized the
house probably wasn't air-conditioned. What kind of guy would
build such a sprawling, expensive house in a Southern state and not
put in air-conditioning? "Let's go." He led me through the kitchen
and, without asking, handed me a Coke from a high-end refrigerator
my father would have approved of. I decided not to ask if he had diet.
He poured himself another mug of coffee and held the door as we
went outside.

The house, I now saw, had been built to take every advantage of
the mountain. Just outside the kitchen was a small, flat area, no larger
than a good-size Manhattan living room. Beyond this little plateau,
the mountainside dropped down at least a thousand feet. Naturally,
there was no fence around it, as Jacques obviously appreciated open
vistas and presumably expected his guests to have enough sense not
to hover on the edge in stiletto heels. He didn't seem to have factored
in visitors with acrophobia. It really was a glorious sight. A thin,
humid mist rose from the trees way down the mountain, softening
the view and giving the panorama a green haze—like in some lesser
Impressionist painting. I decided to enjoy it from the security of a

picnic table and parked myself on the bench that was a safe ten feet from the drop.

"Beautiful," I said.

"It is." He sat on the bench with me, a proper couple of feet away. If he was so intuitive, I wondered if he knew I was speculating on where he'd gotten the money for such an impressive house. The no-air-conditioning business seemed more a conscious choice than a cost-cutting measure, though I couldn't say why I decided that. But I sensed family money more than canny investments or luck at roulette.

"What made you settle here?" I asked.

"I liked it." I was beginning to see why he lived alone. However, I couldn't judge whether his withholding information was affected—Jacques Harlow, Mystery Man Without a Past—or something he felt necessary for his own safety or peace of mind. "Who was your boss at the Agency?" he asked. "The one who kept going to Berlin."

"Benton Mattingly."

"Oh." His response took just a second too long. "Are you still in touch with him?"

"Not really." I cleared my throat. "'Not really' means that naturally, once I got fired, I was cut off from all contact with anyone I'd worked with, including Ben. But I did make that call to him about Lisa Golding a week or so ago. Actually, I was a little surprised he was willing to speak to me. I mean, besides the fact that in the Agency's view I'm forever tainted. Did you know he's head of a big telecommunications company now, and his name is being tossed around as the next secretary of commerce?"

"Did he know anything about Lisa?" Jacques was looking off into the distance, at another mountain not as high as his.

"No. He said he would ask some non-Agency contacts, but he wasn't holding out too much hope. I don't know whether he was just saying that or if he meant it."

"It's safe to assume he was just saying it."

"I guess you've met Ben," I said.

"Yes."

"And you don't like him."

"Not much." He turned toward me. "Not at all."

"How come? I assume this isn't the sort of conversation that interests you, but I'm curious."

"You were one of his girls?" he asked casually, as if not caring whether I answered.

"You mean did I have an affair with him? Yes. Just for three months: he dropped me faster than most. But it was more than a year after that before I was fired. We worked together comfortably enough after the romance ended. And a few months after it was over, I met my husband."

"The man you're married to now?" My arms were resting on the table and he was looking at my wedding ring. Plain gold, now unfashionably wide. When we'd picked out our rings, I'd pointed to it and said to Adam, "That's the one. I'll always feel married in it." At the time, maybe I'd been counting on its width as juju against thinking about Ben.

"Yes. Same guy. He's a veterinary pathologist at the Bronx Zoo. Not into espionage." Without stopping, I asked, "Why don't you like Ben?"

Even in profile, I caught his blink, blink of discomposure. Finally he said, "He put as much energy into maintaining his social position as he did into his work." His voice was slightly hoarse, as if the sentence was being pulled out of him against his will, which I guess it was.

"That's it?"

"You didn't come here to discuss Mr. Mattingly."

I hadn't. But I recalled that Ben's prominence in the mix of new money, journalists, think-tank people, and politicos—the alternative to old-line Washington society—had always been a sore point at the Agency and, obviously, from Jacques's attitude, in the larger intelligence community. Certainly Ben had the intellect to deserve the job

he had. Yet the charm that had made him a dinner party darling and expert seducer had alienated many of the analysts in the Agency. At the time, I'd put most of it down to jealousy of the dull for anyone who sparkled. That could have been true with Jacques as well; men naturally resented one of their own who was able to do what they could not—or would not: marry for money, drive Maseratis, make people laugh, be listened to by powerful people. "What else do you want to know?" Jacques asked. "Substance. I don't have time to talk about personalities."

I sipped my Coke and realized I hadn't had a nondiet soda since sixth grade. It gave me a heady rush, both from its chemistry and also from the pleasure of imbibing an illicit substance, like the first few times I'd smoked pot. "I need to talk about personalities. Well, about people. The other two."

"The other two?" he asked, though he clearly knew whom I meant.

"The other two Germans who came out with Manfred Gottesman."

"Why?"

"Because one of them might lead me to Lisa. Or at least know something about her."

"That's a ridiculous long shot."

"I don't have a short shot."

"This Lisa is a liar. I cannot understand why you would believe her in the first place, that she knows the truth about why you were fired. She could make up anything." Before I could speak . . . actually, before I could even come up with a response, he continued: "If she did have some valuable or dangerous information she wanted to get out to the public, why, of all people, would she choose you to facilitate it? Don't misunderstand me. I didn't mean that at all as an insult. I meant, wouldn't it be more likely for her to go to a journalist, someone who's familiar with the intelligence community?"

"Look," I said, "you're right to be asking those questions. I thought she was nuts when she called. I tried to get her off the phone, until she brought up my being fired. I admit that now I'm curious

about what she wanted to disclose to a journalist, assuming it wasn't some asinine story she made up. Or if she was telling a lie, why? And why to me? But bottom line is, I want to get in touch with her because I want the chance to learn what happened to me."

It was getting toward noon, and both the temperature and humidity were climbing. Jacques's face had a sheen of sweat. I touched my forehead. It felt wetter than a mere sheen. Unlike inside the house, the heat here didn't feel oppressive. I didn't need my usual anti-hotness techniques of imagining myself skiing on an Alp in an unzipped Polartec vest, or, conversely, being a dauntless Israelite wandering around the desert for forty years and never kvetching about the heat. I put my elbows on the table and my chin in my hands.

Jacques, on the other hand, continued to sit straight, as if the bench had a perfectly comfortable back to rest against. "This entire business is most likely nothing. But you never know, do you? I find it strange she called you after—what?—fifteen years. There could have been a purpose to the call, though when you're dealing with someone like her—"

"I know she's a little off. Maybe a lot off. But there are more off types in the intelligence community than in other places."

"No, there are not," Jacques said.

"What?"

"Do you honestly believe there are more 'off types' at the CIA than in your television business?"

When I thought about it, I had to smile. "Actually, there are more crazies in TV. But I wasn't in clandestine services. I was working with a lot of ex-academics and specialists in all sorts of areas."

"As far as I could see, Defense Intelligence reflected the general population in terms of what you call crazies vis-à-vis stable people. Your Lisa doesn't sound as if she were among the stable. She would have lied if she'd been a nun."

"You could be right."

"Could be and am," he said.

"One thing: If Lisa had anything big to say, and if she were dealing with people like her, with her strange moral code, could she be dead? Could somebody at the Agency have gone wink-wink, 'Check out Lisa Golding, who's going to blab and expose us,' and the next day she's history?"

"Because she had a story that was potentially embarrassing?" Jacques asked. "Even humiliating? If that were true, half the administration and two-thirds of the Pentagon would be belly-up. No, I don't see it." He didn't go *Ahem* or move, but he allowed a couple of seconds to go by before he continued: "Now, as to your two other East Germans."

"Yes, my two East Germans. What you called my ridiculous long shot."

"Tell me about them," Jacques asked. "Who are they?"

"That's the problem. I can't remember."

"And?"

"I was wondering if you might consider helping me find out who they are."

At least he didn't guffaw and say, *You've got to be kidding!* "You're mixing up your acronyms. I was in the DIA, not the CIA. I wouldn't know about an operation like that, done by another agency."

"You wouldn't know, maybe. But you yourself told me you'd heard rumors that they'd brought over Manfred Gottesman. If you heard that—and being in the secret police, Gottesman didn't have much to do with Defense Intelligence matters—then you might have heard that two other big shots came over also."

"And if I tell you no, that I didn't hear about the other two?"

"Maybe I'll sense you're telling the truth. Maybe I'll think you do know but you don't want to tell me. What am I going to do, turn you over to the Egyptian secret police and have them beat it out of you?"

"Fair enough."

I waited, and waited some more. Then I realized he was probably

used to sitting and staring out at the mountains for hours on end. "How come you agreed to see me?" I asked.

"Because Huff asked me to. He's an old friend."

"Oh."

"He said you could be annoying, but to help you if I could."

"Huff said that? I'm amazed. Not at the annoying part. I don't think of myself as at all annoying, but I know he does. I'm amazed that he asked you to do anything more than answer a couple of my questions."

"Huff is an interesting character. Not unique. He lived overseas year in, year out, keeping secrets, telling lies. Basically, though, a decent man. He's back now, retired, may do an occasional job for the Agency as a contract employee. And consults for people like you. Huff's as good an American as you can get, but he's not at home here. Probably not at home anyplace. He's the sort who's at his best, most graceful, when he's in danger. Put him at a church bake sale and he'd be awkward as hell."

I traced the wood grain of the table. It wasn't redwood like most picnic setups. It was the same wood as the house. "That's an interesting insight. But do you think it's possible that Huff would have stuck out like a sore thumb at a church bake sale when he was thirteen, and the reason he did the work he did was to get away from all that normality?"

"Maybe."

"I apologize for being negative. But *Spy Guys* is always getting accused of romanticizing the espionage business. It does. But sometimes I think the espionage business romanticizes itself even more. Tragic figure. Doomed to wander. No place is home."

"We do that all the time," Jacques said. "But whatever he is, Huff told me he heard you might have gotten a raw deal when the Agency cut you loose."

I pressed the Coke bottle against my head, but it was no longer cold. Feverish. I felt definitely feverish. The heat was radiating from

inside me, not from the sun overhead. "Does he know . . . Did he say why?"

"No. I don't sense he had much conversation about you when he was thinking about the job on your show. He just had you and a couple of other people at the show checked out. Especially you. He got the okay to work. I suppose in the process, someone who knew someone heard that possibly you got a raw deal."

"I can't tell you how—"

"How much you appreciate hearing it. Right." I gathered Jacques was not a big fan of unreserved gratitude. "This is what I'll do for you," he went on. "I may have a memory of something about the other two. I'll have to reflect. And then I need to find out some more about you."

"I'll tell you anything you want to know."

"I don't want to hear it from you. I want to hear it from sources I'm sure of. So you have a choice. You can stay here for a couple of days." I realized what he was offering was more proposition than invitation. "Or go home to your husband and I'll call you. Either way, you get the same answer."

So I went home.

Chapter Twenty-one

Less than twelve hours to North Carolina and back again, yet as I waited in the taxi line at LaGuardia, I didn't feel I was home. It wasn't one of those *Ooh, Dwayne, look at the tall buildings!* reactions. I wasn't under enchantment from the green beauty of the Blue Ridge Mountains. Sure, as far as mountains went, they were beautiful enough. But the universe I'd moved into didn't have tourist attractions. It did have Jacques Harlow, however. I couldn't get him out of my head.

I was like a character in one of Nicky's fantasy novels; unknowingly, I had tripped through a rip in the fabric of time-space somewhere between Asheville and New York. I was now in a world remarkably like the one I'd left, except instead of normal concerns like global warming, whether to drive or take the subway to Yankee Stadium, and checking out newspaper advice on selecting a good honeydew, this entire universe was about intelligence. Not the intelligence establishment of *Spy Guys*. Nothing bubbly here. Just infor-

mation and analysis, loyalty and perfidy and more dagger than
cloak—Jacques's world, or maybe my cockeyed vision of the world
that he inhabited.

My alternate world was right next to this one, but I couldn't quite
make it back. It wasn't that Adam's greeting was chilly and uninvit-
ing. He'd never been particularly adept as a grudge-holder. While he
was still upset that I'd gone away without him, we had polite sushi in
front of the TV. We switched between the baseball game and *Seems
Like Old Times,* which we agreed made us miss Nicky and his seal-
bark laugh as he watched movies with us. Yet all the while, I couldn't
get the three Germans out of my head. I kept recalling the photo Lisa
had showed me of Manfred Gottesman before she made him over
into Dick Schroeder. I imagined him in a cheesy, pants-too-short
communist suit, flying out of whatever country the Agency had
stashed him in for safekeeping until all his paperwork was final and
he could enter the United States. Not satisfying, so I pictured him
flying into Dulles, then changed it to some obscure military airport.
Wait: a landing field in West Virginia. He was alone on the plane; he
was with a CIA handler; he was seated beside German number two
and across the aisle from three.

Between the movie and the Yankees winning, Adam was in a
good enough mood that a black nightgown and half an hour would
have patched things up. But I was too preoccupied. All I could have
possibly responded to was friction, and with Jacques's "Huff told
me he heard you might have gotten a raw deal" echoing in my head,
even that was questionable. So I went for yellow gingham, murmured, "God, I'm *so* exhausted," and stood on tippytoes to peck
him on the cheek—a posture as close to cute as I ever got—before
we got into bed.

He took the next day off, and we drove out early to spend the
weekend at my parents' place in East Hampton. We didn't have to
force conversation on the way because he had a CD all ready to slip
in, an audiobook on Theodore Roosevelt's trip down Amazon

River tributaries. I said, "Nothing personal," then blocked it out by pushing in my earbuds as far as they would go and listening to my iPod.

A little more than two hours later, we pulled into my parents' driveway. The house, set next to what had once been a potato field, had been built in the early twentieth century by a family who'd apparently bred children for farm labor. Bedrooms galore: for us, Nicky, and my sister, with rooms to spare for other guests. Fortunately, there were none. Nearly all my parents' friends had their own weekend houses with an excessive number of delectably decorated guest quarters, so competition for newly divorced, lost-the-second-house-in-the-settlement-but-splitting-was-*still*-worth-it friends was intense. Even Flippy and Lucy had their own denim doggy beds in the Mexican-tiled laundry room.

"Did you invite Maddy out?" I asked my mother. We were in what they referred to as their "farmhouse kitchen," perhaps believing that farm wives routinely cooked on eight-burner restaurant stoves and displayed blue and white delftware in antique Welsh dressers. She wore one of my father's white chef's aprons over her white cropped pants and white shirt. Her hair was held back in a banana clip so it wouldn't get into the food. This is because she was slicing a radish.

"I did ask her," my mother replied, "but she said she had a million things to do around the apartment." She couldn't look at me as she spoke because she was slicing. My father and Adam had gone off early to fish, vowing striped bass and no bluefish for dinner. By default, lunch had fallen to me. As always, my mother wanted to help, but she was slicing the radish with a paring knife as if it were a live patient on her first day of surgical rotation. Her agonizing precision drove me crazy. I made a big deal over arranging sliced turkey on a plate so I wouldn't have to watch her. At that moment, like some blessed deity descending at the end of a Greek play, Adam strolled in.

"Went to a fish-free zone, I guess," he said.

My father came in a minute later carrying two paper shopping bags and announcing, "We decided we felt like steak and fries tonight!" My mother and I went to kiss our respective husbands, she going on as if he were a Cro-Magnon man bringing home a winter's supply of yak. While he went up for a shower and a change of outfits, my mother volunteered to set the table outside for lunch.

I made a pitcher of iced tea while Adam stole a slice of turkey, then rearranged the platter to hide the loss. "Did you have quality man-to-man time?" I asked.

"Nice morning," he said. My father revered not only Adam's doctorate and scientific knowledge, but also his ease at what my father thought of as manly, all-American enterprises like fishing, spackling walls, pointing out constellations in the night sky. Adam understood how much my father valued his acceptance. Soon after we'd been married, he pointed out that my father's wildly enthusiastic embrace of him had little to do with some secret wish Dad had had for a son, but rather a strong desire to transcend his world of cooking and table settings, which he sensed branded him as feminized. "Did you talk to your mother about Maddy feeling so down?"

"I brought it up, but lightly. Well, as light as you can get about depression. I told her major writer's block is something to get down about, but that I thought Maddy was being honest when she said she'd been a lot worse."

"Did you tell her all she does is stay home all day thinking about the poems she's not writing?"

"Yes. And I also said I don't know how she's going to pull herself out of this if she doesn't move from that apartment. It took my mother less than two seconds to suggest, 'What if I arrange for the two of you to go to a spa?' She said she was sure you would understand, and with Nicky being away . . .'"

"Sure. Go ahead."

I kissed him, then re-rearranged the turkey. "You're such a good guy."

"I'm okay."

"But I told her I couldn't see Maddy and me together at an eight A.M. spinning class. Listen, neither of us are spa people. My mother thinks two hours of aerobics with the stretch class in between and a mango sugar-glow-body scrub is a great way to spend a morning. But the truth is, I couldn't imagine Maddy and me going away together anywhere."

"I don't know. You could go someplace upstate and read."

"A reading festival in two Adirondack chairs. She'd have a snappy collection of poems about the degradation of women."

"So what? You'd have a pile of spy books. At least neither of you would be surprised about the other's reading preferences."

"That's true, but I really don't want to leave you and go away with my sister."

Adam smiled. "I wish I could take that as a compliment, but it's pretty hard to, considering that you'd rather be drawn and quartered than take a vacation with her."

"No. Take it as a definite compliment. Anyway, I said I'd come up with some way to get her out for an airing. But prying her loose from that place—"

My cell rang. Caller ID read *Private*. Though my heart picked up a little speed, it didn't race. Chances were good it wasn't Lisa. Three-quarters of my friends and colleagues in the TV business blocked their ID, probably in the belief that if they didn't, they would appear willing to talk to anyone and, therefore, losers.

My fingers, still slightly moist from my sliced turkey collage, almost dropped the phone. "Hello," I said, a little too loudly.

"Harlow."

"Just a second, please." I turned to Adam. *Oliver,* I mouthed. He nodded and went and opened the refrigerator, looking from shelf to shelf as if he were picking a book in the library.

I took the call in the living room, in the front of the house. "How are you?" I asked.

"All right." I was hoping he'd say something spyish, like *Do you think this is a safe line?* but he said, "I have information."

"By the way, this is a cell phone."

"No sweat," he said. "I spoke to the person who informed our mutual friend that you got a raw deal. At the time the raw deal occurred, people around there thought you were doing a good job — as far as anyone can remember. There was surprise when you got the ax. The person couldn't remember anything more about it other than thinking at the time that someone higher up had it in for you."

I sat down on the rug and leaned back against my father's favorite chair, a cross between a wing chair and a throne. "Thank you," I said.

"You're welcome."

"Do you happen to know what's written in my file?"

"No. Don't and won't." There was silence. I wanted to fill it, but for a few seconds I couldn't think of anything to say. Jacques, apparently, was one of those people who paused between sentences because he said, "Who do you think had it in for you?"

"Honestly, I don't know. My reviews were always positive. I got good feedback about my reports."

"Who were the higher-ups besides your boyfriend?"

Naturally I wanted to say, *Don't call Ben my boyfriend,* but I wanted to seem above his little dig, if that's what it was, because he could come back with *Really? What do you call a man you slept with for three months?* "During my time there, Ben was number two in the Office of Eastern Europe Analysis. Archie Edwards was the chief. But I really didn't deal with Archie. He was kind of snide —"

"I knew Archie. I doubt if it was him. If he didn't like you, he'd just make your life a hell. If you weren't worth tormenting, he'd kick you out fast. So if you don't think it was your boyfriend, and if it wasn't Archie, does that mean you were number three in the department?"

"Of course not. All the analysts were on a much higher level than I was. It's just that I dealt with them on an ad hoc basis, to get what-

ever information was necessary to put in a specific report. Then I had to go back to them and show them a first draft. Once they signed off on it, I wrote a second draft and sent that to Ben. He'd make his comments, and I'd rewrite, then submit it back to him. If it was okay, he'd show it to Archie. It almost never came back to me after that."

Jacques waited after my sentences as well as his own. Finally he said, "Maybe Mattingly found it uncomfortable, you being there."

"No, really, we worked very well together for over a year after the affair or whatever you call it. If anyone felt awkward, it was me. I mean, as far as I knew, there was no etiquette to cover that situation. I just acted polite and businesslike and tried not to seem stiff." When he didn't say anything, I added, "It's not like I was his only ex-girlfriend in the department. I knew about two definites and a couple of maybes before me and one after me. None of them got fired."

I waited. For all I could tell, he was taking down my conversation in longhand, or maybe he'd put down the phone and gone to get a cup of coffee. Finally he spoke. "What about Lisa Golding? Was she in any position to get you fired?"

"Of course not. From time to time I got information from her. Conducted interviews because she wasn't much of a writer. There must have been ten or twenty people outside the department who did projects with us that I had those kinds of dealings with."

I was running my nail through the nap of the rug. The cleaning woman who worked for my parents in East Hampton was doing a commendable job. Just then, my parents tripped down the stairs. I gave them a half wave, half shrug, indicating I had no out. I was stuck on this call. Both of them smiled and waved back with their fingers: *See you whenever!* Sometimes they seemed more yin and yang aspects of the same being rather than two separate people.

All this thinking took place in an instant. Maybe a little longer, considering the length of Jacques's conversational hiatuses. "Was there any connection between Lisa and Archie Edwards or Lisa and Ben Mattingly?" he asked.

"Not that I know of. I don't think so. She was in ICD, the International Cooperation Detail, the unit that got foreign nationals settled here. Huff told me it has a different name now."

"They're good at that."

"I wasn't around long enough to find out. Anyway, Lisa might have gotten instructions from Archie or Ben on dealing with the people our unit had sponsored. More likely she got them from whomever her boss was."

"So she never had a go with Mattingly?" he asked.

"No. I can't give you a written guarantee, but I can't imagine anyone who was less his type. He seemed to like women with minds." I wondered if Jacques was thinking, Yeah, minds he can fuck with. "And as far as Archie went—"

"He didn't," Jacques said. "All right, as to that foreign threesome we'd been discussing . . ." I got up and hurried back to the kitchen. My mother kept a pen and pad on the counter. "So far all I've been able to find out were the original names of the other two. One of them was fairly high up in the SED." That was the communist party in East Germany, the Sozialistische Einheitspartei Deutschlands. "His name was Hans Pfannenschmidt."

"Bet he was glad for the chance to get his name changed!"

It was embarrassing to say something and anticipate an empathetic chuckle and get zilch. Jacques went on: "He was the party's liaison to the criminal justice system and the courts."

"His name doesn't ring a bell. Part of it is that my German is close to nonexistent, so I didn't retain a lot. I was always trying so hard to translate in my head that my comprehension was even more limited."

"I noticed," Jacques said. "When I had the documents up on the monitor, you were looking too hard. I didn't think you were getting anything beyond a sentence or two."

"You turned around?" So much for my keen powers of observation.

"Yes. You were having trouble making it out. And moving your lips trying to read. Your accent is probably lousy."

"Atrocious. What's the name of the third? Is it a woman? I remember Lisa buying shoes for an East German. A woman's size seven."

"Woman. Maria Kurz. She was the secretary to the head of the Presidium."

"That was the smaller group that was over the Council of Ministers?" I asked.

"Yes, and the council was over the Politburo and the party congress. There were sixteen members of the Presidium. Maria Kurz wasn't one of them, but from what I remember, she was more than just a secretary."

"Could the three of them have been friends back in Deutschland?"

"I don't know. I don't have enough information. If I had to guess I'd say Manfred Gottesman could easily have known Hans Pfannenschmidt. Someone near the top of the Stasi could well have known the party's liaison to the criminal justice system. Maria Kurz is simply a question mark."

I closed my eyes. I could feel my energy draining. What were all these names going to do? Lead me to Lisa Golding, who, ninety-nine chances out of a hundred, would also lead me nowhere? The big thrill of the whole conversation was that I may have impressed Jacques by knowing what the Presidium was. That I had a nonsexual or maybe even sexual crush on a retiree, of all things, who was probably just a couple of years younger than my father really creeped me out. D and D, as my sister and I used to whisper to each other when we observed anyone or anything that didn't meet our sophisticated and pristine standards. Dumb and dees-gusting.

"What now?" I managed to ask. *There's nothing more to be done.* That's what I was sure, or hoping very hard, would be his next sentence.

"I'll see if I can pick up anything on their current identities," Jacques said. "If not, at least the identities they were given when they first came here. Now," he snapped, very militarily, "your job: sleep on it. Maybe you'll have a brainstorm."

"And your job," I snapped back. "Try and think of a way to track down Lisa. I can't stop worrying."

"So I've noticed."

Chapter Twenty-two

The following night, I lay beside Adam in our bedroom at my parents' house in the Hamptons and had a brainstorm. Not about anything useful, like recalling the new names of the two Germans left standing, but about Jacques and Huff. Was Jacques's telling me Huff thought I'd gotten a raw deal the truth? Maybe Huff had told him I was a superbitch but gullible as hell when it came to matters of espionage. *Do me a favor,* Huff had requested, *let her go chasing down to North Carolina . . . for nothing. Put on a little show for her. Get her hopes up. Payback for being so snotty with me— downright nasty—ordering me to do her legwork, trying to get me to believe it was for* Spy Guys.

When I tried to think about something else, I started on how hard a time Dani would give me on the final episode. I'd gotten off a first draft to Oliver. He'd said, "Not bad," but Dani and Javiero would read it over the weekend. Javiero would probably ask for one more fight to show off His Highness's fearlessness and pectorals. Dani

would come into the Monday morning meeting and, first thing, exhale slowly and say to me, *I assume you know what ruined my weekend?*

Moonlight lit the fields in a way that made it look as if the luminescence were not coming from the sky, but from a glow in the tall grass. Adam, deep in sleep, smiled. I glanced down the blanket: not an erotic dream. Maybe a dream about zebras. He dreamed of them often and loved them with unscientific passion. Whenever he recounted these dreams, the zebras sounded imbued with magic, like mythological creatures. Grazing on a golden savanna, they were his unicorns. On awakening, he was always delighted when he remembered they were real.

I wished I could have switched my brainstorm for his dreams. No, because I wouldn't wish what was going through my head on Adam. Forget my usual *Spy Guys* angst. Here I was, in the grip of an obsession that had nothing to do with the life I was now living, relying on a stranger who lived alone in the middle of a forest—like a troll with family money—and I had no idea whether he was okay or a liar.

That "Trust your gut" credo was fine for creating a character or arguing a plot point with Oliver. But my gut wasn't working very well in this world of real agents and double agents, ops and multiple identities. How could I trust it? And not just gut. Brain, perceptivity, judgment, sixth sense: my usual assets were out to lunch. All I could rely on was faith. If I couldn't believe in the guy who said he was helping me as a favor to his friend Huff, there was nothing I could do.

Adam turned onto his side. I moved in close and put my arm around him, feeling grateful for his solidity—his common sense, his integrity, his lean and hardy physical self. He was warm, but the day had cooled off into a sweet, humid, hair-kinking night. I could smell the ocean a quarter mile away, the fabric softener in my mother's well-laundered pillowcases.

"You okay?" he murmured.

"Fine. Go back to sleep."

Saturday night we ditched my parents and went out to dinner with friends who were similarly sponging off their parents. At one point, we were arguing about Bush, Rumsfeld, and Iraq, drinking wine, gesticulating so dramatically with forks that strands of linguine flew into the air, laughing when Adam declared us not only knee-jerk New York liberals but *boring* knee-jerk New York liberals. I poured myself a depraved third glass of wine and gave myself a figurative pat on the back: I was having fun. I had a good marriage. Excellent! Move on, I'd told myself, and indeed I had. Until a few minutes later when my cell phone rang. I forced myself not to think that Nicky had been in some hideous accident or had been caught with black-market M&Ms and was being sent home. I choked out a hello and heard, "Harlow."

I covered the mic with my thumb, told everyone, "*Spy Guys* crisis," and walked from the noisy, basil-scented room out the door. Valets were parking so many Mercedeses that it looked like SS Reunion Nacht in Munich.

"Hi, Jacques," I said.

"Where are you?"

"I just walked outside a restaurant."

"Where?" Jacques demanded.

"You know, if this were my show I'd be having one of the leads in front of a computer with a triangulation program, and in two seconds there'd be an extreme close-up on the screen and it would say 'East Hampton.'"

"How realistic," he murmured. "I have two names for you. Do you need to get a piece of paper?"

"I can remember them," I said coolly, and suddenly felt my linguine vongole solidify into a nauseating mass south of my esophagus. What if I couldn't?

"Remember Hans Pfannenschmidt? He had problems in the first couple of cities they sent him to, but he wound up in Minneapolis."

"Were you able to get the name he got when he came here?"

"Yes." I waited. "Bernard Ritter."

"Do you know anything about him?" I asked. "What he does?"

"What he did. Nothing as glamorous as a candy millionaire. He was a salesman for a company that manufactured brake fluid."

"You said 'what he did.' Is he retired? Or dead or something?"

"Dead. In his office, about six weeks ago, the end of May. He was working late. Stabbed to death."

"Oh my God!"

"Police are clueless. Nothing on any of the security cameras, but those are at all the entrances and in the elevators, not in the offices themselves. No enemies. Family man, wife dead several years ago, but two children in school in Minneapolis."

"How awful!" I said. "What do you think?"

"Strange. Interesting. Pick one. Then put that up against a simple coincidence, two of the three dying so close together, one from a nasty illness and the other by violence."

Bernard Ritter Minneapolis late May, I said to myself, praying I wouldn't forget. "And Maria?" Naturally I had a *24* image of an exploding Volkswagen, instantly followed by another of a gray-haired woman choking to death in a cloud of ricin.

"Maria Kurz is still Maria. Her last name is Schneider. Never heard of anyone getting a new identity and keeping their old name."

"Could it be some subtle ploy?" I asked.

"A ploy maybe. I don't see what's subtle about it. And to save you from asking, she's alive, fine, apparently. Sells real estate in Tallahassee." He paused and then said, "I'm assuming you know where Tallahassee is."

"Of course I know. Florida. Where in Florida?"

He sighed. "About where the Florida Panhandle begins. South of Georgia. How did you get out of elementary school?"

"I got out loaded down with prizes in everything except geography."

"And German," he said. "Okay, that's it for me. Good-bye."

Before I could find my voice, he added, "Well, you can call me if you get desperate, but I can't think of anything more I can do for you."

When I called the public affairs office of the Minneapolis Police Department that Monday morning, I was hoping to hear a honeyed yet quirky voice like Frances McDormand's in *Fargo*. Instead, I got one of those happy guys who made his hello into a three-syllable word: "Hel-lo-oh!"

So I managed an effusive "Hello!" back and gave him my QTV, *Spy Guys,* Dani Barber and Javiero Rojas spiel. I probably could have gotten information out of him based on that, but he was actually a fan of the show so I gave him a story about using Bernard Ritter as the basis for a future episode, how an innocent, admirable immigrant came to a terrible, lonely end in his promised land. I added how he, Sergeant Dave Whatever, would get his name in the end credits if we were able to use the material, but even if we couldn't, how very grateful we all would be, including, without a doubt, Dani Barber. And, oh yes, she would be happy to sign a picture for him. Since Dani thought autographing photos was tasteless, she'd have her assistant sign, "To Dave, Warmest personal regards, Dani." He said he'd talk to the detectives involved and get back to me. He did in less than an hour.

"Any other cases like this?" I asked.

"No. Not before. Not after, so far. I'm not saying we haven't had homicides in workplaces. But to the best of my recollection, not like this one. Not like where someone sneaks upstairs like that. I say 'sneaks upstairs' because Mr. Ritter worked on seven and there wasn't anybody on the elevators who wasn't eventually accounted for from morning on. Same thing with the video from the entrances and the parking lot. Not that we positively could identify everybody, but there's nobody we could point to and say, 'Let's check him or her out.'"

"One of the reasons Mr. Ritter is such an appealing character is

that he sounds like a good family man. Solid values." Why I put on that annoyingly wholesome persona when speaking to people outside the Washington–New York–Boston corridor was one of life's mysteries. "What's the family like?"

"Let's see what it says here . . ." Dave made little murmurs indicating speed-reading. "Son, twelve, good student, not a troublemaker. Daughter, ten, pretty much the same thing."

"I understand his wife died?"

"Four years ago. Massive heart attack. In her early forties. Can you believe such bad luck? Her sister is going to take the kids. Sad."

"It is sad. Do you happen to have any information on what Mr. Ritter did before he left Germany?"

I had to wait while he went through the material. "He worked for a tire company. A German offshoot of Michelin tires. Says here he was a salesman. I guess once you're a salesman, you know what you're good at. By all accounts, he was a friendly, outgoing guy."

"Had there been any problems in his life? Women, drinking, gambling? I don't know, maybe some weird person stalking him or something."

"That's the thing," Dave said. "No trouble anywhere. There was no nicer guy. Everybody had a good word for him. You know, you talk about immigrants. This is just the kind of person you want to come here."

"I know what you mean," I said. Those high-ranking communist bureaucrats made such good Americans. "A sad ending to a heartwarming story."

And that left Maria.

Chapter Twenty-three

"QTV IS PLEASED TO ANNOUNCE THAT ITS HIT series *Spy Guys* has been picked up for an unprecedented sixth season," the press release on my desk chair read. I smirked at *hit* and rolled my eyes for *unprecedented*.

Attached to it was a note from Oliver on his personalized, ultra-thick stationery. It was covered with pale blue squares, so it looked like graph paper for high-class algebraists. Occasionally I imagined him drawing, in different color inks, his own, Dani's, and Javiero's value lines sloping up almost vertically, while mine would plunge beyond the deckle edge at the bottom of the paper. Meanwhile, I read, "Congrats. Done deal. Remember I told you last year your next raise wasn't for the next two years even if we got picked up again and we did. Best, O."

I put it into my To Be Filed basket, a cute wicker number lined in the toile fabric of my office. While my computer booted up, I jotted down two columns on a notepad.

BAD GUYS	BAD ACT
Philippine radical Islamists	blow up congressional delegations while they're visiting Iraqi hospital
Colombian drug dealers	digging tunnel under U.S. embassy in Manila
crazed British animal rights people	meeting in Cape Town to plan sabotage of American submarine
Indian pharmaceutical company making degraded blood pressure medicine	planning on putting poison in the vats of America's leading tofu manufacturer

I figured that it would take me about twenty minutes to generate a list long enough that I'd have the whole sixth season. All I'd have to do was draw a line from anything in column A to anything in column B. Then I knitted my eyebrows together and pursed my lips slightly, that intelligent writer's expression I'd seen in movies about Lillian Hellman and Virginia Woolf. That done, I went to Google and typed: *Tallahassee real estate "Maria Schneider."* And there she was, phone number and all, at Orange Blossom Realtors.

"Hello, this is Maria Schneider," her voice mail announced brightly. "I'm either on the phone or out with a client. If you leave your name, number, and a short message, I'll get back to you as soon as I can." She didn't sound like my idea of an East German hotshot. Her voice was adorable, just short of sex-kittenish, like Elke Sommer's in *The Venetian Affair*. She sounded blond, though if she'd been a heavy hitter in the Presidium and not just a secretary with a steno pad, she must be at least in her fifties, a tad past the age of kittenhood.

"Hi, Ms. Schneider. My name is Katherine Schottland." Should I

say I was a writer? No, she could think I was an investigative reporter and there were periods of her life she didn't want investigated. "It's a long, complex story which I'll be glad to tell you when we talk, but I got your number from . . ." Why hadn't I rehearsed this? Should I say I got her number from the Internet based on information given to me by a former Defense Intelligence Agency spook? ". . . Lisa Golding. I'm a little concerned about her and I would appreciate it if you could give me a call, whether or not you have information." I gave her my cell, home, and office numbers. "Thanks so much." I threw in a "Bye!" based on my observation that Germans are always saying, "*Auf Wiedersehen,*" to each other in such happy voices, as if parting was what they liked to do best.

A minute after I called her, I wished I could take it back. She'd probably never heard the name Lisa Golding, as Agency people dealing with outsiders would often use pseudonyms. Of the three East Germans Lisa had tutored, one had been murdered and another had died mysteriously from a rare fungus. Maybe Manfred-turned-Dick had contracted his fatal disease splashing around in organism-rich Ohio River mud, but there was a chance someone could have given him blastomycosis to kill him. To kill him cleverly, because if a Cincinnati sportsman was going to die in some obscure manner, it wouldn't make sense to inject typhoid bacteria into his tube of Colgate; no, give him something local. (I did like the thought of infecting a tube of toothpaste, so I added to my notes, *Injects typhoid into teeny toothpaste tube samples handed out at the Republican convention.* Then, *& Democratic,* so as not to seem partisan.)

Even if I couldn't really believe that someone had murdered Dick Schroeder, I knew that Hans Pfannenschmidt–Bernard Ritter hadn't stabbed himself to death. So if someone was out to stop Lisa from talking—and considered getting rid of those Germans as part of that job—then why had I left my number with Maria? Not just my cell, my home and office numbers also. They'd be tapping her phones. I'd done everything for them except spell my last name.

The shudder that went through me began somewhere between my heart and my stomach, but immediately surged to my head and rushed to my feet. I did recover almost immediately, shaking off the terror, yet I sensed that recovery was merely some ancient self-preservation instinct at work to allow me to keep going. The truth was, getting frightened was a proper response to death by violence and death by bizarre organism. Wasn't it? On the odd chance that Maria returned my call and her future killers were listening in, I decided to simply say, *Yeah, well, Lisa did sound upset, but I overreacted. Sorry to have bothered you, but you know Lisa. Drama, drama, drama.*

I may have been staring at my computer screen nearly the whole time I was thinking, but now I really looked at it. I started typing a list of the sets for some future episode, but after "EXT. DOORWAY IN CAIRO—NIGHT" (which naturally would be some vertical-planked doorway the set designers put up and sandpapered to look etched by years of North African weather), my left hand reached out to the phone on my desk. Except who was I going to call?

I could picture Adam's beeper going off in the middle of his Monday pathology meeting and him calling me back so I could tell him how I lied to him about North Carolina and then talking for an hour to bring him up to date on my craziness. Of all the people I knew, he was the most balanced. But he'd suggested—and would have ordered if he'd come from an earlier generation—that I forget about Lisa, the CIA. So not Adam. Of course not Adam.

Forget my parents. My mother would react more calmly than my father, but their only response would be horror. Whether they shrieked silently or out loud, spoke judiciously or hysterically: *Someone you knew at the CIA vanished? And someone was stabbed to death? And another one died from a rare fungus? Oh my God, Katie honey!* Definitely not my parents.

Dix, on the other hand, was tough-minded and understanding at the same time. He knew why I couldn't let this go, probably more clearly than I did. His first reaction wouldn't be to demand, *Are you*

insane? or to declare, *Sister sweetie, you are over the top.* That was the problem. Dix was a little too much like me. For us, life itself and what was on page or screen tended to have the same weight. Depending on the situation we were in, we'd reflexively compare what we were living to some art form.

Give us a profoundly dark or sad period in our lives and we'd think, Russian novel, or bleak, three-hour Japanese film. Dix coming out and breaking up with Maddy was Ingmar Bergman, but also a little ninety-minute romantic comedy with him as Cary Grant pursuing a young Marlon Brando in construction worker gear; he probably believed the divorce was good for Maddy, because she would wind up with an intellectual Jimmy Stewart. If I tried to explain Jacques to Dix, or attempted to get Dix to help me figure why, out of all the communists in East Berlin, these three had gotten a free pass (plus two of them had also gotten a big DECEASED stamped on their case file), he, as I, might wind up analogizing it to a two-hour thriller that, unfortunately, would not star Matt Damon.

I went back to my script and got lost in it until early evening. The night went well. Adam and I finished a bottle of Zinfandel and made love on the living room floor, which was a little hard on my back, but pretty wild except for one thrashing-about, screaming moment when Flippy trotted in to save whichever one of us needed saving. While we didn't awaken the next morning in each other's arms, both of us wore the goofy morning smiles that come after a night of great sex. So maybe I was recovering from my obsession after all. Whatever was, was. Let it be.

Naturally, I couldn't. At eight-thirty, as I pulled out of the garage to go to work, I called my sister, the smartest person I knew, and asked if I could come over.

Maddy viewed hospitality as a weakness. Its sole purpose was to get people to love or admire you using food or the paraphernalia of gra-

cious living—mother-of-pearl napkin rings, silver candlesticks—as a way to distract them from experiencing your essence. Actually, when she and Dix had been together they had thrown wonderful dinner parties, complete with a collection of porcelain espresso cups and itty-bitty spoons. Maybe she'd decided dinner parties were gay, because after he left she had no more. Or she could have been making a statement: *My father's business is selling the unnecessary to the frivolous and I want no part of such frippery.* In any case, anyone who knew her soon learned not to drop by her place hungry. Or thirsty.

To get a cup of coffee, I met her in front of her building. We walked a block and a half, passing a Starbucks and a coffee shop that came complete with a counter, stools, and the heady aroma of percolating coffee. "Not here. Around the corner," she said. "They have tables outside." Maddy was trying. She'd spruced up. Her bangs were brushed off her forehead and, except for an oval in the back that was still matted from sleep, her hair was smooth, brown with its natural copper highlights.

The place did have tables outside, and they were pretty clean. The same could not be said of the sidewalk beneath, so we made our way around a great gathering of feasting pigeons and sat on those woven chairs they have outside Parisian cafés. Rather than rattan, they were fabricated from some soft plastic, so when we sat we immediately slid toward the front of the seats. As we righted ourselves, a waitress in a black miniskirt, white shirt, and a cotton scarf or handkerchief tied around her throat emerged. I guess her getup was supposed to evoke Gene Kelly in *An American in Paris,* but to me it said the café was a tourist trap. The coffee confirmed it, and considering how decent coffee could now be had on any block in the city, I couldn't figure how such a place stayed in business. We were the only ones seated outside: word of mouth had obviously spread to everyone south of Fourteenth Street except my sister. She had a gift for zeroing in on the worst restaurant in any venue.

The croissant Maddy ordered was the size of a pro basketball player's sneaker. I appropriated a pinch of it and found it tasted more pastry than shoe, but only slightly. She dropped a couple of dollops of jam on a large piece, but before popping it into her mouth said, "See? I gave you my oath. I'm still alive, so this might be a good time to harangue me about carbs."

"Too predictable." I poured a little more milk into my coffee.

"I told you I wasn't that bad, that I'd been much worse."

"At the risk of you thinking I'm even a bigger egomaniac than I actually am," I said, "this isn't about you. This is about me."

"Go ahead," she said warily. More caution than lack of interest, I guessed, though I wasn't sure if it was concern that I might demand too much of her or suspicion I might be diverting her in the interest of her mental health.

"I need your advice," I told her.

"On what?"

"Remember when I told you all about Lisa Golding's call and about going to visit that guy in Cincinnati?"

"Katie, do you think I take an eraser and wipe away the day's memories every night?"

One of the millions of self-help books I'd read over the years had a short list of items to cut from your vocabulary, and one of them was *for once in your life can you/can't you*. That left me with nothing to say for a moment, during which she gave me a jut of chin and a narrowing of eye to let me know she wouldn't take it back. "No, Maddy, I don't think you erase, okay? So let me bring you up to date. Here's the math: three East Germans to whom Lisa showed the ropes on living in the U.S., minus the dead guy in Cincinnati, leaves two. Take away one from two—"

Maddy broke in. "Another one died?"

"He was a high-up party official in East Germany. Here he was a salesman for a company in Minneapolis that made brake fluid. He was in his office on the seventh floor of a building. Found stabbed to death."

"Stabbed?" Too loud. I wanted to shush her, but held on to my *shh* just in time.

"Yes. There are no leads as to who might have done it. I spoke to the public affairs guy of the Minneapolis Police. The German got the name Bernard Ritter. He was supposed to be a sweetie. Widower, two young kids, everybody liked him, et cetera."

She was wearing a beige and brown striped T-shirt, and she stretched the neckline under her throat. "Someone didn't like him." Her shirt was ugly, but cool in its banality, if shirts can be banal. Maddy had never dressed the way some of her poet friends did, with long, wagon-train-women skirts, or in jewelry that looked composed of bent paper clips and blood clots.

"Or maybe someone did like him, or didn't care one way or another—just found Bernard's continued existence inconvenient," I observed.

"Are you going to tell me three take away two leaves one, and you can also take that one away because the third was lured to his death by Sirens?"

"No. The third is a woman. They gave her the name Maria Schneider. In East Germany, she'd been a secretary to the head of the Presidium."

"What's the Presidium?"

"It was kind of like we have a cabinet, but it had more to do with economics, obviously."

"Obviously?"

"East Germany had a planned economy. I forget exactly what the group's precise function was, to tell you the truth. And I don't know what her specific job was. She clearly performed some service people here thought was valuable." I think we both wanted to interject *blow job*, but as this was a serious conversation and we hadn't been jokey around each other for years, we held back.

"She's alive?" Maddy asked.

"Alive and well, so far as I know. She sells real estate in Tallahassee."

"Brake fluid. Real estate. And the third man was a candy distributor?" I nodded. "So many people give their lives over to commerce." Of course I didn't say, *Shut up,* or, *Like your father, who's been supporting you and your poetry habit for over twenty years.* "Were any of them in touch with Lisa?"

"I don't know," I said. "But I can't imagine any of them would have stayed in contact with her. For starters, they probably wouldn't have known her real name. She'd have spent only two or three weeks with them, Americanizing them. Everything from going to a mall to advising them on how not to behave like an officious communist functionary."

"Did she teach them 'Have a nice day'?"

"Did we say that then? They couldn't survive here without it. Anyway, I never thought any of them could give me Lisa's current whereabouts. I just thought going back to the situation—the people—Lisa and I had spent the most time on while we were working together . . ." My sister was shaking her head. "What are you saying no to?" I demanded.

"You can't do this, Katie."

"Oh, please!"

"Do you want me to explain the difference to you between reality and Hollywood movies?"

"That's your ex-husband, not me."

"No, it's you. Dix is too self-involved to be a romantic. Listen: What if you get to talk to this Maria Schneider? What do you think she'll tell you? That Lisa told her back in 1990 that you were fired for adding snide parenthetical asides in a report on the Yugoslavian steel industry?"

"That is such a long sentence for you," I said.

Maddy pushed her bread plate and cup away from her. I was dying to brush the crumbs in front of her into my hand and drop them back on the plate, but I refrained. "You seem to be missing the point. You've involved yourself in a dangerous business."

"You don't think I know that?" I said.

"You know it, but you don't appreciate it. Two people are dead, one of them murdered. You can say, 'This has nothing to do with me,' but someone who kills may not make such fine distinctions. Someone who kills would say, 'That Katie Schottland might discover something I don't want discovered. How should I handle her? Oh, I know. I'll murder her.'"

Chapter Twenty-four

"IT'S POSSIBLE," I SAID, "THAT WHOEVER KILLED Bernard Ritter did it for reasons that had nothing to do with all this."

"It's possible," Maddy said quietly. "It's also possible that this quest you're on has nothing to do with finding Lisa."

This was my sister at her most insufferable, explaining what my motives were in a composed voice, while an invisible chorus backed her up with *Maddy knows you better than you know yourself because she's got double your depth and three times your smarts.* I once punched her when I was ten because she told me that the only reason I volunteered for the robotics project was because Scott Valadares was doing it. Which happened to have been true. "And you're going to explain to me what this so-called quest of mine really means," I said.

"Unless you called me at eight-thirty because you wanted company for coffee."

"Be my guest. Tell me. I'm listening."

"It's a momentous time in your life."

"Are you about to give me the life-crisis business because I'm turning forty? Because if you are—"

"Lisa was just an opportunity that came along. It could have been anything else, an affair—"

"Give me a break. I would not have an affair and you know it."

"Or you would have taken up mountain climbing. Climbed Kilimanjaro with a group of women searching for their inner she-wolf." The waitress poked her head out the door of the café and I waved my hand for her to bring the check.

"Listen to me, Katie. You're looking for an adventure, and for you, what better adventure than something to do with espionage. Not just with espionage, but with your tenure at the CIA."

"You mean the termination of my tenure. That I'm obsessed with having been fired and I'll do anything to find out why."

"No. I'm not saying you're obsessed. But I think the real issue is your life today. Nicky's getting older. He's away for the summer. Adam is Adam and always will be. Not that that's bad: just familiar. Same with your work. You want some excitement. You want your youth back."

"Who doesn't? What are you going to tell me, that I'm getting older and afraid of death?"

"Give me some credit for originality," my sister snapped. "If you want adventure, make it a worthwhile one. Help rain forests." I wanted to say, *Gee, here you are without responsibilities and your parents supporting you—"subsidizing," as you would say—and I don't see you breaking your ass saving rain forests.* "Work for PEN's Writers in Prison committee. Seriously, go visit a country that's throwing writers in jail, or killing them. That has the added attraction that you'd be visiting a place where the government thinks the best cure for creativity is death. Or just play Russian roulette."

"Stop it!"

"I promise to be a good aunt to Nicky."

"Shut up, Maddy! I asked your advice because I respect your intelligence. I can't believe you're talking like one of those old ladies who sit on benches and say, 'Oy! You could get killed crossing the street.'"

"Especially if someone's trying to run you over."

I was still seething at my sister as I emerged from the Midtown Tunnel in Queens, although I had to admit that having gotten her to decide I was nuts seemed to have a salutary effect on her. Besides being angry, I was shaken by the thought that she could be right, if only in saying I was looking for adventure.

But she was wrong about me looking for my youth. Nobody could pay me enough to get me to go back to high school. College hadn't been such a treasure either. Five percent of my time was given over to having sex, 40 to thinking about it. Another 45 went to being miserable about my weight/direction in life/inability to have fun. The final 10 percent was assigned reading.

I was waiting at a traffic light, remembering a quote from somewhere about youth being the Lord of life and thinking, Am I the only one in the world with a memory, the only one who doesn't sentimentalize being young? when a moment of my youth popped into my head. Technically it might be considered postyouth since I must have been around twenty-four, but it was spring and even though I felt very old at the time, I was very young. Ben had broken off with me a couple of weeks earlier. I hadn't met Adam yet.

I was trudging through the parking lot after work, thinking that the last thing I wanted to see driving back to my apartment in D.C. from Langley was the cherry trees in blossom. Not that their beauty and promise would make me break down and weep—the sight would just reconfirm that the world that seemed to be working right for other people wasn't working for me. Suddenly I heard that unmistakable squeak of Lisa's voice: "Kaaaa-tie!" Since it was nearly powerful

enough to shatter the safety glass of all the car windows, I couldn't ignore it.

She hurried up to me. In a black fedora, black vest, and white shirt with rolled-up sleeves, her look was more Boy George than Annie Hall. We hadn't seen each other in a couple of months, so we had a long conversation about what was going on in our lives, which was, essentially, nothing. We couldn't discuss our work, so we chatted in the most general terms while the apple in my purse that I was planning to eat the instant I got in my car was calling to me. Suddenly, in the midst of all her blithering, she asked, "What's new with your boss?"

"Archie or Ben?" I felt a little dizzy, as I did every time I heard "Ben," even if it was my own voice saying it. Dizziness, apparently, was the post–love affair correlative of the pounding heart that happens during the amour itself.

"Who do you think? Name me one thing about Archie that's interesting enough to make me ask what's new with him. You can't, can you?"

Who knows if I gave myself away in my pretense that while Ben barely interested me, I found Lisa's "What's new with your boss?" amusing enough to give the subject a bit of thought. I realized I had leaned against somebody's Volvo during my few seconds of vertigo, so I stood straight and shifted the strap of my shoulder bag a little higher. "As far as I know, nothing's new. Why? Have you heard murmurings?"

"I heard he was having a something with someone in your unit," Lisa said.

I wished I hadn't moved away from the Volvo. Was she telling me something? Did she know it had been me? I couldn't detect any of that *See, I'm looking directly into your eyes so how can I have any ulterior motives?* craftiness. "Lisa, give me a break. He's always having a something with someone in our unit. Why do you think we have such a great record for egalitarian hires? He's got to keep up the

supply chain." I guess I was testing her to see if she knew, if she'd say, *Come on, I heard about you and Ben.*

"Do you know who it was?" she asked.

"No."

Lisa cleared her throat in the manner of politicians about to say something significant. "I have it on good authority"—a slow blink, fraught with significance—"that he's in love, actual love, with someone else and he's leaving the wife!"

"Bad authority."

"No. Good. As good as it gets."

"Lisa, 'as good as it gets' means from Ben himself. Was it?"

"No, but—"

"Listen, his standard operating procedure is to tell the woman up front that he'll never leave Deedee, but in every other way he signals that he's madly in love and that he will leave."

He had hardly bothered to signal me on the subject, I realized, but I'd chosen to believe he would soon be mine anyway. He also dumped me sooner than most. That was doubly painful, because I knew his pattern. Six months: I only got half that. Seconds before Lisa had called out to me in the parking lot, I'd been thinking about what his other women had that I lacked, that they could hold on to Ben for half a year and make him work to convince them he would soon be theirs forever.

"Well, if you pick up the paper and read 'One of Washington's most successful marriage acts is splitting up,' don't say you didn't hear it here first," Lisa said. "Okay, now, on to the big question." She adjusted her Boy George hat, but instead of slanting it to a pert angle, it wound up right on top, so she looked like a Hasid. "Do you think he ever sincerely loved her? Or was it all money, all the time, from the get-go?"

I voted for all money, and got away from her by glancing at my watch, aghast, and saying I was late for a dentist's appointment. As she strolled to her car, the straps on the back of her vest flopping with

each step, it occurred to me that she too had a crush on Ben. Not smitten, because she didn't try hard enough to pump me—as a member of his unit—for information, but she was keen on him enough to get pleasure out of talking about him.

Interesting memory of my youth, Lisa's youth, I thought. As I made a right onto the street that led to the studio, it occurred to me I had told Jacques Harlow that it was unlikely Ben and Lisa had had much to do with each other.

But who knows what happened in the years after I'd left? Maybe too many questions were being asked about all the female hires in Eastern Europe and he'd had to hunt for girlfriends in other units. Could the two of them have gotten together? I couldn't picture Ben being able to bear not just Lisa's lack of discernible intellect, but her voice, high enough to make an ordinary soprano sound like a basso. Nevertheless, if they'd had an affair, I wondered if it lasted more than three months.

Javiero's dressing room was much larger than Dani's, not only with room for a couch, but a small chaise across from it. This commodious size pleased me immensely because it galled Dani. Javiero Rojas, as far as I could tell, was a sweet guy. I wasn't positive because his English was so limited and he, like everybody else, had difficulty comprehending my pre-K Spanish vocabulary. He had come to acting after a successful, though not stellar, career as a singer of Latin love songs. His audience was mostly women of a certain age, i.e., old enough to have significant hearing loss.

He worked with a dialect coach, and learned his lines with a slight, pleasing accent. But having come to the United States from Chile when he was thirty, and with no knack for foreign languages, his untutored English consisted of many nouns and much acting-out of verbs. I was supposed to be getting his notes on the second draft of the script, but since his coach/translator was having one of his mys-

terious, lengthy sojourns in the bathroom, we wound up discussing our plans for the rest of the summer. So far I gathered that he was taking his wife, who looked like Brigitte Bardot, except blonder, to spend time with his family in Arica, in Chile, then flying to some islands off the coast of Spain where they were renting a villa.

"Ocean and pool," Javiero told me, doing an Australian crawl stroke with his arms.

"It sounds wonderful!" I said.

"You, the husband, Nicky?"

"Nicky's in camp." I did one stroke of the crawl and hit a baseball.

"Great!" Javiero said. "I know 'camp.'" His smile was gorgeous, as was the rest of him. Blond hair, brown eyes, sun-kissed skin: it was like having a conversation with a golden idol. "You and the husband?"

"We'll play it by ear" didn't seem to be an idiom Javiero knew and explaining it was beyond my ability, so I said, "*No somos seguros. We* don't want to leave the U.S. because of Nicky."

"I know. Nervous."

I laughed while simultaneously straining to think of how to keep the conversation going until his coach came back from the bathroom. Just then, my cell phone started to play the *Spy Guys* theme song. "It can wait," I told him. "Sorry, I forgot to turn it off."

"No, please. Talk." He tapped the face of his watch. "Three o'clock."

As I waved good-bye and slipped out the door, I opened my cell. A good thing. "Hello. Maria Schneider returning your call."

"Oh, thank you so much. I really appreciate your calling back." I might have run off at the mouth more, but I stopped walking down the hall and leaned against a wall.

"You are looking for Lisa?" she asked.

"Yes. I worked with her years ago. She called me a few weeks ago after . . . well, after a really long time. I happened to remember your name from way back when, and . . ." I felt like such a fool, trying to make my phoning Maria, recalling her name and enough information

to locate her, appear a matter of memory. "I know this is a long shot, and that you might not remember much about her —"

"No, no, we kept in touch. Lisa even told me her true name. Obviously. Back then I knew her as Ann Mc . . . something. She is a great character. What an introduction to the States she was! I couldn't bear to let her disappear, and she said that she had never hit it off so well with anyone before me." Lisa could have gotten into major trouble for getting along so well, but my guess was that after a lifetime of telling lies and getting away with it, she wouldn't worry about an Agency rule or two. "We don't speak so often," Maria went on. "Life has a way, you know. Everyone is so busy."

"Do you happen to remember when was the last time you spoke to her?"

"I'm not sure," she said slowly. "It has been some time. Is there a problem? I don't mean to be too curious, but is it that you don't have a number for her or that you suspect something is wrong?"

"Well, I would appreciate any number you have. But from what I gather, she seems to have disappeared from Washington and when she called me, she was very disturbed about something."

"What was it?" Maria blurted. She sounded upset.

"That's the problem. I don't know. She said she would call me back, but never did. I've tried everything I could think of to track her down, but so far nothing's come of it."

"I don't know what to tell you," she said. "Lisa may not return a call the next day or even the next week, but she wouldn't call someone to say there is trouble and not call again. And she is such an easy person. It is difficult to imagine her saying she has a problem. I'm worried."

"I am too," I said. "Is there any friend of hers I could call? Maybe she's been in contact with other people. I promise you, I wouldn't bother them. I would just give them my name and contact numbers so that if they can locate her, or if she calls them, they can say I've been reaching out for her."

"I'm sure you would be no bother," Maria said. "I really don't know her friends' names. The best one to call would be Ben."

"Ben?"

"Yes. Benton Mattingly. You know him?"

"Of course," I managed to say. "I just didn't realize she and he had, you know, stayed in touch."

Maria laughed. "They've been together how many years now? Fifteen? Twenty? More a marriage than a marriage, as she says. Call Ben. If anyone would know, he would."

Chapter Twenty-five

BEN AND LISA JUST DIDN'T MAKE SENSE. YET I'd seen enough of life, or at least read enough about it, that short of Timmy and Lassie, no coupling would astound me. Home from work, marinating chicken breasts, I told myself, *Here is a man, Benton Mattingly, who has shown himself incapable of keeping his pants zipped. Here is a woman, Lisa Golding, whose lies indicate she is desperate for attention. They work for the same company. They got together. So? This is not the stuff of a banner headline.*

But if it were true, it wasn't true to type. As far as I could see, Ben had had only one long-term connection in his life, and that was to Deedee, or, if not to her, to her money. All the rest of his women were limited engagements, tops six months. Well, there was always the possibility that Maria was wrong, that if Ben and Lisa had something together, it was a friendship or some sort of mutually beneficial connection. Except what was it she'd quoted Lisa as saying? That it was

more a marriage than a marriage? Of course, Lisa could have been lying. That would be in character.

And speaking of connections, what was the Lisa-Maria friendship about? I could see it from Maria's point of view; as a shrewd operator, she would want to cultivate anyone in or near power. But was she such an appealing person that Lisa broke Agency rules and gave out her real name just to keep the friendship going? Maybe. Over the years, Lisa's work—coaching people to live a lie, staying close to them for a few weeks, then leaving—might have gotten to her. It wasn't as if she had a family at home to act as a ballast. Just, it seemed, a very married lover.

I was pondering whether to make rice pilaf or just stick to vegetables when the phone rang. Adam, the caller ID told me, probably telling me he was leaving the zoo.

But he wasn't. "You know Blossom, the Sumatran rhino?"

"Sure. Is anything wrong?"

He sighed, a sign his soul was troubled. "I don't know. The keeper thought she was out of sorts and her vet wants some test run. With Sumatran rhinos, what can present as hemolytic disease can be iron overload syndrome."

"Is it serious?"

"Don't ask. Their blood cells are lacking in antioxidant capacity. Sumatran and black rhinos can wind up with iron pigments deposited in their tissue."

"I hope she's all right," I said.

"So do I."

"You're not coming home for dinner?"

"I need to get things started here." I was about to tell him I'd probably catch up with all the *Queer Eye* episodes I'd TiVo-ed, when he said, "I was going to talk to you tonight."

My heart lurched: that was a sentence that could mean anything from I need you to help me look for my left tennis sneaker to I've fallen in love with a twenty-nine-year-old chimpanzee researcher. "What about?"

"You're still not yourself."

"What do you mean?" I knew what he meant.

"You can't get that Agency thing off your mind."

"I guess I wasn't hiding it as well as I thought."

"No." Adam sighed again, and I realized it wasn't just Blossom the rhino that was weighing on him. "So this is what I thought." I waited long enough to swallow a couple of times—with some difficulty. What was he going to suggest? Trial separation for the summer? And there were a hundred worse alternatives that lay just beyond that one. "I want to help you get past this, Katie. Let's get a lawyer on this. Go public. Now that you're writing about the Agency for TV, you can say you don't want them having something to manipulate you with. Ask them to release whatever it is."

"Someone could have made up something horrible about me."

"Then we'll fight it. I'll be with you. You don't have to do this alone."

"Adam, thank you." I rested my hand over my heart, then remembered that was what they were doing now in commercials— "our pledge to you"—thereby debasing the most deeply felt of gestures. "You could make me believe in reincarnation. How else would I deserve someone as good as you if I didn't do something great in another life?"

His silence told me his instinct was to run to a microscope and look at rhinoceros cells, because he felt obliged to come up with something flowery. Finally he said, "Me too." Eloquent enough.

The next morning, when push came to shove, which it always seemed to, I told Adam I wanted to hold off until I decided what we should do. This was because I didn't want "we." This was all "me." Adam wanted to help me with a problem, yet for whatever reason, I had my arms close around it, clutching it against me as if he were trying to pull away my most cherished possession. *Don't you dare try to help!*

What did this say about me? That in a world where character ought to count, mine was nowhere near as upright as my husband's. I could talk the devoted spouse talk, but if there were indeed reincarnation, in my next life I'd be married to a crooked accountant with a pencil mustache.

I called Ben at Euro-fone's Prague office and left a message with the secretary: Mr. Mattingly and I had spoken recently and, since then, I'd come up with some information about a mutual friend. When my cell rang late that afternoon, caller ID had nothing to tell me. Still, I knew it was Ben. As I said hello, I was calculating what time it was in England and the Czech Republic when he informed me he was in Washington. He asked what information I had come up with and I countered with "I'm glad you're in the States. It would be much better if we talked in person."

"Katie, as much as I'd like to, I'm pressed for time."

"I understand that. So am I. But here's the deal: I'll fly down to Washington tomorrow. Guaranteed I won't keep you too long because I have so many things piled up here in New York."

I heard him setting down something—a glass or a cup. I pictured him doing it impatiently, the corners of his mouth puckered with disgust, *That bitch is milking the situation for all it's worth*. On the other hand, if he was tied as tightly to Lisa as Maria Schneider claimed, he couldn't afford to blow me off.

I can't say I wasn't wary. If Ben had suggested a meeting on a path in Rock Creek Park or even in an obscure restaurant, I might have said no. But he asked that I meet him in his office. Even though I'd seen *Charade* enough times to know how the bad guy put one over on Audrey Hepburn officewise, I agreed. Ten o'clock, which would give me time to drive to La Guardia for the shuttle and get home in time for a late lunch. It was only after I'd hung up that I made a second association with the word *office*.

It was in his own office that Bernard Ritter had been stabbed to death.

I'd pictured some flat, anonymous office building with blue-tinted windows, but Ben Mattingly's Washington office was a town house not far from Dupont Circle. The street had once been residential, but now law firms, lobbying groups, and well-heeled nonprofits had replaced the families so completely that at ten in the morning, the street was lifeless; it might have been taken over by vampires who were incommunicado after a night on the prowl.

Three names were listed on a panel that had a slot for an electronic key card: Euro-fone USA, Mattingly Associates, and B. Mattingly. I pressed the buzzer for B. and checked out the doorway. Neat paint job: no drippies or uneven surfaces. Brass doorknob polished to a refined dull gleam. I was about to reach up and feel how my hair was doing in the Washington humidity when I glanced up and saw a camera. When I realized how grateful I was that I hadn't made that I-have-to-look-just-right gesture, it dawned on me how much this meant to me, and how many years I'd imagined it. Our meeting seemed inevitable; never, not even for a second, had it occurred to me that I wouldn't see Ben again.

I'd put such energy into appearing casual. Liner, lipstick, gloss then blot. I did this three times and refused even the bottle of water on the shuttle. I took out a magnifying mirror to recheck four times on my ride from the airport. That mandated two more applications of Barely Strawberry Glossimer lip shine. Same effort into supposedly au naturel eyes, lashes, skin, shoes, clothes.

Despite having warned myself earlier not to meet Ben in a lonely place, I really wasn't frightened. Anxiety? Only my normal quotient, which had nothing to do with any unusual sense of danger. My apprehension was predictable girl stuff: fretting over my appearance; nervous about the first moment that he laid eyes on me, praying he

would think, She looks fantastic, rather than, I can't believe I ever slept with that.

Unfortunately, walking the few yards from taxi to door had caused my camisole, whose lace was meant to peek naughtily through my white silk blouse, to ride up above what was supposed to have been a non-noticeable midriff bulge. Now, no doubt, it would look as if I'd put on a pink bicycle tire along with my underwear; I couldn't make the necessary adjustment because of the damned camera's bulging eye.

Then I heard his voice saying, "I'll buzz you in. One flight up, door to the right." No electronic buzz or echo on Benton Mattingly's sound system. Clarity the New York Philharmonic would have died for. As I stepped inside, I did a frantic sweep to see if I could spot a camera. None. I pulled out my blouse, unrolled the camisole, and tucked everything back by the time I hit the third stair. When I reached the top, I was nearly panting—not from exertion, but from nerves and sucking in my gut in order to prevent a repeat camisole crisis.

Sometimes you picture what's about to happen without realizing that your mind is a step ahead of you. That must have occurred because I was startled to find Ben's door closed. He wasn't there, waiting for me, clearly on edge despite his restrained (yet still cordial) "Good to see you."

When I knocked, I heard what sounded like a file drawer being shut. A few seconds later a woman carrying some manila folders opened the door. She was easily in her fifties, old enough so that the herpes sore on her lip seemed as age-inappropriate as would low-rise jeans. She held the door open and I entered a room that might have been a parlor in its youth and a doctor's waiting room in middle age. Now it was empty except for a U-shaped desk, chair, and two walls' worth of filing cabinets. The last were mostly beige, along with a couple of those battered old steel-color ones; they looked like dead teeth in a mouth that didn't know from dental hygiene.

"Go right in." She pointed to a tall wooden door with a glass knob. When I lifted my knuckles tentatively to knock, she said, "No, go in, go in."

On the plane, I'd decided that the instant I saw Ben, I'd give a hearty, "How are you?" and extend my hand. I wanted to insure against doing any embarrassing romance novel stuff, like feasting my eyes on him hungrily. I'd also warned myself not to recoil if he looked repulsive. He was now fifty-nine years old. That meant potential liver spots the size of quarters all over his face, or jowls that flapped around his collarbone. No matter what, I would show no surprise.

My "How are you?" came out as planned, but not so hearty; all I could manage was a polite smile—the sort you give to a clergyman not of your religion. Well, Ben Mattingly had not gone to seed. As he came around the side of his desk to greet me, I could see he still had an athlete's body, maybe a little more spread out, as if he'd traded half his tennis time for golf. His face had more lines, sufficient to evidence character, though too few to connote wisdom. As always, his suit jacket hung on the back of his chair. His tie was loosened, the top button of the shirt opened, with the sleeves rolled twice, midway between wrist and elbow.

I could see he expected me to shake hands or maybe even try to give him a kiss on the cheek. I extended my hand and was relieved when I wasn't overcome with passion from his body heat. His palm, in fact, was disagreeably dry. It made me remember what I'd completely forgotten: his hands had been so rough that during foreplay I'd sometimes felt more exfoliated than stimulated.

"You look good, Katie."

"Thanks. You too."

"You've really done well since the last time we met."

"You too."

That over with, he waited until I settled into the armchair he'd offered, then walked to his chair. As he sat, he wheeled back a couple of inches, perhaps concerned I'd vault over his desk to ravish him.

"You wanted to talk about Lisa," he said. Now he seemed comfortable. No tension in his body to indicate unease about seeing me. No sign of concern that something bad had happened to the woman with whom he allegedly had more of a marriage than a marriage, whatever that was.

"When Lisa called me," I said, "she said it was about a matter of national importance. I told you that."

"Right."

"What she wanted was for me to put her in touch with someone at CNN or some other news outlet. She seemed to think that my having something to do with TV gave me entrée to everyone associated with it."

"Do you know people in the news business?" Ben asked. I couldn't tell if it was a polite question or if he wanted to know.

"No, except for a few entertainment reporters, and with one exception, they're all print journalists." I crossed my legs. I had forgotten that the last minute before I left, for some unknown reason, I'd switched my black linen pants for olive green ones. Had I just looked bewildered by my own clothes? Was my distress showing? What in God's name had I thought I would accomplish with a face-to-face interview? I tried to pick a tiny piece of yellowish lint off my right knee, but it turned out to be part of the fabric. "I explained to Lisa that there really wasn't anything I could do, especially since whatever she wanted to discuss had national importance." He nodded and waited. I was the one who had requested this meeting. He didn't seem inclined to do much to make it work. "When I called you," I went on, "you said you would see if you could find out anything about Lisa's whereabouts. Were you able to?"

"No." He glanced at his watch. Oblong, gold, but not glitzy, brown alligator strap. No Rolexes for former CIA bright guys, unless it was part of their cover. If I'd been a Washington insider, I would have been able to read whether his watch-peeking meant he was checking the time surreptitiously, because he felt he had a million

other things to do, or intentionally, because he wanted me to feel as if I was a burden and would therefore feel pressured to hurry up and get out of his life. "To be perfectly candid, Katie, I didn't make any calls. I'm up to here"—he drew an imaginary line high across his forehead—"with work."

It hit me that he was waiting for me to pardon him, to tell him that I understood perfectly that a man of his stature didn't have the luxury of time for doing favors, especially not for people who had left the Agency under a cloud. What also hit me was that while Ben still looked good, with strong features and a rich man's relaxed posture, he'd lost something. His magnetism. I'd expected to have to fight being inexorably drawn to him. There wasn't even a tug. It wasn't his being older, though once he sat down, there was enough overhead light that I could see his scalp through his hair. Jacques Harlow was even older than Ben, nowhere near as good-looking, had a C-minus in social skills, and was beyond odd in the personality department. Nevertheless, he'd had a manliness about him that could register on a Geiger counter.

Who knew? Maybe Ben still had magnetism coming out of his ears. Maybe it was I who'd changed. I'd had fifteen years to meet a world of men. Friends' husbands, neighbors, publishing guys, TV guys, veterinarian and pathology guys, socialites at Wildlife Conservation Society events I went to with Adam. Among them were a small number of charmers—men whose eyes and body language said, *You want me, and for good reason.* Except after a while, I must have started to see that the reason wasn't so good.

These hot guys may have liked sex, but they weren't so crazy about women. When it came to "love 'em and leave 'em," leaving brought these men far more pleasure than loving. That's why they left so often, to find someone new, so they could leave again. They weren't man enough to stick with a relationship with one woman: when that id voice cried, *I want her,* they lacked the balls to tell it, *Tough shit. You can't have her.* And if they tried marriage, as Ben

had, their wives would know what was going on, even if they pretended not to. And they'd know again and again and again. The other women weren't just a source of pleasure; they were a weapon used to inflict pain.

"Do you have any idea," I asked, "what Lisa was talking about? That matter of national importance?"

"No. I told you, I barely knew her." The Agency trained ops to read body language, but I didn't need formal instruction to know that Ben's leaning forward in his chair meant he was on the verge of getting up to escort me out.

"You did tell me that." I smiled. "What can I tell you? I write fiction."

He clasped his hands and rested them on the edge of his desk. "Then why don't you stay with fiction?" Ben may have come from a poor Arkansas family, but on his climb up the ladder, he'd picked up enough of the East Coast upper-class snottiness to know how to ask a nasty question in a congenial manner.

"Because Lisa called me," I said agreeably. "She sounded terribly upset. I'm worried about her."

"Then you should have called Personnel Security at the Agency. Or the D.C. Police if you thought she'd gone missing. With all due respect, Katie, I don't see why you're bringing me into this." Maybe he was genuinely exasperated. Maybe he was feeling threatened and wanted me to feel unwelcome enough to go away and leave him alone. Naturally he was confident I'd respond to the cold shoulder. Ben would be positive that I'd carried the torch, flame ever-burning, for years. Well, I had. Or, to give him credit, maybe he was acting pissy because he didn't want a sticky situation, like me throwing myself at him.

But my guess was he was somewhere between keeping his distance and pushing me away because he didn't want to show how concerned he was over Lisa's call to me and what I might know. (I knew this act-cold ploy: the TV business would go bust without it. The

VIP feigns indifference or distaste at what you had to offer in order to induce desperation. With desperation come tactical blunders and concessions.) Ben wanted to make me desperate enough to say, *Of course I'll get out of here and drop this nonsense immediately.*

"I'll tell you why I'm bringing you into this," I told him. "Lisa didn't need me to get to the media. A few phone calls, a big, credible story to tell, and she'd be sitting across from Katie Couric. She came to me because I had something she wanted." Ben sat back in his chair. If he was tense with anticipation, I couldn't see it. Quite the opposite. CIA cool dude, his foot up on something, a wastebasket. He rocked gently back and forth while I continued. "What she wanted from me must have had to do with our work together."

" 'Must have?' " he repeated.

"Yes. Look, Lisa and the truth weren't always on speaking terms, as you may or may not know." I withheld a knowing smile. Why confront him about his "more than a marriage" with Lisa, especially when all the proof I had was Maria Schneider's allegation? "But Lisa wouldn't call me and go on about a matter of national importance if all she wanted was for me to take her to the studio so she could watch *Spy Guys* being taped."

"Maybe she had some other crazy reason. Maybe she was making up a story and then lost interest. That could be why she never called you back."

"Possibly. Except she left the Agency a year and a half ago."

"She told you that?"

"No."

"Then how did you find out?" He was still casual, still rocking.

"Through some contacts who know people who know people."

"What in the hell is that supposed to mean?" I could hear a trace of his Southern accent in the way he broke *hell* apart, as though it had a diphthong in the middle. Usually, he spoke the standard, educated American English of a PBS announcer.

"Come on, Ben. You know what it means. Somebody gave me a

little information and in return I gave my word that I'd keep the source to myself."

I could see he was trying to read between the lines, except he couldn't figure out where the lines were. I was an outsider; who could I possibly know? "What has Lisa been doing since she left?" he asked.

"I don't know."

"That's some great source you've got." When I didn't respond, he continued: "I'm still trying to understand where I fit into your story."

"I'll get to it. But I do believe Lisa came to me for a reason rather than as a matter of whim."

"Why?"

"Why not? I don't see the potential for any grand scam here. A friend from the past calls, says she's in trouble, sounds like she's in trouble. I didn't sense a practical joke or that she was overdramatizing." I still wasn't willing to tell him that she'd offered to trade her knowledge for my assistance. "If I track her down, I can find out if she still needs my help—or if she's full of shit."

Ben put his head against the high back of his chair and gave me what I assumed was The Look, the Agency cold stare that would supposedly turn your bones to marshmallow and make you babble on and on in a futile attempt to ingratiate yourself.

I didn't bother staring back. I knew not to: instead of one of those self-proclaiming T-shirts that said BORN TO RAISE HELL, mine would say BORN TO BLINK FIRST. "I asked myself what Lisa and I could have worked on together that could possibly have ramifications today. That's where you come in. I worked for you. There's nothing I did that you didn't request that I do, and nothing that you didn't check."

"Do you expect me to be able to"—he snapped his fingers—"go like that and come up with what particular reports you wrote? And out of those reports, am I supposed to tell you which ones Lisa had something to do with? Because if that's what you want . . ." He shook

his head. "Katie, I'm blessed with a good memory. But do you have any idea how many cases I worked on over the years, how many reports I wrote myself or supervised?"

"Probably thousands," I conceded. "I'm just asking: Does anything ring a bell? Something that Lisa and I might have done together in eighty-nine or ninety?"

If he considered my question at all, it took him about a second and a half. "Nothing."

"One report sticks out in my mind," I told him.

No reaction, although by the same token, I couldn't imagine him gasping and shrieking, *Oh my Gawd!* "What's that?" he inquired casually.

"The report on those three East Germans we brought over here." No reaction here either. Yet I sensed, or maybe imagined, a change. For all I knew, it could have been atmospheric, the way some dogs can forecast a thunderstorm. "Do you remember them?"

"Yes. Why those three in particular?"

"Because I only dealt with Lisa on a couple of matters and out of those, this was the only one important enough that it could possibly have repercussions fifteen years later."

"Germany was officially reunified in 1990," Ben said. "October third, 1990." Did he expect extra credit for the exact date? "What possible meaning could any of those three have now?"

"I'm not sure."

"Does your contact who has contacts have any ideas?"

"Well, I was able to find out some interesting information."

"Am I supposed to play games with you or are you going to tell me?" He spoke in the same even tone and without moving even the tiniest muscle to change his bland expression. Maybe that's why it seemed menacing, even when he did not.

"Of course I'm going to tell you. Two out of the three are dead."

"Go on."

"Manfred Gottesman, aka Richard Schroeder, died from a rare

fungus. Rare, but it can be found around the Ohio River. I don't know if you remember, but we settled him in Cincinnati."

"Your contact told you that?"

"No. I was able to trace it myself. Do you remember the other two?"

He nodded slowly. "I don't have the names on the tip of my tongue. And even if I did, I couldn't give them to you. You know that. And let me tell you, whoever your contact is—"

"—is guilty of a mortal sin and violation of section 798 of the U.S. Code for disclosing classified information. I know. I'm sure my contact or contacts know it too. Anyway, I, personally, find it discomforting that a guy dies from an obscure fungus that's so hard to diagnose that by the time the doctors figure out what's killing him, he's dead."

"So you're imagining someone pouring a vial of fungus into Gottesman's ear?"

Now I sensed he wanted to be complimented on his allusion to *Hamlet,* and in the old days I would have. Instead I said, "The second guy was Hans Pfannenschmidt. He was way up in the SED, liaised between the party and the criminal justice system."

Ben's eyes widened just a bit, but for him that was a three-ring circus of amazement. "You were able to trace—?"

"No. Found out through a friend. When he got here Hans's name was changed to Bernard Ritter. Anyway, he was recently stabbed to death in his office in Minneapolis. The police are clueless."

"Jesus Christ!" By the time he took a deep breath and exhaled, he thought enough to ask, "How is this linked to Lisa Golding?"

"I don't know. That's why I came to see you."

"Why?" His voice was a little harsh but his posture remained easy.

I didn't buy it. This whole business had to mean something to Ben. Otherwise he wouldn't have agreed even to taking a phone call, much less this meeting. So how come his body seemed so loose he could have been smoking weed for three days straight? I decided

what I was seeing was the result of training and practice: hiding fear, tension, anger. That's what an operative had to do. But there was a problem here. Ben hadn't been an operative. An analyst, a policy maker, a person paid to think about Eastern Europe. But a spy? No. He was an office guy who obviously had learned to hide his emotions to survive and thrive in the Agency and, later, in the multinational corporate world.

I knew I had to tread carefully. Even though I was pretty good at reading people, I never had that gift of sending them just where I wanted them to go: always able to make the sad glad, calm the hysterical. I decided it was best to deal straightforwardly. Ben was historically immune to my charm and underwhelmed by my intellect. I could manage a clear sentence, however.

"When it came to bringing anyone over from Eastern Europe," I began, "there were only two people in our unit who had any say about that, you and Archie. Okay, it had to be approved higher up, but to a large extent, you could make it happen. And even more important, once it was okayed, you guys worked hand in glove with . . . whoever the woman was who was Lisa's boss. I forget her name."

"And?" he demanded. Instead of merely looking at his watch this time, he rotated it a few degrees around his wrist.

"And, I was hoping you could remember something about Lisa's involvement with their resettlement, the extent of it." He started shaking his head, so I quickly added, "Do you think she had any sort of continuing relationship with any of these three?"

I guess Ben had had enough of hiding his emotions, because he took his leg off the wastebasket, sat straight, and glared. "I have to ask this," he said. "Are you nuts?" He didn't give me a chance to consider, much less answer. "Do you think I'd disclose Agency policy or practice to someone like you?" I waited for him to follow that with *Look, I don't want to hurt your feelings*. He didn't. "Did your friend Lisa have a continuing relationship with any of the three?

Let's put it this way. If she had and anyone found out about it, she would be out on her ass faster than the speed of light. Possibly prosecuted. Furthermore, how would I know if some underling from another unit had a relationship with any of those three people? I'd stopped thinking about them fifteen minutes after their plane landed here."

I don't know if it was that instant, but at some point it hit me that Maria Schneider could be as much of a liar as Lisa Golding. Maybe her assertion that Lisa and Ben had been lovers for years was a fabrication. On the other hand, she hadn't called me saying, *Pssst! Want some dirt on Benton Mattingly?* I'd been the one to call her, and when she learned something might be wrong with Lisa, her immediate response had been, "The best one to call would be Ben." Ben and Lisa, an instant pairing, like bread and butter.

If that was true, wouldn't Ben be more cautious? Why would he have agreed to see me? To find out if I knew anything, or what I knew. But maybe there was no need for caution because he knew Lisa was alive and well.

But suddenly I got scared. I didn't get that chill that's always written in for characters at scary moments of TV scripts—which actresses invariably take as a signal to rub their upper arms while squeezing their breasts together. Why it had taken me so long to get frightened was a mystery, but looking across the desk at this nice-looking man with loosened tie and rolled-up sleeves, the thought came to me, Maybe he killed Lisa.

Maybe she had given him an ultimatum because her biological clock had only a short time to tick before its final chime. Only God knew what his relationship with his wife was, but if Lisa had threatened the big reveal to Deedee or to make public their long-term "more a marriage than a marriage," he could have decided to shut her up permanently.

If that were the case, though, why would Lisa have told me she had information of national importance? Anyone who'd lived in

Washington as long as she had and wasn't totally disconnected from reality would understand that for a potential secretary of commerce, having a longtime affair wouldn't be a career killer.

So if it wasn't their affair that she considered of national importance, what was the real deal? What had she really wanted that could have motivated her to call me? And what was her disappearance about? Not just her never calling me back, but her dropping out of sight. I couldn't push Ben any further than I already had. I was too scared.

So I decided to ask him something else. "Why was I fired?"

"What?" But he'd heard me. "Even if I wanted to, and actually I do, I couldn't . . . I can't tell you, Katie." This was the Ben I remembered: head cocked to the side, eyes moist with yearning. But whatever response the sideways head and the shiny eyes were supposed to evoke, he wasn't seeing it in me. And this must have burned him because he uncocked his head and blinked the yearning right out of his eyes. "I'm going to do you a favor," he said. I could feel the freeze coming. "I'm giving you a friendly warning. You seem to have a nice life. Husband, kid, fun job. Stick to that. You're really not in any position to be poking around in Agency business, even if it's old business. Face facts. You are persona non grata."

"These days I'm pretty grata," I said. "Where do you think I'm getting all my information?" From a couple of weird guys who might like me or feel I got a raw deal and wanted to help? Or from the same two weird guys for whom time stopped when the Cold War ended, two weird guys who maybe had some old scores to settle with Ben Mattingly on behalf of themselves or their friends? "I'm sure it's obvious to you that I'm getting some information from individuals with connections to the intelligence community. Having a TV show called *Spy Guys* that's had a five-year run with two semi-well-known leads is a big plus." I picked up my handbag and stood. He stayed in his chair. "You probably know my show is not a monster hit. It's definitely not realistic. But it is show business. And in

today's culture, Ben, show business trumps all business. Including the spy business."

I walked to the door and opened it. Ms. Herpes was busy at her computer. From her sudden burst of activity, I figured she'd been doing a little online shopping or porn watching. I turned back to look at Ben. "I appreciate your time," I said in a tone I hoped was low enough that only he could hear. "And just so you know, those friends of mine? They told me about you and Lisa. 'More of a marriage than a marriage.'" No predictable response, no bugged-out eyes or dropped jaw. Instead, unflappable Ben kept jerking his head, right, left, up, down, as if he'd just put something somewhere and now, for the life of him, couldn't find it. "If you think of anything I might like to know, you have my number." Then I added: "And my friends have yours."

"Katie, I might not be a nice guy, but I'm not a bad guy. Don't lose sight of the difference."

Chapter Twenty-six

SINCE OUR APARTMENT HAD BEEN BUILT BEFORE the first world war, it was loaded with features to please upscale Edwardians: two minuscule maid's rooms, a butler's pantry off the kitchen, two fireplaces, and a cube, more closet than room, with a huge porcelain slop sink. I'd seen photographs at the New York Historical Society of immigrant Irish maids in full-length aprons emptying the buckets they used for cleaning floors into such a sink. Now, Adam was bathing Flippy in it. The two of us had a mutual animal pact: I'd agree to no pets sharing our bed, while he'd put up with my decree of no pets in bathroom tubs and sinks, including Nicky's fish when we cleaned the tank.

Lucy, our beagle, sat beside me, watching them guardedly, as if she expected Adam at any moment to grab her as well. Periodically I patted her head, but mostly I was holding a beach towel. That wasn't necessary, but I liked to be there watching Adam. His mere presence was comforting to animals. Flippy stood in the sink, serene instead of

having canine hysterics as she did the one time I tried to bathe her. Now she comported herself like a supermodel getting her hair done before a major runway show. "You are going to look sooo beautiful," Adam murmured to her. He was wearing an ancient T-shirt, shorts, and flip-flops and was as wet as the dog. "Angelina Jolie is going to say, 'I can't take the competition. Flippy is too hot.'"

I hadn't said a word to him about having spent the morning in Washington. Flying down, I'd been such a wreck about a plane crash—not fear of dying, but that Adam would ask himself for the rest of his life *What was she doing on that plane after I said I wanted to help her?* The only thing that had kept me from popping a Xanax was knowing it might make me dopey during my meeting with Ben. On the ride back, of course, I was so absorbed by trying to make sense of what he'd said and hadn't said, as well as attempting to translate all his body language, that no other thought entered my mind.

What had I learned? Ben was still denying he knew Lisa well. For all I knew, it could be the truth. How could I base any conclusion on the word of Maria Schneider, a woman I hadn't even met? What else? I'd seen, or rather sensed, Ben trying to mute any movement that would give hints at what he was thinking. But what did that signify? Maybe he was trained in such control, it was an aspect of his style I'd never noticed, or he'd learned it post-me.

Big deal, I'd finally gotten what I'd wanted. I'd seen Ben. I tried not to think that the reason I insisted on the meeting had been only that, to see him. But I couldn't get that notion out of my head. A teenage crush, with all its arrogant self-deceit, is an exceedingly unattractive trait in someone about to stumble into middle age.

Yet the trip hadn't been a total waste: I had learned something. Ben had tried to scare me away from digging any deeper. That had to mean something. When he told me to stay out of it, his vehemence was way past a scornful "The CIA's business is none of your business" warning.

Adam pulled out the hose and tested the water with his wrist

before starting to rinse Flippy. I willed myself to relish watching big, cute husband bathe big, cute dog, but I could feel my spirits slide. What if I had been completely wrong in believing there was a link between the three Germans and Lisa? I'd zeroed in on that case because, as they say in the entertainment business, it had legs. It harkened back to an important time, the end of the Cold War. And it was a big deal: How easy could it have been sneaking those three out from under the noses of their own compatriots—to say nothing about the noses of our own allies, the West Germans? But in the end, what if it turned out Lisa was calling me about something else entirely, like the crazy Albanian general's crazier daughter whom the CIA had brought over and put into the plumbing supply business?

"Are you going to bathe Lucy?" I asked.

"No. I didn't plan on this, but Flippy stank. Didn't you smell it?"

I shook my head, then realized his back was toward me. "No. I mean, she didn't smell like she doused herself with Marc Jacobs, but I honestly didn't notice." He reached out and I handed him the towel. He swaddled her, then did one of his neat vet tricks, lifting her out holding her legs together so she wouldn't panic because she wasn't on a firm footing. Considering she weighed about 120 not soaking wet, he did it with notable ease. He rubbed her some more, stepped back while she shook herself. Then he opened the door so she could do her after-bath mad dog dash through the house. Lucy gave us an "I'm outta here" glance and took off after her. I could hear the crazed scratching of their claws on the wood floors.

"Hey, if you didn't get a whiff of Flippy, something's wrong with your nose," Adam said. "Don't get too close yet. She was rubbing up against me and you could spontaneously recover your sense of smell. I'll take a fast shower."

"Take a slow one. I want to go down to the crypt and look for something." I didn't have to look to see his disappointment at my not leaping at the chance to get him sooner rather than later, so I added, "Don't worry, I won't be long."

This time, scooting past the laundry room, I didn't have to sing "Born in the U.S.A." to keep up my courage. My mind was whirring much too fast to perceive fear. I decided: it *had* to be the Germans Lisa was calling about. Okay, that kind of thinking wouldn't pass a logic test, but I based my conclusion on the dubious theory that where there's smoke, there's fire.

Maybe Lisa had no knowledge of the deaths. The point was, two of the three had checked out suspiciously in the last couple of months. Bernard Ritter's death was just plain murder. Had anyone in Cincinnati wondered, Isn't there something curious about Dick Schroeder's death? He could have been the victim of a brilliantly planned, scientifically shrewd, and well-executed homicide.

That left Maria, alive and talking. If she could be believed, there was a strong Lisa/Ben link. Since I had concluded that Lisa's matter of national importance had something to do with the Germans, her concerns might have involved Ben as well. What else would explain his show-no-emotion act as well as his "friendly warning" about my not continuing to poke around in Agency business?

I kept trying to recall Agency business, specifically Ben's going back and forth to Berlin in 1989. Because Germany was divided then and Berlin was in the east, you couldn't fly directly there from Washington. You had to grab a flight to someplace in West Germany, Frankfurt, I recalled, and, from there, take another plane to Berlin. A tough trip. When Ben got back to the office, he always looked like hell—jet lag coming and going, shaving on the plane with an electric razor, dressed in a suit, shirt, and tie still creased from his suitcase.

By that time, when Ben was off to Berlin so often, he and I had been split for more than a year. I was married to Adam. Happily. Still, I couldn't forget how my feelings for Ben welled up when I saw how worn he looked. I wanted to put my arms around him and comfort him. Okay, so it wasn't just *sweetie, baby, snooky-pie* solace. I imagined him recognizing, as he broke down in my arms and wept from

sheer exhaustion, that this was what he had tossed away: a woman who had a magnificent balance of heart and mind.

I opened the lock to our section of the crypt. Everything neat as I'd left it, all the wicker baskets and rattan boxes stacked up, the sheet over the treadmill. This time I couldn't afford to sit and leaf through my notes. Adam could stay in the shower for only so long, and since I was already feeling terrible about keeping my trip to D.C. a secret, I wasn't going to compound my guilt by staying downstairs long enough to make him suspect I was not in the mood. Which I was not.

I got out my economics texts and rushed through my notes. A couple of times I almost ripped a page in my hurry to get out of there. Sure enough, I had noted Ben's trips to Berlin with a "B2B." I couldn't believe I had done anything that obvious; it had all the sub-tlety of a sixteen-year-old writing in her diary, "I F Joey tonite." I actually was writing such insipid stuff after I was married? Yes indeed. The evidence was right there on the page. I read the dates out loud: "October sixth, October twentieth, November third, November seventeenth, December first." That led to a quick head/fingers calculation. At that time, when all the protests were breaking out in East Germany and soon after, when the Wall had come down, Ben had been going to Berlin every other week. Wow, I'd forgotten it was so often. There had been B2B trips earlier than that; now, quickly checking, I realized those had occurred regularly as well, every two or three months.

When I got upstairs, the shower was still going. Grateful, I hurried to the computer and brought up a 1989 calendar. Each time, late in '89, Ben had left Washington on a Friday. Every two weeks. I wasn't sure whether he'd flown on commercial or government air-craft, but I had zero memory of him being out of the office the following weeks. Definitely nothing in my notes about it. But why would he have gone on a weekend?

Even if he was willing to forfeit his Saturdays and Sundays, why would he want to go to Berlin on those days? Whatever he was

doing, getting briefed, talking to operatives or diplomats, wouldn't he be better off doing it during the workweek, when offices were open? Sure, those months in '89 had been crisis time, but even then, some bureaus and departments must have been closed on weekends.

I got up from the computer and walked slowly into the bedroom. No sound of water from the shower. I had to think fast. Why would someone from the Agency travel to Berlin over a weekend? Perhaps to see a person or people there who could not meet during the week. If you had secret business to take care of, you went there at a time that was safer for the people you were dealing with. Like Hans, Manfred, and Maria.

Or maybe—I heard Adam putting his towel back on the rack. Maybe what? All that control I'd observed this morning, Ben's mastery of muscle and expression. What was I looking at? An operative's training. Could it be he had been using his desk job, deputy chief of the Office of Eastern Europe Analysis, as a cover for other work? Like work as a CIA clandestine op?

Chapter Twenty-seven

THERE MUST HAVE BEEN LIMITS TO THE DELIGHTS of shooting coyotes and admiring neighborhood mountains, because when I told Jacques Harlow I could not go back down to North Carolina, and please, could we talk about this on the phone, he let out a deep sigh and said, "I'll come up."

An immediate image of him with a dirty duffel bag full of hideous tourist clothes, like Bermuda shorts, support socks, and FDNY T-shirts sprang up. He'd ring my doorbell, expecting to stay at the apartment for a night or two. Before I could suggest a place for him to stay, he'd barrel past me with an electronic bug sweeper and ask, in a loud voice that Adam couldn't help but hear, *Is your husband in town?*

He called me the following afternoon from the Peninsula, a good hotel in Midtown, and asked me to meet him for dinner. I expected someplace out of the way, like eastern Queens, or over-the-top tacky, serving NASCAR-themed food. To my surprise, we wound up at a

Mediterranean bistro I knew well, three blocks from my parents' apartment on the Upper East Side. It was casual and noisy, one of those neighborhood places, overpriced naturally, where everybody knows everybody—Applebee's for the rich.

"I remember coming here for the first time when I was ten or eleven," I told Jacques. "It was a lesser coming-of-age ritual. You had to have the self-control to sit with both sides of your"—I pointed to my butt—"on your chair for the entire meal, and that meant from Shirley Temple through dessert."

"I didn't realize it had a history for you," Jacques said. "Do you want a Shirley Temple?"

"Some form of white wine would be fine."

He ordered a single-malt scotch, neat. Between that and his shirt with minuscule black-and-white checks and a black sweater tossed over his shoulders, he was fitting so perfectly into the scene that he might have been coached in the Park and Seventy-sixth lifestyle by someone like Lisa.

"Remember I told you it was unlikely that Lisa and Ben knew each other very well?" I asked.

"Yes, but don't tell me now." I glanced around. No one was passing by to overhear me, and though I'd waved to my parents' friends Jane and Jonathan on the way to our table, they were far enough from us that even had they been tempted, which I couldn't imagine, they couldn't have heard what we were saying. I couldn't see anyone studiously avoiding looking at us—the dead giveaway of eavesdropping in espionage novels. All I got was a wink and a micro-smile from a guy I knew from when I'd been on the board of the Writers Guild who obviously thought I'd been staring at him. "I'm not worried about anyone listening," Jacques explained. "Huff should be here any minute."

He downed his scotch fast, as if it were apple juice, then signaled for another. I wasn't surprised that he was one of those men waiters tune in on, and his second drink all but flew over. After two sips of

my Sancerre, I put the glass down on the yellow tablecloth. The restaurant's palette was yellow and blue, which to me has always said Sweden; when I'd been fifteen and obnoxious, I'd inquired about it and the owner told me they said sun and sea to him.

During a lull in our conversation, I kept myself amused with a little anxiety, like imagining Jacques ordering a third drink, followed by a fourth, then being loud and slurry enough to blurt out something to mortify me, probably about Jews. Or he might scoot his chair right beside mine and, in a repulsively sloppy old-guy fashion, drape his arm around me and let his left hand dangle over my boob. My face was feeling hot from the awfulness of it, but then the maître d' brought Huff to the table.

"He knows what I know," Jacques told me as Huff sat.

"Does that mean you know what I told Jacques?" I asked Huff.

"Right." Huff sat beside me. No Lisa-style lessons on how to fit in for him. His shirt was a stiff khaki that could have come from the wardrobe department during the shoot of *Five Graves to Cairo*. He ordered Bombay Sapphire gin, chilled, no ice, which sounded pleasingly spyish.

"I told her to wait until you got here," Jacques said. Huff put his tongue on his canine tooth and nodded. "Do you want to get started?" Jacques asked me. "Don't worry about talking in front of Huff. He'll keep quiet. Not a word to your show. I told him if he didn't keep his mouth shut, I'd kill him." That seemed good for a laugh. While they chuckled away, I reached for a breadstick. "Go ahead," Jacques told me.

"You're not doing this because I got a raw deal, are you?" I asked.

"You and a lot of people got raw deals," Huff said. "Shit happens."

"Let's put it this way," Jacques said, "you happened to come along. This is no formal thing, no cabal of ex-ops righting wrongs and all that. But Huff and I . . . we want to see justice done. Why wouldn't we? The intelligence community has a terrible rap, and it didn't just begin in 2001. No doubt about it, we did make mistakes that cost

lives. We badly misjudged certain situations. But we also made some brilliant calls and performed in ways nobody gives us credit for. With the secrecy of our work, we can't take credit. What galls me is that over the years, people have come to see everything we do as illegitimate. Any half-assed conspiracy theory on the Internet about the American intelligence community is considered one hundred percent credible."

"Sometimes you deserve the hit. Tenet and Iraq," I said.

"How fucked up was that?" Huff agreed.

"Sometimes we do deserve it," Jacques told me. "But you've got to distinguish between the political decisions that are made by a few people in the directorate of an intelligence agency and the recommendations from knowledgeable people those few didn't listen to. When the few ignore or misinterpret the work of the many, is everyone to blame?"

"No," I said. "But if an institution can be so screwed up by its management, then that institution isn't doing us much good."

"Well," Huff began. Then he stopped.

I peered down. I had finished my wine. Jacques signaled the waiter and pointed to my glass. "I'm assuming what you're saying about the few people who make decisions contrary to all the great advice and scholarship they're offered has something to do with Benton Mattingly."

"Yes," Jacques said. Huff tapped his chest to signal *me too*. "He was one of the few. Smooth, smart, and incredibly cagey. And dangerously wrong."

"But he hasn't been in the Agency for years," I said. "So what does it matter?"

"You're not in the Agency anymore either," Jacques said, "and it seems to matter to you."

Considering how quickly I'd been to brush off whatever their beef against Ben was, I realized how amazing it was that Jacques and Huff were helping me. Then I decided the word *amazing* should be

replaced with *lucky*. But since I had no idea what they themselves were getting out of helping me, I wasn't up for *luck* either. Between the double whammy of all those spy novels and movies—Treachery! Intrigue! Wickedness beyond your wildest dreams!—and my experience of getting fired, caution kicked in. Maybe even their "helping" wasn't accurate. Maybe they were leading me to a place I shouldn't go.

For all I knew, when I'd first asked Huff for information about Lisa, he might have run and told Ben. And maybe Ben said, *Go ahead. Lead her on. And bring Harlow into this. He can control a loose cannon.* I could have innocently stumbled into the middle of some huge cover-up of a dastardly plot I'd never even heard of. By the same token, maybe I was having dinner with two demented retirees who would sneak out after the nougat mousse leaving me with nothing except the check.

Despite all those nasty possibilities, I believed these two were on my side. I had never been superstitious, but that day, that night, all signs felt right. I could trust these guys. Why? I didn't know. The world itself felt auspicious. It was a perfect July evening. Still hot. The buildings wouldn't let go of the day's heat. Only an occasional damp breath of cooler air came down the side streets from the East River. No one could walk a block without getting a patina of moisture on her face. Since the time I was old enough to get out of going to summer camp, I had worn that sweat proudly. It separated me from the weenies who still had to go to camp, from the wusses who started fleeing Manhattan after Memorial Day.

Another good sign was that I'd escaped having to lie to Adam about going out. He'd called a little before three and asked if I minded if he went to see a Yankees-Angels game with a pathologist friend from Montefiore Hospital. An hour later, an e-mail from Nicky began with "I learned to sail!! Me and Nathan and the sailing counselor Aalbert that's a funny way to spell it but he's from Holland sailed across the lake to Camp Chipinaw!!!!" I was on a roll, so I chose to believe Jacques and Huff were out to help me. Neither the

Scarlet Pimpernel nor Jack Ryan would make a decision that way. My own His Highness would mock it. Jamie would demand, *How can you be such a moron?*

"I spoke to Maria Schneider," I told them. "She suggested I ask Ben about where Lisa might be."

"Ben?" Huff pulled back his head in surprise.

"Maria said Lisa and Ben had been lovers for years. She didn't actually say 'lovers.' They'd been together, was what she said. More a marriage than a marriage." Jacques too seemed taken aback at the news, and it did appear to be news to them both. They were nodding slowly with a similar brows-brought-together expression of concentration.

"Of course," I added, "Maria could be lying. She could be misinterpreting what she heard. Or there's another possibility. Maybe she was just repeating a lie that Lisa told her."

"We know that," Jacques said. I was surprised by his tone, which wasn't snide. Close to courteous. "When you're not sure what you're dealing with, any fact can have an enormous number of interpretations. Just get the facts out first."

"After I talked to Maria, I remembered back to when I was there, at the Agency. Lisa had pumped me for information about Ben. It struck me then she might have a thing for him, but she was so not his type. He liked very bright women, because to fully grasp his wonderfulness, you had to have brains, along with some interest in geopolitics, or at least the ability to fake it. Lisa wasn't dumb by any means, but not at all book smart. She just had an amazing ability to read style and to remake anybody to match their new identity."

"Did you ever meet any of the people she remade?" Jacques asked.

"No. But everything I ever heard about her indicated she was a whiz at her job. Still, she was superficial in that she wasn't interested in what was going on in the world, unless it was a handbag sale in Paris."

"Maybe it was pure sex with him and Lisa," Huff said.

"Even if pure sex can stay hot for more than fifteen years, I never

saw Lisa as someone who could be hot to anyone. Just her voice alone: it would have been like doing Minnie Mouse. Who knows? Maybe there was something magical about her for him, but even then, how did he find time for her, much less energy? He had the Agency, his Deedee life, and he was involved with someone from our unit at least seventy-five percent of the time."

"How often would Ben have dealt with Lisa on CIA business?" Jacques asked.

"I can't say for sure, because all I knew were the cases I was assigned to write about. Even though Lisa's unit was nicknamed the Welcome Wagon, I can't imagine the Agency was bringing over hundreds of people from Eastern Europe to settle here. And her unit wasn't just servicing us. They had all the other units, people coming in from all over the world, to deal with. So my guess is, Ben and Lisa dealt with each other on a case no more than a few times a year. Even then, Ben would have been dealing less with her than with her boss. That doesn't mean that they couldn't have fallen madly in love and had a long-term affair. It just means they didn't work together a lot."

The waiter came and handed us menus. "What's good here?" Jacques asked.

"Pretty much anything, except they have a meat loaf they call à la Greque. Loaded with raisins. It's fairly dreadful."

"All right," said Jacques as he ran his eyes down the menu, then set it aside. "Maybe they were having an affair. Or some sort of working relationship you didn't know about."

"It's possible. He went to Eastern Europe a lot, every other month for a long time. From what I know, he always stopped in Berlin. That would have made sense in the late eighties. And toward the end of eighty-nine, he began going to Berlin every two weeks. On weekends. So this is what I was wondering." I didn't say to Jacques, *Tell me if this sounds crazy,* because I had no doubt he would. "Do you think it's possible that besides being second in command of our unit, dealing with Eastern European intelligence, he could also have

been using his job as a cover for some sort of clandestine operation? I mean, the Soviets would know he was in Berlin, but they'd yawn and say, 'Boring intel guy is here again.' "

Huff seemed on the verge of answering, but whether by a signal I missed or prearrangement, he kept quiet. Jacques said, "I'll tell you what I thought at the time. I was in Berlin during the late eighties. Don't forget, it wasn't just us versus the Soviets there. There were the French and British sectors also. Militarily, it was a potential nightmare. It also had the possibility of being a dream, because the USSR was changing so fast, stepping down its commitments in Eastern Europe. Mattingly came to Berlin regularly enough that some of us suspected he was running an operation, but certainly not anything big enough to require real watching. I viewed it as the harmless little hobby of a desk-bound bureaucrat. My guess was he had a connection with somebody out of Poland because of his expertise on the Solidarity movement."

"I didn't know that about him," I said. "I mean, that he was an expert on Solidarity."

"He wasn't an academic, but he had quite a bit of knowledge about postwar Polish politics. In any case, I assumed his contact was someone high up in the Polish government who knew the plans for dealing with the Solidarity movement. But about a month before the Wall came down, I heard about Mattingly coming more often. On weekends. That's when I started to think he was running an agent in the Soviet sector and that whoever he was, he wasn't a high-ranking Polish diplomat or official. The Poles saw the writing on the wall. They weren't rushing to visit Berlin. Whoever Mattingly was running would be an East German, someone also reading the tea leaves a hell of a lot better than Ben was. The East German knew it was just a matter of days or weeks before his government went down in flames. If that happened, he'd be done for. He wanted out, and fast."

I was so absorbed with what Jacques was saying that when the waiter came back and asked, "Are you ready to order?" I let out a

squeal of surprise. That led Jacques and Huff to glance at each other. *Amateur night,* they were telling each other silently. The waiter mumbled, "Be back in a few when ya ready to order."

"So I think you are on target about Mattingly using his job as an analyst and adviser as a cover for some kind of an operation," Jacques went on. "What I've been wondering is whether your friend Lisa was involved in it."

"I don't know. She claimed she was an army brat. Another time she said she was the daughter of a troubleshooter for an American company in Europe, had gone to a Swiss boarding school. If the Europe part of it had a kernel of truth, she might have spoken several languages. That could have been useful to him."

"Everyone in the Agency speaks at least a couple of languages," Huff declared, obviously never having seen my file. "That's no big deal."

"What was a big deal," I said, "was that her job required her to move around all the time, to stay in whatever area she was settling someone for weeks. If she was working with Ben, her assignment with the Welcome Wagon was a built-in excuse for being away from the office. If they were lovers, they could meet anywhere—here, Europe—and have a tryst. The lover thing would have been a major time management problem for Ben in D.C., because he had his wife and all her demands, plus taking care of whichever one of us from the unit he was seeing at the time."

"Whether Lisa was his girlfriend or just on his team is irrelevant," Jacques said, crossing over the border into impatience.

"Excuse me," I said, "but it is relevant. If they've been involved romantically or emotionally for fifteen years plus, it's one sort of tie. If he dumped her, that could have set her off. If they were paired by the Agency, then it's possible that the call she made to me had something to do with—who the hell knows?—fearing something from him. There are so many choices: every one of them can produce a different plotline."

"For Christ's sake, stop talking like this is one of your television shows," Jacques said. He was just short of snarling, and he shook his head and compressed his lips in that *She's hopeless* manner. Huff worked on looking expressionless. Whatever their operation was, Jacques appeared to be running it.

"Don't patronize me," I told him. It's bad enough to be looked down upon by some jerk, but ten times worse to be condescended to by someone you respect. "If one or both of them are motivated by love or anger or rejection or some other man-woman emotion, I can run rings around both of you when it comes to interpreting it." I picked up a breadstick and snapped it, which admittedly was no great demonstration of power.

The waiter came and announced daily specials that sounded as if the chef had bought too much saffron. We ordered quickly, including another round of drinks, taking care only to distance ourselves from the Greek meat loaf.

"Let's talk about that report you wrote, the one on the three Germans," Jacques said. "Think back. Was there anything unusual about it? Did you ever write other reports about individuals your unit brought in to be resettled?"

"Yes. A few times. I didn't view it as a major part of my job because it really dealt more with personalities than with issues. We had to write those sorts of things now and then because of some problem—a person we brought over was giving us a lot of trouble, like threatening to go to the press, or to go home and make a huge confession and beg for forgiveness. We'd write it to explain what happened, what we'd done to solve the problem. Usually there was to be a follow-up report at some point."

"Was there a particular problem with any of these three?" Jacques asked.

"Now that you mention it, no. They had only been here a month or so, but I guess they were all doing well enough, considering."

"Then how come the report?"

I closed my eyes and played with the hem of the tablecloth. Why had the report been requested? "Ben had me do it," I said finally. "Well, he was the one who always gave me my marching orders. He told me to speak to Lisa because she could give a positive spin on how well the three were doing here. I guess the reason he wanted it written was . . . Give me a second to think." I did the eye-closed/table-cloth-feeling business again. Then I said, "It had to be as a justification for all the money we spent on the operation. All Ben's trips, settling them here. This wasn't some Eastern European labor movement guy we slotted into a low- to middle-level job at the AFL-CIO. These were VIPs in East Germany. They needed more kid glove treatment, plus a lot of cash so they could give capitalism a shot. You had to treat them well. You can't take someone who is one of the key players in the East German secret police like Gottesman, a supersmart guy who's a genius at duplicity, and give him a job filling uniform requisition orders for the LAPD."

"All three of them did all right here," Huff observed. "I guess that says something about something. But I don't know what."

"This is what I think the 'what' is," Jacques said. "From what Katie is saying and from what I've heard around—" The waiter came with our drinks. Jacques swirled his scotch, then took a sip. More of a slug; about half the whiskey evaporated. "After you left my place," he told me, "I talked to a couple of friends who talked to a couple of their friends. As friends are wont to do." I nodded. "What you're describing to me is classic cover-your-ass intelligence community procedure. What that says to me is that Mattingly, in bringing those three here, had to have gone beyond standard operating procedure. Not only that, the cost must have been way out of line. Something was wrong, and he was trying to hide it, probably by overstating the Germans' value to us and then bringing in Lisa to give it all a happy ending. You wrote that report when?"

"I think early February 1990. Pretty soon after they came here. Come to think of it, I thought Lisa was overstating their great adjust-

ment, because how much adjusting could they have done in a few weeks? The reason it stuck with me is even though Ben took it out of the report, Hans Pfannenschmidt couldn't speak any English. That was a problem. Remember you told me they had to move him almost right away because he was so unhappy."

"Did that move make it into the report?" Jacques asked.

"Of course not. As far as I can recall, the report was about how the operation was worth every single penny and how these three had risked their lives providing us vital information. I only wish I could remember what the information was, but I can't. I can't remember what the total cost was either. I assume it was in the report, but that part's a complete blank."

"You wrote the report in early February and you were fired in a matter of weeks." Jacques was rotating his glass between his palms. Huff was studying his gin. To maintain the mood, I took a glug of Sancerre as if I were Alec Leamas in *The Spy Who Came In from the Cold*. I wanted to come off looking knowing and world-weary, but my heart was thumping and I sensed my eyes blinking like a strobe light. I was both afraid of and agog at what Jacques was going to say. "By writing the report, you were complicit with them, or at least with Ben, in a cover-up."

"But I was totally clueless—"

"That's how he wanted it. The problem was, when all was said and done, Ben couldn't be completely sure how much information you'd come across in preparing the report. As you just told us, he made you delete a couple of things. There might have been more he told you to drop."

"There probably was," I said. "He would never delete only two things and say fine. And for all I know, he might have rewritten some of it on his own. I doubt it could have been all of it because he was a clunky writer."

"Do you remember if you talked to or got information from anyone besides Ben and Lisa?" Huff asked.

"I must have. I would have endnoted the names of anyone I dealt with. Ben couldn't just have me write a report clearing him of any misjudgment or overspending based on his own word and someone as low-level as Lisa. Also, whatever I wrote would have had to go through Archie, the head of our unit."

"Would it?" Jacques wanted to know. "Don't you think Mattingly could have found a way to end-run him on the report? Because chances are that's what he did on the operation itself. I don't think Archie knew. Ben wasn't authorized to order or even approve anything like that."

"It's possible Archie didn't know. I'm guessing here. I wasn't privy to how they ran the unit. But all hell was breaking loose in Eastern Europe then, so maybe our internal controls weren't functioning the way they were supposed to. Maybe Ben ingratiated himself with someone in Clandestine Services, offered to help. I can't imagine anyone saying yes, but who knows? Do you think there could be an outside chance he did it on his own?"

"Yes, because I can't imagine anyone giving him the green light. It's not because he was Intelligence. It's that everyone knew his abilities, but they also knew he was something of a dilettante. If you're mentioned in society columns too often, people suspect you're not working hard enough. If you're known to be carrying on all the time with girls young enough to be your daughter—"

"If you started having children early," I interposed.

"—then you're not working hard enough. And if you're so oblivious to the consequences of fooling around with girls you're supposed to be supervising, then you don't have the judgment to be an operative."

But Ben was so glamorous. I was swept up. Being with him, I felt as if I were a character in the most thrilling espionage story in the world. Strange how it didn't occur to me that so many of those novels and movies end with the spy's girlfriend dead on a rainy street and the spy walking off into the night.

"This is what I think happened," Jacques continued. "Ben was afraid of what you knew, even if you didn't know you knew it. There was always the chance that when things slowed down, you'd think, Wait. What was that all about? And naturally, he worried that whatever doubts about him you had that might come to the surface, you had a motive for talking. You would have gone to Archie or someone from Security."

"Ben would think my motive was that I was bitter because he'd dropped me?"

"Yes. So he went to Archie and told him a story about you. Archie bought it."

"Do you know this as a fact?" I demanded.

"Yes. He signed a statement that you were incompetent. Mattingly claimed that on two occasions you'd told him you had mistakenly shredded documents."

I went numb. I couldn't think. I definitely couldn't move. Alive, but only in a rudimentary way: I could hear the *hmmm* and gurgle of the air conditioner. Maybe I breathed. "What?" I finally croaked.

"A cable from one of your people in Sofia. And some daily briefs from the embassy in Bonn." Jacques stopped for a minute, then realized I was dazed. He kept going, but more slowly. I think he wanted to make sure I could absorb it. "His complaint against you was on the basis of incompetence."

"But they didn't just fire me!" I managed to say. "I was accompanied from Personnel by two guards. They went through everything in my office before I could pack up. Then they took me to my car. A mobile unit from Security followed me until I was actually back on the public road."

"There naturally was some question whether you actually did shred or—"

"I didn't!" I understood now why he had chosen the restaurant. It wasn't noisy enough that you couldn't hear people at your table,

but it was loud enough to keep others from listening, even if you inadvertently raised your voice.

"No one here is saying you did anything. Look, you write stories. Your dismissal was brought about by Mattingly's story, a pretty good one. He indicated there was some question whether you shredded that material on purpose, not accidentally. He even speculated you might have taken it off premises. The cable and the briefs themselves were relatively unimportant, as it turned out. That was his doing also. The last thing he wanted was to have you prosecuted. He couldn't have you or a lawyer questioning what had happened or subpoenaing any Agency documents—not that they could have gotten any. He just wanted you out of there. Out and stigmatized. He didn't want anyone feeling sorry for you. That's why the guards."

I had no idea how long we sat in silence. The waiter came with our appetizers. We sat there as if we hadn't yet been served.

"Why did Lisa call me now?" I was finally able to say. "After so many years?"

"If Mattingly gets nominated for secretary of commerce, there will be hearings. He can't risk a Clarence Thomas, having someone from his past come up and start accusing him of misconduct in office or worse—and I'm not referring to sexual misconduct. He may have sent Lisa to find out what, if anything, you remembered. It would seem natural. She'd come crying to you with a sad story about something. She'd get around to the Germans and your report in due course. There you'd be, two former colleagues, two women, talking about old times."

"And then what?"

"Maybe nothing. If her take on you was that you were no threat, that would be it. Whatever story of so-called national importance she had would fizzle. Maybe she'd call you back and tell you she'd found someone to talk to at *The New York Times,* but thanks anyway."

"And if she thought I had information? I don't, but what if all she had was her own paranoia?"

"I don't know," Jacques said. "Maybe you'd have an unfortunate accident."

All my life, I'd gone around imagining so many ways I could die accidentally. Going for a run in the park, I'd routinely picture myself being attacked by a swarm of bees, tripping over a tree root and smashing my head, getting run over by an out-of-control in-line skater. This was the moment I comprehended the difference between anxiety and actual fear: the idea of being killed in a so-called accident didn't just preoccupy me, it dizzied me. I deeply regretted the Sancerre.

Huff touched my arm. I assumed unspoken kindness until he said, "Something I want to tell you." He exchanged looks with Jacques, and Jacques shrugged what I took to mean *Up to you*. "I was married," Huff said.

Since he seemed to be waiting for me to respond, I managed, "I didn't know that."

"She worked for the Agency. An op. Sometimes we got to work together. But in eighty-six, she was in Bucharest. I was in La Paz." He picked up his spoon and began rotating it back and forth, tapping first the bottom on the table, then the top. "I'll make a long story short. Mattingly was in Bucharest a few times. I hear he cultivated her, you know, to get something. Probably dirt on the chief of station, but that's a guess, what a friend of hers thought. He did the usual routine. Charmed her. Slept with her. Got what he wanted. Dropped her. She killed herself six weeks later."

"I'm so sorry."

"Maybe it had nothing to do with him," Huff said to the spoon.

"But you think it did?"

"Yeah. I lost her. After that, the icing on the cake is that when your spouse commits suicide, that's it for your career at the Agency. Wherever you are, that's where you stay. You're not going anyplace

higher. So let's say I had a grudge. When I got asked about being an adviser to *Spy Guys,* I had you and Oliver checked out. It sounded like you could've gotten a raw deal, but that's life. What interested me was that Mattingly was the one who signed your death warrant. So bottom line? I never cared about your raw deal. When you asked me about Lisa Golding, I said to myself, Hmmm. Didn't mean much, a little strange, but who knows. You worked for Mattingly and maybe in the course of the events, I could find something I could use against him. That's why I asked Jacques to see you."

"Thank you for telling me." I tried to imagine a marriage in which a couple could be split up for a year or more, and what it had been like for his wife to have been stuck in what must have been a hellhole, Ceausescu's Romania. I couldn't.

"You're welcome," he said. "I didn't feel sorry for you."

"Getting back to the subject at hand," Jacques broke in.

Huff didn't look as if he thought this was rude. They seemed to be waiting for me, so I asked, "Why didn't Lisa ever call me back?"

"Could be she was acting on her own," Jacques replied. "Maybe she lost interest. Maybe Mattingly found out she was trying to get you to tell her what you knew, so he called her off. He might have decided it was better to risk your knowing something than to get rid of you. You might not realize the import of what you knew. On the other hand, you make your living writing a TV show about the Agency. You're on record saying you worked there. This is an age of conspiracy as well as conspiracy theories. Your accidental death could raise questions that might lead to his name being brought in."

I took a long, shaky breath. "Do you think it's likely Lisa was working on her own? Or that she broke with him for some reason and that . . ." I swallowed.

"That he killed her?" Huff completed my sentence.

"It's possible," Jacques answered. "More likely, if he wanted it done, he'd delegate the job. Or Lisa might have just decided to take a powder on her own after she called you. Whatever happened, the

intention of her call was not to excite you into getting the truth about why you were fired. In all likelihood, she only threw out the firing idea because you didn't seem that interested in talking to her. She needed a hook. If that hadn't worked, she would have gone on to something else. I doubt that she understood how large that firing loomed in your life."

"It's funny, though," Huff said, "how she dropped out of sight."

"Maybe she was busy checking into how the Germans were doing," I said. "And isn't it something? Now two out of three are dead."

Chapter Twenty-eight

At FIVE MINUTES BEFORE NINE THE NEXT MORN-
ing, I sat in my car telling myself I should be happy. I had what I
wanted, the reason I'd been fired from the CIA. Happy, but not
ecstatic because I had no way to turn injustice into justice. There
wasn't any secret Agency Retirees Tribunal to which I could bring
my case against Benton Mattingly and call Jacques, Huff, and all their
friends to testify. Except I wasn't happy.

There I was, stuck in the Midtown Tunnel in a monster traffic jam
on the way to work. No inching along. The car was in park, my satellite radio dead, and I was inhaling noxious car exhaust while thinking
that if I had to put a name to what I was feeling, it would be unsatisfied. What would satisfy me? Ben's death? My reinstatement with
both a letter of apology ("Dear Ms. Schottland, All your friends here
at Central Intelligence want to say how darned sorry we are ...") and
back pay? Clearly if I couldn't put this behind me, I would remain
unsatisfied for the rest of my life. Maybe dissatisfied, because I'd

always been forgetful when it came to negative prefixes, and I didn't have a dictionary in the glove compartment.

I started worrying the car would overheat if I sat there with the air-conditioning on, but if I turned off the engine and opened the windows, I could get asphyxiated, plus get disgusting semicircles of sweat on my sleeveless chartreuse tank dress, which was surprisingly flattering, especially with big hoop earrings, although who would care when they pulled my dead body out of the car?

What was I going to do, spend the rest of my life like Huff Van Damme, waiting and hoping for the chance to get even? I wondered how much of his bitterness was aimed not at Ben, but at his late wife—for leaving him that way and, in the process of killing herself, killing his career. Damn it! I hated to be stopped dead in traffic, and of course being stuck in the middle of a 1.3-mile tunnel was a claus-trophobe's nightmare. Not that I was truly claustrophobic, though there were more comfortable places for me than crowded parties and stock-still cars in underground locations.

Of course, in New York, there was always that subliminal whis-per of *Is something wrong?* In threatening situations, it became a howl. Terrorists! I was in the middle of the tunnel, probably a little closer to Manhattan than Queens. Could something have happened at either end? A bomb, then a gradual collapse of the structure, the tunnel caving in on itself like a line of toppling dominoes?

When I first understood that tunnels were built underwater, I was always a little panicky in them, swiveling my head back and forth looking for the dribble that could turn into a flood. I remember being in a car with my father, most likely in this very tunnel, and staring as drops of water went *Ping!* onto the windshield. "Are you scared?" he'd asked and I flared up, "No!" "Because it's perfectly normal to be scared," he went on, as if I'd said yes, "with drops of water coming down. But the tunnel is safe."

Later I'd learned that a tunnel wasn't an eel-shaped tube stretched along the bottom of a river. It was built by excavating under the

riverbed. Big help. I shut my eyes and tried a breathing exercise I'd read about that was supposed to calm your mind. I breathed in through my nose, making sure the air went down to my stomach. Then opened my eyes. I couldn't drown in a tunnel, but if I went into some kind of meditative state, I might miss the fun of watching the mudslide that would bury me alive.

Think pleasant thoughts. Fine. I thought about driving up with Adam to see Nicky on visiting day, then Nicky, slimmed down but not gaunt, his gorgeous smile wide, running toward us with arms wide open. And talk about pleasant: Look what I had! Look at my life! A solid marriage versus my sister's loveless liaisons. Devotion and stability versus whatever Huff had with his wife, giving up the comfort of closeness to serve their country—or maybe their own craving for adventure. Adam and I? How could what we had be compared with Ben and Deedee's arrangement?

Throughout the tunnel, drivers were honking their horns. Or maybe slumped over on them, already dead. Who knew? At this hour, my father would be playing tennis in his club, my mother seeing a patient, my sister sleeping. But Adam would just be arriving at the zoo. Should I call him and say, *Hey, were you listening to the radio? Did you hear about any terrorist attack on the Midtown Tunnel?* Then he'd say, *No, jeez, let me turn it on now. I'll call you right back.* I'd press redial, but by then all the circuits would be busy and I'd never get to say that last *I love you.*

How could Ben live with himself? Easily. You can't feel remorse when you don't have a conscience. He could tell himself with absolute sincerity that he never led a woman on. He was always up front that he would never leave Deedee. Right after having said that, of course, he would then use all his brains, charisma, and sexuality to announce, much louder, *I really don't mean what I said!* But to him, those deceits didn't count. Neither did lying about me and getting me fired, because that had been in the service of covering up something—I guessed eyebrow-raising expenditures—that might damage

his career. No doubt he'd been right up front with Huff's wife too, telling her, *You have such incredible insight into what's going on at this embassy,* along with *I don't want you to tell me anything you don't feel comfortable telling me. Please [Mary/Jenny/Kelly], don't feel pressured.*

The cars in front of me must have been creeping for several seconds before the ones in back of me started honking for me to move. A couple of minutes later, I was through the tollbooth. All right, I told myself, blasting the air-conditioning. This was it. My search was over. I had found out what I needed to know. Time to put the past behind me. I had to. Think quality of life. What quality did all those Cold Warriors have who still couldn't cut loose from history, the world's and their own?

My shoulders ached. I was so tired I wished I could pull over and take a nap. Already I felt as if I'd done a whole day's work and then stayed up too late straightening the linen closet. One question remained. How could I leave the past behind when there was still unfinished business back there?

What ever happened to Lisa? And what about Maria Schneider? Two down, one to go? Unless Maria had killed Bernard Ritter and Dick Schroeder. But I had trouble picturing a Tallahassee real estate agent, even an ex-commie bigwig, traveling up to Minneapolis, sneaking up to Ritter's office, taking care to avoid security cameras, and stabbing him repeatedly. Even if she had been one wicked woman with a knife, I didn't see how that could translate into her having the resources and technical knowledge to come up with some blastomycosis and convey a hit of it into Schroeder.

"Hi, Maria," I found myself saying to her voice mail when I got into the office. "This is Katie Schottland calling again. I really hate to bother you, but I'm still concerned about Lisa. And there's another thing that's come up that might possibly involve you. I'll be brief, but I really would appreciate hearing from you. The sooner the better."

■   ■   ■

"I don't get it," Jacques said. I'd called him at his hotel. He sounded hungover enough to make me curious about what he'd done after our dinner the previous night. His voice was hoarse and muted, most likely because any loud sound could make his headache press even harder against the inside of his skull. "You called Maria?"

"Yes," I said patiently. "She didn't answer. I left a message."

"All right, if I were you, this is the extent of what you should do. If she calls back, maybe pussyfoot around a little, see if she'll open up about how come she and the other two were the lucky ones who got a new life here instead of prison there. But going down to meet her? No."

"Why not?" I asked. "Do you think she's dangerous?" I tried to speak clearly, but the phone kept slipping. The twenty-seventh screenwriting program I'd bought in my life was on my desk and I was trying to get the plastic wrap off the jewel case without the use of teeth.

"Dangerous?" repeated Jacques. "I actually wasn't thinking about her being dangerous. I'm figuring that if Gottesman didn't die of natural causes and what's-his-name was stabbed to death, that would increase the likelihood that Maria herself is in danger. It's bad policy to stand next to a target. Don't they teach you that in New York?" I was tempted to scream *Yes!* to really throw his headache into high gear. But I needed him to be able to think. I gnawed an opening in the plastic and peeled it off. Jacques, meanwhile, did some throat-clearing business, along with a couple of coughs—fortunately without anything in the audible expectoration department.

"Girlfriend talk on the phone is fine if you've known somebody forever," I explained to him, "but I can't imagine someone I've never met opening up about her deal with the Agency—or her dealings with Ben and the U.S.A.—to a stranger."

"You're probably right," he said.

"Probably?" I set the CD aside because slicing or peeling off the killer adhesive strip from the top without breaking the plastic case required my full attention.

"If you know so much, you don't need any suggestions from me."

"Relax, I was just joshing you a little. You North Carolina guys know from joshing, don't you? Anyway, I would appreciate any suggestions you have."

"Meet her in a public place where there are a lot of people. I'm not talking about something that's so crowded you can't move. Restaurant, coffeehouse. A busy store is okay, but not a supermarket or store where there are aisles."

"Anything else?" I asked.

"Can you take a little crudeness?"

"You just pointed out I'm from New York."

"Right. Watch your ass. And don't get into any cars with anybody, especially her. For a pro, a moving target is easy pickings."

Jacques's warning came so close to the dialogue I wrote for *Spy Guys* that it was too comfortably familiar to frighten me. His "a moving target is easy pickings" was a little bit country for either of my characters, but His Highness and Jamie were always admonishing each other to be careful: *Keep your eyes open for bolo machetes, or cyanide in the marzipan tart.*

Only two things held me back from wanting to go see Maria. I knew that, unlike my trip to Washington, I couldn't sneak this one by Adam, though it would have to be a fast trip because we were going up to visit Nicky at camp. Another thing: July in Tallahassee wouldn't be April in Paris, and New York was oppressive enough for my taste. Still, when Maria called back at the end of the afternoon, I made sure not to give away too much. I still hadn't heard from Lisa, I reported, but now I had a bigger worry. I really couldn't discuss it over the phone, but two of her colleagues from the class of '90 were

dead—and I had certain concerns about her own welfare because of that.

"Do you mean—" she began.

"I don't think we should use names."

Naturally, if anyone was tapping her phone and had an IQ higher than mayonnaise, he would know I was talking about Hans-Bernard and Manfred-Dick. However, having a minor familiarity with listening in because I'd researched it for a couple of scripts, I knew that the chances of 24/7 monitoring on a tap were unlikely. I also recalled from some of the reports I'd written at the Agency that, on occasion, the designated listener indeed does not have a higher IQ than mayonnaise.

"If you could just give me a little more information," Maria said. I heard concern, but no panic. Still, I wanted an invitation to Tallahassee, though I realized there was a chance that she had been brought over separately from the other two. Ben may have run all three of them as separate operations, possibly because he'd negotiated different deals for each of them. They might not have even known each other in East Germany, though with Manfred-Dick in the Stasi and Hans-Bernard as the party's point man on the criminal justice system and the courts, I felt the two of them probably had been acquainted. Maria was a different case, because her job description as secretary to the head of the Presidium was so unclear.

"I really can't talk about this on the phone," I said. "I'd like to meet you. You can pick any public, reasonably busy place and I'll be there. I want you to feel comfortable."

I solved the Adam problem by being direct, if not completely honest. The details of my talk with Jacques could come later. I told him there was a former East German official the CIA had brought over in 1989. She was now a real estate agent in Tallahassee and I needed to speak to her face-to-face for a couple of hours. That was it, my last attempt to clarify what had happened to me. If nothing came of it, I gave him my word of honor I'd drop my search. I also invited

him to come along. And blessedly, he said he couldn't get away. I'd been counting on that.

A park right near the Florida state capitol sounded like a good idea. I pictured lots of guys in white shirts and a few southern gents in seersucker suits and Panama hats that they would tip when a lady passed by. As usual, reality had little to do with my fantasy life. While the air was not hot enough to scorch the lungs, I seemed to be the only person nuts enough to be sitting on any of the benches along the curved path.

Well, there might have been a sniper hidden behind the giant privet hedges twenty feet back, but if that was the case, he/she and his/her Uzi submachine gun were out of sight. However, the privets looked extremely inviting. Even in the noonday sun, they offered a strip of shade. Nevertheless, Maria had said, "I'll meet you at the benches," and I had to play by her rules. Since I couldn't imagine her belonging to the kill-her-in-broad-daylight school of preemption, I assumed she had chosen the spot not only because she wanted to see me in bright light, but to make certain I was alone.

And vice versa. Jacques had warned me Maria might be a target and to be cautious. But he'd said it on the phone. I'd called him from my office desk, where I did most of my work on *Spy Guys*, so his words had a make-believe ring to them, as if they were dialogue. A thing spies say to each other. Thrilling, menacing, great entertainment. Now, under the feverish Florida sun, I tried not to think that I was a sitting duck.

Then I spotted a person who had to be her—no one else was around—strolling down the path with a brisk, long-legged stride as if it were an autumn day in New England. Dove gray cotton pants, a white, crocheted-looking cap-sleeve shirt, heels, and, unlike me, a sensible straw hat on her head. She carried a pink straw tote. From her walk alone, I decided she couldn't be much more than fifty.

"Katie?" I stood and smiled, hoping it was in an ingratiating manner. "Of course! Who else would it be?" she asked. "Sorry to have picked this spot. Mad dogs and Englishmen, or whatever that saying is. I'm not one or the other, but I'm outside every chance I can get."

"Happy to meet you anywhere," I said, trying not to gasp from the heat. We shook hands. A firm but not bone-crushing grip, a shake perfect for a real estate agent: it said Neither overbearing nor lacking in confidence.

"Do you mind sitting here?" In person, she had even less of an accent than on the phone. She was pleasant-looking, with light skin and light brown hair that hung straight down from under her hat. Her brows kept her from blandness. They were dark and unplucked, and reminded me of Hillary Clinton's college picture.

"No. This is fine," I lied. I'd probably find out what I wanted to know. Then, as I got up to leave, I'd die of heatstroke.

We sat. She reached into her tote bag and pulled out a small plastic shopping bag that said DELI DIVINE. "I bought sandwiches so we could picnic. Turkey or cheese. So many people are vegetarians these days."

"I'm not, but I'll take the cheese if that's okay."

"No problem." She handed me an overlarge sandwich wrapped in white paper. "It's on seven-grain bread."

"This is so nice of you."

"Please, it's the least I could do," Maria said. "You flying down here."

"I'm glad to do it. Let me give you a little background." While I told her about having been at the Agency—though not about how I'd left it—she brought out two bottles of Evian and a few packets of mustard, yellow and Dijon. As she took out a wad of luxurious, thick paper napkins, I gave her two sentences about writing the *Spy Guys* show. There was a distant quality about her that made me want to work to get on her good side, so much so that I had to squelch the temptation to lie and promote myself to writer-producer. While I

unwrapped the sandwich, I decided hers was a cool that came from self-confidence. She didn't have to sell herself and she knew it. I didn't get even a whiff of arrogance. "Lisa helped you get settled here and you remained friends, right?"

"Yes," she said. "Sometimes we didn't see each other for a few years, but if not, we would visit on the phone."

"It struck me as surprising that Lisa kept up a friendship with you—it being against Agency rules. She must have valued your company."

"We value each other's company," Maria said. "And I think we both had a sixth sense right from the first, that we could trust each other. In the world I was in then, that was worth more than gold." A drop of sweat made a slow slide from behind her ear down her neck, but she didn't appear to notice. "I don't know you, but I feel that about you. You have a nice openness about you. So completely American."

"Thanks."

"You're welcome."

"Did you know the other two men who were brought over when you were? One was in the Stasi, the other was a big shot in the party."

"Yes, of course." She sneezed. After I blessed her, she said, "A summer cold, but the sun is the great healer. Hans and Manfred."

"Did you know them well?"

"From what you said when you phoned . . . They're both dead?" On *both,* her voice broke slightly. "I knew Hans only slightly. Manfred and I had been . . . close. This is so much ancient history." It became so silent I could hear her breathing.

Chapter Twenty-nine

"WE HAD BEEN LOVERS. HE WAS MARRIED, YOU know. In Germany."

"I didn't know."

"Yes. Manfred told the Americans his wife didn't want to leave Germany. I always wondered if that was true." Her voice sounded sad, but she was looking down at the sandwich on her lap and the brim of her hat shaded her eyes, so I couldn't be sure. "He made the deal. He and I, together, a package deal. I don't know what would have happened to me if I'd stayed there. My position was not . . ." She searched for a word. ". . . exalted. A secretary. But there were letters that had been dictated to me, papers I typed. I attended so many meetings. My job was to make my boss's job easier. He gave me some of his responsibilities." She looked up. Her eyes were dry, her glance direct. "I must be crazy, saying all this. You could be . . . I don't know. A reporter. Journalists cultivate trust. Overnight they become people's best friend."

"I'm not a journalist."

"An avenging angel." She laughed, but it sounded tight, caught in the back of her throat.

"I am who I say I am," I told her. "What we talk about here will never be public, much less in print. And I don't want vengeance." Well, at least not against Maria Schneider. "You and Manfred split up? When?"

"*We* didn't split up. We were split. They said it was too difficult and dangerous to keep us together. Our situation, relationship, was not much of a secret among those who know. *Knew*, I guess is what I mean. If a person wanted to find us in the U.S., they would look for a man and woman together. We had one night before they separated us. We were in an apartment—I think it was near Baltimore. Naturally we were under guard, but they let us stay alone in a bedroom. At six in the morning, they came and took me someplace else for more debriefing. I don't know where. A couple of hours from Baltimore. After that, I was taken to Tallahassee by a woman named Jessica. Or she called herself Jessica. I had asked to be in a warm climate, a place with palm trees."

I took a few sips of water. I would have settled for one palm tree at that moment. Just put my back against its trunk, gaze up at the shadowing fronds, and wait for a breeze. Despite the water, my mouth was so dry the insides of my cheeks felt glued to my teeth. "Did you ever find out what happened to Manfred Gottesman?" I asked.

"That's why I will be grateful to Lisa forever. When she came a couple of weeks later, to do what she did, educate me, she told me he had been taken to a city in the Midwest and seemed to be making a good adjustment. She said she could lose her job and go to jail just for telling me that. She couldn't tell me the name of the city or his new name. Of course not. I didn't expect her to." She gave what is described in chick lit as a tinkly laugh. Bright, carefree, knowing. But it had a quality that would make a sound editor drop it from a laugh track for being just a little weird. "But several years later, she told me

he had become quite the entrepreneur. I laughed so hard! How strange life can be! By that time, I was nicely settled here." I pictured her smiling, leading clients into the living room of one of those nine-million-square-foot town houses and pointing out the remote-controlled shades. "When did Manfred die?" she asked.

"About two weeks ago."

"A long illness?"

"No, but an unusual one. He died from an infection caused by a rare fungus."

She blinked twice, very hard, so that her eyes shut tight and her cheeks rose. "Where did he catch it? Or get it? I don't know the terminology for a fungus."

"It can be found in riverbank soil near his area, but it's quite rare."

For a moment, it seemed as if she was trying to speak—leaning forward, mouth open slightly. But language seemed to have deserted her. At last she pushed out some words.

"Was he married?" I nodded. "I am glad he had someone at the end. He was a strong man, but always needed a woman." She lifted her sandwich off her lap to cross her legs. For someone who must walk miles a day showing real estate, she was wearing surprising shoes, white patent pumps with three-inch stiletto heels. Pretty ugly, I thought, like what a nurse would wear in a porn movie. As my mother would have remarked, *They cheapen a perfectly nice look.* "Is there a suspicion about the way he died, it being unusual?"

"Not officially. Not that I know of. People say that's more the stuff of fiction. But Hans Pfannenschmidt is another story. He was stabbed to death in his office a couple of months ago." Her mouth formed an O, but she definitely wasn't as emotional hearing about him as she had been about Manfred-Dick's death. It was the O anyone's mouth would make when hearing that someone she knew slightly had been murdered. "That's one reason I wanted to come here and talk with you. Whoever killed Hans seemed to have planned it. The police weren't able to find anyone on the security cameras

who might be of interest to them. They're at a loss as far as suspect and motive. He was a widower with children. From the little I learned, he seemed to have been a nice, responsible person. Do you know what he was like in Germany?"

"Not nice. I know Manfred didn't like him. He said Hans was sneaky and for himself only. Hans was a small man, and skinny. Manfred called him the Weasel. His judgment was usually correct, but I only knew the man slightly, so I can't tell you for myself." Finally she took a bite of her turkey sandwich. I'd been getting just the teeniest bit edgy, having glommed my sandwich almost immediately before wondering if there could have been strychnine between the cheese slices. I might have disguised whatever taste it might have had by putting on so much mustard.

"Lisa seems to have dropped out of sight in Washington," I said. "Look, Hans was killed. Then Manfred died from a rare infection that took so long to diagnose that it was too late to do anything for him. I'm worried about her."

"You think Lisa is dead too?"

"No. Actually, I don't know. But she called me more than a month ago, talked about a matter of national importance—she didn't say what it was—and said she'd call back the next day. She never did. Did she ever mention anything that, in your opinion, could have turned into something big?"

She smiled fondly. "No."

"Did you know that she had left the CIA?"

"Yes."

"Why?"

"She was tired. That's all. Always traveling, living in motels or, you know, the ugly houses the government keeps with linoleum on the living room floors. She wanted a normal life."

"Couldn't she have had a nice life living in Washington? She owned a house there and I bet it didn't have linoleum floors. Why do you think she disappeared?"

"I don't know. I can't explain it. She had a lovely house in Washington."

"I saw another house she had once," I said. "She bought it while I was still working for the Agency. Great location that was becoming gentrified. Couldn't have been cheap, plus I got the impression she'd put some money into upgrading. How was she able to afford living like that on a government salary?"

I expected to hear something like *She comes from a wealthy family,* but instead Maria said, "Ben."

"Ben?" She nodded. I got the impression she thought I was a little dense for being surprised. "Do you think his wife knew?" I asked. "She was the one with the money, so it must have come from her—whether she knew about it or not."

"No," she said dismissively. "Of course she didn't know."

"Did he have control over her money?"

"I don't know. I have no idea how he—what's the word?—diverted it."

I gave her a minute on her turkey sandwich, not so much out of politeness, but because I'd read a mystery ages ago about a murderer taking a single bite of something knowing it didn't contain enough poison to kill him—while his victim ate the whole whatever-it-was. Actually, I had taken off on that once in a script, with Jamie taking only a tiny taste of poisoned beluga caviar and setting it aside—she being too Brooklyn, too down-to-earth for caviar—while the evil agent of North Korean nuclear interests watched in frustration.

"Did Lisa do a lot of work for Ben?" I asked.

"Not so much, I don't think. She worked with him closely on, you know, the three of us. Not only getting us familiar with U.S. ways of doing things. I know she came to Germany with him several times before we got out, though I didn't meet her then. She stayed in West Berlin when he came to see us. I only found out later." I pushed my hair behind my ears. My scalp was soaked and I knew my hair would start frizzing from the roots out, until I'd look like one of those

pathetic kinked girls in Woodstock photos who never got any, even during the Summer of Love. The top of my head throbbed. Maria, on the other hand, looked as if she had arranged a private, cool breeze. My mother once said something about insensitivity to heat being a sign or symptom of something, but I couldn't remember what it was.

"Do you know what Lisa was doing for him regarding the three of you?" I asked. She shook her head. "Did you know that Ben is being considered for a job in the cabinet? It's expected to open up soon."

"Months ago, Lisa told me he wanted to leave his company. It was too time-consuming. He found it tedious. There were a couple of very important jobs in the government he was hoping to be considered for."

"Hans and Manfred are dead now," I said, "so you're the only one who can give me an answer. Was there any reason Ben Mattingly might not want the three of you around? Like being up for an important government post and being afraid something would become public?"

"I can't . . . Truly, I can't think of anything."

"So the possibility that Ben sent out Lisa to get rid of Hans and Manfred doesn't strike you as realistic?"

"No. Lisa as an assassin? That's laughable." But Maria wasn't laughing. For an instant, she attempted a small smile. "I've known her for a long time now. Not deeply, but well enough to understand she has a lot of troubles."

"Like troubles with truth," I suggested.

"Yes. She lies all the time. Well, often. I cannot tell you how many times I've said, 'You're making that up.' Sometimes she says yes, sometimes she swears it's the truth. Her knowing I'm aware of her lying never makes her stop."

"But you told me that you had a sixth sense that you could trust her."

"Lisa's lies are never big, about business or matters of the heart. They are lies to make her look good, or to get sympathy."

"She'll give two or three different stories, lies, about the same thing."

"Yes," Maria said. "But truthfully—if I can use that word in this discussion of lying—were you ever fooled by her? She never chose one version of a lie and stayed with it. If you knew her for any length of time, you would hear different stories and know precisely what she was doing."

"Then how were you able to get so close to her?"

"The answer is, we aren't close. But I like her very much and also feel sorry for her. It doesn't matter which of her stories you believe. At bottom she is a lost soul, an American child moving around Europe, rootless. Her parents . . . I don't know about them. They were either bad parents, cruel, or parents who gave her no attention. I would have loved to see her CIA file, because she may have told the truth there."

"So if Lisa was a victim," I asked, "was Ben a villain?"

I'd seen too many actors take a long beat before responding to wonder whether Maria was thinking this over or just pausing for dramatic effect. Finally she said, "Yes, Ben was the villain."

When she didn't elaborate, I asked, "In what way?"

"I'm tempted to say in every way I can think of, but that isn't true. He could be charming. He was very intelligent, very thoughtful about capitalism and communism, not only the Cold War politics, but about their philosophies and, you know, how the philosophies turn out in practice."

"But?"

"The *but*," she said. "He was a man who was unable to say no to himself. It wasn't because he had no self-control. He just didn't believe he should say no to himself, not ever. He wanted money, so he married it. He wanted to be important and worldly and powerful, so he went to work for the CIA. He wanted someone who would live only for him, so he got Lisa. He wanted women, so he got women."

"Did Lisa know about the other women?"

She clapped her hand against her forehead. A theatrical gesture, as if as a child she'd been exposed to too many over-the-top German operettas. "I can't believe it. Well, I can. She spoke about it. Of course she knew. He had woman after woman after woman, like a parade. And Lisa excused it by saying they meant nothing to him. She called them his orifices. She said, Ben is very European in his attitude. I told her that was not European, that was sick. Sometimes he didn't see her for weeks because he was too busy with his wife and a woman."

"Did she ever have anyone else?"

"Of course not. She loved him completely."

"And you don't think she would kill for him?"

This time her long silence was believable. "She might. If he worked on her long enough, he probably could get her to see anything his way."

We spent the next few seconds with our water bottles. Then I asked, "Are you at all concerned about your own safety?"

"I don't think so, though of course, if Lisa was forced to choose between Ben and me, she would choose him."

"And kill you?"

"She would try to. I assure you, I will be very cautious from now on. I am a realist and I understand I cannot be sentimental in a situation where there are all these . . . questions." She smiled and said, "You must be too hot here. Every day when there is sun, I have lunch outside. My friends at the office tell me I'm crazy. Come, we can get coffee right over there. Inside. Air-conditioned." She pointed to some office buildings.

"One more question," I said.

"Okay."

"How were the three of you able to get out of Germany?"

No pause this time. "Blackmail," she said.

Chapter Thirty

"BLACKMAIL," I REPEATED CALMLY, AS IF THE word occurred in my life as frequently as *cappuccino*.

My reaction seemed right. If I'd gasped like a complete amateur, Maria might have held back. Not that I was conning her with my composure. She realized she'd said something startling. But she made no attempt to get up and go. Instead, she took off her hat and raised her face to the sun. As she closed her eyes, I noticed her Evian bottle was still three-quarters full. Mine had no more than one swallow left. Screw this: I could write off my obsession with the past, snatch her hat and water, and be out of there. Good-bye Sunshine State. Except even with her porn heels and at least ten extra years, she would out-run me.

I was so sick from the heat. All I could do was stay motionless. The hot, thick air itself was fighting me. Any movement made me feel as if I would keep going in that direction, until my unconscious body hit the bench or ground. Either she enjoyed the heat or had

chosen the park because she figured being out in the midday sun would make anyone at least a little dopey. If so, she knew she could take it because she was made of the toughest stuff—like the Spartan who put a fox under his garment and hung tough while it ate out his guts.

Finally, she put the hat back on and turned a bit to face me. "Let me try to remember. Manfred met Ben around 1985. It was at a meeting in Charlottenburg, in the British sector, though it was really a U.S., DDR dispute. About radio towers, which doesn't sound like much, but it had become a nasty business. Ben was in Berlin at the time and was brought along, probably a courtesy, like a host would take a guest to a show to keep him amused. Ben's cover was State Department, but Manfred said he was too confident for . . ." She paused. The sun must be getting to her, I decided. Suddenly, she was looking lousy, crimson-faced. Her eyes seemed momentarily unfocused. But then she simply blinked and said, "Forgive me, I've never thought about this in English. Ben acted too confident for someone claiming to be at the middle level at State. Manfred knew immediately what he was, of course, or rather, who he was with. For a reason even he couldn't say, he didn't think Ben was a spy. More of a policy man and very smooth.

"They talked, very friendly. You wouldn't think someone in the Stasi could be so polished, but Manfred was. Ben was trying to cultivate him, which of course Manfred understood. They made a point of seeing each other after that. Ben came into East Berlin on a Polish passport. He was fluent in Polish. If he had used a U.S. passport or one from anyplace else in the West, he would have been followed as he entered East German territory. Of course, Manfred was also trying to cultivate Ben during these meetings. He saw in Ben someone very turned on to two things, money and power. Women also, but Manfred didn't think women were as much of a weakness. At the beginning, Manfred gave him some information that he was permitted to give. Like bait for fish. He also introduced him to Hans some-

time later, I don't know when. The head of the Stasi, Manfred's superior, told him Hans had to be involved and that the order came from the highest level.

"Manfred spent almost two years meeting Ben. Very friendly. They had something in common. Two charming men, secret work. Both unfaithful to their wives. With mistresses. The difference was, I was Manfred's only woman. Not even his wife. She didn't matter anymore to him. We lived in my apartment most of the time. He only went back to his wife for short periods, to make things look good. Her father was very high in the party."

I wondered how much truth there was in Manfred-Dick's explanation to Maria of why he didn't leave his wife, and how much Maria simply chose to believe because she loved him. On the other hand, Manfred had brought her out of Germany with him. In similar circumstances, I would have bet big money that Ben would have found an excuse to leave Lisa: He deserved a new beginning. He didn't want to schlepp an extra suitcase.

"After two years, Manfred understood Ben was having trouble keeping Lisa satisfied. In the money sense. Obviously he couldn't go to his rich wife for help. One thing led to another. Since they were giving each other bits of unimportant information, Manfred said to Ben, 'Look, we're two grown men. Let me help you a little. Just give me what information you've already been giving me and I can arrange some cash. I won't put your name on it. I'll say it's for someone else.' Ben didn't fall for it, but in another few months, he allowed himself to be convinced. Not great amounts of money, but not small, Ben being an American with a high lifestyle.

"Manfred really never got much from him, but he didn't expect to. He had what he needed, his reports on all the transactions. Of course the two of them were also photographed together. He said having Ben was like having a Swiss bank account. You don't draw down on it from week to week, but it's there for something big. And for the future also. He thought Ben was a man with a future. He was

wrong on that, because of Ben's inability to see how the DDR would come crashing down.

"Manfred saw it though. A few months before it happened, he began putting the pressure on Ben. Then more pressure. He showed him the photographs. Ben got angry, so Manfred handed Ben a list of people at the CIA who would get letters and pictures if Manfred didn't place a certain call—which he would make only when he was safe in the U.S."

"Where was Hans during all of this?" I was trying to concentrate one hundred percent, but I began worrying about dehydrating and getting arrhythmia. Despite the humidity, my lips were so parched it slowed down my talking.

"Hans was with them sometimes, which Manfred hated and so did Ben. Such a nasty little man." She sniffled and, as if she'd developed an instant postnasal drip, began to cough. She held up her index finger—*Wait a minute*—until she could speak again. "Sorry. I'm allergic to pines. I take shots, but sometimes . . . Where was I? Oh yes, in October of eighty-nine, Hans came to Manfred and told him he must push Ben to help get the two of them out of Germany. Manfred was shocked. He thought Hans was such a good communist. He was convinced Hans was reporting on him, because the very top men could never trust a Jew who had grown up in Moscow. They would feel his loyalty was to the USSR, not to the Deutsche Demokratische Republik. You knew that about Manfred? His history?"

"Yes. Saved from the Nazis by the communists."

"He told me he would never have thought to make such a proposal to Hans. He thought Hans would report it so fast he would be arrested before he could even say, 'I was joking.' But it became the two of them from that moment on. It wasn't until we were out of Germany entirely that Hans learned I was part of the package. Interesting, because he also left his wife behind. But maybe Manfred told him it would be impossible to bring her. Who knows? Even if that was so, who could Hans complain to?"

Maria stood and stretched her arms up and out, then took off her hat and tousled her hair. Then she did a few wrist rotations, which gave me a second to do what I hadn't before, check out her ring finger. Bare. I was dying to ask her if she'd ever married or had a boyfriend. In fact, I was incredibly curious about her life. What had it been like, moving from a despotic regime she was part of, being torn from the man she loved, then sent alone to the freedom of Tallahassee? Had her early childhood been tough, living in Soviet-dominated East Germany, or had her family sheltered her from politics? And what were they like and what had they been doing during World War II? I thought, This is a woman who ought to write her memoirs. What a story she must have!

I got up from the bench slowly, delighting myself that I was able to stand without swooning. The air-conditioned coffee place in the distance glimmered the way the Emerald City must have for Dorothy. Had it been up to Maria, we might have racewalked there, but I kept it at a reasonably poky pace.

"What are your thoughts about Lisa?" I asked.

"I'm not sure. I can't say I'm not nervous, of course. If she killed the other two . . . She could come to my office and . . ." She raised her thumb and pointed her index finger and said, "Bang-bang. I'm dead. That's my nerves speaking, especially after the way Hans was killed. Manfred? Who knows. Maybe, as you say, stories like that are for fiction, but it makes me wonder. From the minute I got here, I felt safe. I have to laugh, everyone living in gated communities. I know. People here have different fears. I myself could walk in any city in the U.S. at two in the morning and feel safe. That's crazy, but it happens to be true." It probably was true, but as she said it, it sounded over the top. No, I told myself, not over the top: a little wild. Maybe she needed swagger to get through life, and now some bombast as well to face a possible threat from an old friend.

"From what you're telling me, you seem to think that Lisa is alive," I said.

"That's my hope. Also a little of my fear because of what she might do if Ben ordered her to, but mostly hope." Then she repeated, "Hope."

For some reason, I remembered, when I was about ten, my mother reading Maddy and me the Emily Dickinson poem that starts "Hope is the thing with feathers," and Maddy loving it, genuinely, with tears in her eyes. I'd smiled and nodded sagely. My mother seemed so pleased at our reactions. She gave us her soft-faced my-beloved-daughters look. What I'd really liked about the poem was hearing her read out loud. She had a sweet voice and spoke naturally: none of that business of pronouncing each word as if it were a gem. But, as my sister would put it, as an aesthetic experience? Sure, I got the thing about the bird, but I thought, What crap. Why not "Hope is the thing with blueberries" about a muffin?

"What do you mean that it's your hope that Lisa is alive?" I asked. "Do you have serious doubts?"

"Yes, I do." She stopped walking. For a moment she looked the way I felt: close to keeling over from the heat. But she pulled herself together and started walking again, seemingly unaware that she had stopped. "Lisa isn't the type not to call back when she says she will. She may take longer than most people, but eventually she calls. After calling you and saying it was a matter of national importance, even if she changed her mind, or Ben changed his mind, she would call you again and tell you her problem was resolved. Not just to be polite. So you wouldn't do exactly what you're doing, what I would do too—worry and then try to trace her."

"What's your theory then?"

"My theory is Ben may have killed her. Years ago I would have thought 'had her killed.' But he's been out of the CIA for years now, and he wouldn't, you know, hire someone else because it would expose him to blackmail again."

Emerald City was getting closer. I was so grateful. My head pounded and the cheese sandwich had reconstituted itself and now lodged behind my breastbone.

"Do you think she had anything to do with the two deaths?"

"If she could be convinced that Hans and Manfred were a danger to Ben, then yes. And I think he could convince her of anything."

"So you think one of them, or maybe both, was blackmailing him again, threatening to expose what he'd done when he'd been in the Agency?"

"Yes. Though it could have been the threat alone, the potential of dangerous information coming out, that frightened Ben. If it was blackmail, most likely Hans did it. He was a little weasel. Lisa told me that Manfred had become an entrepreneur, so I don't think he would. If he had enough money, what could Ben give him? Maybe because Manfred and Hans had been a package deal coming out, Ben could have assumed they were in any plot together. Or Hans might have told him Manfred was in it. But I have another hope."

"What's that?"

"If Lisa is dead, then—I know this sounds terrible—I would be safer, maybe even safe. If I'm right about Ben not risking hiring a stranger, and if he's not willing to do it himself, then who would go after me?"

I was thinking that was a lot of ifs, but I said, "Good point. But if Lisa did all that for him, why would he risk killing her?"

"Good question." Maria smiled. She seemed to be enjoying the game of figuring out who did what to whom and why. "All right, this is how I see it. He wanted to make a clean break once and for all. Blackmail and the threat of it have been hanging over him for—what?—fifteen years or more."

"Look, I don't want to get you upset, but why wouldn't he let her do the job on you first before getting rid of her?"

"Maybe she refused to do it. I don't know. We've been friends. For him, that would cancel out everything else she did for him in all their years together. What's that expression? Oh, she would have signed her own death warrant. It could be something else; he didn't

think I had anything to do with any new blackmail scheme. In his eyes, I was not an important figure. I was just somebody's former mistress." We were nearing the street now and she added, "I'll give you the bottom line. I think Ben may have wanted freedom from blackmail and also freedom from Lisa. She wasn't getting any younger, you know. If he gets to be in the cabinet, he will have his choice of girls like her who are willing to do anything for a man they worship." I was lost in my own thoughts, to say nothing of my own headache, so I didn't immediately respond. "And one more thing, if I may."

"Yes, definitely." I offered an encouraging smile, not at all phony. She was terrific at exploring possibilities, and for someone whose life might be on the line, pretty cheerful. I would have loved to have her with me when I plotted out an episode.

"By getting rid of her, he gets rid of a big expense. Don't forget, it was his difficulties in keeping her living as nicely as she did that brought him his troubles in the first place."

Now what do I do? I was thinking. This was all guesswork. Lisa could be anywhere. I could walk into the coffee place with Maria and—surprise!—Lisa would greet her with a gun in her hand to finish the job for Ben. Assuming, of course, that our conclusions about Ben were correct. The question I was asking myself as we crossed the street was: Before I leave the past behind me, is there anything else I want? The answer: Yes, I want justice. Not a lot, but—

Who knows if luck—good or bad—is the thing with feathers too, or if you make your own, but at that moment I happened to look both left and right just to make sure no eighteen-wheeler had turned the corner and was bearing down on us. Safe. Or at least from a truck, but I caught a glimpse of Maria's face. She was deep in thought, but not so deep that I couldn't see that whatever she was contemplating pleased her. So I figured it wasn't the notion that Lisa might still be around to kill her. Conversely, I didn't think she would be gladdened by Lisa's death. Nor could she be pleased by Manfred's

death and the end to any fantasy she might have of seeing him again. And since every form of logic and illogic I had at my disposal couldn't come up with a reason for Maria to have murdered those two men, I decided she wasn't gloating at putting something over on me.

While before she'd been easy to talk to—I supposed a necessary quality for a real estate broker—now she turned uncommunicative. We sat across from each other in a blissfully frigid little store drinking iced coffee and sharing a pie-size oatmeal cookie. Her head moved up and down rhythmically as if she were keeping the beat to a happy tune only she could hear. Or telling herself, *Yes, yes, yes.*

That was it. Yes, Ben might be responsible for Manfred's death, and maybe Lisa's, but yes, Maria Schneider was going to keep him from profiting from his crimes. What if there were no crimes by Ben, only a naturally occurring fungus and a crazy person who broke into a Minneapolis office and killed a guy? Then Ben had at least inflicted endless insults and pain on Lisa. And he also was a traitor to his country. Why should he be rewarded with a cabinet post?

"Are you okay, Maria?"

"Fine. Sorry, I'm having to digest all that I learned today."

She was digesting such awful stuff with that contented expression and the nodding business? Not likely. Well, if she wanted to zing it to Benton Mattingly, she could be my guest. "I guess that will take a lot of digesting," I said, just to be sociable, though I don't think she heard me. Her head was going up, down, up, down, like one of Nicky's New York Yankees bobble-head dolls.

But what if Maria's plan wasn't getting even in that way, by going to the media or somehow getting the word out on Mattingly? What if instead she decided to supplement her income by taking up the blackmail again? Would she put herself at such risk? Maybe, if she could think of a way to insulate herself better than Hans or Manfred had. But where would that leave my search for justice?

"I really have to run now," she said suddenly, and only then made

a big deal of glancing at her watch. "Why don't you meet me for dinner? I'll put a steak on the grill and mix a salad. I'll tell you what, I'll be with clients all afternoon so I'll let you buy the wine. I'll pay you for it."

"No, really."

"It would be my pleasure," Maria said.

"I was thinking about taking a late-afternoon, early-evening plane back to New York. Surprise my husband. But thanks so much for—"

"Don't say no. Please." She took a business card from a case and jotted something on the back. "Here's my address." She jotted some more. "And here's a little map. Very little, but you can still read it."

"I'd love to—"

"I understand. If you want to get home to your husband, of course go. It's only that I would have liked to spend some time with you not discussing, you know, horrible things. Nice things. Funny stories about Lisa. And to show you my villa."

Chapter Thirty-one

Frankly, I thought calling it "my villa" was tacky. It was like telling someone, *Oh, you must drop by my mansion.* But Maria was in the real estate business, so maybe that's what they called a certain kind of house in Tallahassee. Unless she was being ironic and actually had a bungalow.

The iced coffee followed by a sports bottle of water and a couple of Excedrins didn't improve my headache and dizziness, so I drove around for a few minutes, checked into a Holiday Inn, and called Adam. "I cannot tell you how awful I feel," I said and then proceeded to tell him.

"Keep drinking water," he told me. "Sounds like you're seriously dehydrated. You're probably better off leaving tomorrow morning."

"You're holding back from saying, 'How could you sit in the blazing sun in ninety-five-degree heat for three-quarters of an hour?'"

"You're right."

" 'Without a hat.' "

"Right again. Besides being crazy and giving you a cheese sandwich on a park bench, how was that woman?" he asked.

"Not bad. A little weird. She must bathe in SPF 45 every day or she'd be dead by now. Anyway, I'll tell you all about it, but it will take the whole six-hour trip up to camp, and maybe even the trip back."

"Give me a hint."

I felt so sick I didn't have the strength to hold back, so I could think about how to present it to Adam. The words just fell out. "Benton Mattingly. He wanted me out of there for reasons that had nothing to do with my work and everything to do with hiding the fact that he was—I can't think of what to say."

"Not like you," Adam said.

"I know. Okay, duplicitous and traitorous. An unmitigated shit. It's too much to go into now. I think I'm still overwhelmed that someone I worked with on a daily basis could betray me so easily. Anyway, I'll tell you more tomorrow. Please, I have to get some sleep."

"Water first."

I was about to say good-bye, but something popped into my head. "Fine. One quick question. On allergies. Did you ever hear of an allergy to pine trees? I never did."

"Animals have a broad range of allergies, and I'm pretty sure pine is up there. Are you talking about in Florida? I could check it out."

"Not in animals. In people."

"You want it now?" I heard the click of his keyboard, so I knew he wasn't waiting for an answer. After some seconds he said, "Yes. Down there, Australian pines are an issue."

"This woman says she takes shots, but she was still coughing."

"Well . . ."

"Why?"

"Wait, let me get it back up on the screen. Okay, tree pollen sea-

son generally runs from mid-December through early spring, and Australian pine can come again in early fall. So it's probably another allergen. Don't worry about her. Worry about your needing water and getting some rest."

I woke up at four feeling better, though not enough to face Maria, to say nothing about Maria's steak, which I sensed would taste like a flip-flop with garlic salt. Instead, I turned on the TV to see if they had any good spy movies.

They didn't, so I watched a few minutes of a dreadful one that was mostly about people chasing each other through the backstreets of Hong Kong, with carts being overturned so melons would cascade over the street and trip the bad guys, Asians, all of whom were poorly costumed and looked as if they'd been yanked out of one of those anti-Japanese World War II yellow peril movies by a lazy casting director and put into a 2004 production that had been made solely to take advantage of a tax write-off.

I switched it off before its conclusion, which no doubt would have had much balletic swinging from clotheslines and shooting, and went out to a bookstore. Forty-three dollars later, I was driving back to the hotel when my cell rang.

"Katie, are you still in town?" Maria, sounding hopeful.

I told myself that no matter what, I would not go to her villa and eat rubber steak. "Yes. I was afraid I wouldn't make my plane in time, so I'm leaving in the morning."

"You're welcome to stay here. I have so many guest rooms and—"

I stopped her. "That's really nice of you, but I've already checked in to a hotel. I had a little too much sun today and—"

"I feel terrible. I should have realized, but when you said a public place, the park was what came to mind."

"How's your allergy, by the way?"

"Better, thank you. How about this? I have two more houses to show and then I can meet you at my villa. Forget the wine. We can have a nice meal together and get to know each other a little better.

Girl talk. No DDR, no death. I promise you'll be back in your room by nine at the latest."

I wanted to get into bed with my books, but I realized this could be my chance to convince Maria that getting even with Ben Mattingly was better than . . . I could hardly say, *Ultimately, ruining his chances for a cabinet post will give you more satisfaction than blackmailing him, plus, if you can afford to live in a villa, you don't need the extra pocket money.* Naturally, I wouldn't use the word *blackmail.* I would talk in a very high-minded manner about revenge—no, I'd call it justice. So I said, "I may not be an enthusiastic steak eater because my stomach is a little off, but I'd love to spend some time with you."

"Great! I'll meet you there at . . . Let's see. Would seven be too late for you? I'm sorry but I can't get rid of these clients and get home earlier than that. If you have an appetite, the steak is defrosted in the refrigerator and the gas grill gets hot in no time."

"No problem," I assured her.

Except there was a problem, I realized after I returned to my room. Maria herself. For someone who had been tough and shrewd enough to make her way in the upper reaches of the East German power elite, she had been surprisingly open with me about Manfred and Hans blackmailing Ben. Open about being Manfred's lover as well. And how come she'd told me about her friendship with Lisa, a relationship that probably violated three-quarters of the Agency's regs and rules? The conversation that had seemed so natural in the park, one woman opening up to another about her life, felt wrong in the air-conditioned, room-deodorized, comfortable artificiality of my hotel room.

And talk about feeling wrong, why had she agreed to see me in the first place? In my normal life, I would have come up with reasons: She was worried about Lisa. She was still gaga about Manfred-Dick and figured anyone who knew about Lisa might have a lead to him. She was lonely and the prospect of a visit, even from a stranger, was appealing. But this wasn't my normal life and Maria wasn't your typ-

ical real estate broker. I'd known enough women in the business to recognize that most of them didn't have "important functionary in corrupt communist government" on their résumés.

Then what could Maria want from me? Information. There was something she wanted to find out about Lisa. Or about Ben. *Stop it!* I told myself. What else could I possibly know that would be of interest or value to Maria Schneider? If I had been with anyone, I might have made the effort to chuckle over my own silliness. But I was alone. So I went down to the gift shop and bought two bottles of water. Keeping my fingers crossed that Maria really was taking clients to two different houses and wouldn't be home until seven, I left the chill of the hotel and walked out into the late-afternoon inferno.

The little map Maria had drawn on the back of her business card was easy to follow, so much so that I got there in less than fifteen minutes. To me, the word *villa* conjured up something venerable, an old farmhouse rising from the earth on a hill in Tuscany. The houses on Plantation Way looked as though they'd been built within the last ten years and that the sole aesthetic criterion had been Big. Some were pretty. There were Spanish houses with red-tiled roofs, houses so closely modeled on Tara that they lacked only slave quarters, and one New Englandy place with shingles and shutters. The rest were a strange fusion of styles; California redwood with Hamptons cantilevered modern, Western ranch in white-painted brick.

It was a long street and a prosperous-looking neighborhood, more hilly than the endlessly flat South Florida I was familiar with, and had as many deciduous trees as palms. There were some pineylooking things that might have been Australian. Having been raised in Manhattan, I wasn't very good at estimating acreage, but while the houses on Plantation Way didn't appear to have enough land to grow cotton, each had sufficient space that it stood proudly independent of its neighbors.

The end of the street was a cul-de-sac. Maria's place took up most of it. At first glance, my reaction was, Well, this is some residential style I've never seen before. At second glance, I thought, God almighty, is this ugly! Stone, stucco, and an ironwork pattern on the doors and fence that looked like ovaries attached to fat fallopian tubes. The walls had black timbered beams, the kind in Tudor houses, but they seemed to have been placed by the whim of someone who had never actually seen even a picture of a Tudor house or, for that matter, studied architecture. I was surprised Maria had chosen it because, except for her white, porn-nurse high heels, she seemed to have okay taste. Maybe she'd gotten a terrific buy and was about to start work on curb appeal. Or maybe her taste in houses equaled her taste in shoes.

A long drive of some yellowed version of cobblestone led to the house. The ride was bumpy enough to rattle my teeth. A fountain stood in front, a great round stucco thing with a lot of curly ironwork rising up into a teepee shape. The water was having some problems, spurting on and off erratically. It only rose about three inches before it gave up. I got out of the car for a second just to look at it. What a mess! The outside of the fountain itself wasn't stucco but—I looked closer—beige-painted concrete that was chipping, so there were small patches of gray. The house, I saw, was suffering from the same problem. The inside of the fountain was so clogged with algae that it looked lined with green velvet.

Major mistake, coming here, I told myself as I walked up the five steps to the front door. I wanted to make sure she wasn't home, so I rang. No chime. A buzzer that had a crude honk, like some guy on the subway blowing his nose. No answer. I waited a courteous minute, then rang again. I decided to take a quick stroll, which turned out to be not so quick because the house itself was an example of sub-urban sprawl. The entrance to the garage was just around a curve in the drive, to the side of the house. I peered into a garage window. Empty. I contemplated trotting back to the car, bumping down the

driveway, and flooring it, then calling to leave a message that I wasn't feeling well. But that wasn't the way to persuade her to help me bring Ben to justice.

What the hell had made me come here? I had to ask myself. It's not like I have some plan to break into her house. I strolled to the car and took out my tote bag, recalling I still had some yogurt-covered nuts and raisins I'd bought at Kennedy Airport that morning, convincing myself that it was a healthy snack. I was getting hungry and I couldn't wait until seven, when she'd return home and offer me hideous hors d'oeuvres, probably olives stuffed with marshmallow slivers. Immediately following that thought, I felt guilty for reacting in the snotty manner that Adam suggested was the reason half the country hated New York. The cheese sandwich Maria had given me was a perfectly fine cheese sandwich if you liked Jarlsberg, which actually I didn't. I strolled toward the back of the house.

If the fountain had been gross, the back could have qualified for federal disaster relief funds. There were hunks of grass here and there, indicating there had once been a lawn. Now it was bare, brown ground. Way off in the distance, I could see metal outdoor furniture. A table was upside down and two of the chairs lay on their sides. They looked forgotten, as if blown over by a hurricane the year before.

Then I made the mistake of looking in through a bay window into what was Maria's breakfast nook. A round table was covered with place settings of food-encrusted dishes, in various stages of disgustingness, looking as if they'd been there for days on end—she'd set a place for herself, never cleared it, and just moved on. I saw egg yolk on a blue plate and a tablespoon in the middle of the table covered in what was probably cottage cheese. A cereal box lay on its side, the flakes scattered about it. On the floor was a piece of toast with one bite taken out and an empty, twisted Equal packet. I averted my eyes, afraid of seeing the famed Florida version of the New York cockroach—probably around the size of Maria's size seven shoes—enjoying cocktail hour.

Suddenly it hit me: Maria was insane. Admittedly, *insane* wasn't a diagnosis that could be found in my mother's volume of the DSM-IV. But it was accurate. This wasn't a messy person's home. What chilled me was that she had seemed so normal at first, except for the sun worship. Then slightly off. But I had found her interesting, admired her even. Believed what she told me.

Did Maria comprehend what her place looked like? Had she invited me over in order to scare me? One thing was certain: if what I was looking for was a way to help me find justice, this was not the place to find it. For all I knew, maybe it hadn't been Hans-Bernard or Manfred-Dick who had been a threat to Ben Mattingly's ambitions. Maybe Maria had been in on it all along.

Had I been so sunstruck or focused on myself that I hadn't seen there was something profoundly wrong with her? The chaos and neglect in and around her villa was like a sign proclaiming WACKO! Smart and canny, maybe, but here was a woman who had been the mistress of one of the top men of a despised secret police force that had been famous for its viciousness. Here was the former secretary to the head of the Presidium, who had probably been intimately familiar with every sort of repression. She'd said to me, "He gave me some of his responsibilities." She might have done everything from typing out the death warrants for her fellow citizens who were trying to escape to the West to signing his name on them. Take away her power, take away her lover, bring her to a strange country and give her freedom—and what would she become?

I'm out of here. The last thing I wanted to do was deal with a person who might be crazy enough to want to sign my death warrant.

On the other hand, she wouldn't be back for more than an hour. If she was so demented and disorganized, maybe she hadn't thrown away . . . What? Information that could lead me to Lisa. Ridiculous. But maybe, and I did have a safe three-quarters of an hour. No, safer, thirty minutes. Then I could leave without risking passing her driving home—having been stood up by a client—along Plantation Way.

What I would do with that half hour was another issue. Considering that her algae fountain smelled like year-old spinach salad, I didn't want a whiff of her breakfast nook. Not that I was about to break in. She probably had a burglar alarm anyway. I had once had my character Jamie take her shoe and carefully knock out several panes of glass along with whatever those crisscross bars that separate the panes are called. That way, the window frame remained locked while she cautiously climbed through the opening she'd made. Of course, the windows Dani Barber broke were made specifically to shatter safely, and did so on the show with a nice, satisfying, Foley artist–generated sound. Also, even with her giganto implants, Dani could get through a smaller opening than I.

Just for fun, I pulled my shirttail out from my pants and sauntered over to Maria's solid-looking wood back door, with four panes of glass set into the upper part. I turned the knob with my shirt covering my hands and fingers. Naturally, it was locked. Only then did it occur to me to look around to see if I could be spotted by neighbors. No, from the villa's setting on the cul-de-sac, no other houses were even in sight.

How often would she use the back door? I wondered. She had no swimming pool in back. And the gas grill she'd mentioned wasn't even around. From the nearly bald ground that had once been lawn to the upended metal furniture, I couldn't imagine her cavorting out back. The garage was attached to the house so when she pulled in her car, she probably went through a door that led directly inside. If she had guests, which I was finding it increasingly hard to imagine, they would come in the front door. She might not even look at her back door for days at a time. Weeks.

When Maddy started college she was always babbling about life imitating art. Maybe it had been vice versa. However, glancing down at my sandals, I saw they were not imitative of art, although calling *Spy Guys* art was, admittedly, chutzpah. I longed for the steel-heeled stiletto Dani had used to knock in the windowpanes. Was I as nuts as Maria? How could I possibly be considering breaking and entering?

Without opening the buttons, I pulled my shirt over my head, wrapped it around my fist and wrist, and with all the delicacy I could muster, tried to knock out the pane of glass nearest the doorknob. I got it on the fifth try. Then, making sure once again to cover my palm and fingers, I gingerly put my hand through the hole I'd made and unlocked the door. And opened it, but only a fraction of an inch. I didn't want to be standing around in my bra if an alarm went off, so I shook out my shirt about ninety times to get rid of any fragments of glass, and put it back on.

I held my breath and pushed open the door with my hip: no alarm. That second, I realized she might have a silent alarm, which at that very moment could be lighting up the switchboard at the Tallahassee Police Department. *Run!* I commanded myself. Instead, I walked right into Maria Schneider's house.

I should have stayed outside. True, the air-conditioning was blasting so hard it was a relief from the heat, but it was so freezing I immediately longed for gloves and socks. But that was nothing compared with the kitchen. It wasn't the stench: I was breathing through my mouth so I wouldn't smell it, but nothing, including the hum of the AC and the refrigerator, could obscure the *bzzzz* of the flies in there. I stuck my head in for just an instant, of course imagining hideous, decomposing bodies, but most of the flies, which seemed to be suffering from an epidemic of obesity, were busy at the breakfast nook table. A small contingent of fly foodies had broken off and were working at the dirty dishes in the sink and open dishwasher.

I gagged, and before I could work myself up into a major nausea festival, I rushed off the other way, looking for some kind of home office, or a desk. I found it, or something like it, in a room paneled in some light wood, oak maybe, with floor-to-ceiling shelves for books and show-off stuff: those Etruscan urns or chinoiserie people bring home from vacations, or their collections of Disneyana. The shelves were almost bare. Whoever had owned the house before Maria must have had a giant TV. Hers, in the space in the middle of the shelving

unit, was of such ordinary size that it didn't even hide the electrical outlet. Besides the couch on the opposite wall from the shelves, the only furniture was a desk and chair. I glanced at my watch: I would give this five minutes.

I didn't even need that. The narrow drawer under the top of the desk was filled with narrow drawer things: pans, paper clips, a staple remover, and a couple of old floppy disks. The disks were labeled, but I had trouble reading Maria's European-style handwriting, the kind that looks neat but is close to illegible. In any case, there was no computer in the room and I wasn't about to steal the disks, though why I was suddenly having moral qualms after smashing her window and breaking into her house was beyond me. The drawer on the right had about ten unopened envelopes—including MasterCard, American Express, Southern Bell, and something from the Tallahassee traffic court. The drawer beneath was a file. All bills marked paid, alphabetized. It looked messy, though, with too many papers stuffed into a single drawer. And the wastebasket I found underneath the desk was overflowing with discarded catalogs.

Still, this wasn't the room of a deranged person, not in the way the kitchen was. She wasn't neat, but she hadn't been an utter slob. But a person has to eat every day. I, for one, could go weeks and, on one occasion, a couple of months without opening a bill. Maybe what I saw as Maria's craziness was not a long-term business. Maybe it had something to do with Lisa.

Then I realized that Maria did have to get dressed every day. So I went upstairs. She had one of those master suites: a giant bedroom with an unmade bed and discarded tissues on the floor, a blue-tiled bathroom only slightly smaller than the Mediterranean—surprisingly neat except for a sliver of dirty soap on the sink. Behind that was another enormous room—one really big closet. It was a mess. Not that she had a huge wardrobe. In fact, the room was so gigantic and her clothing so minimal that the place looked as if it had been looted. I made my way around strewn pants suits, slacks, scarves, matronly

cotton bras and panties, dressy T-shirts, and shoes all over the floor. Everything was white, gray, black, or some combination.

A few things were still on hangers, including a flapperlike dress, sleeveless, black on top, and, starting at the hips, widening into a white pleated skirt. It still had the price tag: $89, reduced from $139. There were no sports clothes in her drawers and no sneakers or flip-flops on the near-empty shoe shelves. One pair each of black flats, black heels, white flats, and brown faux alligator heels.

Except something made me look at the brown pair. These alligators weren't faux. I checked out the label. They were Manolos, so I assumed they cost about one or two thousand. I was a little taken aback, both by the intrusion of brown amid all that black, white, and gray—and by the price. I picked up a pair of Maria's flats; I'd never heard of the label, but being my mother's daughter, I had enough shoe knowledge to recognize they were fairly inexpensive and not at all stylish. And sure enough, size seven. I put the flat back down and picked up one of the alligator numbers. I, personally, could never spend that amount of money on shoes, but I had to admit, despite my husband's protectiveness toward large reptiles, they really were beautiful and I wouldn't mind having a pair.

Then I looked again. They were a size nine. Shoes that I bet would fit Lisa Golding. And if they were Lisa's, what did that mean? That Lisa and Maria had met recently? That . . . I couldn't think anymore. All that was in my head was *I'm out of here!*

And I would have been, except just then I heard a car bumping up that awful stone driveway. What in God's name could I do?

Run. Hide. And pray I could figure something out.

Chapter Thirty-two

WHILE HER CAR WAS STILL BUMPING UP THE driveway, I had broken into a run. I'd wound up in a thicket, if a thicket means shoulder-high bushes that smell like Juicy Fruit and have branches with what look like fuzzy little things on them, except the fuzzies are vicious thorns. I didn't know if this was meant to be a natural barrier, upper-middle-class barbed wire, but every part of me not covered with clothes was crisscrossed with bloody scratches.

Maria's car door opened and she called out, "Katie?" Then louder, and still louder. Closer too, as she came around the house into the back. "Katie, is that you? Did you get here early?" I couldn't see where she was because I was scrunched down sideways. If I turned my head, the thicket might stir. "I checked the pocket-book in the car out front. It is you. Oh, Katie, are you hurt? I'm so worried. Can you call out to me? Try to make some noise. Don't panic, I'll find you." Naturally I started to cry, but silently, and not the "[CRIES SILENTLY]" I've written into scripts, which always turns

out looking phony and gets cut. The crying made everything worse because there was no way I could lift up my hand through the thorny branches to wipe my nose, which I then realized was a primal instinct, because the compulsion to do it was so powerful I had to consciously fight it. My earliest ancestors may have survived because of their nose-wiping gene.

I had another fear that made me stop crying. With so many scratches emitting tiny bubbles of blood, a dark cloud of insects would zoom into the bushes to feast on me. The extended family of the flies I'd seen in the kitchen. Maria would see a great buzzing cloud rushing straight to my part of the thicket, a living arrow pointing out my hiding place. Except right after I stopped crying, my lenses got so dry it felt as if my eyelids were on the verge of being glued shut.

"Katie? Is something wrong? Please, give me some sort of signal. That's all. Then I'll go inside and call the police. They'll come and look for you, bring an ambulance."

Sometimes she came close, but then her calls to me came from a farther distance—way on the other side of the house. I tried envisioning the lay of the land, which isn't so easy when you're stuck in a thicket. Being at the end of a cul-de-sac, I took a guess that her property was pie-shaped, albeit an ineptly cut piece of pie. I had made it to the back of the crust, somewhere near the left. When she was off to the right, there were minutes that I could no longer make out her words, only the sounds of vowels urging me to reveal my location. "Aaaaaaa-eeeeee!"

For the first half hour or so, there was still a little goody-goody inside my head, hands on her hips, scolding me, *Maria's so nice and has had a hard life. She's just a bad housekeeper and look what you've done: made up a story about her being a nut job and/or a terrible person. Listen to her: She is so worried about you! You owe her an apology!*

What finally shut her up—the voice in my head, not Maria—was the realization that any person truly concerned about the welfare of

another would have called the cops. No one of goodwill would be yelling out to bargain, *Tell me where you are and then I'll call the police.*

Other than it was big, I had no sense of the size of her property or what was on it. The immediate area around the house was bare, and all I had was a vague recollection of a clump or clumps of trees in the distance. I thought I recalled the land sloping downward when I'd passed the window in her bathroom. There might just be one small grouping of trees between her and my thicket. Or the trees could be a mini-forest—maybe several mini-forests—and she could spend the time until nightfall tramping in the woods, watching out for snakes. A mistake, snake thinking. I had never recoiled at the zoo when Adam would pick one up to show me something interesting, but suddenly all I could imagine was the hideous, chokey exhalations snakes make in movies, and maybe in real life. Then giant fangs would sink into my flesh. Singing "Born in the U.S.A." inside my head did not help.

Okay, time to think. What would Maria do if she found me? Say, *Ooh, you're so scratched up. Let me get the Neosporin?* Attempt to reason with me by saying, *Ben Mattingly is a bad man and deserves to be extorted so please don't interfere with what I've been doing or plan to do?* I didn't think so. She would kill me.

Crying was too weak a word. I began weeping again, still silently, thinking how devastating my death would be to Adam. Nicky too, of course, but kids have resilience that comes in part from not being able to comprehend the true dimensions of loss. Adam was self-possessed, strong, practical—all those solid qualities that allowed his forebears to travel to the middle of nowhere, endure frightening weather and soul-wrenching loneliness, and survive. But for all his being a man from the West, there was an Eastern aspect to his view of life; he seemed to see the two of us as one soul. He had never said it directly, but over the years he told me a hundred times, with and without words, that he never felt whole until I came into his life.

I couldn't bear to think about my parents' grief. Maddy, finally the only child, would discover what I would feel if something happened to her, that we comprised some other kind of spirit. Who would Oliver hire to write season six? A jerk. Maybe it wouldn't be a jerk. The *Times* TV critic would say, Spy Guys, *old and, from the start, tired, has suddenly sprung to life . . .*

Maybe my mother would call me to chat and Adam would say, *She decided to stay overnight in Tallahassee.* Then she would call my sister and, in the course of their conversation, mention Tallahassee and—I knew I'd told Maddy about going to Cincinnati and visiting Dick Schroeder. But I couldn't remember whether I said anything about a real estate agent in Tallahassee. Had I known about Maria then? Had I told her Maria's name? As Oliver was gracious enough to point out with some frequency, "Your sense of continuity sucks the big one." But maybe I had. She'd call Adam and pour out everything about Maria—wait, they'd conference call with my parents on the line.

From somewhere between me and the house, though a blessed distance away from me, I heard her sneeze three times: "Choo, choo, choo," without any Ahs.

Adam would call me at the Holiday Inn and on my cell phone, which would ring and of course not be answered. He'd think, Something's wrong. He'd be quick-witted enough to look at my calendar on the computer and search "Tallahassee" and find Maria's name and Orange Blossom Realtors. Within thirty seconds, he and my father— because Adam would be too polite to push him off—would be on the phone with the Tallahassee Police. Soon, any minute, I'd hear sirens. Maybe not sirens, because that would tip her off.

A perfect *Spy Guys* dénouement. My specialty, unreality TV. *They all lived happily ever after.* That old saying "Where there's life there's hope" trying to fight off "Abandon hope, all ye who enter here." Of course there was also that stupid thing with feathers, but that probably only worked if you were a New England WASP.

Maria would kill me because she had killed before. Not the two men. I recalled her kitchen and decided that even before she'd gone bonkers, she'd had neither the organizational skills to arrange Bernard Ritter's murder nor the laboratory resources to pull off Dick Schroeder's—if indeed his death had been a homicide.

But could she have killed Lisa? Maria's surprise, even sadness, on hearing about Manfred-Dick's death could have been a pretense. She might have gotten his new name years earlier from Lisa. If she'd heard he'd died of a rare disease, her second (if not her first) thought would be: CIA. And to Maria, the Agency meant Ben. And with Ben came Lisa. So it was possible Maria was prepared for trouble when Lisa came by. Or maybe knowing Lisa so well, something she did might have aroused Maria's suspicion. Or something she said. Lisa had always been a lousy liar.

I couldn't get over those alligator shoes. I couldn't imagine any-one, other than a committed animal-rights type or a billionaire with incurable bunions, who would voluntarily give up a pair of Manolos like that. Okay, I had an overactive imagination; that's how I made my living. There could be an innocent explanation. Assuming the Manolos belonged to Lisa, maybe she'd brought an overnight bag to Maria's house. Say there had been an argument. Lisa stomped off and Maria, in a rage, tossed the bag. As I recalled, Lisa's clothing size had probably been a six, and Maria's was double that, and even the most optimistic I'll-start-Weight-Watchers-Monday type wouldn't have kept the clothes. But even a nonfashion person in these label-conscious times would have had trouble chucking those shoes.

But a noninnocent explanation seemed more likely to me. As I'd seen, Maria was tough stuff. And if she was suspicious of her friend Lisa? It's one thing to be a suspicious regular person—third-grade teacher, Pizza Hut franchisee. It's another to be suspicious when you'd spent a good part of your life as an insider in a totalitarian state that dealt with annoyances by exterminating annoying people.

And what about Lisa herself? Did she have a conscience? Who

knew? There might have been something within her that made her hesitate to kill a friend, if friendship can actually exist between two such defective people. *Damn, it's hard putting a gun to a girlfriend's head and pulling the trigger,* she might have confided. She could even have disclosed what happened to Dick Schroeder and Bernard Ritter to Maria, either voluntarily or under duress.

Where did I fit in? The more I considered it, the less I believed that Lisa had called me that day to set me up as a murder victim. I had written the report on the three Germans, but I'd never met them. There would have been no way I knew they'd blackmailed Ben. So I wasn't an imminent danger, just a possible glitch. Also, Ben wouldn't have ordered my death because any homicide investigator would recognize that the only curious part of my life had been when I had worked for the CIA, and he had been my boss there. No, that would be too close for comfort for him. Most likely he had dispatched Lisa to find out what I knew.

How come she hadn't followed up? She was pressed for time; she still had to get to work on Dick Schroeder. Or maybe Ben had decided getting me to talk was too chancy. It could start me remembering what I'd once forgotten. Lisa might have picked up the phone on her own, though. Either she got discouraged or Ben ordered her to leave me alone.

A crash. I heard a crash in the distance, and then almost immediately a scream. All I could imagine was that it was Maria tripping over all that awful, turned-over outdoor furniture. Broken neck, I thought, CAMERA MOVES IN. ECU HEAD AT UNNATURAL ANGLE, EYES STARING AT NOTHING. The next instant, a long and vicious curse. I couldn't tell if it was in English or German because she was too far away. And then a coughing fit, surprisingly deep and barking and long-lasting. The next thing I heard were clanks of metal. I hoped it was just that she was getting up, or righting the chairs, and not assembling an AK-47.

I'd been bent over, hiding in the thicket for so long I was afraid

that if she found me and commanded *Stand up or I'll shoot*, I wouldn't be able to. She'd shoot me through the bushes. Would she leave me there, the way she'd left her breakfast dishes? Or would she pull me out and risk scratching her arms? Maybe she had gloves that went above her elbows, like on those debutantes in 1930s movies, so it wouldn't be so hard.

If she had killed Lisa, where had she put her?

Almost dark. What time could it be? Around eight-thirty? Was there a difference between Florida and New York sunsets because New York was farther north? It was then that I realized I hadn't heard her calling me since a few minutes after the crash, the cursing, and the coughing. How long had that been? Awhile. That was all I knew, but because I hadn't been able to see my watch in the thicket, I had no way of telling whether Maria had been silent for five minutes or half an hour. But I thought the violently bright light had been softening when that happened, that time before dusk that's referred to in scripts as magic hour. Now it was so near dark that the branches all around me were an out-of-focus haze instead of individual sticks.

This would be my only chance to move. If the branches within inches of my eyes weren't clear, in moments I wouldn't be able to see a thing. Getting out could be treacherous if Maria was around. I had to stay silent but fighting my way out of the thicket—the brush and rattle of thorny branches against each other—could give me away. But maybe she had gotten hurt when she'd fallen, even a little bit, and decided to go inside and clean her wounds.

I could have stayed there debating myself, but then some large birds flew overhead. They weren't anywhere near as loud as geese. But just for an instant they were squawking enough that while it wasn't camouflage, it was all I had.

Going into the thicket hadn't been this terrible. I clawed my way out, my head down, my eyes squeezed shut. I could feel thorn after thorn seeking my skin, piercing it, then slicing, not letting go until I

pulled away. One dug into my neck right under my chin and kept cutting as I moved forward, all around the side.

I was out! I touched my neck and looked at my hand. A line of blood, but not the jugular. I was not going to bleed to death—unless something wrong had just come up with my clotting factor. Okay, I had to get to my car because I'd left the keys in there, as well as my handbag, which had my cell. I guess I was doing an *On your mark, get set* when I realized she might have gone to my car and taken the keys and my handbag too. Had I left the car door open? All I could remember was grabbing my tote because it had the raisins and nuts and telling myself, *I'll just take a quick look around.*

Decide! Of course she had gone into the car! She said she'd checked my pocketbook. And the minute I went to the front of the house, she'd see me and— So dark. Any minute she'd turn on the outside lights. I looked around. Trees. Nothing. More trees. Down the hill, the toolshed. She'd probably looked in there already. Go! I couldn't, not right then, because I had been bent over so. Standing upright enough to try to make a run for it made me groan in pain.

A light came on in the house somewhere on the first floor, and the glow lit the kitchen and the breakfast nook. Hunched over, I seized the moment to dash down the hill to the toolshed. I yanked at the door and it gave a nasal whine of protest. I tried again. Locked. So I ran behind it, praying that since I was on an even lower level, she wouldn't be able to see me from the house. I could wait there. Maybe the moon would rise. Then I could . . . I had no idea what I could possibly do.

Anyway, that's where I am now, behind the toolshed, sometimes sitting, sometimes leaning against the rough wood wall. Mosquitoes and gnats are having a banquet on the blood from my scratches. The jumbo-size insects prefer to dive-bomb and make their own puncture.

Behind me, there's some water feature. A koi pond? No, fish

would probably go belly-up from the heat before the day was out. A puddle from a semitropical rainstorm? A swamp? Alligators! I can't believe it's taken me all this time to think about alligators, especially after seeing Lisa's shoes! And I also absolutely cannot believe I once read somewhere what to do if you think an alligator is going to attack you. Now I can't remember if it's stay still or back off slowly or run as fast as you can.

Why hasn't she turned the outside lights on? Can it be that her life is as bad as her kitchen and that burned-out bulbs weren't replaced?

Some things sliding across the tops of my feet feel like something other than insects, but I can't even think about what they could be. Whatever energy I have left I'm spending smacking them away. Mortal peril is one thing. Revolting, abominable-beyond-all-imagining animal life is another. It's so hard keeping control and not screeching with revulsion. I'm scared that as the night goes on, I'll let my defenses down for a second and feel something unspeakable, like a bat alighting on top of my head, and I will scream so loud and long in horror that she'll know my precise location.

Oh God, the outside lights just came on. She's back, searching. A flashlight is beaming a V of illumination that I can see moving side to side. The central part of the backyard is lit, so she's heading toward the side, to some trees. I guess she's planning to search the entire part of her property that's dark with her damned high-beam flashlight. She'll walk slowly, methodically, and eventually she'll come to me.

What is Adam going to think when he keeps calling my cell, then the hotel, and I don't answer? *Oh, she went to a movie?* How long have I been here now? I should have done something smart, like sing the score of *Grease* or *Annie* in my head so I would know, well, it's been . . . however long a musical score is, forty-five minutes, an hour. Then I could say to myself with some confidence that it's three in the morning and sunrise is a couple of hours away.

She's coming closer. Close enough that I can hear her cough. Then a big-time sniffle. If she has allergies, why doesn't she carry tis-

sues? Is she so crazy she can't think to blow her own nose? Will she come behind the toolshed? Does she know right behind it is some kind of water? She could tell herself that I wouldn't be hiding submerged in a swamp. Maybe she won't say that because it isn't a swamp after all, that thing less than a foot behind me. Just a puddle from after a hard rain.

Chapter Thirty-three

I've got to get out of here, now! I can't really see, but at least I can feel. Well, the one thing I can see is Maria, or at least her flashlight. The beam arcs back and forth, first on the ground, then rises a few feet before she lowers it again. Not that I have any idea of what to do if I can make it back toward the front of the house, but hopefully something will occur to me along the way. That may be the wrong usage of *hopefully,* but I don't give a shit.

I'm past the toolshed, climbing. I turn for a second to look behind, but there's just blackness. Every once in a while she coughs, and a couple of times I heard her gathering something up in her throat and then spitting, loud and defiant. Maybe she thinks that will make me abandon all caution and start screeching, *That is revolting!* My father said he understood how much the city had changed when signs in the subway cars went from PLEASE DO NOT EXPECTORATE to DO NOT SPIT.

Still walking. What possessed me to put on sandals this morning?

Except in the immediate aftermath of 9/11, people usually didn't get dressed assuming that later in the day a catastrophe would occur and they'd be better off with sneakers. But how could I have forgotten that in going through the metal detector at the airport I'd have to take off my shoes and walk barefoot, an experience vile beyond belief? Anyway, the soles of my sandals are completely soaked through and will probably disintegrate.

Forget shoes. What am I going to do? Make as wide an arc around her disgusting villa as possible. Somehow, find if there's a way to check my car, see if the key and my handbag are still in it. Unlikely. How could she not take them? I'll have to see if getting close to the car would expose me too much. I can't see the flashlight anymore. Maybe I'm just at a bad angle. Is Maria still outside? Did she go in?

I'm in a bunch of trees. A copse? Is that the word? There's a little more light out, but it doesn't stop me from tripping over . . . What? I get up, brush off the damp dirt. But the dirt shouldn't be this moist. Damp, yes, enough to seep into my sandals over the hours, but this place is different. A slight rise in the soil, that's all. Just not as packed down as the rest of the ground. But my body knows what that wetness is about before my mind does. And the rise. Soil that's been dug up. I heave, then heave again. Nothing comes up except acid. Lisa is right beneath me. How do I know? I don't. Yet I know. I rush on, my arms flailing in front and to the sides in the blackness.

Now I can make out something: I'm about two hundred feet from the house, not that I really comprehend what two hundred feet looks like, but it sounds like a reasonable distance. I'm amazed I was able to get as far as I did when I heard Maria's car coming up the drive. If I keep along this circle, there are a bunch of trees way behind the overturned furniture that I can hide behind. But before I come to that, there's that frighteningly long, naked space of the backyard that except for a few tufts of dying grass is just flat, packed dirt.

Should I tiptoe or run for it? Maybe it doesn't matter, because she's waiting for me near the front of the house and she'll get me the minute I come around from the side and move to my car. Even if I forget about the car, and make a giant loop, there's no way she won't see me.

Forget tiptoeing. I've lost all track of time. Assuming I get to where I can make out my car, birds could be chirping, greeting the bright morning. But I've got to do it. Now!

I pray it was only a piece of rotting fruit I just stepped on. But I'm not grossed out; I'm too hysterical. My heart is speeding, and it's not from my running. Her semicircular drive, with the fountain in the center of it, is a small hill. I think I may have run a little too far. Now I'll have to go back up, but what do I care? Is that my car? Yes. Maria's too. In the darkness, it looms like an ocean liner beside my tugboat of a rental car. I guess you need a big car to take clients around. I can't see her anywhere. I don't know if that's the good news or the bad news.

I'm so out of breath, almost to my car, trying to breathe through my nose so I don't wheeze or pant. Crouched down now, near the driver's door, which is the side that doesn't face the house. Villa. What if it's like a slasher movie and when I rise up to look inside the car window, she'll pop up with a hunting knife? I'm not really sure what a hunting knife looks like. Move it!

They're gone. My handbag and the car key. The buttons are down, so she even locked the car. I have to run for it. I hope I don't collapse before I can get to the nearest neighbor's and start scream-ing. What if the neighbors are away and my screaming focuses her and she jumps in her car—

Oh, that'll be great, running down her endless cobblestone drive-way in a pair of sandals in the blackest part of night. And if Maria comes chasing after me with her flashlight with its eternal-life battery or, worse, in her car with the headlights on high beam, I'm as good as dead. No, just dead. But maybe her battery has died after all. I haven't

seen its arcing light in . . . How should I know? It's too dark to see my watch.

I've got to get to her car. When I first heard her get out of it and start calling for me as she moved around the house to the back . . . Did I hear the door actually shut? I can't remember. Now, still crouched down, I rush from my car to hers. I probably look like Groucho Marx. The driver's door is open a few inches, as if she'd already been running and didn't wait to see if it closed. I grope along the dashboard, past the steering wheel. The key. Oh my God, it's in the ignition! But the inside light isn't on, so maybe the battery had died. But I'm getting in. I don't care. I'll lock all the doors. What if the car won't start? She'll come out with a shotgun, blast me, and tell the police she caught me trying to steal the car. Wait, I know, I'll—

Dear God, she's here! Right behind me, grabbing hold of my hair with both her hands, nails slicing into my scalp just before she clenches her fists. I'm screaming like I'm the crazy one. She's not making a sound. What's she going to do? I grab her wrists but her arms are so drenched with sweat I can't get a grip. "Please, Maria, please just listen. Please." Amazingly, she eases up but my hair is still in her clutches, so much so that my head is pulled back at a horrible, throat-baring angle. I try to remember all the research I did on hand-to-hand combat for *Spy Guys,* all the martial arts people who came to coach Dani and Javiero, but my mind is too overcome by terror to do any remembering. "Listen to me," I plead, "I have information—"

"Shut up!" All my life, I've seen movies with evil characters or crazy characters, but I've never heard a voice so harsh, so filled with hate. "Give me Ben's home address," she orders, "and don't tell me you don't know it!"

I don't. Yet before I can even say a word, she's pushing my head forward. I'm almost doubled over. What's she— She's trying to smash my head against the car. I shout, "Thirty-seven Lincoln Street," praying that sounds Washingtonian enough to satisfy her. Maybe. For

now, she seems to have stopped trying to crack open my skull, but that doesn't seem cause enough for optimism.

"Corner?" She demands. *Corner?* I think stupidly. "What's the cross street?"

Does she think I'm fucking MapQuest? "I don't know," I cry. "It's in Georgetown."

And now she's at it again. My head bangs against the driver's window. Not too hard, but now she's doing it again and— She stops. A horrible coughing fit. I crash my elbow backward into her ribs, except her ribs aren't there because that second she lets go, she's coughing so hard— What kind of person doesn't cover her mouth when she coughs? I pull open the door of her car some more. If I can get in fast enough and lock it, at least I'll have some temporary protection.

She's moving again, and grabs me, but this time all she's got is the front of my shirt. Either it's close to dawn or my eyes are getting used to the darkness, but I can see her now. Her face shines with sweat, her breathing is labored. The heat from her hand grasping my shirt burns into my chest. "Maria, just listen for a second. Did Lisa inject you with anything? Or maybe give you something to eat or drink? Because if she did, it might be what she gave Manfred, and I can tell you—"

"Shut up!" She's shaking me, and the strength of that one arm is incredible. My head is bubbling back and forth. She shrieks, "You're all so stupid it makes me sick!"

I would think, Great, I've engaged her in conversation. That's what you're supposed to do in hostage situations to remind the crazy person of your humanity, but the crazy person has let go of my shirt only to reach for my throat with both hands. A prayer, I have to say a prayer before—

Wait, that martial arts guy, Bob, Bob Wyatt, who taught Dani how to land a punch. He kept after her about . . . What? Aligning the hand, wrist, and arm so the force gets transmitted up the entire arm

into the body, some law of physics. Except her hands are around my neck and her thumbs are pressing into my—

I raise my knee and kick her with all my might where I'd kick a guy in the balls and she's so surprised, maybe hurt, that for a second she drops her hands and—*align, align*—I punch. And it's like something on *Spy Guys*: She drops to the ground. Except not slowly like on the show, just *klonk!* she's down. The side of her head hits the cobblestone and actually makes a sound and I feel sick. I realize it's not a knockout punch because she's moaning, but I'm in her car.

Turn key, engine starts. I put it in drive and I'm careening down the cobblestones, trying to close the door at the same time. I don't care, I will not stop and put on my seat belt. I will not look in the rearview mirror. I don't want to see her picking herself up, rubbing her head, then running to get the keys to my rented car.

There could be a car chase. I grew up in the city. I'm not the world's greatest driver. Did they have an autobahn in East Germany? I'm off her driveway now, onto Plantation Way, and I floor it. Her pink tote bag is on the passenger seat, but I will not check if her cell phone is in it so I can call Adam. I will not put on the headlights or step on the brake unless it's absolutely necessary. All I can do is drive.

Chapter Thirty-four

I DID NOT FLY HOME INTO ADAM'S ARMS. THAT was because as I turned off Plantation Way and resumed going seventy-five miles per hour, two thoughts hit me. Number one was that I was driving a stolen car. I slowed to fifty-five and began checking the rearview mirror every ten or twenty seconds. Number two was that there was no point heading for the Tallahassee airport because my only photo ID—my driver's license—was in my wallet, which was in my handbag, which was probably in Maria Schneider's house. There was no point going to the Delta Airlines counter and sobbing out an elaborately crafted tale about a stolen handbag. At that very moment, Maria could be on the phone with the police filing a complaint that I committed God knows what crime. Unlikely, but I couldn't risk it.

Her gas tank was nearly empty. I pulled into a vacant lot behind a lumberyard and picked up her tote bag. Lots of used tissues, so I pulled down the sleeve of my shirt to go through it. Orange stuff,

what appeared to be many smashed-up Cheez Doodles. Six dollars and change in a purse. Visa and American Express cards, which I didn't dare use. Her cell phone was there, but when I turned it on, it signaled "low battery" and died.

Somehow I found my way to a service station near the main highway and asked a truck driver which was closer, Miami or Atlanta. He looked like a guy who would have chuckled under normal circumstances. But I noticed he was checking out my scratches. I realized how awful I must look when he asked, with a gentleness I hadn't previously associated with vast numbers of tattoos, "Do you need any help?"

"I'm all right. Thanks, though."

"If you're in trouble, I can give you some money to tide you over."

He wore a dark green uniform with short sleeves. Right above his shirt pocket was an embroidered logo, BOSTON STREET ICED TEA, in block letters, each letter a different color, deliberately friendly. The name tag on the pocket said Andrew William Turner. I thanked him profusely and told him I'd been camping and stumbled into some brambles—a scenario that would surprise no one who knew me. Still, I didn't think Andrew Turner bought it.

"Do you need money?" he asked. I wouldn't have even thought about my seventy dollars and credit cards currently residing at Maria's until I was faced with paying for gas. "I think . . . I need money for gas. That's all." He reached into the pocket of his green cotton slacks and pulled out a wallet, its leather cracked with age. He opened it and pulled out three twenties. As an afterthought, he handed me another ten.

"I don't have words enough to thank you," I told him. I began to cry, but added, "If you give me your address, Mr. Turner, I'll get the money back to you right away."

"No need."

"Really, I—"

"Do unto others . . ." he said. Then he added: "I bet you any

amount of money that you're the kind of girl who would do this for someone."

"Yes, I would." I wiped my eyes with the points of my shirt collar. "Sorry. It was a rough night."

"I figured. Now Atlanta is closer than Miami by a lot. You basically want to go I-75 north." Before I could ask for his address again, he said, "You take care now," and got into his truck. "God bless." Then waved good-bye.

Even with the flickering, yellowish light in the gas station's ladies' room, I could see the wreck he'd pitied. Besides looking as if I'd gotten into a literal catfight, with long scratches all over my face, hands, and feet—some of them more like gouges—my cheek was swollen and discolored. Noting that my shirt was several degrees beyond filthy, I changed breakfast plans from a Burger King feast to a couple of granola bars and Diet Cokes I bought when I paid for the gas. Then, my hands shaking, I used the pay phone and called home. Adam was not only there, he was as beside himself as I'd ever known him.

"Hi."

"Katie!"

"I'm okay. I'm sure you called, and I know you must have been worried, but—"

"Where were you all night? Katie, for Christ's sake, I had the hotel manager go into your room to see if you were all right!" His voice was thin, as if he couldn't get enough air into his chest. Raspy, too. He was exhausted. "I looked up that Tallahassee woman on your Outlook, that Maria whatever, but she wasn't answering. I left message after message."

"I'm sorry. I'm so sorry. It was terrible. She turned out to be crazy and—I'm sorry. She took my handbag, so I don't have any driver's license or credit cards or anything. I don't have my cell. I don't know how I'm going to get home. I want to come home."

I broke down again, and he said, "Don't worry. Calm down, sweetheart. Give me a minute to think."

"You have a perfect right to—"

"Take it easy, okay?"

"You can hold this against me for the rest of your life and I wouldn't blame you."

"I don't operate that way."

"I know. Sorry, Adam. I look scary. I'm scratched all over. I have a shiner, and the side of my face is swollen."

"You'll be fine. Where are you now?"

"In a gas station somewhere in Tallahassee. But I can't stay here." I cupped the mouthpiece of the phone and whispered, "I stole her car."

I heard something that sounded suspiciously like a laugh, but quickly Adam said, "Okay, the biggest city near there is probably—"

"Atlanta. I asked a truck driver."

"Good. We should head to a good-size city so I won't have to wait all day on a layover between flights. We want to be together as soon as possible."

"Oh yes."

"This is what I'll do. I'll get the first direct flight to Atlanta and bring your passport. Are you okay to drive there? It's probably a couple of hundred miles. That could take about five hours."

"If I get tired, I'll pull over and nap," I told him. "But I'll call and let you know. Oh, could you bring me some clean clothes? And sneakers and a pair of my tennis socks."

In Atlanta, I parked Maria's tank of a car in a long-term parking lot at the airport. After a three-second debate, I decided to leave the keys in it and give some stranger the chance to steal it. For good measure, I threw in her pink straw tote bag. As I was getting out, though, I had another debate. Should I look in the trunk? What if I'd been wrong and I hadn't tripped over Lisa's grave? What if she was in the trunk—along with my fingerprints all over the car?

The words "God forbid!" burst out of me, just the way my father's mother, Grandma Rosie, would have blared them, at full volume, in case God was hard of hearing. If Lisa was in the trunk, I

didn't want to see her. The only thing I wanted in the world was Adam. He wouldn't have any trouble looking in the trunk; in his whole life, only two things had grossed him out—an African millipede and anything crawling with maggots. My list was probably a thousand items, and included the slimy edges of overripe honeydew.

I compromised by taking the keys and opening the trunk about an inch. Tentatively, I sniffed. Trunk odor, not dead person odor. I opened it a little more. Nothing, just a pair of black flats in a paper shopping bag and a bunch of maps in a small brown grocery store carton. Unlike her kitchen, this at least showed a capacity for organization. I opened the trunk lid all the way. A lantern flashlight. A stack of manila envelopes, the size to hold regular typing paper, held together by a thick rubber band—probably one envelope per client. I said to myself, *Don't*. Then I dumped her black flats, stuck the envelopes into her shopping bag, and put her keys back into the ignition.

Adam was already there, waiting in front of a Cinnabon on Concourse A. I made a major "Don't hug me, I'm filthy" protest, which I knew he would ignore. I was too wiped to refuse when he bought me two Cinnabons and a container of milk—whole milk. While I was eating, he checked out my scratches so gently that I could understand why orangutans gazed at him with eyes filled with love.

He pronounced I was a mess, unfit to travel. He made a call and got a room at a hotel five minutes from the airport, one of those places with an atrium where corporate travelers who hate their jobs stay. After I took both a bath and a shower, Adam dressed all my scrapes and scratches with some ointment he'd brought along. Then, because I'd fallen at least once or twice, he gave me a tetanus shot. "Get some sleep now," he said.

"You brought down a syringe?"

"Yes. From what you said, it sounded like you must have gotten some soil in the scratches."

"Is the tetanus stuff for people or—"

"I'm not sure if it's tetanus immune globulin. Some guy was about

to throw it onto the subway tracks, but I bought it from him for two bucks."

"So it's for people."

"Of course it's for people."

"Let me tell you about Maria. I got to her place and she wasn't there yet—" My thoughts were so jumbled I couldn't arrange them in order. All that seemed to come up clearly was random sounds, like Maria's car bumping up the stone driveway and the clatter of metal against metal when she fell over the outdoor furniture. The only image I could conjure was one of the absolute blackness of the moonless night.

"You'll tell me later." He pulled down the blanket. "Get some sleep."

"Is it tomorrow that we have to drive up to camp?"

"The day after. Your parents will drive up separately. Maddy may go with them."

"You're kidding."

"I spoke to her before my plane took off. I asked her to pretend to be you and report your driver's license and credit cards lost. When we were about to hang up, she said she wanted to see Nicky and would hitch a ride with your parents. Go to sleep, Katie."

The sheets were probably polyester-blend hotel sheets, nothing fancy, but as I slid under the cover they felt utterly smooth and cool, like the highest-count Egyptian cotton. "How can I explain what I look like?" I could feel myself slipping into sleep, as if I'd taken some fast-acting and marvelous drug. "Nicky will be shocked."

"I e-mailed him this morning that you'd gone berry picking with a bunch of your friends and that you fell in a raspberry patch and got scratched up. I told him not to be surprised if you look like you went one-on-one with a mountain lion."

"Don't let me sleep too long because then I won't be able to fall asleep tonight."

I didn't wake up until the next morning. Thankfully, Adam had

remembered to bring my sneakers and socks. And despite my worst fears, he hadn't packed a silk skirt and black lace camisole to go with the sneakers. Sensible blue pants and a white cotton sweater, an outfit he could understand because it was the female equivalent of what he would wear. And best of all, he handed me my passport. I could go home.

On the flight back to New York, I gave him the "I'll understand if you hate me for the rest of your life for keeping all this terrible stuff hidden from you" preface before giving him some sense of what I'd discovered. I found myself, though, jumping back and forth from the three Germans to Lisa and Ben to Jacques and Huff. I kept using the names Hans and Bernard and Manfred and Dick interchangeably and confusingly, so Adam had me make a chart on the back of my boarding pass that looked like the dramatis personae listed before a play: "Hans Pfannenschmidt—comm. party liaison to crim. justice, later Bernard Ritter, Minneap. brake fluid sales, stabbed."

Somewhere, probably over Pennsylvania, I asked him, "Are you angry?"

"I've been in your family long enough to say 'at some level.' Why couldn't you come to me right away?"

"I don't know. Partly because it was more an obsession than a problem to solve. Partly because you made it clear, or at least that's how I took it, that you had heard enough about it and that I should forget it. Get a life. Maybe I was wrong, but that's how I read your reaction."

"That was pretty much it. So I guess I should apologize to you for being, whatever. Insensitive."

"Okay."

"I'm sorry," Adam said.

"Accepted." I kissed his cheek. "Remember that being insensitive isn't as big a deal as what I did."

"I guess not. But don't start up with that 'You're going to hate me for the rest of my life.' You know I don't hold grudges."

I did know. We gave each other that married couple public kiss with puckered-up lips accompanied by a smacking sound. Then he picked up his Harlan Coben novel and I reached into Maria's shopping bag for the *Gourmet* I'd bought at the airport, figuring that would take my mind off all that had happened in Tallahassee—unless it was an issue devoted to the art of the cheese sandwich. Except what I touched first was the rubber band around those manila envelopes I'd found in Maria's trunk. I pulled out the tray from the arm of the seat, put the rubber band around my wrist, and picked up the first one. Clasped but not sealed.

Adam looked over. "What's that?"

Funny, but my instinct was to get creative. I fought it. "I found them in the trunk of her car."

"You just took them?" I nodded. He gave me slightly raised eyebrows that I interpreted as "Thou shalt not steal" and went back to his book.

I opened the envelope and found a sheaf of paper that had nothing to do with real estate. All in German. Single-spaced. It looked boring. Most likely typed rather than computer-generated because it had that fuzzy quality from a tired old typewriter ribbon. Maybe she had written her memoirs after all. I didn't even attempt to translate any of it but quickly leafed through a few more pages. Boring, boring, and then I stopped. Letterhead. It said *Ministerium für Staatssicherheit*. Ministry of State Security. The Stasi. In the upper left-hand corner was a small logo, a bare arm holding up a rifle and bayonet, the rifle serving as a pole displaying the East German flag.

"Oh boy!" I said and handed it to Adam, who reluctantly put down his book. "Can you read it?" He had studied German because it was a requirement for his doctorate, and could read 100 percent more than I could, which, while being nothing to be ashamed about, did not qualify him to become a Thomas Mann scholar.

" 'State Ministry—' "

"I know. It's the Stasi, their secret police force."

" 'The something or other was followed to . . . a store in the Mitte district. There he meets, met, something Manfred Gottesman.' " Adam took the list I'd drawn up from his book, where he'd put it to mark his page. "That's one of your guys," he said.

"I know. Can you see . . ." I ran my finger slowly down the page until it came to *Benton Mattingly*.

I felt as if I'd been away for ages instead of just two days, but rather than go home, hug the dogs, and get together the books, cube-in-a-cube brainteaser, and swim goggles I'd bought for Nicky, I dragged Adam to the bank and opened a safe deposit box in both our names. I put all the manila envelopes into it—the ones with all the Stasi files on Ben, including Manfred's dictated memoranda with his signature at the bottom of each, the party's own reports, written by Hans, and my personal favorite, the envelope of photographs of Ben and Manfred together. Six of them were taken at the same time, one right after the other. They were seated at a small round table inside a café. From their sequence, it appeared that Manfred was taking a regular white business envelope out of a big, hard-sided briefcase, peering inside it, licking it to seal it, handing it to Ben, Ben holding it between thumb and index finger, staring at it as if it were a small menu, and finally putting it into his inside jacket pocket.

"You know what it is," I'd said to Adam, "but someone could look at it and say the order was reversed, and that Ben was the one handing over the envelope to Hans."

My husband, fortunately, was the man who spent a good part of his professional life looking at cells under a microscope and discerning subtle differences among them. "Look," he said. Above what I guessed was a coffee bar, there were two boxes of cookies, evidence of the scarcity of consumer goods in East Germany, and above that a row of old black-and-white photographs of men boxing. On top of those was a large portrait-style photo of Erich Honecker, the head of

the East German government, who had resigned in mid-October 1989. And over that, almost at the top, was about three-quarters of wall clock. The top of it was cut off by the frame of the picture. Adam pointed to it.

"What?" I demanded. "What are you pointing at?"

"Look close," he said. I squinted, but was still mystified. "The clock has a second hand. The pictures start with Manfred digging in his briefcase. See? The one with Ben putting the envelope into his pocket is three or four seconds later."

I'd imagined visiting day at camp so often that I didn't even need a DVD of it: Nicky running with outstretched arms, Nicky showing me a lamp base he'd carved and stained, Nicky sailing a Sunfish, separated only by years from crewing on the boat that would win the 2020 America's Cup.

Not quite. My DVD did not have footage of grandparents and assorted other relatives waiting behind a line made by two traffic cones and thirty feet of string. My parents, both wearing white, looked ready for an afternoon of croquet or a Ralph Lauren ad. Maddy was in full makeup—lip gloss—and had on black cropped pants, a blue Henley shirt, and a *Poets & Writers* baseball hat. After kissing me almost everyplace I wasn't scratched, my mother held my hands a lot, peered into my eyes, checked my scratches one after another without asking me if I was okay; then, as if I were unable to speak for myself, she asked Adam, "Did she get a tetanus shot?"

My father refrained from his usual bear hug, kissed my forehead, and offered to send Adam and me on a cruise of the Greek islands so I could recuperate. When I told him I was fine, he said, "Trust me, whatever you've been through, you don't get fine just like that."

My sister gave my hand a gentle squeeze, then started crying and hugged me. This triggered my mother, who sobbed embarrassingly

loudly. She embraced us both at the same time, no doubt with equal compression. Then she reapplied her eyeliner.

At noon, Lionheart's campers, fat, medium, and downright trim, were released from their bunks and variously raced, ran, and galumphed to the other side of the string. Nicky? Nicky? At least a quarter of the boys' hair was sun-bleached, the way Nicky's got every summer. I didn't recognize him at first because he looked so much taller then he had just the month before and he'd slimmed down, so now he resembled someone else's husky football player son. I couldn't believe he was only ten years old.

No outstretched arms. He sauntered over, allowing us time to admire him and, finally, to hug and kiss him. "Hey," he said to me as we strolled toward the picnic tables, "why were you picking raspberries?"

"I don't know. It seemed like a summery, back-to-the-land thing to do."

"Mom, stick to Fairway from now on," he advised.

We ate grilled chicken, grilled vegetables, and fruit with lots of flies. We watched Nicky play tennis and shoot a rifle. We admired the stay-fit Web site he was designing, Nicky's Slim Pickings, and the mahogany-stained mini-cabinet to store his iPod and CDs—with wood pegs to hold earphones. We visited his bunk and gave him his gifts under the watchful eye of a counselor guarding against contraband Reese's Peanut Butter Cups. At parting, back near the parking lot, Adam and I got all choked up. My parents had that beatific *our grandson* look. My sister's eyes were glazed with dread at the prospect of the six-hour ride home with my parents, so I took pity on her and invited her to drive with us. Nicky kissed us perfunctorily, said, "See you in three and a half weeks," and moseyed back to his bunk.

Chapter Thirty-five

WEEKS EARLIER, WHEN I HAD SPOKEN WITH Constance Cincotta, the Washington lawyer who had spent twenty years in the Office of the General Counsel in the CIA, she'd told me there wasn't anything she could find out about why I'd been fired. Nothing could penetrate the Agency's wall of silence.

On Monday I spent two hours on the phone with her telling her what had happened. I admitted that I'd gotten some "guidance" from a couple of friends, but I wouldn't give her Jacques's or Huff's names. Not that I didn't trust in the attorney-client privilege, but I wouldn't name names.

Then I hit the bank vault and spent the rest of the day in the apartment, scanning all the documents and photographs I got from Maria's trunk, and e-mailed them to Constance. Then, just because I would have had Jamie do it in a script, I burned a CD of all the data. I hid it in the bottom of the bin where I kept the dogs' kibble and brought the manila envelopes back to the bank.

On Tuesday and Wednesday, Constance and two of her associates were at work on my case. On Thursday morning I was in her office, handed over to her the manila envelopes, and got many receipts for the papers and photographs. She put them all in her law firm's safe and together we drove to the Central Intelligence Agency.

Walter McKey, the general counsel of the CIA, was the most distinguished-looking man I'd ever seen. He could have been cast as president, at least in an era before presidents came from the South and pretended to be modest. He had steel gray hair neatly combed back and an exquisitely trimmed steel gray mustache. His voice was deep and so assuring it made me want to salute. Plus he looked me in the eye and said, "I'm sorry."

My lawyer, Constance Cincotta, had another great voice, full and melodic. "There's a reason for sorrow. This is a blight on the Agency. Even more, it has been a blight on Ms. Schottland's life for fifteen years."

"I understand," Walter McKey said.

Maybe being a lawyer wasn't enough. You had to mesmerize. To get hired for the general counsel's office, you had to outdo Churchill in the vocal department. For a couple of minutes, I'd been so entranced listening to them that I had trouble concentrating on what they were actually saying. Also, just being back at the CIA had shaken me. We were in a small conference room, sitting around an oval table. Walter McKey had held my chair for me, which I'd thought extremely gallant at the moment. It probably was, but I was also directly opposite a giant CIA seal on the opposite wall, and its eagle, looking left, was giving all its attention to McKey.

"What can you do to make it better?" Constance asked him.

I wanted to say, *Listen, just get all the bad stuff out of my record and we'll call it quits. But fair is fair. You can at least tell me what you're going to do about Ben Mattingly. Can you do anything?* But

lawyers had to cover all possibilities. It would not have been seemly for me to say, *Hey, cut to the chase.*

At this moment, they turned to Joanne Sexton, the representative from the Directorate of Intelligence. She'd been notably silent up to this point, although she had said hi when we were introduced and gave me a hearty but not bone-crushing handshake. From her hi, I guessed she couldn't make a career from her voice alone. As she pronounced the word "Hah" followed by an incandescent smile, I imagined her spending her early years as the happiest cheerleader at Tuscaloosa High School before deciding to become a substantive person and serve her country. "You seem to be settled and successful in your career, your life in New York. Am I mistaken? Are you thinking you might be interested in coming back here?"

"No. I have a good life where I am."

"Ms. Schottland's termination, her consequent inability to find another job—all of that cannot be brushed aside," Constance declared. She gripped the edge of the table and leaned toward Walter McKey. "We would expect some sort of gesture."

"Connie," he replied, "we have a proposal." Joanne Sexton nodded with great enthusiasm, as if Tuscaloosa had scored a tiebreaking touchdown in the last three seconds of the big game.

"Please, go on."

"Everything in Ms. Schottland's records in regard to any complaints and to the termination will be expunged. Her records would reflect the fine work she did during her tenure at the Agency, and will include a letter of commendation signed by the director of intelligence. We will also strongly recommend that she be awarded a presidential citation for gallantry and meritorious service to the country to reflect the work she did in bringing this matter to our attention."

"What are the chances of such a recommendation being honored?" Constance inquired politely.

"Very high," Walter McKey said.

"That means she'll get it," added Joanne Sexton. "The presidential

citation will be a matter of public record, although naturally the details must remain classified."

"Katie?" Constance asked. "Would you like to think this over?"

"No. That sounds good. It's justice being done and I'm fine with that."

"Do you have any questions?"

"Yes. Are there any consequences for me because of breaking into Maria Schneider's house?" I paused. "Oh, and stealing her car and taking the stuff from her trunk?"

"None," Walter McKey said. He smoothed his perfect mustache and added, "We've already taken care of that."

"And what about . . ." I took a deep breath. Every once in a while—well, five or six times a day—I'd be overcome with a flash of fear. Post-traumatic stress: it's one thing to give it a name, another to feel your guts liquify every few hours. "What about Maria Schneider?"

"She'll be indicted for murder," Walter McKey said. "They found material under Lisa Golding's fingernails. Skin cells that match Maria Schneider's DNA."

"So they found Lisa," I managed to say.

"Yes. Your assumption was correct. She was buried there."

I shuddered visibly. Joanne Sexton asked, "Do you want any details?"

"Yes."

"The local medical examiner said there had been a fight. Ms. Golding was choked to death. That's really all they know at this point. Maria Schneider's house was in such a chaotic state that the authorities are still trying to piece together where the murder occurred."

"What about Benton Mattingly?" I asked.

"We have to proceed judiciously," Walter McKey said.

"What does that mean?" Constance asked.

"The scans of the documents and those photographs you for-

warded to us seem authentic, though of course we have to examine the originals. They're in your possession now?" Constance nodded. "Even if she would cooperate with us, it's doubtful Maria Schneider has direct knowledge about the agreements and the payoffs. She's no good to us. Presumably we will have talks with the German government to see if there are any former East German officials who have firsthand knowledge about the arrangements between Benton Mattingly and Gottesman and Pfannenschmidt. That could be of enormous value if it were to come to a trial."

"For murder?" I asked.

"With Lisa Golding dead, it's going to be either difficult or impossible to tie Mattingly to anything that happened to Pfannenschmidt." He glanced down at a yellow legal pad. "Ritter," he amended. "As to Richard Schroeder's death, we've been told it would be close to impossible to prove it a homicide."

"I'm no lawyer," Joanne Sexton said cheerfully, "but the documents and photographs look to be darn good evidence of treason."

"Treason is a capital offense," Constance remarked pleasantly.

Walter McKey reached toward the middle of the conference table, pulled a law book toward him, and cleared his throat. "Section 3281 of the U.S. Code states," he said to me in his glorious voice, "'An indictment for any offense punishable by death may be found at any time without limitation.'"

"So there's no statute of limitations on treason?" I asked.

"None," he said. "Now, I must be up front with you. I've spoken with some colleagues in the Department of Justice, and there are no guarantees. You and Connie will be speaking with some people at the FBI, and your evidence, what you found in Maria Schneider's car, would be the basis for any case. Preliminary translations of those documents are damning. But this is where Germany comes in: to make a capital case, the Bureau needs to come up with some testimony that what was in the envelope Benton Mattingly pocketed was, in fact, money."

"That means Mattingly's lawyers could work out a deal," Constance said. "The government might not seek the death penalty, though of course they would use that as a bargaining tool."

"But it's good-bye secretary of commerce," I said.

"At the very least," Joanne Sexton said. "And with luck, hello United States Penitentiary at Lewisberg. I must say, the U.S. Attorney is an eager beaver, and though it's unseemly for me to say so, I'm just thrilled with his determination."

Walter McKey cleared his throat. "I detest gossip." I waited, but when he didn't say anything more, I nodded. Now that we were in agreement, he went on: "I have heard Mrs. Mattingly is quite unhappy with the entire turn of events vis-à-vis her husband. Excuse me, I am not being precise. She is unhappy *with* her husband. Murmurings of treason can put a crimp in a couple's social schedule. She is said to have suggested that he take a hike."

"You're not cut out for this," Jacques observed a few days later.

"Maybe not," I observed, "but you'll notice I'm still alive."

"I noticed. How are you doing?"

"Same as yesterday. Fine."

"Bullshit," Jacques said. He and Huff had been calling me every day. The day before, he had stopped asking permission to be crude.

I sat in the glow of my yellow toile office. Downstairs, they were shooting the season's final episode of *Spy Guys* and then we'd be on hiatus. "Well, that night in Florida was not a night I'd care to repeat," I admitted. "Speak to anyone interesting lately?"

"Yes. A few people. Listen, remember right after you got back from Tallahassee, I told you that one of them—Mattingly or Maria—would be dead within two weeks? They'd be trying to kill each other and the worst one would probably be the one to survive?"

"I remember."

"Well, Maria Schneider was taken to the hospital three days ago."

"Oh God, I knew it!" But then I thought to ask: "With what?" Along with pens, I always kept a few pencils in a yellow mug on my desk. I didn't use them except to chew on during tense conversations, usually with QTV executives. I found myself gnawing with frightening enthusiasm.

"A fever of unknown origin. You know how I read it? Somehow, your friend Lisa got to her before she got to Lisa. What did we say when we were kids? 'There's a fungus among us.'"

I put down the pencil. "Where is Maria? I mean, do you know the name of the hospital? I guess . . . I guess there's a moral obligation to call them and tell them about the blastomycosis that Dick Schroeder died from. If that's what it is. I actually tried to tell her, because she was coughing and cold-y, but she wasn't in a listening mood. Maybe it's something else, something peculiar to her area, but—"

"No, it turned out to be the blastomycosis. Sort of trips off the tongue, doesn't it?"

"How is she?" I asked.

"Dead," Jacques replied. I picked up the pencil, but I was way past chewing. "This morning. Huff and I assumed you would bring up the moral obligation business."

"How could I not? I mean, I can't tell you how relieved I am that she's dead, but I couldn't have *not* called."

"That's why we didn't tell you until now."

"You mean, you knew?" I think I sounded amazingly calm as I said this.

"We'd been tracking her after a fashion, just to make sure . . . We wouldn't have wanted her to pay you a surprise visit up in New York. But the next night, the night after you were there, she called 911 and asked for an ambulance."

"She was coughing that night, but to go from that to some fatal infection . . ."

"Virulent stuff, I guess. But it's not from the Agency. Huff checked it out. It isn't on their agenda these days. He thinks Mat-

tingly got whatever he got—the fungus and the means of delivering it—from a private contractor. Like the kind of guy who caused that anthrax scare a few years ago. Or maybe he just had Lisa doing the work of coming up with some bug that would be catastrophic. I guess we'll never know."

"What's so weird is I told Maria about Manfred dying of a rare fungus."

"Maybe she didn't put two and two together. You'd be amazed how many smart people can't add. Or maybe she wanted to die. You never know. The point is, she's dead and you're alive and all the moral obligation stuff is on our heads."

"How can you . . ." There's no graceful way of asking somebody, *How can you live with yourself?*

"How can we live with ourselves? Is that what you're worrying about? You start losing sleep, you wind up losing your edge. We're fine."

"Thank you for everything, Jacques. You saved my life in more ways than you know."

"All we did was give you a helping hand, Katie. You saved your own life."

Come to think of it, I guess I did.

Acknowledgments

Help! Well, I asked for it and got it. My thanks to the following generous and patient individuals who answered all sorts of questions. When their facts didn't fit my fiction, however, I went for the story. The inaccuracies are mine, not theirs. Arnold Abramowitz, Janice Asher, Jack Baruch, Mary FitzPatrick, Kim Gibbons, Debra LaMorte, Abby Ross, David Ross, Deborah O. Thompson, Paul Tolins, Clare Vance, and Susan Zises. Three gents, current or past employees of the Central Intelligence Agency, were informative and reflective: Stanley Sporkin, James Zirkle, and Chase Brandon. Emily Silverman, a senior researcher at the Max Planck Institut for Foreign and International Criminal Law in Freiburg, helped me understand a crucial aspect of German criminal law. And Dee McAloose, head of pathology at the Wildlife Conservation Society (aka the Bronx Zoo), enabled me to give life and intellect to my character Adam Grainger, a veterinary pathologist.

The following people made generous donations to charities by

"buying" characters' names in this novel. Harvey Aiges, Constance Cincotta, Karin Eckert (who used the name of her late husband, Walter McKey), Jacques Harlow, Jo-Ellen McCracken Hazan, Joanne Sexton, Merry Slone, Andrew William Turner, and Toni Wiener.

Blessings on the heads of the fine people at my publisher, Scribner, including my editor, the awesome and delightful Nan Graham, as well as Susan Moldow, Suzanne Balaban, Katherine Monaghan, Anna deVries, and their colleagues. And hail to Susanne Kirk, plot-meister and logician. I'm so lucky to be on their team.

I am grateful to the staffs of the Port Washington (New York) Public Library and the New York Public Library.

My assistant, Ronnie Gavarian, knows everything, plus she is resourceful, diplomatic, kind, fun, and brilliantly accessorized. What a terrific dame!

Richard Pine is a great tactician and a wise, organized, and honorable man. He could run countries or corporations. Happily for me, he decided to become a literary agent.

I keep learning about life from my wonderful children and in-law children: Elizabeth and Vincent Picciuto; Andy and Leslie Stern Abramowitz. Two philosophers, a lawyer, a teacher: what *nachas*!

Some writers have muses named Thalia or Clio. Mine are called Nathan and Molly Abramowitz.

And after all these years, my husband, Elkan Abramowitz, remains the best person in the world.

About the Author

Susan Isaacs is the author of eleven novels, including *Long Time No See; Red, White and Blue; Lily White; After All These Years; Compromising Positions; Shining Through;* and *Any Place I Hang My Hat;* and one nonfiction title, *Brave Dames and Wimpettes.* A former editor of *Seventeen* magazine and freelance political speechwriter, she lives on Long Island with her husband.